A TIME TO CHANGE

CALLIE LANGRIDGE

Storm
PUBLISHING

Ebook ISBN: 978-1-80508-097-8
Paperback ISBN: 978-1-80508-098-5

Previously published as *A Time to Change* by Bloodhound Books.

Cover design: Eileen Carey
Cover images: Midjourney, Shutterstock and Stocksy

Published by Storm Publishing.
For further information, visit:
www.stormpublishing.co

For Pete. For everything x

'But, dying, has made us rarer gifts than gold'

The Dead (*I*) by Rupert Chawner Brooke, 1914

PROLOGUE

It's dark in the old stable block and it smells like bonfires. Beneath a hole in the roof, there's a pile of burnt wood. The big boys from the estate broke in on Bonfire Night, smashed up the cobbled floor and set fire to what was left of the place. A fire engine put out the flames and the next day a workman came to block up the windows and doorway. But it will take more than a sheet of metal and a snarling dog on a poster shouting: *WARNING. DANGEROUS BUILDING. TRESPASSERS WILL BE PROSECUTED!* to stop ten-year-old Lou squeezing into her favourite hiding place.

'27, 28, 29, 30. Ready or not, here I come!'

Footsteps thump outside. She crouches closer to the wall, covers her mouth so that her brother won't hear her breathing. She waits and when the footsteps disappear, she grins. Stephen's only one year older than her but he thinks that means he should beat her at everything. Winning at hide-and-seek is her only way of getting revenge for all the times he's hung her *My Little Pony* by its neck from the loft hatch. He's only playing with her now because Mum wants them out from under her feet so she can bath their baby brother. Stephen would much rather be at home watching cartoons or hanging out with the big boys in the car park of The Hill House Arms.

When Lou is sure the coast is clear, she picks her way over the broken cobbles and burnt wood and squeezes back through the gap in the stable wall.

It's getting dark outside. She wanders into the walled garden where gardeners once grew flowers and vegetables for the kitchens inside the house. They learned about it at school. They learn a lot about the history of Hill House at Hill House Primary. But Lou can't remember a time when there was glass in the long row of greenhouses or walls around the garden. In her whole life, she has only ever seen the place full of weeds as tall as men.

She skips down the side of the main house, dragging her hand over the boards covering all the doors and windows and picking at the moss between the bricks.

She reaches the front of the house and peeks around the columns holding up the roof above the front door, in case Stephen's there, but she can't see him. Standing on her tiptoes, she peers through a gap in the board covering a window. She presses her nose to the wood. She sees what she always sees. Darkness beyond. She squints. Inside, something shines. Something glitters. She looks away and looks back. It glitters again!

She spins around. 'Stephen!' she calls to her brother, who is running away down the long drive. 'Stephen! There's tinsel inside. I see tinsel!'

'You're such a weirdo!' he shouts. 'Ghosts don't have Christmas trees!' When Stephen reaches the end of the drive, he climbs the high gates and drops to the ground on the other side. He runs up the steps of the footbridge that crosses over the top of the motorway, linking their estate with what's left of Hill House.

Lou stands on her tiptoes again. But there is only darkness now. Stephen was right.

She takes her time walking to the end of the drive. She is still small enough to squeeze through the gap between the padlocked gates, dodging the branches of overgrown trees that reach out to snag her coat.

Out on the pavement, she takes hold of the rusty metal bars of the gates and looks back up the drive. The sky is pink now. How sad the house looks, sitting all alone on its hill. She would love to be able to ask someone what it was like to live in that huge house when there was still glass in the windows, servants in the basement kitchen, horses in the stables; to sleep in the bedroom with the big windows above the front door. But everyone who lived in Hill House is long dead and buried, some of them in the vault inside St Mary's Church at the end of their garden.

Lou waves at the house in case any ghosts are watching and feel lonely. She's not scared of ghosts. She *was* scared, for a while after their dad went away, when she didn't want to sleep in her own room because of the dead people in the graveyard.

'Don't worry, sweetheart,' Mum had said, when she tucked her in and kissed her goodnight. 'The dead can't hurt you. It's the living you have to worry about.'

ONE

1 DECEMBER 2013

'Hello . . .? Mum . . .? It's me.'

'Lou? Is that you, love? It's a terrible line. Are you at the takeaway?'

'I'm having a quick drink at The Arms with the girls from work.'

'Oh. Will you be back for dinner?'

'I can't hear you. I've got Christmas songs blasting in my ear. I'll stop at the takeaway on my way home. It's my turn to get dinner in.'

'No, love. Stay and have a nice time with your friends. I'll go. Dean's been hassling me since four o'clock. I swear that boy has got hollow legs.'

'Oh – oh, well if you're sure, I'll have chicken pie and extra mushy peas. Keep it warm in the oven for me, would you?'

'I was thinking we could put the tree up tomorrow and make some mince pies and gingerbread and—'

'I've got to go. My drink's coming.'

'Okay. See you later then. Love you.'

'Yeah. See you later.'

Lou hung up, shoved her phone into her bag and watched

Mel squeeze back through the payday scrum at the bar. Mel plonked Lou's pint of beer on the table, edged onto the bench seat, and slipped the straw from an odd-looking blue concoction into the corner of her mouth. 'Was that Andy?'

'No-o. We split up last week, remember?'

'Oh yeah. Shame.' Mel slurped her drink loudly.

Was it? Lou thought. Two months was good going by her standards, but it hardly qualified as the romance of the century. A series of uninspiring dates involving a few disappointing meals barely qualified as a romance at all.

'I wouldn't kick him out of bed,' Mel said. 'Just so long as he didn't fart under the duvet and waft it in my face like that guy Joe did, remember?' She cackled before launching into a croaky rendition of 'Deck the Halls'.

Lou laughed and took a sip of her pint. 'Where've Becca and Shelley gone?'

'Toilet. Becca's spotted that Luke bloke she likes. Shelley's giving her an emergency makeover. Reckon she's in with him. Lucky girl.'

'Luke Smedley? He only split up with his wife a few weeks ago.'

'Fair game, then. A butcher doesn't put his meat in the window unless it's for sale.' She elbowed Lou in the ribs.

'Is that all you think about?'

'What else is there?'

Here it comes, Lou thought.

'We haven't *all* got the brains to be teachers, you know,' Mel said.

Lou cringed. She should never have let slip to the girls at work that she was considering teacher training. 'Just because I've got the application form, it doesn't mean I'm going to do anything with it. Anyway, it takes two years of studying and where am I going to find ten grand to pay for a PGCE?'

'A PG-whatty?'

'It doesn't matter.'

Mel drained her glass and slammed it down on the table. 'Are we having another or what?'

Lou placed her hand over the top of her glass. Mel looked at her as though she had just refused a share of a lottery jackpot.

'Giving up already? Not even a teacher yet and already too good to be seen out with the likes of us. . .'

Lou took a ten-pound note from her purse and put it down on the table. 'You win!' God, she was weak. But what was waiting at home apart from rubbish gameshows on television and a soggy chicken pie?

At some point around ten o'clock, Lou stumbled into a waiting taxi. An unnecessary payday extravagance.

'Don't forget you promised to get your mum to make some of those mini chocolate cakes like last year. Oh, and her famous gingerbread!' Mel said, hanging out of her own taxi. 'She's a legend, your mum is.'

'You wouldn't say that if you had to live with Mrs Christmas.'

'See ya tomorrow!'

'Laters, sweetie!'

The cab pulled away and Lou tried to focus on the orange strands of light from the streetlamps trailing across the dark night sky. She bloody loved those girls. Her workmates were the only friends she had here in her hometown since Katie had got hitched and moved away to Manchester. She fell back into her seat. Was she a terrible person then for wanting to escape too? For wanting to do something with the three years she'd spent studying history at the University of Sheffield, expanding her brain and her horizons, experiencing the world beyond this small town.

Her head began to swim. Was she thinking too hard? Or

was it the second vodka chaser. Or maybe the third pint of beer? She pressed her forehead to the cold glass and frowned at her reflection. Seven years since graduating and not even out of debt yet and here she was, contemplating another loan to put herself through teacher training. All so she could stand in front of a class of fourteen-year-olds and share her passion for the past, when they were only interested in the future. She giggled. She must be crazy.

Just short of the parade of shops on the edge of town, the cabbie made an unexpected stop. He nodded to a police car blocking the road. 'I'll have to take a detour.'

Lou looked out at the crowd of boys milling around behind blue and white police tape tied to lampposts. 'Fine,' she said and slumped back in her seat.

After paying the cabbie, Lou stumbled up the path and into the house. She kicked off her shoes, dumped her bag in the hall and tripped over the Christmas tree and a box of decorations at the bottom of the stairs. How many times had she told Mum not to go up that rickety old loft ladder on her own? One of these days she was going to fall and break her neck.

'Hey, Mum,' she called, 'there's a police car blocking the road at the parade. Do you reckon someone held up the take-away? Was it assault and battery? Get it? A salt and batter-y? Did you get me that pie?' She grabbed a strand of silver tinsel from the box and wrapped it around her neck, making a twinkling boa. She giggled and was still giggling as she made her way into the living room and fell into two police officers in hi-vis jackets. Her brother Dean was on his knees in the middle of the room with Stephen and a female police officer standing over him.

'I don't believe you,' Dean sobbed. 'I want my mum. Get me my mum!'

TWO

TWO WEEKS LATER

It was only three o'clock, but the day had already turned to night. Through the window of the Freezerfayre supermarket, Lou watched a flurry of empty food packets and burger cartons tumble down one of the deserted 'boulevards' and swirl around the drained fountain in the central courtyard of Hill House Shopping Arcade – or the Arc, as the single-storey 1960s shopping precinct was known to the locals.

Lou ran the barcode of a frozen pizza over the scanner and handed it to a harassed young woman struggling to pack her shopping while keeping a toddler strapped into its pushchair.

'£17.58, please,' Lou said.

The young woman emptied the contents of her purse on to the conveyer belt. Lou counted out the coins and crumpled notes. It was sixty pence short, but she decided to say nothing. If her till was down at the end of the day, they'd deduct the shortfall from her wages. The young woman loaded the bags onto the handles of the pushchair and was followed out of the store by a teenage girl who didn't stop to pay for the chocolate bar shoved up her sleeve. She gave Lou a sideways glance as she pulled up her hood, hiding her impressive mane of auburn hair.

． ． ．

When her supervisor pulled the shutters down at the end of the day, Lou slipped quietly away, saving her colleagues the embarrassment of having to ask whether she would be joining them at the Christmas party they had been excitedly talking about across the aisles. All day she had been aware of the awkward stares and pitying looks from the other checkout staff. After the initial hugs and the well-meaning flood of, 'You all right? You sure you haven't come back too soon?' they had kept their distance, whether out of tact or embarrassment, Lou wasn't sure.

Lou pulled her parka on over her gingham uniform and stepped out into the snow. Tying her scarf tighter around her neck and pulling up her hood, she crossed the yard and walked the short distance to the bus stop. From beneath her damp hair, she watched the headlights of cars, their tyres churning the newly fallen snow into slush, until the bus pulled up to the kerb.

With the driver battling against the heavy snow, the bus took twice as long as normal to wind its way across town. Lou rubbed a hole in the condensation. The further they travelled from the centre of town, the greyer the buildings grew until they arrived at the sprawling estate on the outskirts. Once upon a time the residents of Hill House Estate had tended their gardens and planted hanging baskets. Children – including Lou, her brothers and Katie – had played tag on the greens. A few of the older residents still planted daffodil bulbs each year but it had been a long time since the greens had been used as anything other than a toilet for dogs and a place for the estate teenagers to congregate and intimidate any passer-by who dared to look at them.

Lou zipped up her parka and stepped from the bus. With the cold biting her cheeks, she turned in to the very last street on the farthest edge of the estate. The snow had a strange, calming effect, muffling the roar of traffic coming from the motorway just beyond the houses. It settled on parked cars and filled potholes in the road. Twinkling lights shone out from windows, and lights shaped like icicles nailed to porches and fences, blinked and rattled in the wind. In one garden, a huge, inflated Homer Simpson dressed as Santa Claus bobbed and weaved on a rope tethering him to the ground.

Lou stopped at the gate of the only house not decorated for Christmas and looked up at the dark windows. Above the roof, the spire of St Mary's church was just visible, its weathervane creaking as it spun. A shout came from the direction of the green and a car revved its engine. She opened the gate, ran up the path, dropped her keys, stooped to pick them up. Her hands shook so violently it took three attempts to force the key into the lock. Once inside, she slammed the door and leant against it. Danger seemed to lurk everywhere on this estate now. She no longer knew how to be in this place where once she had felt so safe, whose alleys and streets she had run along as a child.

When her pulse settled, she switched on the hall light. Everything looked as it always had; coats draped over the banisters and hung on the hooks beside the door; shoes piled up at the bottom of the stairs; Dean's rugby boots upturned, each stud encased in a crust of dried mud and twisted grass. But a glance along the hooks revealed that one coat was missing. And a pair of fleece-trimmed boots was absent from the pile of shoes. The police had kept them as evidence.

'Dean! Are you in?' Lou called, her voice sounding more desperate than she would have liked. 'Dean!' she tried again. 'Bring your sports stuff down, I'll put it through the wash.'

A door opened upstairs, and the stairs creaked as Dean lumbered down. 'How was college?' Lou asked.

Dean shrugged and grabbed his coat from the banisters without a single glance in her direction.

'Where's Stephen?' Lou said.

'Where do you think?'

The pub. It was always the pub. Even before the events of the last few weeks, Stephen had been as much a fixture of The Hill House Arms as the collection of horse brasses behind the bar.

'What about your dinner? I'll make you something. Sausages?' She wasn't even sure there was anything in the freezer except an empty ice cube tray.

'I'll get something from the kebab van.'

'Do you want to help me put the Christmas tree up tomorrow?' Lou injected as much cheerfulness into her voice as she could muster. 'I'll get some gingerbread. It'll be like old times.'

'No, it won't.'

Dean opened the door. The cold air rushed inside before he slammed it behind him. Lou stared at the net curtain quivering on the closed door. He was right. She could promise all the sausages and gingerbread in the world, but it would never be like old times again.

The letterbox rattled and she collected the free newspaper from the doormat. Almost on autopilot, Lou unfurled the newspaper and scanned the headlines. She stopped, the newspaper trembling in her hands. Shoved between a report on the recent spate of metal thefts in the area and a story about the Scouts' Christmas jumble sale, was the headline:

FUNERAL FOR JOYRIDING VICTIM

The funeral was held on Monday last for Mrs Maureen Arnold (50), the much-loved local woman tragically killed in the latest incident of a joyriding epidemic plaguing Hill House Estate.

*The private service, attended by close friends and family,
was held at St Mary's Church. The Revd George Reeves paid
tribute to a devoted mother and lifelong resident of the town.*

*Sylvia Mather, who witnessed the tragedy, said, 'I
remember when this estate was a lovely place to live. Now it's
just a breeding ground for thugs and criminals. They don't
care about anybody but themselves. They left that poor woman
to die in the gutter without a single thought and with her
dinner spilled all over the road. They're animals. Plain and
simple. Prison's too good for them.'*

*Police continue to look for witnesses and ask anyone with
information to come forward . . .*

Lou dropped the newspaper, turned out the light, and ran
up the stairs. Passing the door of her own room, she fell onto the
bed in the room at the front of the house. Crawling beneath the
duvet, she placed her head on the pillow, and breathed in the
lingering trace of *L'Air du Temps*. The tears she had been
holding back all day finally came. She wept for the hopelessness
of the loss that gnawed her stomach raw. There was nothing she
could do to make this better. She wished she could turn back
the hands of time to alter the moment she'd decided to stay at
the pub to get drunk rather than coming home for a soggy pie
and an evening of crap television. If she hadn't let her mum go
to the takeaway in her place, then none of this would be
happening. Sobbing into the darkness, she repeated her now
nightly chant – 'It's my fault, it's all my fault' – until she slipped
into a shallow, restless sleep.

THREE

Lou woke to the sound of children laughing and shrieking on the street outside. For a single, perfect moment everything was right with the world. And then reality crashed through the fantasy. Lou peered out from the safety of the duvet and watched dust swirl in the shafts of winter sunlight breaking through the gaping curtains, settling on trinkets crowding almost every inch of the dressing table; the jewellery box Stephen had made in woodwork class, the yoghurt pot Dean had smeared with finger-paints at nursery, and the photo frame Lou had painstakingly decorated with pasta bows at Brownies.

The frame held Mum's favourite photograph, taken on their one and only family holiday. Was it really possible that those three kids sitting in the saddles of Daisy, Dobbin and Daphne on the glittering sands of the Golden Mile in Blackpool, smiling for Mum's old Kodak, were the same people who now shared this house? The same people who just a few days ago had clung to each other in the front pew of St Mary's, their raw grief binding them together in a way that being siblings never had? Now they were strangers again. Numb and facing a future where the glue that had held them together was gone.

Pulling herself up, Lou sat on the edge of the bed, and clutched the duvet around her. On the chair in the corner of the room, next to a pile of clean laundry still waiting to be put away, was a carrier bag stuffed with tubes of Christmas wrapping paper. No matter how hard it had been on her part-time wages from the Post Office, and without a single penny in maintenance from their feckless father, Mum had always managed to make Christmas special. It would break her heart to see the house the week before Christmas without a turkey in the freezer, a bottle of Baileys in the fridge or a single string of tinsel wrapped around her ornaments on the mantelshelf.

Standing in the shower, Lou made a plan. It was her day off, she would go shopping and have a homemade shepherd's pie on the table by the time Dean got home from college and Stephen finished work. It wasn't much, but it was a start.

With her hair still wet, Lou ran downstairs. But by the time she reached the bottom, the brakes screeched on her plan. Through the open kitchen door, she saw her brothers sitting at the table, surrounded by the previous evening's squashed beer cans and kebab wrappers. Stephen and Dean never spent any time together. Yet there was Stephen, in his Manchester United dressing gown, stirring sugar into a mug of tea and pushing it across the table to Dean. 'Drink this,' he said.

Dean stared into the rusty orange builder's brew. He was barely recognisable as the Dean who used to start each day by running down the stairs, gym bag slung over his shoulder, snatching a slice of toast, and kissing Mum goodbye on his way out of the front door.

'I miss her, Ste,' Dean said, cuffing his eyes.

'Finish your brew.' Stephen shifted in his chair. 'I'll take you to the café for a fry up. My treat.'

Dean collapsed onto the table and buried his face in his

arms. He began to sob. Stephen stubbed his cigarette out in the overflowing ashtray. He reached his hand towards his brother, then pulled it away. Lou watched as he sat for a few seconds and then reached out again and patted Dean's shoulder. 'She wouldn't want to see you like this, mate.'

'I kept going on and on about wanting stupid dinner,' Dean sobbed. 'I should have gone . . . I could have run out of the way of that car . . . I could . . .' His words disappeared in a cry that made his shoulders shake.

Guilt churned in Lou's empty stomach. Abandoning the safety of the staircase she burst into the kitchen. 'Dean, it wasn't you, it was me. It was my fault, I—'

Stephen leapt from his chair. 'Drink your tea!' he barked at Dean. He grabbed Lou's arm and manhandled her out into the hall. Slamming the door behind them.

'What the hell are you doing?' Lou said, following him into the living room. 'We're not kids anymore. You can't bully me and push me around.'

Stephen tried to push past Lou to get back to the kitchen, but she stepped into his path. There was something unusual about Stephen's behaviour. He wasn't shouting and yelling. He could hardly bring himself to look at her. His lips were tight in barely contained anger. No, it was more than anger. It was fury.

A wave of nervous energy rushed through Lou's chest. 'You know, don't you? You know it's all my fault. You know it should have been me that night, not Mum.'

Stephen turned to face the wall, leaving Lou to stare at the back of his creased dressing gown. He slammed the heel of his hand into the chimneybreast. 'You couldn't leave it, could you? You had to interfere like you always do. Shit.'

'I don't know what to do,' Lou said, pouncing on his reaction. 'Let me help pay for the funeral. It's the least—'

'You're joking, aren't you?' Stephen braced himself against

the chimney. 'I bet you hardly scrape minimum wage at that poxy supermarket.'

It was against every fibre in Lou's body to back down from an argument, especially with Stephen – they could push each other's buttons without even trying. But she should make allowances. Stephen was lashing out and didn't he have every right to?

'Well?' he pressed. 'What is it? Two hundred pounds a week?'

Don't take the bait. Don't take. . . 'I . . . I—'

'Not much to show for three years at your precious university, is it?'

'What's that got to do with this?'

'Nothing. Everything. Going off there. Thinking you're better than the rest of us.'

Don't Lou, don't . . . 'At least I had ambition.' The words exploded from her mouth before she could stop herself.

'And ambition pays the bills, does it?'

'It's not my fault a checkout assistant doesn't get paid as much as a plumber. I pay my way as best I can.'

'Oh yeah, because the fifty pounds you bung in the kitty every month goes a long way to paying the rent and the gas and the electric and the council tax and the food and the water. And it puts shoes on his feet and clothes on his back.' Stephen flicked his head towards the kitchen. 'But don't you worry, Lou, you stick your brainy head in the sand and leave the rest of us to do what we have to to get by. Because a plumber's wages *really* covers all of that, doesn't it? Along with everything else.'

'What's "everything else"?'

'Forget it.' Stephen started to walk away but suddenly turned back. 'You know your problem, don't you?' he said, glaring at Lou. 'You live in Cloud Cuckoo Land. Always have, always will.'

'Who the hell are you to judge me and my life? *I'm* not the one who ran out on his fiancée the month before his wedding and came crawling back here because he couldn't face up to the commitment.'

'Like you'd get the chance to run out on anyone. No one in their right mind would take you on.' A horrible smirk darkened Stephen's face. 'You know, I pity the guy that ends up lumbered with you. He'll have to be mad. Or a saint.'

Lou dug her fingernails into her palms. Why did they have to do this? Why couldn't they speak to each other like normal human beings and find a way to comfort each other? 'I'm trying to be nice today. I was going to make dinner and maybe put the Christmas tree up and—'

'Why? A few stupid baubles aren't going to bring her back, are they?'

So he did blame her. He really did. 'I'm going to tell Dean it was my fault,' Lou said. But as she made to leave, Stephen grabbed her arm again. 'No, you're not.'

'He can't go on believing he's to blame, it's killing him.'

'Do you think I don't know that? I'll convince him it's not his fault. Somehow.'

'Why are you protecting me?'

Stephen released her arm and laughed. 'Don't flatter your-self. And if you give a shit about that kid, you'll drop it. The last thing he needs is you messing with his head.'

Lou grappled with the meaning behind Stephen's words. 'Would you and Dean be better off without me? Is that what you're saying? Do you want me to move out?'

Say no! Make me a cup of tea and hug me and tell me every-thing's going to be okay. Be my big brother too.

'Do what you want, Lou. You always bloody do.'

Stephen pushed past her and made his way back up the hall. Lou stared after him. For the second time in two days one of her brothers slammed a door on her. Supressing the sob rising in her throat, she grabbed her coat and let herself out of the front door.

Out on the path, Lou hunched her shoulders to the cold morning air and pushed through the gate. Ignoring the children laughing as they built a snowman on the green, she wiped the hot tears that spilled down her cheeks as she ran along the alleyway at the end of the road, heading for the one place where she knew she could guarantee to be alone. She ran up the steps of the footbridge, her shoes slipping on the icy concrete as traffic hurtled through the freshly sprayed salt on the motorway below.

It had been a long time since the Council had sent anyone to lock the gates of Hill House. For years the single track, dead-end road on which they opened had been a dumping ground for battered sofas, stained mattresses, and bin bags spewing rubbish onto the pavement. The snarling dogs on the posters warning trespassers to keep away had long since been silenced by graffiti. Only the rusty barbed wire wound around the top of the gates served as a reminder that someone had once cared enough to protect this place.

Lou eased through the gap created where the gates had collapsed onto each other. At least here there was nobody to hate her. Nobody she could do harm to without even trying. Wiping her wet hair from her face, she walked up the path towards Hill House. Frost had turned the metal grilles covering the windows of the ground floor white, like the bloom on choco-late past its sell-by date. Icicles hung from the shards of glass clinging to the sash frames of the unprotected windows in the floors above. Even with a bellyful of guilt, the sad beauty of the three storeys of weathered Portland stone, decorated by nature, still had the ability to take her breath away.

Over the rumble of the motorway, the clock of St Mary's chimed the hour. Eleven peals echoed around the snow-covered landscape. As a kid, playing hide-and-seek here, the other kids from the estate had thought she was brave since she was the only one bold enough to ignore the tales of ghosts and hide in the dark outbuildings. They had no idea it was curiosity pushing her on: the desire to see more of the house they had all learned about at school. While the rest of the class had yawned over the old photos of Hill House and made paper planes out of the photocopied worksheets, it had sparked something inside Lou – ignited a passion for history. Much good that had done her. It had been seven years since her degree, and here she was, living back at home, working in the supermarket, still paying off debt – desperately filling in applications in the hope that a school might sponsor her through teacher training, up against kids fresh from uni.

Stephen was right; she really did live in Cloud Cuckoo Land. And the events of that morning had made it clear that her brother didn't want her anywhere near him. She had nowhere to go. And nobody who wanted or needed her.

The snow began to fall again. At first, fat flakes, like feathers, floated from the sky, but within minutes it turned into a blizzard. Lou ran the rest of the way up the drive and took shelter beneath the portico. She shook the snow from her hair and looked out at the white sky meeting the white ground. What would the little girl who used to play on that snow-covered lawn think of the woman she had become?

Lou slumped against the grille covering the front door and felt something shift. She turned around. The padlock that should have been securing the grille hung unlocked and redundant from the bolt. Lou took it in her hand. She had been in and out of the dilapidated outbuildings more times than she could count but had only ever dreamt of roaming the panelled rooms to marvel at the hand-painted wallpapers and interiors she'd seen in the black-and-white photographs on display in the school library.

Before she could change her mind, Lou grabbed the padlock, pulled it free and placed it on the step. A shudder of excitement raced through her as she eased the bolt across and slowly opened the grille. Beneath the crude metal was what must have once been an imposing door. It was at least twice the size of any domestic front door, with exquisitely carved panels. Lou tentatively pushed it and it swung open slowly, groaning on its hinges. Decades of rust and old, blue paint fluttered to the ground. Lou stepped over the threshold into a vestibule and was instantly plunged into darkness. She covered her nose in an attempt to block out the stench of urine mixed with mould and the bitter scent of charred wood.

It was common knowledge that the last baronet was a bachelor who had died a sad and lonely recluse in a flat in London. On selling his land to the Council and abandoning Hill House after the Second World War, he had disposed of every stick of furniture and anything of value to pay off huge debts. But what Lou saw when she stood in the centre of the hall, her eyes gradually growing accustomed to the dim daylight breaking in around the security grilles and through the open door, made her heart sink. The utter destruction wreaked on this beautiful house was beyond anything she could ever have imagined. Every trace of decoration was gone, each wall stripped back to bare brick, blackened by fire and green with mould from the water dripping unchecked from above. There were no doors or frames around the many entrances leading from the hall. A huge hole in the chimneybreast, like a toothless, gaping mouth, gave the only clue that there had once been a fireplace. Whatever had covered the floor had been ripped away to expose the rough boards beneath. Even the vast staircase that had once swept up the centre of the hall was gone, leaving a void in the ceiling and the innards of each floor suspended skeletally above.

And what the final baronet had started, the vandals and the Council's neglect had finished.

Lou kicked at a piece of burned wood. As it disintegrated, she became aware of a noise coming from one of the rooms. She peered into the darkness. It was a rat. It had to be. The noise grew louder. If it was a rat then it was a bloody big one, wearing what sounded like boots. Before she could make a run for it, a staggeringly bright light burst through the gloom. Frozen in fear, she could just make out the outline of a person. For the briefest moment, the figure paused before letting out a bloodcurdling scream.

'Jesus, Joseph and Mary! I thought you were a ghost!' A short middle-aged woman in a pink anorak stepped from behind the beam of a torch, clutching her chest.

'No,' Lou panted, her heart hammering at her ribs. 'I'm not a ghost.'

The woman laughed nervously. 'You're not from the Council, are you? I wouldn't want to get into trouble. One of the doors at the back was open. I parked out on the road. We haven't done any harm, I promise.'

'Don't worry,' Lou said, still catching her breath. 'I'm trespassing too.'

'Thank heavens!' The woman puffed out her cheeks. 'Oh, I'm Julie.'

Before Lou could introduce herself, a muffled call came from the room behind the woman.

'It's all right Uncle, don't fret,' Julie called back, then turned to Lou. 'Come on,' she said, 'come and have a nosey in here. It's the ballroom, apparently. Looks more like a bombsite if you ask me.'

Lou followed Julie, picking her way over the rubbish strewn across the floor. Once inside the ballroom, Lou's only sense of the scale of the room came from the sweep of Julie's torch. No matter how hard she peered into the darkness, she couldn't make out any detail.

Julie directed her torch to the centre of the room where an old man sat in a wheelchair. Bundled up against the bitter cold, he barely registered their presence. Lou had never seen a person who looked so old. His upper body was bent and his shoulders hunched, so that he seemed fixed in a position where he sat permanently forward. His chin rested on his chest and the harsh torchlight cast shadows in the deep creases etched into his face. His only reaction was to flinch at the light of the torch and then again when Julie went over to him and tucked the blanket tighter around his knees, as though their presence was a surprise to him.

'This young lady's having a bit of a snoop around, like us.' Julie raised her voice before lowering it as she turned back to talk to Lou. 'Uncle Bert grew up here when his parents were in service. Hard to imagine that he was once a little boy, isn't it? When I was small, he used to tell me stories about riding a tricycle in the corridors downstairs and taking tea with the family in the grand morning room on Sunday afternoons. He filled my head with pictures of such grandeur that I was expecting to find Blenheim Palace, not a haunted house! When I asked him what he'd like for Christmas this year, he said his only wish was to see this house one last time. And it had to be today. Insistent on it, he was. Isn't that right Uncle? He probably can't hear—'

'Such parties this room has seen,' the old man interrupted, his voice creaking like one of the old floorboards. 'Such laughter and music and dancing. You never saw more handsome men or prettier girls. Every one a belle of the ball!' He struggled to lift his chin from his chest and pulled his hand from the folds of the blanket. With a bent finger, he pointed to the ceiling. 'Two crystal chandeliers glittered like fairyland up there, hundreds of candles turning night into day.'

'That's lovely, Uncle.' Julie patted his shoulder. She

lowered her voice again. 'Most days he can't tell you what he had for breakfast, but he can go on for hours about things that happened ninety-odd years ago.'

The old man turned to face Lou. She shifted uncomfortably.

'Go on,' Julie said, 'he wants to talk to you. He's harmless.'

Lou moved closer and knelt beside the wheelchair. With a huge effort, the man raised his head and leant in so close that Lou could see the wiry, feral hair growing in and on his nose. 'You remember that last party, don't you? The Christmas Ball the year before the Great War. Every guest bedroom full, every fire lit, maids and footmen rushing around. I should have been asleep in the kitchen maid's room, but I slipped out to watch the arrival of the guests through the banisters.' He smiled as though peering through the banisters again. But as he rubbed his finger across his dry lips, his smile turned to a frown. 'The life went out of this house when Captain Mandeville died. He would have made the best master Hill House had ever seen. He was the first we lost to that war, but not the last. Including my own, dear father.'

His voice caught in his throat and a wheeze rattled in his chest. Julie stepped forward but he held up his hand, deter-mined to finish.

'Master Edward could never hope to fill his brother's shoes. Wasn't cut from the same cloth. His bad eyes saved him from the draft. Sensitive he was, bookish. But all that book learning didn't help him manage the estate's finances. It's not my place to question, but did he have to marry his sister off like that? Miss Charlotte was an angel.' He lowered his voice to a whisper. 'An accident, the police said. I say she threw herself down those stairs at Caxton Hall. Couldn't stand to bear a child to that brute of a cousin. He killed that poor girl as surely as if he'd pushed her with his own hands.' He nodded at Lou. 'But you know better than most what George Caxton was capable of.'

'I'm sorry,' Lou said. 'But I think you've confused me with somebody else.'

The old man lowered his voice still further. 'One in, one out. It's the way it's always been. It's the way it always will be.'

'I'm sorry, I really don't understand.'

He smiled again and nodded. 'No, but you will. You will.' With that, the old man sat back, his chin sank to his chest and the spark in his eyes disappeared, like a candle snuffed out.

'Pay him no mind,' Julie said, fussing over his blanket as Lou got to her feet. 'He gets confused.' She reminded her uncle that he needed to save his energy for the carol concert at his home that evening. She spoke to him as though he were a child, not the lucid man Lou had just talked to.

Julie handed the torch to Lou. 'Keep it, you'll need it if you want to have a nosey. It was lovely to meet you, but we'd better be getting back. Matron doesn't like it if the residents are late for dinner. Will you be okay on your own?'

'Yes. I think so.'

Julie spun the wheelchair around and headed towards a door at the far end of the room, the wheels crunching in the debris. As she eased the chair through the doorway, the old man suddenly called out, 'Je reviens, Miss Louisa. Je reviens.'

By the time Lou had collected her thoughts enough to realise what he had said, Julie and her uncle had disappeared. How had he known her name? Had she told him?

Turning the beam of the torch around the vast room, Lou found it followed the same depressing pattern of destruction as the hallway – no fireplaces, no decoration, walls stripped back to bare brick and tainted by scorch marks and mould. She directed the beam to the ceiling and saw that huge sections of plaster were missing, leaving the joists above naked, like ribs in a dead man's chest. If Hill House were a dog, it would have been put out of its misery years ago. Surely there was only so much punishment a building could take. It could only be a matter of time before its structure became compromised so completely that it collapsed in on itself. Or was razed to the ground by a fire at the hands of vandals.

Lou picked her way back out to the hall. If this was to be her only chance of exploring Hill House, then she knew exactly where she wanted to go. Sweeping the torch around, she found the door she was looking for. It was small and narrow. An entrance designed with function, not form in mind.

Passing though the doorway, she relied on the beam of the torch to make her way in the inky blackness. The plaster crumbled beneath her fingertips as, with her free hand, she felt her way along the damp wall. She plunged deeper into a network of narrow, low passageways, into the part of the house that had never known wood panelling or elaborate furnishings. These passageways were utilitarian and modest, like the people who had once passed through them, unseen and unknown to the family they served. Lou imagined the servants moving from room to room, floor to floor; housemaids struggling with buckets of steaming water; footmen running from the kitchen to the dining room, desperate to deliver hot food upstairs; the hall boy struggling with scuttles of coal to the upper floors in the dead of night, ready for a maid to make up the fires in the bedrooms before the family woke.

Lou thought back to her dissertation in her final year at Sheffield – *To assess the impact of nineteenth and early twentieth century global conflict on the politicisation of women in Britain*. As part of her research, she had visited countless historic properties – including Caxton Hall, the grand stately home across the valley – in an attempt to immerse herself in the conditions of working women of that era. Each property had proved disappointing; sanitised for visitors, with whitewashed walls, gleaming brass pots, tour guides warning you not to touch anything, printed bookmarks in the gift shop, and cream teas in the café. She should have broken in here sooner to find out what it was really like instead of playing at understanding peoples' lives.

She turned and the beam of the torch picked out a series of bells high up on the wall. The pulleys and springs, connecting each one to a room, were intact, as though only moments earlier they had summoned staff to the rooms indicated on the plaques above - *Dining Room, Drawing Room, Library, Ballroom.* But how had these bells survived when the rest of the house was crumbling around them? Was it because they were so specific? There couldn't be many people in need of a set of bells denoting the bedrooms of *Sir Charles, Lady Mandeville, Mrs Hart, Captain Thomas, Mister Edward* and *Miss Charlotte,* but surely, they would have a value as collectables.

Lou shone the torch along the names again. The Mandevilles and their guests at that last party in Christmas 1913 could have had no idea that, in a few short months, the war already brewing in the fractious politics across the Channel would sound the death knell for their comfortable Edwardian world. That their life of house parties, hunts, and hand-painted wallpapers was about to come crashing down around them.

Pressing on down the passageway, Lou wrinkled her nose; she swore she could smell school dinners – meat in gravy and boiled cabbage. Her mind must be playing tricks on her. She should have eaten breakfast. She came to a staircase that led down, and grinned as she placed her boot into a groove in the top step worn smooth by centuries of feet passing this way. Making her way down, in search of the kitchen – the beating heart of the house – she noticed how the walls of the staircase appeared to have been recently whitewashed and how it was much lighter down here than in any other part of the house. It quickly grew so bright that by the time she reached the flagstone floor at the bottom, she no longer needed the torch. She switched off the light and placed the torch on the floor.

She looked around, struggling to take it in. At the end of a long corridor was a door to the outside, its glass intact. Unlike the windows upstairs, there were no grilles shutting out the world and Lou could see an external set of steps leading up to ground level. The doors to various rooms off the corridor stood open, daylight casting squares of light on the floor; a floor clear of dirt and debris. Everything gleamed, sparkled. This wasn't possible. It didn't make sense – unless some kind of house-proud squatter had taken up residence.

'Mon Dieu!' a heavily accented man's voice shouted. 'I said salt not malt. What is wrong with you, girl? How am I to create meals fit for ze table when you cannot follow a simple instruction!'

Lou felt a chill go through her. With her mind full of gory movies set in abandoned houses, she spun around and ran slap bang into the broad chest of a man.

FOUR

18TH DECEMBER 1913

'I'm so sorry,' the man said, water slopping from the bucket he was carrying. It appeared to contain a large and rapidly melting lump of ice.

'It's me who should apologise,' Lou said, finding her voice now that she was faced with a handsome young man instead of the chainsaw-wielding maniac she was expecting.

The man shifted awkwardly, seemingly reluctant to make eye contact. He was tall, mid-twenties, his short hair parted and oiled neatly to one side, dressed in what Lou could only describe as the livery of a footman – dark blue knickerbockers, a blue and gold striped waistcoat, crisp white bow tie and matching stockings. When he noticed her glance at his shirt-sleeves rolled up to his elbows, he hurriedly placed the bucket on the floor and rolled his sleeves down.

'I shouldn't have burst in on you and . . . well, whatever this is,' Lou said. 'Are you some kind of re-enactment society? I like the wooden pail, nice touch. Very authentic.'

'A society?' The footman frowned. 'I'm not sure I under—'

'William is that you?' the foreign man yelled. 'How long

does it take to collect a bucket of ice from ze icehouse? How am I to make pineapple ice cream without ice?' A short, skinny man with a pointed nose and wild, staring eyes, dressed in chef's whites, appeared in the doorway of the kitchen. A young girl craned to see around him. She wore an apron splattered with grease. A grey dress, made for a woman twice her size, hung loosely on her slight frame and unruly strands of dark hair escaped from beneath her mob cap. She couldn't be more than thirteen, fourteen at the most.

'Ah, I see,' the chef said, looking from Lou to the footman. 'You are too busy making small talk to—'

'I think this lady is her Ladyship's visitor, Monsieur Gotti,' the footman interrupted. The girl gasped and looked to the floor.

'Please accept my apologies.' The chef removed his hat and bowed. 'William, why do you not ask if madam would like to wait in Mrs Moriarty's parlour while you go to find Mr Bainbridge?'

'Mr Bainbridge is out with Sir Charles. They're checking on the birds for the shoot.'

'Then fetch Mrs Moriarty.' The chef attempted a smile, but it turned into a grimace. He didn't look like a man who smiled much.

'Please,' Lou said, 'don't go to any trouble. I found my own way in, so I can find my way back out again.'

'If you'll excuse my impertinence, madam,' the footman said, 'I think Mrs Moriarty would prefer it if you were to wait so that she might escort you herself.'

Here we go, Lou thought. Whoever was in charge of this funfair was going to come along and send her away with a flea in her ear. Accepting her fate, she followed the footman to a room where he asked her to wait. Lou watched as he closed the door behind him. Everything fell into place. The Council must have rented out the basement to these historical enthusiasts to generate a bit of revenue. That's why the front door had been left unlocked; to give access to make possible the creation of the kitchens and this cosy parlour, authentic down to the small hard-looking sofa, dark wooden table stacked with piles of accounting ledgers and heavy curtains at the windows high in the basement walls. There was even a potted aspidistra sitting on a doily on a plant stand and a pair of blue and white Staffordshire pottery dogs standing sentry at either end of the mantelshelf. This re-enactment society must have scoured every antique fair, car boot sale and online auction to assemble such an array of props. Especially the calendar beside the clock that revealed the date they were 'living' – 18 December 1913 – one hundred years ago to the day.

There was a scuffle on the other side of the door and hushed voices.

'Mr Bainbridge won't be happy that people are wandering into the house without a by-your-leave,' a young girl's voice whispered. 'I'd like to know how she found her way down here. And *why* would she *want* to find her way down here?'

'She found her way on her feet, how do you think, you stupid girl,' the chef answered dismissively. 'And how Mr Bainbridge runs the house is no concern of yours. Do you reckon to know the role of a butler when you can hardly manage the job of kitchen maid? Go and pour two glasses of ale for Pennymore's deliverymen, they are due any second. Even you cannot get that wrong.'

Lou's eyes were wide, and her hearing primed for the next exchange. This was incredible; these people were staying in character even when they were on their own, incorporating her unexpected arrival into their Edwardian world.

With an ominous warning from the chef, connecting the girl's continuing position in the house with how quickly she could clear the breakfast pots still in the sink, they left. Or so Lou thought.

'Mary Parkinson!' a woman whispered forcefully in a broad Belfast accent. 'What on Earth do you think you are doing, sneaking around at my door?'

'Sorry, Mrs Moriarty. I was keeping an eye on the visitor. We don't know how she found her way down here or why and—'

'When I need your appraisal of a situation, I shall be sure to ask for it. Until that time, get about your chores. If Monsieur Gotti has no need of you then with all the bedrooms to air and make up, I am sure I can find a hundred and one things to gainfully employ your time.'

'I'm to clean the pots from breakfast and pour the beer for the deliverymen,' Mary added quickly.

'Well, you better get on with it then. And change that filthy apron. What will it look like if the maids and kitchen staff arrive from Caxton Hall to find you looking like a waif dragged in from the workhouse? I don't want them returning to Lady Caxton after Christmas saying I do not run an orderly household. Have you made up the rooms for them in the attic yet?'

'Yes, Mrs Moriarty. Sorry, Mrs Moriarty.'

Footsteps hurried away up the corridor. The door opened and a woman dressed entirely in black entered. With her auburn hair pulled back severely from her face, a single streak of white at each temple, she carried an aura of authority intensified by the large chatelaine of keys hanging from a belt at her middle. She stood before Lou, her eyes dipped. There was an uncomfortable silence.

'Good morning?' Lou tried.

The woman looked up. 'Good morning, madam,' she said and curtseyed, her dress pooling like a black lake on the floor around her. 'I am Mrs Moriarty, the housekeeper. I cannot apologise enough that nobody was here to greet you on your arrival.

It is no excuse but I'm afraid that with the preparations for the party, our normal routines are somewhat disturbed. Please, won't you follow me?'

Like her fellow role-players, this woman was acting her part to perfection. So much so, that Lou felt like she was standing before the headmistress, accused of bunking off class.

'I'm sorry but there's been some kind of mistake,' she said. 'I only came in because the front door was unlocked. I'm not part of your . . . group. I'm really not expected.'

'Not expected!' The housekeeper's composure slipped. She took a small notebook from the pocket of her dress and consulted a page. 'I took instructions from her Ladyship this morning. We are to expect the arrival of Miss Louisa Arnold today. You are Miss Louisa Arnold, are you not?'

Lou looked about her but there was no answer for any of this to be found in the eyes of the statues staring at her from the mantelshelf. 'Yes, but—'

The housekeeper snapped her notebook closed, just a hint of a smile turning up the corners of her lips. 'Please, Miss Arnold, won't you follow me?'

Trying to work out if she had actually let her name slip to this woman or any of her troupe, Lou followed the housekeeper out into the corridor. They were met with the commotion of the footman and a small army of men hauling crates and packages down the outside steps. The chef leant over an open hamper, inspecting a haunch of meat packed in hay. The young maid, Mary, stood to one side, wearing a clean apron, holding a tray containing two glasses of beer. Up at ground level, Lou could just make out the wheels of a cart and some horse's hooves. A horse and cart! There were no local farms. They must have shipped it in from miles away.

'Please, this way, Miss Arnold,' the housekeeper said. Lou followed her back up the stone steps, waiting for the woman's act to slip and for her to deliver a tongue-lashing for gate crashing the party. Instead, Mrs Moriarty's spine remained ramrod straight, keys chinking against her hip as she led the way down the network of passageways.

Lou was sure they were retracing her earlier journey, but they couldn't be; these passageways were well lit and clean. They passed a set of bells and pulleys high up on the wall. Did houses have two sets of bells? Finally, they came to a door. Convinced she was about to be unceremoniously ejected into the outside world, Lou braced herself for a blast of cold air.

When Mrs Moriarty held the door open for her to step through Lou's breath escaped in a long gasp. She was in the hall. It couldn't be . . . but it was! Gone were the charred remnants of the interior, the mould and the rubbish. Every window was now glazed and, high up in the ceiling, two floors above, sunlight flooded through a glass dome. She looked down; beneath her feet was a floor of intricate mosaic tiles; a pattern of tulip-like bronze flowers on a background of white. Statues and busts of the purest marble sat on plinths in recesses in the pale wood panelling cloaking the walls. Two stone fauns flanked the fireplace, bearing the weight of the mantelshelf on their shoulders, one playing a flute, the other, a lyre. Sweeping down into the centre of the hall was the staircase; a continuous swirl of finely carved wood decorated with small creatures and fruits. Every tread, every stair-rod holding the scarlet carpet in place, even the exotically carved pineapples topping the newel posts, were intact. And above the roaring fire in the hearth, the chimneybreast was clad in a single slab of Portland stone. It bore a crest in relief of two lions holding aloft a globe: the coat of arms of the Mandevilles.

'Please, Miss Arnold,' Mrs Moriarty said, holding out her open palm, 'won't you take a seat in the morning room so that you might be more appropriately received.'

Unable to form a reply, Lou mutely acquiesced. She stopped just inside the room and stared in open-mouthed awe.

Paintings of pastoral scenes in gilt frames hung on the dusky pink walls. An immense rug with a pattern of climbing roses covered the floor and the sofas and chairs arranged around a low table before the fireplace were upholstered in pinks and greens, matching the velvet curtains at the three long windows looking out over the snow-covered drive. Lou turned to look at a display case packed with ornaments which ran the entire length of the far wall and a writing desk of pale wood and delicately turned legs which stood in one of the windows. A fire in the hearth made this feminine room feel more welcoming, homelier, than Lou had ever imagined a room in Hill House would be. Imagined! What was she thinking? She was imagining now. This wasn't real. That painting of sheep grazing on a purple heather covered hillside and the gold-cased clock ticking on the mantelshelf were figments of her imagination. She was dreaming, yes that was it; she was fast asleep at home, in bed, dreaming the most vivid dream of her life.

She closed her eyes, fully expecting to find herself back in her bedroom when she opened them. Instead, she came face-to-face with her reflection in the mirror above the fireplace and, for the second time in just minutes, she gasped. It was her, there was no doubt of that, but . . . she looked down at herself, running her fingers over the long blue skirt and pink blouse and touched the silver brooch at her neck. With her hair piled up and held in place by a silver slide, she looked . . . Edwardian.

'It's French.'

Lou wheeled around. A woman had entered the morning room.

'Rococo,' the woman added, pointing to the mirror. 'And a rather exquisite example. It's been here as long as the house. Mrs Leonora Hart.' She held out her hand to shake Lou's. 'And you must be Miss Louisa Arnold.'

'Yes, yes I am, but . . .'

'I'm sure after your journey you won't say no to a spot of tea unless you'd rather change out of your travelling clothes first?'

Change? Into what? A hippopotamus? A giraffe? A tiger leaping from a pomegranate? 'No. I'm fine. Thank you.'

'I can see that you are a young woman after my own heart.' Mrs Hart smiled. She encouraged Lou to sit next to her on one of the sofas and pulled a cord beside the fireplace, ordering tea from the maid who answered. Lou noticed how the tasselled, jade-green shawl around Mrs Hart's shoulders gave her an exotic air, quite at odds with this conservative room.

When the maid left Mrs Hart turned to Lou. 'I have to say, the letter from Elizabeth Goodwill rather came out of the blue. I'm afraid we lost contact after she married and went out to Calcutta with the Major. It's awful how we can allow good friends to drop from our lives. Still, Elizabeth was always an impeccable judge of character so when she recommended you and said you needed a place to stay, I was glad to help.'

'Thank you?' Lou said, for want of something to say.

'This is my brother's house. I'm something of a glorified tenant myself, but my brother's wife, Lady Mandeville, is happy to have you stay. She was sorry not to be here to greet you herself. She is a stickler for formality. Now Louisa, I may call you Louisa, mayn't I? I find titles so unnecessarily formal.' Without waiting for Lou to respond, she continued. 'Tell me something about yourself. We are so remote here that I find myself living vicariously through the experiences of visitors. Elizabeth mentioned that you had suffered a sadness recently. Is it something you wish to talk about? I pride myself on being a good listener.'

She looked at Lou, kindly. Waiting.

This might be a dream, but it didn't make the prospect of a revelation any less painful. 'My mother died,' Lou said quietly.

'Oh, my dear!' Mrs Hart took hold of Lou's hands. 'Oh, I am so sorry. Hang my stupidity! I am a good listener but an equally good contortionist if I am judged by my ability to put my foot in my mouth.'

'It's all right—'

'No! Don't make excuses for me. My lack of tact is a fault I am in constant battle with. But I *am* sorry. I know how devastating the loss of one's mother is to a daughter.' She squeezed Lou's hands. 'And do you have family at home to help you through this trying time?'

'I have two brothers.'

'And your father?'

'He's . . . he's no longer with us.'

'Oh my, you poor dear. I don't doubt that as the only woman you are left to shoulder the responsibility for the household, as is the lot of every woman.'

Mrs Hart showed such compassion that Lou felt guilty for letting her believe her dad was dead. But this was her dream, and she could live out any truth she wanted.

The door opened and the maid placed the tray on the table. After thanking then dismissing her, Mrs Hart poured two cups of tea and placed one before Lou.

'I'm glad that you have found your way to us. It would appear that you are in need of a sojourn from your troubles. Sugar?'

Lou shook her head.

'You must make the most of my brother's hospitality. Hill House has a reputation for entertaining, which is indeed well-earned.' Mrs Hart blew across the top of her tea before taking a sip. 'And you have fortunately timed your visit to perfection. With the ball in a few days, there will be so many people to meet and so much to keep you occupied that you will be too busy to dwell for long. And if you prefer the outdoors, I'd be happy to show you some of the winter walks. This was my childhood home, so I know how to enjoy it in all seasons. Do you know how long you intend to stay with us?'

'I'm not sure.'

The door flew open and a young woman burst in. 'Aunt Leonora!' she exclaimed, brandishing a newspaper. She could be no more than eighteen-years old, with fair hair, a nose that turned up at the tip and wide blue eyes. On seeing Lou, she stopped. 'Oh, I'm so sorry. I hadn't realised your guest had arrived.'

'Charlotte, dear, this is Miss Louisa Arnold. Louisa, I would like to introduce my favourite niece, Miss Charlotte Mandeville. And Charlotte, don't worry. I think that in Louisa we have an ally for our cause.'

Cause? What cause? A small, knowing smile passed between aunt and niece. Lou rose briefly to shake hands with the girl who laughed. 'Don't be fooled by my aunt's flattery, Miss Arnold,' she said, flouncing back into an armchair. 'Since I am my aunt's only niece, it goes without saying that I must be her favourite. I may call you Louisa, that's not too familiar, is it? You must call me Charlotte, I insist.' Charlotte looked from Lou to Mrs Hart. 'You haven't dressed for tea. What *would* Mama say?'

'Happily for us, since your mother is attending the Christmas assembly at the village school, she is not here to reprimand us. For one afternoon at least, Louisa and I have agreed to say fie to formality.' Mrs Hart flashed a wicked sort of grin, making Charlotte laugh again.

'Oh, Aunt. You are so rebellious,' Charlotte said, adding two sugar lumps to the cup of tea that her aunt poured for her.

Lou couldn't take her eyes from this young girl who was continually watching, taking everything in, like a young owl. With a sudden, sinking sensation, Lou remembered the old man's earlier prediction about Charlotte Mandeville's future.

'Aunt Leonora says that a friend of hers from India asked that you might come and stay with us for a while,' Charlotte said, sipping her tea. 'I would so like to go to India. It seems so very colourful and exotic. One of my favourite stories is *Ali Baba and the Forty Thieves*. I know that's not exactly India but it's similar, don't you think? With all of the spices and perfumes.'

'You will have to excuse my niece,' Mrs Hart said. 'She has so many thoughts racing around her head that they crash about like young birds leaving the nest for the first time. But don't let her beauty or her silliness fool you; she has a brain the size of a planet. And never play her at bridge. I have often thought about taking her on a trip on a paddle steamer up the Mississippi. Charlotte would make our fortune beating those Yankee card sharps at poker!'

'I'm certainly not that good,' Charlotte protested. She took a plate of biscuits from the tea tray and offered them to Lou. 'Please, do try one. Monsieur Gotti, our chef, bakes them. He's from Switzerland. Aunt Leonora and I spent the summer in Switzerland when I was sixteen, didn't we Aunt?'

Mrs Hart smiled indulgently. 'Indeed, we did. My intention, Louisa, was to give my niece an education in art and music; instead I spent most of the month fending off potential suitors. But Charlotte is above such silly things as admirers, aren't you, my dear?'

Charlotte's cheeks flushed. She held the plate to Lou. 'Please, Louisa, won't you try one.' Sensing Charlotte's embarrassment and her desperation for a diversion from talk of romance, Lou took a biscuit and bit into its buttery surface. It melted on her tongue.

'How would you describe it?' Charlotte asked, placing the plate back on the tray.

Lou thought for a moment. 'Like eating a mouthful of cloud.'

'Yes it is! How perceptive you are.' Charlotte clapped in delight and picked up her newspaper. 'There's a fascinating story in here about a scientist in the Lake District. He's attempting to capture a cloud in a huge net so that he can study its construction and design a machine to shoot clouds into the sky to make rain in very dry climates. How clever! Have you read it?'

Lou said that she hadn't, and Charlotte proceeded to recount every detail she could remember. Mrs Hart threw herself into the conversation wholeheartedly, humouring her niece and steering her back on track when her enthusiasm veered off onto scientific fantasy rather than fact. There seemed to be real affection between aunt and niece; gentle laughs, a shared language of short cuts and in-jokes. Lou experienced a pang of longing. To distract herself, she studied the ornaments in the display cabinet; small vases decorated with Highland scenes of stags on high, craggy peaks and delicate porcelain creatures – foxes, hedgehogs, badgers. A wave of tiredness washed over her. She attempted to stifle a yawn but Mrs Hart, who seemed to miss nothing, saw her.

'Charlotte, dear,' she said, 'I'm afraid that we have lost Louisa somewhere in our conversation.'

'I'm sorry,' Lou said. 'I didn't mean to be rude.' She felt ready for bed, but surely she should be about to wake up.

Mrs Hart held up her hand. 'There should never be the need for apologies between friends. I'll ring for Jones to show you to your room. I'm sure you will be glad of a rest before dinner.'

'Thank you, yes, I'd be glad of that.'

Glad of that! When had she started to talk like Bobbie from *The Railway Children*? All the rainy Saturday afternoons spent immersed in Nesbit, Kipling and Hodgson Burnett hadn't gone to waste after all. At least she was managing to sound like these people.

Mrs Hart pulled the cord to summon the maid. She appeared within seconds. 'Rest well,' Mrs Hart said as Lou followed the maid from the room.

'Dinner is at eight o'clock sharp,' Charlotte called after her. 'Don't be late! Mother does not tolerate tardiness.'

Lou followed the maid, Jones, across the hall, and up the stairs they went, up the scarlet carpet, Lou running her fingers along the handrail. The maid showed her to a room at the front of the house on the first floor. Lou looked around at the pale wooden dressing table positioned between two tall windows and matching wardrobe on the opposite wall. Beside the bed, a door stood open, leading to a bathroom.

'Just ring the bell, Miss, if you need anything at all,' the maid said. She stood in the doorway, turned away from Lou. When Lou tried to get a better look at the girl's face, she twisted away.

'Do I know you?' Lou asked, taking in the red hair which was pulled back and topped off with a crisp white cap.

'I . . . I don't think so.'

'You look familiar.'

'I've got a familiar face. Or so I'm told.'

'What's your name again?'

'Jones.' She gave her name so quietly, it seemed she would rather not have given it at all. 'If that's everything, Miss?'

'If what's everything?'

'Can I go? Sorry, may I go, Miss?'

'Yes, I suppose so. Don't let me stop you.'

The maid didn't waste a second in closing the door behind her.

Lou stood in the middle of the bedroom which was bathed in the afternoon sunlight. Outside, beyond the trees, the clock of St Mary's chimed the hour. She went to the window and looked out. The snow-covered landscape was empty save for a handful of cottages just beyond the gates. There was no motorway splitting Hill House from St Mary's and no Hill House Council Estate.

Lou lay down on the bed, nestled into the inviting feather

quilt, and closed her eyes. This was some crazy dream. But if it was a dream, why did the taste of the buttery biscuit still linger on her tongue? How could she feel the soft linen of the pillow against her cheek and smell the lavender in a glass bowl on the nightstand . . .?

FIVE

Slowly Lou became aware of someone knocking at her bedroom door. She opened her eyes. The room was dark – no moonlight, no streetlamps. The snow must have caused a power cut. She rolled over. 'My bag's in the hall. Take what you can find in my purse.'

Silence.

'Dean, I said take what you want. Order a pizza if you're hungry.'

The door opened a crack.

'Miss Arnold,' a female voice said.

With a start, Lou sat up.

'Would you like me to turn on the light?' the woman asked.

'Yes. Okay. All right.'

A bright light shone from overhead. Momentarily dazzled, Lou peered around the strange room until shapes began to make sense: the wardrobe with its matching dressing table, yellow curtains at the window and a yellow quilt, dented with the imprint of her body. How could she still be in this dream?

'I'm so sorry to disturb you, Miss Arnold,' the young woman said, hovering expectantly in the doorway. She wore a black dress and a crisp white apron, a white cap perched on her head. 'It's after five o'clock. I thought you might want me to wake you so I can help you dress for dinner. I'm Morrison, I'm to be your lady's maid for your stay here.'

'My lady's maid?'

'The groom collected your trunk from the station this morning.' The young woman closed the door and crossed the room. She opened the wardrobe to reveal a rail crammed with clothes in fabric covers and then pulled out drawers which contained garments wrapped in tissue paper. 'I hope you're happy with how I have unpacked your clothes.'

Her clothes? Realising that the young woman was waiting for a response, Lou said, 'Thank you. Yes, they look lovely . . . Sorry, I'm a bit confused. What was your name again?'

'Morrison, Miss.'

'No, your real name, your Christian name.' She might be in a dream, but she couldn't bring herself to call another woman by her surname.

'Sally, Miss. But everyone knows me as Morrison.'

'Would you mind if I call you Sally?'

'As you like, Miss.'

'And you can call me Louisa.'

'Oh no, I couldn't do that. It wouldn't be right.' Sally's eyes widened in a look of horror, as though Lou had asked her to call her darling or sweetheart. 'Would you like me to draw you a bath?' Sally added, clearly keen to re-establish the natural order of things. 'You must have had quite a journey. Did you come directly from India?'

'India?'

'Mrs Moriarty said that a friend of Mrs Hart's—'

'Of course, yes, India.' – what was one more fabrication? – 'Sorry my mind's all over the place.'

'It is?'

Sally took a step back. It was clear that she thought she had been sent to wait on a madwoman. Lou dredged up memories of every period drama she had ever watched and every historical novel she had read, desperate for a reference point for how she should behave. It ran against every feminist instinct in her, but finally she said, 'Is the offer of a bath still on? I'm afraid I'm terribly tired and not sure that I'm making any sense. A soak will put me right.'

'Very good, Miss,' Sally said and hurried through to the bathroom.

Sitting on the edge of the bed, Lou heard the gush of water. She leant over to remove her boots but stopped halfway down and let out an involuntary yelp. There was something digging into her ribs.

Sally rushed from the bathroom, a towel draped over her arm. 'Oh, Miss,' she said, placing the towel on the bed. 'Let me help you undress.'

'No!' Lou said sharply and then remembering herself added, 'I'm fine, I can manage.'

Sally gave her a quizzical look. 'Not wanting to contradict, Miss, but you won't be able to manage your corset without help.'

Lou touched her ribs and found that she was indeed trussed from waist to bust. 'All right,' she sighed. What choice did she have?

Kneeling before her, Sally unlaced Lou's boots and eased them free before helping her to stand. Expertly she unhooked dozens of tiny buttons running down the back of Lou's blouse and gradually worked her way around, unfastening and unhooking. She eased down the skirt for Lou to step from, unclipped stockings and set to work unlacing the corset. Lou folded her arms across her chest. In her normal life, she couldn't bring herself to use a communal fitting room and preferred to hang around shivering after a swim, waiting for a cubicle to become free, rather than face the humiliation of being naked in front of other people. By contrast, Sally appeared completely at ease in the presence of Lou's increasing nakedness, peeling away layers of clothes with no more ceremony than she might peel the skin from a banana to reveal the pale flesh beneath. The irony wasn't lost on Lou. Here she was, a twenty-first century woman and even in a dream she was more squeamish about her nudity than a woman who lived in a rigid, prudish society.

Mercifully, Sally stopped short of relieving her of the final item of clothing – a flesh-coloured silk slip. After Sally unpinned her hair, Lou hurried to the bathroom. She closed the door behind her, removed the slip and stepped into the bath. Warmth inched up her legs as she sank into the water up to her chin and peered over the edge of the roll-top bath. The sink, bath and toilet were encased in dark wood and the walls and floors were cloaked in white marble shot through with thick blue veins, like ripe Stilton. An open bottle of rosewater sat on the edge of the bath. Lou breathed in deeply, letting the perfume waft from the water and fill her nostrils. If this was a dream, then it was the most vivid, most wonderful dream she had ever experienced.

Thinking back, she retraced her steps, piecing together how she had arrived at this state of affairs. The last memory she had of anything normal was venturing down to the basement of the derelict shell of Hill House. It was then that things had started to take a strange turn, with the scrubbed floor and light pouring in through the windows and the people in costume. Could she have fallen and hit her head on the stone steps, knocking herself out cold? Was she, right now, lying in a hospital bed in a coma, hooked up to machines? If she was, then these people must be doctors and nurses that her drug-addled brain was somehow turning into residents of Hill House, cobbling them together from the snippets of history she knew of each and inventing those that she knew nothing of. It was utterly mad. But the more she thought about it, the more this most farfetched explanation seemed the only one that made any sense. Hadn't she wished to turn back the hands of time to change history? This must be her unconscious brain living out that fantasy. And hadn't she always had a very vivid imagination? Slipping further under the water, the knots in her shoulders unwound. It must be the drugs kicking in. Morphine possibly. A sensation of relaxation she hadn't experienced in weeks, inched up her arms and legs. She briefly thought back to her real world, to the row with Stephen, and to Dean's distress at the breakfast table, before holding her breath and slipping beneath the water, immersing herself completely. If this was a coma, then she was in no rush to wake up.

Emerging from the bathroom in a robe she found hanging behind the door, Lou sat at the dressing table. She watched Sally work around her reflection in the mirror, marvelling at how she skilfully pinched strands of her hair, twisting them and pinning them in place, building up the volume with handfuls of wadding. How did she know so much detail of early twentieth century hairdressing to project onto Sally? She must have read it somewhere.

After helping her into a pale green satin dress, Sally stepped aside. When Lou saw her finished reflection, she touched her hair and ran her fingers over the fine fabric of the dress.

'Are you pleased, Miss?'

'Pleased? I'm . . . speechless. You've performed a miracle.'

'I don't know about that,' Sally smiled modestly.

Lou thought for a moment. If she was going to spend time in this dream world, she might need an ally to help her navigate her way through. 'Can I confide something in you, Sally?'

'Of course, Miss.'

'It's just . . . well, you see, I'm normal. That's to say, I'm only a guest here by some strange stroke of luck.'

'Because you're a friend of Mrs Hart's acquaintance in India?'

'Yes, something like that. But since I'm not the lady everybody seems to think I am, I may need some help, especially in how to behave. You seem to know exactly what to do.'

Sally's cheeks flushed. 'Well, it is my job to look after you while you're a guest, not only to dress you.' She paused and Lou could practically hear the cogs in her brain whirring. 'If it's not too forward, Miss, may I say something else? It's just that you've nothing to be ashamed of. You'd give any of the grand ladies that have stayed at Hill House a run for their money.'

The sound of a gong rang throughout the house. Sally smoothed down the skirt of Lou's dress. 'You'd best go down now, Miss. Lady Mandeville doesn't like latecomers. The family assemble in the drawing room which is the next door along from the morning room.'

SIX

Lou paused outside the door to the drawing room. She took a deep breath – not easy in a bone-crushing corset – and stepped inside the dark panelled room.

'My dear Louisa.' Mrs Hart rose from a chair beside the fire. 'How lovely to see you looking so refreshed. You know Charlotte, but may I introduce you to my brother's wife, Lady Mandeville.'

The woman seated on the sofa beside Charlotte stood up. She had the same wide eyes as her daughter and, although her face had lost the plumpness of youth, she was handsomely beautiful. Her fair hair was flecked with soft grey and she wore a dignified dress in a dark blue lace. She took hold of Lou's hand and shook it warmly.

'Welcome to our home, Miss Arnold. My husband's sister has told me something of the unhappy circumstances that have brought you here. I hope that in some small way we can provide a pleasant distraction.'

'Thank you, your Ladyship,' Lou said. 'I'm very grateful to you for letting me stay.'

'How sweet. Please, Miss Arnold, won't you walk into dinner with me?'

A footman opened a connecting door for them to pass through. The long table in the centre of the next room was set for five with silver and crystal and a vase of beautiful purple flowers in the centre. Lady Mandeville sat at one end with Charlotte beside her. Lou was shown to the seat beside Charlotte with Mrs Hart opposite. An empty place remained beside Mrs Hart.

'My son, Edward, will join us,' Lady Mandeville said, 'just as soon as he returns from town. He knows my feelings on tardiness but recently. . .' she glanced at the footman who was pouring wine. 'Well, he has been busy and sometimes forgets.'

'Forgets,' Charlotte laughed. 'Yes, he does forget his way home when he has spent all afternoon in the public bar of The White Lion Inn.'

'Charlotte!'

'Sorry, Mama.'

Two footmen, one of whom Lou recognised as William from earlier, served them a starter of melon formed into perfect, small spheres. As they ate, an older man hovered around the table. Dressed in a black suit with a bow tie at his neck, he had a horseshoe of perfectly white hair. He was small and rather wiry, but what he lacked in stature he more than made up for in the force of his presence. From the way he wordlessly directed the footmen with a series of nods and hand gestures, Lou guessed that he was Bainbridge, the butler. He surveyed the room constantly and when a ball of melon slipped from Charlotte's plate, all it took was a nod to send the second footman forward to scoop it up. When William removed Lou's plate, she turned to think him but quickly stopped herself, remembering that it wasn't the done thing. She should treat him as though he was invisible, even if she had spoken to him just a few hours earlier.

'I am told that the help has arrived from Caxton Hall

today,' Lady Mandeville said as William offered her a plate of carved chicken. With a silver serving fork and spoon, she served herself a small portion. 'Were it not for the generosity of my husband's cousin with his staff, I am certain I should not be able to cope with all I have to do for the shoot and the Christmas Ball. Are you acquainted with Lord and Lady Caxton, Miss Arnold?'

'I'm afraid not,' Lou said. She could hardly say that she had traipsed around the bedrooms and kitchens at Caxton Hall and eaten a cream tea in what had once been their buttery. Copying Lady Mandeville, she took a small sliver of chicken from the plate William offered and helped herself to a scoop of vegetables from the tray offered by the second footman.

'I had not expected so many guests to accept my invitation,' Lady Mandeville said. 'It is sure to be our largest Christmas Ball yet.'

Charlotte grinned and leant towards Lou. 'Mama has invited everyone we know and many that we don't! She hopes to have good news to announce and wants an audience. Although I'm not sure that my brother, Tom, is aware yet that he is to be the stuffed goose at Mama's festivities.'

'Charlotte!' her mother chided her, but she could hardly contain a smile. 'Is it not my duty as a mother to present my children with opportunities? Even if I cannot second-guess what any of you will do. In my day, children were obedient; they did their parents' bidding. I really do not know what has become of this generation. I am sure—'

The door flew open and a young man staggered in. 'Good evening family,' he slurred, waving his arms before he fell against the wall. 'What a pleasure and a delight it is to see you all.'

As one, Bainbridge and the footmen put down their serving plates and stepped forward to help him into his seat at the table. 'Why, thank you, Bainbridge,' the young man said, collapsing into the chair. 'What an absolute gent you are. Have I ever told you that? No, I doubt that I have.'

'Thank you, Mister Edward,' Bainbridge said quietly before returning to his post beside the sideboard, directing the footmen to continue the service.

Edward ran his fingers through his thick, strawberry blonde hair, making his fringe stick up. 'That's it, Bainbridge. Return to your work. One mustn't converse with the staff, must one? It makes everybody uncomfortable. Lord knows what would happen if we were to treat you as fellow travellers on the journey to the grave.'

'Edward!' Lady Mandeville said.

Edward pushed his wire-framed spectacles further up his nose and turned to face her. 'Mother?'

'You could at least have dressed for dinner. Especially since we have a guest. This is Miss Arnold.'

Edward draped his arm over the back of his chair. He took a moment to focus on Lou through the thick glass of his spectacles. 'Good evening, Miss Arnold. What a pleasure it is to make your acquaintance. May I ask, does it offend you that I present myself at dinner in my tweeds? Is the world as we know it going to come crashing to an end simply because I failed to change my suit?'

'Really, Mama,' Charlotte objected. 'It is too much to bear that he thinks he can behave like this in front of our guest.'

'Oh, don't mind me,' Edward said, grinning. The second footman placed a plate before him. He pushed it away. But when his wine glass was filled, he drank it in one go and wiped his mouth on his sleeve. 'You all go right ahead and talk about me as though I am not here. What does it matter what I think? My opinion is of no significance to this family.' He leant forward and pointed at Lou as though to emphasise his point. 'You see Miss Arnold, I am the spare. The sediment that sank to the bottom of the bucket while my brother, Thomas, is the heir, the cream that rose to the top. I am the chaff. A thorn in the side. A spare part. A—'

'Edward!' Lady Mandeville said again, this time successfully silencing her son. She dismissed Bainbridge and the footmen, saying that she would ring when they were next needed. Lou wished she could follow them rather than sit here to witness this young man's meltdown.

When the door closed behind the staff, Lady Mandeville turned to Edward. 'How can you be so indiscreet?' she said coldly. 'If your father were here he—'

'Well, he's not, is he? He's in Town. Not that I would know anything about that. He has never invited *me* to his office in The House to introduce *me* to his parliamentary friends. I suppose he's afraid I'd want to discuss Keats and Byron and Rosetti. Unlike the magnificent Captain Thomas Mandeville who knows exactly what to say to those old Tories on the subject of policies. Head Boy, captain of the rugby team, cavalry officer; now there's a son any father can be proud of.'

Charlotte slammed her cutlery down. 'You're drunk. And nobody here cares to listen to your bile.'

'I may be drunk but that doesn't mean I'm not correct.' He downed another glass of wine. 'Do you know, Miss Arnold.' – Lou squirmed, why was he directing his outpouring at her? – 'My sister is to be presented next year. Mother will find her a husband with land and money because that's what our family does, you see, they make matches for Lady Wealth. God forbid anything as tawdry as love should get in the way of a politic match.'

'I do not need you to speak on my behalf,' Charlotte said. 'And I have no intention of ever marrying. So there.'

'Oh, Charlotte. Dear, dear, Charlotte.' Edward shook his head and smiled in a way that wasn't at all kind. 'You poor misguided little kitten. You will be married. But if our perfect brother is not allowed to make his own match, then what hope is there for you and I? You will be a broodmare soon enough.'

'Really,' Lady Mandeville said, her neck flushing. 'This behaviour is insufferable.'

Mrs Hart placed her cutlery down on her plate with a controlled chink. She took her napkin from her lap and wiped her lips. 'Edward,' she said. Standing up, she took hold of his hand. Edward got shakily to his feet. He fell against the table and Mrs Hart helped steady him before escorting him from the room.

'I must apologise on behalf of my son, Miss Arnold,' Lady Mandeville said, 'since it would seem that he is currently incapable of doing so for himself.' She rang the bell to recall the staff. As though Edward's outburst had had as little effect on the meal as a pebble dropped into the English Channel, she took up her cutlery and regaled Lou and Charlotte with the details of new glass baubles she had ordered from Selfridges. Bainbridge and the footmen recommenced their well-rehearsed dance, placing dishes on the table, removing them and replacing them. Lou looked from mother to daughter. Rich or poor, stately home or council house, families were all the same. The Mandevilles just had more space and better clothes to conduct their squabbles in than the Arnolds.

At the end of the meal, Lou pushed her pineapple ice cream around the bowl until it melted to a yellow slick. The fun had gone out of the food as well as the dream.

'You look tired, Miss Arnold.' Lady Mandeville said and with exquisite tact, added; 'Do not feel obliged to take coffee with Charlotte and I if you would rather retire.'

'It has been a long day,' Lou said. She got up and placed her napkin on the chair, glad of the excuse to leave.

'But you will join us for church in the morning,' Charlotte said. 'It's the Christmas carol service for the village school. It's always held on the last Friday before Christmas. All the staff attend. Mother takes the car but it's just a short walk to St Mary's. Won't you join me after breakfast?'

'I would like that,' Lou said.

Leaving mother and daughter to their coffee, Lou made her way into the deserted hall. But just short of the stairs, a movement in another downstairs room caught her attention. Edward was slumped in a chair beside a billiard table, his head in his hands, Mrs Hart perched on the arm of the chair. Lou stood in the shadows and listened.

'Oh, my darling, what is wrong? This is so unlike you,' Mrs Hart said. 'You seemed so happy this morning when we were out on our walk. What can have changed in these few short hours? Has something occurred to make you feel lost, is that it? You must find something to occupy your time. It's not enough for you to stay around the house all day. Why don't you write to your old headmaster? I am sure he would be only too happy to have a bright young man like you on the staff at Harrow.'

'It's not that.' Edward shook his head. He took his hands from his face, removed his spectacles and rubbed his eyes. 'It's . . . it's . . . I can't eat, I know I shan't be able to sleep. I can't bear it. I don't want to live anymore.'

'Please my darling,' Mrs Hart said, 'don't talk so. You make me fear for you.'

'She's gone. We were supposed to meet in the library. I went looking for her in all of the places where she might be. She's gone. I can feel it.'

'Who, Edward? Who has gone?'

With a sob, Edward collapsed onto Mrs Hart's shoulder. She wrapped her arms around him and held him as he wept.

In an attempt to put a stop to this young man's pain, Lou closed her eyes. Since this was her dream, surely, she should have some level of control over it? But when she opened them, she saw that Edward was still there, his tears darkening the shoulder of his aunt's dress. Gathering up her skirt, Lou ran up the stairs to her room. Once inside, she had barely caught her breath when Sally appeared, to help her undress. Lou sat listless as she was unpinned, unfastened, unhooked, and a heavy linen nightdress was slipped over her head. When she proved unresponsive to conversation, Sally diplomatically fell silent. Like a child, Lou gave in to Sally's tender kindness.

After Sally left, Lou lay in the darkness, the orange embers of the dying fire glowing in the hearth. Eyes open, eyes closed, all she could see was Dean and Stephen sitting at the kitchen table that morning. Like Edward, Dean had seemed so lost, his heart breaking. In the real world, were her brothers sitting beside her hospital bed, talking to her, willing her to wake from her coma? Or were they thinking how, in the long run, it would be better for them all if she never woke up again?

She rolled onto her side and hugged her knees to her chest. She didn't deserve this dream world where she dressed in fine clothes and feasted on fluffy biscuits and melon balls. Of course, it was all just her overactive imagination reacting to the drugs, taking her to the kind of world she had always wanted to inhabit. She was escaping – if only for as long as she remained in this dream – while her brothers were left at home. They were the ones who deserved respite from the life she had thrust them into. It was her fault that Mum was dead, and here she was, escaping the fallout. Guilt churned in her stomach like curdling cream. That was the single thing she would never escape. Guilt. It would follow her wherever she went, even into her dreams.

SEVEN

19TH DECEMBER 1913

All night Lou drifted in and out of sleep, her thoughts crowded with faces that kept her from true rest, until at some point she became aware of a scraping sound in the darkness. She fumbled for the lamp beside her bed, but it wasn't in its usual place. There was a knock at the door.

'Come in,' she murmured.

'Good morning, Miss.'

Lou sat up and in the dim light watched Sally cross the room. So, she was still in the dream. Sally placed a tray on the dressing table and opened the curtains. She turned and looked towards the fireplace, and her lips parted to speak, but shut before she uttered a word. Lou followed the direction of Sally's sharp stare and saw a girl crouching there, her hand in a coalscuttle, her apron black.

'Mary Parkinson!' Sally snapped.

The girl, who Lou recognised as the kitchen maid, scrabbled to her feet. She stared at her boots and brushed her hair away from her face, leaving a trail of black ash across her forehead.

'I'm sorry,' Mary said, her voice barely audible. 'I'm a bit behind this morning, what with Alice leaving yesterday.' She grabbed the scuttle and a bucket of ashes and headed for the door.

'Don't touch the handle. Not with those filthy hands!' Sally scolded. She crossed the room and held the door open. As Mary passed through, she whispered, 'And less talk of Alice. Mrs Moriarty will tear a strip off you if she hears you've been talking about the staff in front of the family or their guests again. Go on with you.'

Mary disappeared, leaving Sally to close the door. 'Did you sleep well, Miss?' she asked, fussing with the sheets, straightening them over Lou's legs, tucking them into perfect hospital corners.

'Who's Alice?' Lou asked. If she was going to spend another day in this world, then she may as well play along.

Sally placed the tray of tea and toast in Lou's lap. 'You don't want to be bothering yourself with that.'

'Perhaps. But I'd like to know.'

'As you like.' Sally paused before plumping the pillows. 'Alice Jones was a housemaid here until last night.'

'Jones? The maid who showed me to my room yesterday?'

'I daresay. Anyway, while we were all still fast asleep, she packed her bags and slipped a note under Mrs Moriarty's door. Upped and left without a word to anyone. She hadn't been here more than a month, but we'll miss her; she was a good worker. Poor Mary is having to take on some of her chores. It's odd though, I . . . Oh, it doesn't matter.' She ran her hand over the sheets as though to smooth them out, even though they were already quite flat.

'Go on,' Lou said.

'It's just that Mrs Moriarty said Alice mentioned something in her letter about being homesick and wanting to see her family. Only I could have sworn she said she was an orphan with no home to speak of. Still, I suppose we only know as much of a person as they choose to tell us.' Sally collected a blanket from the floor where Lou must have kicked it in the night. Folding it, she placed it back on the bed. It was clear that she had decided the conversation about this Alice character had come to an end. 'Breakfast is at eight and the family always leaves for church on the dot of eight forty-five. I'd best draw your bath or you'll be late.'

Lou sipped her tea. She could get used to being brought a cuppa in bed every morning. 'Is everything done to a schedule in this house?'

'Yes, Miss. Sir Charles was in the army and likes everything to run to time. It makes it easier for us all to know what is expected and when. The staff in a household this size need to be kept in order.'

'Don't you ever tire of fetching and carrying and running around after other people?'

'Tire of it! I don't have the time to be tired.' Sally let out a little laugh. 'Anyway, this is the best job I'm ever likely to have. Her Ladyship has been kinder to me than another employer would have been in my . . . my situation.'

'Your situation?'

'I'd best be getting on.' Sally made hastily in the direction of the bathroom, bringing their conversation to an abrupt halt.

After her bath and while Sally dressed her in a long brown skirt and a white blouse with a close-fitting jacket – 'You'll need a dark skirt if you're walking to church, so that it won't show when the hem gets damp.' – Lou had to resist the urge to press Sally on her *situation*. That level of nosiness would surely be pushing this fledgling friendship a step too far.

Once dressed to Sally's satisfaction, Lou made her way down to the dining room. If the weather outside was chilly – which, judging by the rime on the windows, it was – then the atmosphere around the table was positively arctic. Edward sat at one end, his forehead resting in his cupped palm. He was pale and exuded misery, not to mention beer fumes. Lou briefly held her breath as she passed him to take the chair that Bainbridge held out for her.

'Good morning, Louisa,' Mrs Hart said across the table. Lou wished her a good morning in return. But gone was the cheery Mrs Hart of yesterday and in her place sat a woman who stared at her nephew over the rim of her coffee cup as though her constant gaze alone was stopping him from shattering into pieces. Lady Mandeville and Charlotte, on the other hand, behaved as though Edward was not there at all.

'Did you sleep well, Miss Arnold?' Lady Mandeville asked, vigorously buttering a slice of toast.

'Quite well, thank you,' Lou said and took a sip of the tea William placed before her.

'And do you like your room?' Charlotte scooped a mound of jam onto her toast. 'It's my particular favourite. It has the most wonderful view of the drive, don't you think? It's the perfect place to watch the guests arrive for the Christmas Ball. Wait until you see it lit up with Mama's Chinese lanterns; it's truly splendid. Perhaps I'll come to your room on Christmas Eve so that we can watch the guests arriving together.'

'I must apologise for my daughter, Miss Arnold. She is rather too inquisitive in nature and often too forward. Traits that I do not encourage.' Lady Mandeville glanced briefly at Mrs Hart. 'Charlotte is never satisfied until she knows the business of everybody in the house. Do try to remember, my dear,' she said, addressing her daughter, 'that not every person you meet will want to be as candid with you as you would like them to be.'

Charlotte slumped back in her chair. Lady Mandeville gave her a sharp warning to sit up straight; nobody liked a girl with rounded shoulders. 'Sorry, Louisa,' Charlotte said. 'I didn't mean to be so forward.' She appeared deflated.

'Thank you for your consideration, Lady Mandeville,' Lou said. 'But I'd be happy for Charlotte to come to my room any time she likes.'

The frown that had darkened Charlotte's features turned into a broad smile. She sat forward. 'I knew you wouldn't mind, Louisa. But of course, Mama is right, I can't deny that I like to know what makes people think and behave as they do. Have you read any books on the subject of psychology? It's fascinating. Take Edward for example, I should like to know what caused him to get into such an appalling state yesterday that he made a spectacle of himself and sits here now like a ghost in—'

'It is as well to leave a science that you do not fully understand alone,' Mrs Hart said flatly. 'Meddling in a discipline with only half-formed theories leads to incorrect and unsubstantiated conclusions.'

But as determined as Mrs Hart seemed to be to quieten her niece, Charlotte seemed just as determined to press on. She left the table and helped herself to a plate of food from the silver warmers on the sideboard. On her way back to the table, she stepped closer to Edward than was necessary.

'Mmmm, kippers, my favourite.' She paused to waft the fishy scent towards her nose, breathing in deeply.

Edward threw back his chair so that Charlotte had to jump out of his way. He grabbed a napkin and held it to his mouth. 'If you'll excuse me,' he said, rushing for the door.

'Will you be joining us at church?' Charlotte called after him. But it was too late; he was already gone.

Charlotte took her seat and began to flake the flesh from the fish's bones.

'Really, Charlotte,' Mrs Hart said. 'I had thought you sensible enough to appreciate that sometimes we need those we love to understand what it is like to inhabit our skin. I can see that I was mistaken.'

'But Aunt—'

'Never forget that it takes compassion as well as intelligence to make a fully-rounded human being. Now if you will excuse me, I am going to prepare for church.'

After William had closed the door behind Mrs Hart, Lady Mandeville turned to her daughter. 'Your aunt is right,' she said. 'Edward has been punished enough for his behaviour last night. Perhaps he found a dead squirrel out on his walk yesterday. You know how the smallest thing can upset him. So, for the sake of my nerves, please leave him be.'

'But Mama—' Charlotte whined.

Lady Mandeville held up her hand. 'I won't hear another word on the subject. I want this house to be a picture of tranquillity when your father and brother return today. I have asked chef to prepare Beef Wellington for dinner tonight; it has always been Thomas' favourite. And I do not want anything to spoil his homecoming. I trust I am making myself understood.'

Charlotte folded her arms across her chest. 'Yes, Mama.'

'Good. Now finish your breakfast or you shall be late for church.'

Following breakfast, Lou returned to her room where Sally pinned a wide-brimmed hat to her hair and buttoned her up in long woollen coat. How did the women in this era bear the rigmarole of dressing and undressing so many times in a single day?

After Sally handed her a pair of beige kidskin gloves, Lou was free to make her way downstairs. Finding herself alone, she wandered around the hall, admiring the statues and paintings lining the walls. What an amazing thing the human subconscious was that it could conjure up this labyrinth of a house and decorate it with such fine works of art, no doubt amalgams of paintings she had seen on her many visits to galleries and stately homes. There were portraits of men in powdered wigs sitting side on to the artist, and portraits of women, the folds of their silk gowns so realistic that Lou felt if she reached out to touch them, they would be soft. In one painting, a large lady clutched two Pekinese dogs to her and in another, a proud man sat with his hand over a globe. In others, ruddy-cheeked children posed with hoops and hobbyhorses and dolls. These paintings told the story of the wealth and luxury the Mandevilles had enjoyed for two centuries.

Lou stopped at a vast painting, at least twice the size of any other. It was hung to the rear of the hall, opposite the doorway to the billiard room. She studied the man, in military uniform, who sat astride a black stallion, his height and power matched by the beauty and strength of his horse. His uniform of a dark blue with a red breast to the jacket, was adorned with swathes of intricately twisted gold braid. His black boots gleamed, and a sheathed sword rested against his hip. He sat upright, his legs bent in the stirrups. The scarlet plume of feathers decorating his gold helmet appeared to blow in the wind and the peak was pulled down so far that he was forced to tip his chin up and look down the sides of his nose. The man and horse were framed by foliage and, in the background, stood Hill House. The identity of the sitter on the nameplate came as no surprise to Lou – Captain Thomas Charles Oliver Mandeville. So, this was the heir. Poor Edward didn't stand a chance against this hulk of a man. The piercing blue eyes of the future baronet stared directly at her, defiant and superior. He was the centre of the world he inhabited, the chosen one, the firstborn son. Why would he not believe himself invincible?

Something inside Lou sank. This world she was in may not be real, but the people who had welcomed her so warmly had been, once. If only she hadn't learnt quite so much about the history of Hill House. It pained her knowing that the demise of this proud man, barely two weeks after war was declared, was to sound the death knell for his entire family. Hill House Primary had spared its pupils the exact circumstances of Captain Mandeville's death – they were only taught that he had died a 'hero' – but he looked just the type of man who would throw himself into battle, without a thought to the result. And in his bravado and desire for glory he would start a chain reaction, which nobody could stop. The downfall of the Mandeville family rested squarely on the broad shoulders of Captain Thomas Mandeville. Where was the heroism in that?

'Apparently my brother is considered handsome,' Charlotte said. She had approached without Lou noticing. 'I can't see it; he's just silly old Tom. But our cousin, Emma, will be the envy of everyone we know if he proposes this week.' Charlotte smiled up at the painting. Would she be smiling if she knew the fate waiting for her? Edward's words the previous evening echoed in Lou's ears – that Charlotte was little more than livestock. But Edward could have no inkling that his sister's destiny, moulded by their older brother, would rest finally in *his* decision to marry her off to their cousin.

'Miss Caxton has a brother, doesn't she?' Lou said, watching Charlotte, waiting for her reaction. The way Charlotte's lip curled at the mention of her future husband, confirmed Lou's worst fears. 'You don't like your cousin? You wouldn't want to marry him?'

'Marry him!' Charlotte laughed, her eyes wide. 'I should as soon marry Attila the Hun as *George Caxton*.'

'I'm sorry,' Lou said quickly. 'I just thought, with your brother and Miss Caxton . . .' It might be more commonplace to marry a cousin in wealthy families, but it didn't make it palatable. 'Take no notice of me. Shall we leave? We don't want to be late for church.'

EIGHT

They stepped outside, the cold pinching Lou's cheeks and pricking her nostrils. Had someone in the real world opened a window? Perhaps. In this world, she walked along the snow-covered path beside Charlotte, breathing in the crisp, fresh air. She may have known Charlotte for less than a day but she already knew her silence to be quite out of character.

'You don't think Aunt Leonora was right, do you?' Charlotte said finally. 'That I lack compassion?'

'Your aunt is worried about Edward, that's all. I'm sure she didn't mean to upset you.'

'I wish I could be so certain. I've never known Aunt Leonora to say *anything* she doesn't mean. And I don't ever intend to be cruel to Edward. It's just that . . . it's just that he is always *there*. I spend more time with him now that he has come home from Cambridge than I do with almost anybody else. Except for the last three weeks, that is, when he has seemed preoccupied . . . He's often sullen but yesterday was by far the worst I have ever seen him. I make it my job when he is unhappy or blue to try and goad him out of it. Does that make me cruel?'

Lou laughed. 'No, it makes you his sister.'

Charlotte lifted her eyes. Her cheeks and the tip of her nose were nipped to a healthy pink. 'I don't know how you do it, Louisa, but you seem to know exactly the right thing to say.' She slipped her arm through Lou's. 'Wouldn't it be marvellous if you could stay with us forever? I'm sure we would be the very best of friends. You are quite simply the kindest person I have ever met.'

'Really?' Lou said, embarrassed but touched. If Charlotte knew the truth, she might not be so gushing. 'I think my brothers might disagree with you. I have been known to be quite cruel to them.'

'Cruel! I don't believe it for a second.' Charlotte squeezed Lou's arm. 'Let's say "pooh" to brothers. They are nothing but silly boys.'

Lou laughed. 'All right then. Pooh to brothers.'

Arm in arm they walked through the freshly fallen snow, their skirts and boots growing increasingly sodden as they made their way towards the beacon of St Mary's spire.

They didn't need to leave the grounds; the church was within the boundary wall of Hill House. Taking the path around the side of the church, the view became more familiar to Lou – bushes and hedges, ancient headstones green with moss and lichen – although beyond the front gates stood a row of neat redbrick workers' cottages, surrounded by woodlands and evergreens, not the back fences of council houses she was used to. Churchgoers milled around the open door; men in suits, women in dark dresses and children in smart little outfits, mirroring the adults. The staff of Hill House were amongst them, and Lou spotted Sally holding the hand of a little boy in a pale blue coat, a shock of blonde curls escaping from beneath a cap. There were more worshippers here today than she had ever seen at St Mary's, and they all moved aside to let her and Charlotte pass, the men and boys removing their hats, the women and girls curtseying.

Inside the vestibule they were greeted by the melancholy sound of the organ echoing around the stone walls. Lou was about to follow Charlotte into the church when a sudden and unexpected memory stopped her dead. It was no longer daytime but a cold evening in late December. A breeze whistled through the churchyard into the porch. She was a small child. She was with Stephen and Dean, bundled up against the cold in scarves and hats, each clutching an orange decorated with red ribbon and a small candle. Their eyes gleamed in the tiny flames and Mum smiled as she held the door open for them. The scene transformed. They were all older. Stephen and Dean looked uncomfortable in their newly-purchased cheap black suits. Heads dipped, they walked slowly in time with the undertakers, bearing the weight of Mum's coffin on their shoulders.

Lou's legs buckled. She felt hands taking hold of her as Charlotte's face swam into view.

'Louisa! Louisa!' she heard Charlotte cry. 'Please someone, help. Have Dawson bring Mama's car around so that we can take Miss Arnold back to the house.'

'No,' Lou stammered. 'I'm all right.' She turned to look at the men holding her up and thanked William and Bainbridge, adding, 'Really, I'm quite all right now.' She had to reassure them for a third time, before they reluctantly released her. 'Please,' she said to Charlotte, 'I don't want to cause a fuss. Can we go inside?'

Charlotte gripped Lou's arm and led her down the aisle to the front pew where Lady Mandeville, Mrs Hart, and Edward were already seated. Helping her to sit, Charlotte leant past and whispered to her aunt, 'Louisa had a fainting spell outside. I said that she should go back to the house, but she insisted on coming in. Don't tell Mama. Louisa doesn't want a fuss.'

Lou fixed her gaze on the herringbone weave of her skirt and listened to the creak of wood and the rustle of clothes as the congregation filled the pews behind. Mrs Hart leant in so close that Lou could smell her exotically spiced perfume, full of ginger and jasmine. She gave Lou a sympathetic smile. 'We feel our losses keenly at this time of year, don't we?' She slipped a handkerchief from the pocket of her coat and placed it in Lou's lap.

The vicar stood in the pulpit. 'Welcome one and all,' he said. 'It is truly wonderful to see so many smiling faces here today. I hope you have all brought your loudest singing voices.'

Mrs Hart took Lou's hand. She held it through the entire carol service, only letting go when they knelt to pray. The warmth of Mrs Hart's hand gave Lou the strength to stay in her seat and not run from the church. Eventually she stopped trembling.

When the service came to an end, Lou was glad to escape into the fresh air. Lady Mandeville thanked the vicar and took the car back to the house and Lou joined Mrs Hart, Charlotte and Edward in making their way on foot.

After checking that Lou was well, Charlotte walked ahead with Edward, her arm slipped through his. His shoulders were rolled and he walked slowly while Charlotte almost skipped beside him, turning to grin at him every so often, plainly attempting to make amends.

Mrs Hart took Lou's arm. 'I'm afraid that I sometimes forget just how young my niece is,' she said, a softness in her voice. 'I'm hard on her, I know, but not nearly as hard as the world is on young women. I suppose in my own way I'm attempting to make her stronger. But I think I may have gone too far this morning. I will apologise to her later.'

'I think she would appreciate that,' Lou said. 'And thank you . . . for being so kind to me in church.'

Mrs Hart turned to Lou and smiled. 'I have been an aunt for so long that I seem to slip naturally into the role of confessor and comforter. An aunt should never judge, but always love and try to understand her nieces and nephews.'

They walked in comfortable silence for a while until Lou, remembering the earlier gathering, said, 'I saw Sally at the church. She was with a little boy.'

'Sally? Oh, you mean Morrison. That would have been Albert. He's an adorable little creature, isn't he?'

'Is he her brother?'

'Why no.' Mrs Hart's laugh rang around the frozen landscape. 'Albert is Morrison's son.'

'Her son!'

'It is unconventional, I know, to have a mother as an employee, but one thing you should know about my brother's family, Louisa, is that they have a sentimental streak as wide as the Atlantic.'

'Sally isn't married?'

Mrs Hart laughed again. 'Oh my dear, they are sentimental, not revolutionaries. Morrison is married to William, my brother's footman.'

Lou put two and two together. Bingo! So that was Sally's *situation*; she had been allowed to marry and keep her job. 'I had no idea.'

'And why ever would you? Charlotte could tell you their story better than I, but as I understand it, the Morrisons both entered my brother's service as young people. They fought to hide their feelings for each other – neither of them could afford to lose their good positions – but it's impossible to keep such things secret for long. Love will always find its way in the end. And when Lady Mandeville became aware of the relationship, rather than have them dismissed, she convinced my brother to allow them to marry. Sir Charles is not foolish. He understands the benefits of keeping good staff. And he has indeed been proven correct. The Morrisons are a content little family living down in one of the workers' cottages by the church. My brother may not be able to exhibit his liberalism in his professional life, but he can at least exercise it for the benefit of his household.' She leant in closer to Lou as though sharing a confidence. 'Anyone with sense can see that these are changing times, Louisa. People like us can no longer expect those in our employ to deny themselves the freedoms we enjoy ourselves.'

People like us. Did Mrs Hart think she was one of them? She was doing a good job of fooling everyone.

They arrived at the house as Lady Mandeville stepped from her car. William held the front door open. Somehow the staff had made it back before them and had even managed to change their clothes. Lou fell into place beside Mrs Hart heading inside when a noise like the buzz of a bee in the distance made Lady Mandeville spin around.

'He wouldn't,' Lady Mandeville said, straining to see down the drive, a look of alarm crossing her features. 'He knows my feelings on that contraption.'

'I'm afraid that it rather sounds as though he has,' Mrs Hart said.

Charlotte left Edward's side and ran part of the way down the drive. She spun around and ran back, holding her hat in place. 'He's here! I can see him. He's coming!' she yelled and pointed as though she had just glimpsed the circus arriving in town.

Lou watched a motorcycle manoeuvre through the open gates and speed up the drive. With its chains and innards exposed in a green metal frame, the machine looked more like a souped-up pushbike than any motorcycle she had ever seen. It slid on the gravel – causing Lady Mandeville to gasp – before coming to a sudden stop, the back-tyre skidding in the snow. Without waiting for the engine to cut out completely, Charlotte squealed and ran to the rider who was dressed in a long leather coat with a dark fur-trimmed collar. He dismounted and whisked Charlotte off her feet, spinning her around. When he deposited her back on the ground, he whipped off his flying helmet and goggles to reveal a face covered in grime, except for two clean circles around his eyes, making him look like a panda in reverse. He smiled at the assembled crowd. Lou would have recognised those piercing blue eyes anywhere.

'Thomas,' Lady Mandeville said, holding out her hands. Dispensing with formality, her son threw his arms around her and kissed her on both cheeks. She stepped away, blushing.

'Mother,' Captain Mandeville said, ruffling his hair. 'You're a sight for sore eyes.'

'And you are filthy and so very cold,' Lady Mandeville said. Looking past her son, she frowned at the motorcycle. 'Why do you persist in riding that *thing* when I have made my feelings clear? It is so dangerous.'

Captain Mandeville patted the saddle of the motorcycle. 'The old girl hasn't let me down yet. She was even as good as gold when we went for a spin around the track at Brooklands last summer. Anyway, it was a mere sixty miles from London this morning and I only came a cropper on the icy country lanes outside Bletchley, once. Perhaps twice.'

'Oh, Thomas!' Lady Mandeville said, putting her hand to her chest. 'You will send me to an early grave. And where is your father?'

'I left him at his club. He's planning on catching the 12.30 from Euston but I wanted to surprise you all by arriving early.'

'You have certainly done that. We're nowhere near ready.'

'For what? As long as there's a bed to rest my head on and a fire to warm my feet by, I'll be happy.'

'You are not in barracks now, Thomas.' Lady Mandeville gently reprimanded. 'You must allow your poor mother to indulge herself and spoil you. For the short time you intend to stay with us at least—'

'Mother . . .'

'All right, I know, I mustn't take on so.'

'Thank you.'

From her position beneath the portico, Lou watched
Captain Mandeville greet the rest of his family. He stood head
and shoulders above the women and was a good few inches
taller than his younger brother. She watched as he removed his
gauntlet-like leather gloves to shake hands with Edward. Lady
Mandeville hovered slightly apart from the family group. Was
she holding back? Lou wondered. Clinging to her reserve and
maintaining her stiff upper lip? If she had lived a century later,
Lady Mandeville would have felt no need to hide her emotions;
a son returning unscathed on leave from the army was something to celebrate. As it was, Lady Mandeville kept her distance
and watched on as Charlotte and Mrs Hart showered her son
with the affection she seemed unable to.

With the family welcomes complete, Charlotte dragged
Captain Mandeville in the direction of the portico. For a leader
of men, he seemed unable – or perhaps unwilling – to resist his
determined little sister.

'Tom, let me introduce you to my very good friend, Miss
Louisa Arnold,' Charlotte said. 'Louisa is staying with us as a
guest of Aunt Leonora. I hope to convince her to stay indef-
initely.'

'Well,' Captain Mandeville said, 'any very good friend of
my little sister's is a very good friend of mine. It's a pleasure to
meet you, Miss Arnold.' He tucked his gloves beneath his arm
and took Lou's hand in his, shaking it warmly. 'Please let me
know if there is anything I can do to prolong your stay.
Anything to keep this silly little bird quiet.'

'You beast!' Charlotte tapped her brother's arm.

Captain Mandeville smiled at Lou and shrugged. His teeth
were straight and so very white, contrasting with the grime
smeared across his face which made him appear boyish rather
than a man pushing thirty. Could this really be the pompous
cavalry officer from the painting in the hall? In the flesh, with

his fingers pressed into her palm, he felt incredibly real. Incredibly human.

'Come, Thomas,' Lady Mandeville said. 'Let's go inside to the warm.'

Lou had left it too long to respond. When Captain Mandeville's hand slipped from hers, she silently kicked herself. What would he think of her? He'd think she was a dumb idiot, that's what.

Returning to his motorcycle, Captain Mandeville unstrapped a small, battered leather case from the back. Then he led the way into the house, his family following close behind with Lou dragging up the rear, kicking at the snow.

The staff had formed a line in the hall. Bainbridge stepped forward to take Captain Mandeville's suitcase, which he then handed to the second footman.

'Really, old friend,' Captain Mandeville protested, 'I'm quite capable of carrying my own luggage up a few flights of stairs. Anyway, how have you been? How is the pheasant this year?'

'I'm sure you will not be disappointed, Captain Mandeville,' Bainbridge answered.

'I was sorry to have missed the grouse. Father said it was a particularly good season.'

Bainbridge confirmed that it had been, before guiding Captain Mandeville along the line of staff beginning with Mrs Moriarty. Each woman curtseyed and each man bowed. When Captain Mandeville came to the end of the line – where poor Mary shook so violently that her cap quivered – he placed his hands on his hips and turned around beneath the glass dome high in the ceiling. Silence descended, disturbed only by his leather soles squeaking on the tiled floor and the rhythmic tock of the long-cased clock at the far end of the hall.

'It's good to see the old place still standing. Ten months is rather a long time to be away.'

'Too long,' Lady Mandeville said. 'Especially when you appear to have forgotten how to use a writing block. Now, won't you take some tea?'

Ignoring his mother's dig, Captain Mandeville said, 'I can think of nothing I'd like more. The cookhouse has so far produced nothing to compare to Monsieur Gotti's scones. But if you'll excuse me, I'll go and make myself presentable first.'

Captain Mandeville took the stairs two at a time. His mother, aunt and sister all followed his progress, smiling. None of them appeared to notice, as Lou did, that Edward had slipped away through the billiard room.

In a flurry of activity, the maids circled the ladies to remove hats and coats. Lady Mandeville told Mrs Moriarty that they would take tea and instructed her to ensure that Monsieur Gotti provided a plentiful supply of scones. There was a brief discussion on the appropriateness of scones in the morning, but since they were Captain Mandeville's particular favourite, convention was set aside.

Once in the morning room, Lady Mandeville took a seat beside the fire. Charlotte settled beside her mother, leaving Lou to share a sofa with Mrs Hart.

'What a lovely surprise it is to have Thomas home so early,' Lady Mandeville said.

'Indeed, it is,' Mrs Hart said. 'The foreign climate has clearly agreed with him.'

'I don't believe I have ever seen Thomas looking more handsome or so healthy. If a little too tanned underneath the dirt.'

Charlotte grinned. 'I'm sure cousin Emma won't mind.'

'Charlotte!' Lady Mandeville said sharply but failed to hide a smile.

William and the other footman brought in trays of food, which they arranged on a side table. When they left, Sally appeared in the doorway. She curtseyed. 'Would your Ladyship still like to see Albert today? I thought perhaps with Captain Mandeville's arrival you may prefer just family.'

'Why no!' Lady Mandeville exclaimed. 'Please Morrison, you must bring him in. Charlotte would never forgive me if she were denied her pet.'

Sally pushed the door wider. She beckoned and the little boy from the church came charging into the room. He was dressed in a blue and white sailor's suit and his blonde waves bobbed as he ran directly to Lady Mandeville and Charlotte, clambering up onto the seat between them.

'Oh Mama, doesn't he look adorable! We knew that suit would look well on him, didn't we?' Charlotte gushed. She dusted the boy's face with kisses. 'Oh, my lovely little boy. Have you been good for your mama and papa this week?'

The boy nodded.

'Have you been practising your French?'

He glanced up to the ceiling as though silently rehearsing the words before giving them voice. 'Oui, mademoiselle,' he said carefully. 'Comment ça va?'

Charlotte shrieked with delight and Lou joined Lady Mandeville and Mrs Hart in giving him a round of applause.

'What an absolute genius,' Mrs Hart said. 'Barely four-years old and already mastering foreign tongues. I see a future in the diplomatic service beckoning.'

Charlotte cupped her hand around the boy's ear and whispered something. He slipped from the sofa and walked the two strides to Lou. Standing before her, he stared at her. 'Good morning, Miss Louisa Arnold,' he said very seriously. 'My name is Albert William Morrison, and I am very happy to make your acquaintance.' He bowed, eliciting another rapturous round of applause from his audience.

'I'm very pleased to meet you too, Master Albert Morrison,' Lou said, enchanted by this little boy with his mother's kind eyes.

'I think somebody has earned his treat today.' Lady Mandeville said. 'How would you like some scones and jam?'

Albert nodded enthusiastically. Mrs Hart filled a plate with treats and handed it to Charlotte who broke off pieces of scone. After smothering them with jam and cream, she fed them to Albert and when the plate was cleared, she took a napkin and wiped his mouth. 'What an absolute pet,' she said. 'Now you may go and play.'

Albert skipped away and sat cross-legged on the rug before the fire, where a selection of toys had been arranged for him. He ignored a hobbyhorse, a train and a small army of tin soldiers, and settled on playing with a dolls' house – a replica of Hill House in miniature.

'That was my favourite plaything when I was small,' Charlotte explained to Lou. 'Of all the toys we put out for him, it's his favourite too. Given the chance, he would play with it all day.'

Albert took up a wooden cigar box and removed the lid. Lying in compartments inside, were all manner of residents for the miniature Hill House – men and women, staff and children, dogs and cats. Turning his attention to the house, he removed the figure of a maid from the basement kitchen. He smoothed down her apron and red hair and after gently placing her in the box, selected the figure of a finely dressed woman and placed her in the morning room, joining three other ladies on the sofas.

'Is that Miss Arnold?' Charlotte asked.

Albert nodded and set about arranging little plates on the table.

'Look how he concentrates,' Mrs Hart mused. 'He plays like a child well beyond his years. He is quite the old soul.'

'Not too old to want a piggyback, I hope.'

All heads – including Lou's – turned towards the door to see Captain Mandeville stride into the room. He had changed from his travelling clothes into a blue flannel suit. His face was clean, his hair combed and oiled to tame the unruly waves. In the winter sunlight flooding the room, Lou noticed that his hair was not quite as dark as it had seemed in the dim hall – now each wave had an auburn hue. Pinching the legs of his trousers, he crouched before Albert, his elbows resting on his knees.

'My, my, but how you have grown!' he said, ruffling the boy's hair. 'You remember me, don't you?'

Albert studied Captain Mandeville's face briefly before selecting the figure of a man from his box and placing him in the morning room of the dolls' house. 'You are Captain Thomas Mandeville, and you are an officer in the cavalry. You ride a horse every day and that makes you very, very lucky.'

'I suppose it does.' Captain Mandeville looked up and smiled at the women. 'What a clever little chap you are, Bertie. I may still call you Bertie, mayn't I? Even if you have grown into a strapping young man.'

The boy nodded. He peered into Captain Mandeville's face and ran his finger along his own top lip.

'And observant to boot!' Captain Mandeville said. 'We'll make a scout for the battalion out of you yet. I have indeed shaved off my moustache as I found it fiendishly tickly. Tell me, Bertie, are you still ticklish?'

Albert shook his head.

'No?' Captain Mandeville said, feigning surprise. 'Then you won't mind at all if I do this.' He gently tickled Albert's arm, making him giggle and shrug his shoulder to his ear. 'Bertie, do you remember the game we used to play when you were still a terribly small chap?'

'Of course. You were my horse and I was the General.'

'Precisely!'

Without warning, Captain Mandeville scooped the little boy up, balanced him on his shoulders and to squeals of delight, charged out into the hall. 'Hold on tight, Bertie,' he shouted, and Albert gripped the captain's chin, holding on for dear life.

'Stop, Thomas, do,' Lady Mandeville called out. 'You will make the child ill.'

Captain Mandeville reappeared in the doorway. 'Nonsense. The General has a cast iron constitution. Isn't that right, General?'

'Yes!' Albert shouted. Tom whinnied and charged into the hall again.

'He loves children and they adore him in return,' Mrs Hart laughed. 'Thomas was born to be a father. Perhaps the events of the coming week may see that destiny realised all the sooner.'

'I do hope so, sister, really I do,' Lady Mandeville said. 'But speak more quietly. Thomas must believe that an engagement is his idea. If he thinks, even for a second, that this has been engineered in some way, he will not entertain the notion. You know how stubborn he has always been, even as a small boy.'

'True,' Mrs Hart nodded. 'My nephew certainly does know his own mind. But he has always been so fond of Emma.'

Charlotte pouted. 'We are all fond of Emma. It's just a shame that she comes with the rest of her family.'

'Charlotte, do not talk so!' Lady Mandeville snapped before lowering her voice. 'I want nothing, including your low opinion of your cousin George, to come between Thomas and Emma. Do you understand?'

'Yes, Mama. Sorry, Mama,' Charlotte said.

Captain Mandeville cantered past the doorway again, Albert bouncing on his shoulders, shrieking with delight.

Watching him, Lou's heart sank. She was the only person here who knew that Thomas Mandeville would never have children. Because by this time next year, he would be four months dead, buried in a grave on a battlefield in France.

Captain Mandeville charged back into the room, his cheeks flushed. He swept his fringe away from his face. In his civilian clothes, he was far less imposing than the proud cavalry officer in the painting. Stripped of his finery and braid, and with no sword at his side, he seemed smaller somehow. More vulnerable.

Lou stood up. 'If it's all right with your Ladyship, I think I might go to my room.'

'You won't take tea?' Lady Mandeville asked.

'I don't feel very thirsty. I'm sorry.'

She made to go but stopped when Albert hollered, 'Please, put me down.'

Captain Mandeville came to an abrupt halt. He lifted Albert from his shoulders and deposited him on the floor. Albert made straight for the dolls' house. Reaching inside, he removed the newly arrived, finely dressed lady from the morning room and eased the maid from the wooden box. 'Do you see?' he said to her, holding a doll in each hand. 'One in, one out.'

It took a moment, but Lou's mind flashed back to another day in this house. A day when it was a charred carcass, its walls caked in mould and dripping water. 'I beg your pardon?' she said, unable to trust her memory.

'One in, one out,' Albert repeated. Lou knelt before him. She looked first at the dolls and then into the little boy's eyes. He smiled – a smile she recognised – even though last time she had seen it, the lips were thin and the teeth not his own.

'You're Bert,' she whispered. 'Julie's Uncle Bert.'

He blinked and, still smiling, returned to his game. He placed the maid back into the box and the lady into the house. Lou was only vaguely aware of the babble of conversation around her. Something felt odd. Something that she couldn't put her finger on. Why had her brain summoned up a version of Bert as a child, when she had only met him once before and hardly thought about since?

Instead of returning to her room as she had intended, she settled back on the sofa to watch Albert play with the dolls. She wasn't sure how much time had passed when eventually Sally returned to take him home.

At lunch she spent more time mulling over Albert's words than eating. *One in, one out.* Whatever did that mean? And why, of all the things that old Bert had said to her that day in the derelict house, had her memory dredged up that phrase?

When the lunch party dispersed, Lou returned to her room and lay down on the bed. Sally soon appeared to help her begin the process of dressing for dinner.

'It'll be more formal tonight, what with Sir Charles and Captain Mandeville at home,' Sally said, inspecting the contents of the wardrobe and settling on a lilac satin dress with black straps and a black bandeau.

After her bath, Lou sat at the dressing table, watching Sally's reflection as she constructed her hair. 'Albert's a lovely boy,' she said.

Sally let out an exaggerated sigh. 'When he wants to be.'

Lou fell silent. What else could she say? Didn't Sally think it odd that the Mandeville women treated her son like a pet? Wasn't she worried that they might tire of Albert and abandon him like an old ball gown? Although questioning the motives of the Mandeville women would at least make more sense than revealing that she had already met Sally's adorable, fresh-faced little boy as an arthritic old man confined to a wheelchair.

'He was beautifully behaved today,' Lou said. 'You must be very proud of him.'

Sally smiled, almost reluctantly it seemed, although Lou detected a glimmer of pride. 'I'm just thankful that he minds his manners for Her Ladyship and Miss Charlotte. He's a handful for me and for my mother when she looks after him. William is the only one he really listens to. I suppose men are better at understanding boys, I know I never shall.'

Lou busied herself with unscrewing the cap from a tub of cold cream. She rubbed a dollop into her knuckles. If she spoke, it would be to warn Sally to make the most of every minute of her life with William, to cherish every hurried kiss as her husband was on his way out of the door. She looked at Sally's reflection again, at the tip of her tongue sticking from her lips as she concentrated on securing a hairpin. It was against Lou's nature, but she knew she had to stay silent. If she couldn't tell Sally that she had met her son as an old man, she could hardly tell her that her husband was destined to die in a war.

NINE

The dinner gong couldn't come soon enough for Lou, and she was already on her way downstairs when the last ripple rang through the house. The door to the drawing room stood ajar and voices raised in conversation floated into the hall. She hovered outside, waiting for a convenient moment to make her entrance. Taking a breath to steady her nerves, she peered through the gap between the frame and the door. Most of the family had assembled and Bainbridge and the two footmen were waiting on them. Lady Mandeville, Mrs Hart and Charlotte sat together on a sofa like three exotic birds on a perch with plumages of bright silk and satin. Captain Mandeville stood before the fire, a highly polished black shoe up on the grate. Another man – Sir Charles Mandeville, Lou presumed – sat in a chair beside the fire. Like Captain Mandeville, Sir Charles wore a black tail suit. Even sitting down, he cut an imposing figure, with an impressive sweep of grey hair, parted to one side. The sherry in his glass glinted in the light from the fire. With the thumb and forefinger of his free hand, he rolled the tips of his moustache to fine points and laughed as Captain Mandeville recounted the high-lights of his journey back to Hill House earlier that day. Lou looked from father to son; another twenty years and it wasn't difficult to imagine Captain Mandeville taking that seat beside the fire. Only he never would.

'You should have seen the look on Mother's face when I told her I took a turn around the track at Brooklands,' Captain Mandeville said, striking a match against the hearth. He lit his cigarette before throwing the spent match into the flames. 'Imagine if I had told her about my plans to invest in Hugh Locke King's new venture. A flying school.'

Lady Mandeville's shoulders drew back as though controlled by elastic. 'Why do you delight in tormenting me, Thomas?' she said. 'I still can't understand why Ethel would allow Hugh to build that awful track across the beautiful grounds at Brooklands House. I can't imagine anything worse than hordes of people traipsing across your garden every weekend to watch cars, of all things, speeding around your land. It's quite awful. Promise me Charles that you will never consider turning this land over to such a . . . a ghastly pursuit.'

'A ghastly pursuit!' Captain Mandeville laughed, responding on his father's behalf. 'It's called progress, Mother. The way I see it, Hugh has stolen the march on the rest of us. We must all look for new ways to make our lands viable. Lame elephants soon find themselves in the hunter's sights.'

Lady Mandeville patted her neck. 'Must everything come down to money with you men? Where is the harm in preserving our homes just as they are? I honestly believe that all of these ideas are just fads. New playthings to amuse you.'

Captain Mandeville's jaw clenched, and his good-natured banter evaporated along with his cigarette smoke. In a movement mimicking his father, he ran his finger and thumb from his nostrils down to the corners of his mouth as though stroking an imaginary moustache.

'As I understand it,' Mrs Hart said, 'the building of the race-track was as much Ethel's idea as it was Hugh's. She is a forward-thinking woman. Frederick thought so. He was very fond of Ethel and Hugh. He always looked forward to our trips to their parties at Weybridge and Hugh and Ethel were so kind to me when Fred . . .' Her voice trailed away. Sir Charles, who had sat impassively throughout the exchanges, waved for Bainbridge to refresh Mrs Hart's glass.

'Weybridge is on my way back to camp, Aunt Leo,' Captain Mandeville said gently. 'I'll stop in at Brooklands to give the Locke Kings your regards.'

'Thank you, Tom,' Mrs Hart said quietly.

'Oh, Thomas,' Lady Mandeville said. 'How can you talk about leaving, when you have only just returned? Won't you consider resigning your commission? Ten years in the army is surely long enough. You do know that Lewis retired earlier this year and that your father is yet to replace him. There is nobody better placed than you to take over as estate manager. Nobody knows Hill House and its land as well as you.'

Sir Charles sat forward. He cleared his throat and his family all turned to him. 'Thomas is his own man,' he said. Lou waited to see if he would say more, but that was it, short and to the point. He'd said what he had to say succinctly, leaving no room for interpretation or ambiguity.

Captain Mandeville threw his cigarette into the fire. He made his way to the sofa and stood behind Lady Mandeville. While Charlotte engaged Sir Charles and Mrs Hart in a conversation about the weather machine in the Lake District, Captain Mandeville leant over the back of the sofa. He kissed his mother on the top of her head before coming to sit beside her. They were close enough to the door for Lou to hear the quiet words that passed between them.

'I'm sorry, Thomas,' Lady Mandeville said. 'But your aunt and I, we read in the newspapers about the unrest in Europe. They all assure us that war is coming. I worry about you . . . oh, I know you will tell me that I shouldn't, that you are old enough to look after yourself . . . but I can't help but remember what happened to your poor Uncle Frederick. Please, won't you come home?'

'Mama,' Captain Mandeville said softly, 'the army really is no different from school. I spend my days playing polo and barking orders at men, just as I did as house captain. Why, I have been out to India and Africa, and I don't have a scratch to show for it. If there ever were a war – which I am not saying there will be – but if there were, I'd be sure to stay well away from enemy lines. I'm sure Father could arrange a desk job for me somewhere or—'

'You, in a desk job!' Lady Mandeville interrupted. 'I am sure I will never live to see the day. I know my son and I know that he cannot sit still for more than five minutes at any one time before jumping up to search for adventure.'

Captain Mandeville laughed. 'I suppose I ought to know better than to attempt to fool you. But I have no appetite for war and will be sure to stay out of trouble. So, you see, there really is no need to worry yourself on my account.'

Yes, there is, Lou thought as she watched Lady Mandeville lean into her son. He was a fully-grown man, but he allowed his mother to stroke his hair. Lou shrank away from the door, embarrassed at having gate crashed a moment of private tenderness. She pictured Stephen sitting beside Mum on the couch on the day their dad left, holding her for hours as she cried, telling her over and over that he would take care of her, that he would never let anybody hurt her again. Mum's brave little soldier.

'Louisa!' Charlotte called and rushed to the door. 'Whatever are you doing out there on your own? Come and meet my father.'

Before Lou had the chance to compose herself, Charlotte took her hand and dragged her towards Sir Charles. He rose from his chair.

'Miss Arnold, we meet at last,' Sir Charles said, shaking her hand, his broad features breaking into a smile. 'My daughter hasn't stopped talking about you all afternoon. Apparently, you are to be her very good friend. You have my deepest sympathies. My daughter is about the silliest creature on God's good Earth.'

'Father!' Charlotte said. She frowned, pretending to be cross, before slipping her arm through his. 'My father delights in teasing me, Louisa,' she said and kissed him on the cheek.

'And my daughter is an unruly and wilful child, Miss Arnold. Ever since she was this high' – he placed his hand so that it was flat beside his knee – 'she has had opinions on every subject, which she has not been afraid to air. Including to the Home Secretary himself when he and his wife came to stay for a weekend.'

'And you wouldn't have it any other way,' Mrs Hart chipped in. 'You would soon grow tired of a daughter who behaved like a doll, whose only ambition in life was to look pretty. Remember how proud you were of Charlotte when she was just seven-years old yet held a perfectly lucid political conversation with Mr Lloyd George?'

'Perhaps.' Sir Charles patted Charlotte's hand. 'But it might be nice to have a daughter who spent her time in more ladylike pursuits – tapestry or embroidery or whatever it is you women enjoy – rather than with her nose stuck in the pages of *The Times*.' Before Charlotte or Mrs Hart could respond, he indicated for the second footman to offer Lou a drink. She took a glass of sherry from the silver tray, wondering what it would feel like to have a father that actually cared about her. Sir Charles looked past her. 'At last,' he said. 'I thought we were never to be graced with your presence.'

'Sorry, Father.' Edward stepped into the room. Without lifting his eyes from the floor, he said, 'I hope you're well.'

'Never better. Which is more than can be said for you. You look as though you haven't seen the sun in weeks.'

'Edward is now nocturnal, Papa,' Charlotte grinned. 'He

stays in his room *all* day and only comes out after dark to growl at us like a wild beast. Last night he—'

'Shall we go through?' Lady Mandeville rose to her feet. 'Monsieur Gotti does get terribly upset if we keep him waiting.'

The table in the dining room was laid with more crystal, more silver and more candles than the previous evening. Sir Charles sat at one end, with Lady Mandeville at the other, the purple of the flowers in the vast arrangements perfectly matching her gown. Mrs Hart sat to her brother's left with Edward beside her.

Lou waited to be shown to her seat between Captain Mandeville and Charlotte. She ate every spoonful of the soup placed before her and devoured every flake of trout. For someone who had spent most of the last two days either at a table or preparing for a meal, she had eaten surprisingly little. She was ravenous; far too hungry to concentrate on the conversation bubbling around her.

As she tore into the Beef Wellington, her silence was disturbed.

'Charlotte tells me that you have two brothers, Miss Arnold,' Sir Charles said. 'Would I have met them at a hunt or a shoot?'

Lou paused with her fork midway to her mouth. 'I don't think so.'

'They are in India, Papa.' Charlotte said.

'Of course. Well, when they are next in the country, depending on the season, they must join us on a shoot or to fish. The trout in the stream are particularly good and Edward's rods are always available since he gave up fishing as a pastime some years ago. He'd rather pass the day with his nose in a book or milling around the grounds. Isn't that right, Edward?'

Across the table from Lou, Edward pushed a potato around

his plate; his head drooping like a marionette's with the strings cut. Stripped of the protective blanket of alcohol, he cut a far less belligerent figure.

'We all share a passion for this old house, Charles,' Mrs Hart said, stabbing a slice of carrot. 'But not all of us share a desire to annihilate the creatures that exist on its land in the name of sport. Why go to the trouble of maintaining a library if you expect nobody to read poetry? And why pay a small army of gardeners to maintain the grounds if not to walk in them?'

Sir Charles smiled. 'As ever, Leonora, I can rely on you to point out the error of my ways.' He called for the second footman to refresh Edwards's wine even though he had barely touched it. 'Please ensure that Edward's glass is never empty tonight. As I understand it, my son has developed quite a thirst in the last few days.' He paused. 'Remind me, Thomas, of what you were telling me earlier about how you instruct new recruits to engage with the enemy.'

Like his father, Captain Mandeville smiled. 'I advise that one should never engage in close combat with the enemy unless you can be pretty sure you have the upper hand.'

'Indeed,' Sir Charles said. 'Advice we could all learn from.'

Lou glanced at Mrs Hart, who ate her food angrily, spearing her vegetables. Edward stared at his rare beef, as though he might throw up at any second. Lady Mandeville and Charlotte ate polite mouthfuls while Sir Charles and Captain Mandeville shared little grins as they tucked into their meals. Deciding to steer clear of taking sides in the power game at play around the table, Lou retreated to the relative safety of her beef. But after only one more mouthful, she found that her ever-tightening corset made it impossible to force down another morsel. She placed her knife and fork on the side of the plate and gazed longingly at the remaining pastry and meat.

'I had quite a long conversation with Mr Churchill in the lobby of The House yesterday,' Sir Charles said to his wife.

Mrs Hart made a noise like a snort.

'Do you have something you wish to say, Leonora?' Sir Charles asked.

Mrs Hart pushed her plate away. 'I suppose that *man* still refuses to support the fight for votes for women.'

'You might not be so hard on him. A man in his position must often mask his true opinions for the sake of his party.'

A small laugh escaped Mrs Hart's lips. 'Would you have us believe that the man who was once home secretary and is now first lord of the admiralty, is afraid to voice his honest opinions?'

Sir Charles dabbed his lips with his napkin and smiled. 'I suppose you will not be satisfied until Mr Churchill shares the opinions of your friends in south-west London. Remind me, Leonora, didn't you visit your friend in Richmond in February.'

'You know full well that I did not visit Clarissa until March,' Mrs Hart countered.

'Ah yes. Just in time for the trial and, if I'm not mistaken, you knew the accused.'

'Knew of them. There is a difference, Charles.'

Again, Sir Charles smiled. 'Why suffragettes should feel the need to set fire to the refreshment pavilion at Kew Gardens, I don't know. What can they hope to gain by sending somebody's livelihood up in smoke?'

'The right for women to have a livelihood too.'

Sir Charles appeared to feed off Mrs Hart's anger and it was left to Lady Mandeville to cut off his energy supply with her singsong voice. 'It's such a shame. The pavilion was a lovely spot to take tea on a summer's day. I do hope it is rebuilt.'

Lou took a sip of wine. Couldn't Lady Mandeville see that in trying to keep the peace she was taking her husband's side over the suffragettes, helping, in some small way, to perpetuate the position of women in society? Or was that too harsh? Was Lady Mandeville simply trying to keep the peace around her dinner table?

Lou looked up and found herself in Sir Charles' line of sight. Ignoring his wife's attempt to add a full stop to the conversation, he said, 'Miss Arnold, where do you stand on the question of suffrage for women?' He rested his elbows on the table, pushed his fingertips together and pressed his forefingers to his bottom lip.

Lou placed her glass down. 'I'm not . . .'

'Charles,' Lady Mandeville said. 'It's not fair to tease our guest.'

'Who's teasing? Is it not the role of a politician to listen to all sides of a debate and appreciate every opinion and point of view? Miss Arnold?'

All eyes turned to Lou. Her cheeks grew warmer as she thought about Sally upstairs, waiting to pander to her every need; young Mary kneeling beside the hearth that morning, her hands and apron blackened by coal; all of the women scurrying around downstairs without a voice.

'Why shouldn't women have the same rights as men?' she said. 'Why shouldn't we have a say in how our lives are controlled by the government?'

She was sure she heard someone gasp.

'Come now, Miss Arnold,' Sir Charles said. 'Women have the vote in council elections. They can even serve as councillors now, surely that is concession enough. Why should women have the vote in parliamentary elections when they do not fight in the army? When there are very few who are doctors and lawyers?'

Don't rise to it. Don't rise . . . 'Only because your society does not allow it.'

'My society?' Sir Charles arched an eyebrow.

'Our society.' Lou quickly corrected herself.

'Let me make sure I understand you correctly. You are suggesting that not only should we allow women to have a say in how the country is run, but we should also remove them from their rightful place in the home, raising children, so that they are free to take up any role they choose?'

'If a woman wants to fight for her country, why shouldn't she? If she wants to study law or medicine or dig for coal down a pit, why shouldn't she?'

'Because the ability of a woman to acquit herself in these roles you mention is unproven.'

'How are we ever to prove ourselves if we aren't given the chance?'

'Thomas,' Sir Charles said to his son, 'can you imagine being given a troop of girls like your sister to train into soldiers?'

Captain Mandeville laughed, making Lou bristle. What would this father and son double-act say if they knew that one day women would serve at every level in the armed forces? That before this century was out, a grocer's daughter would rise to the very pinnacle of politics in Britain, influencing the balance of power across the entire globe. She wanted to tell them to wipe the smug grins from their faces. But she knew better than to insult a host at his dinner table. She settled on a compromise. 'Charlotte would make as good a soldier as any man.' She glanced at Charlotte who looked back, open-mouthed.

'An interesting position,' Sir Charles countered. 'How so?'

'She has compassion and kindness as well as strength of character.'

'Even if that were true,' Sir Charles said, glancing at his daughter doubtfully, 'you must at least concede that women lack the physical and mental strength of men.'

'A woman who puts her mind to it can be anything she wants to be.'

'Are you suggesting that women are better than men?'

'No. What I'm *saying* is that we are equal to men, not better. By the end of this decade women will have the vote. You can be sure of that!'

'You seem very well informed, Miss Arnold. Do you have

intelligence direct from the policymakers in the cabinet? Or do you possess a crystal ball which foretells the future.'

'No, sir. What *I* possess is common sense.'

A stunned silence fell across the table. Even Edward lifted his head and peered at Lou from beneath his fringe. Mrs Hart and Charlotte looked at her first with surprise then something that resembled awe. Sir Charles stroked the ends of his moustache.

'Well, well, well, it would seem that my sister is not the only firebrand at my table. What do you say to that, Tom?'

Captain Mandeville sat back in his chair. 'I say that if the suffragettes who torched the refreshment pavilion are in need of reinforcement, then they need look no further than your dining table, Father.' He gave Lou a sidewise glance and smiled before tucking into another mouthful of beef.

Lou fell silent, mortified that she had gone too far. They must all think she was mad. For the remainder of the meal, she studied the pattern on each plate placed before her, while Lady Mandeville steered the conversation to the safer topic of the trip she had planned for the next day to visit a friend with Charlotte and Mrs Hart. When Lou looked up and caught Sir Charles' eye, he raised his glass to her and smiled. At the end of the meal, when the women stood to make their way through to the drawing room, leaving the men to their whisky and cigars, Sir Charles called out to Lou.

'Miss Arnold, won't you stay with us to take a drink? You might find the conversation with the men more to your taste.'

Sir Charles was mocking her, but she could hardly be rude to her host again. 'No, thank you,' she said.

After coffee, she was finally free to return to her room. Sally arrived to help her undress and prepare for bed. Lou submitted but she couldn't help feeling furious at how wrong it felt. That night a woman down in the kitchen would wash the dishes from *her* dinner, tomorrow another woman would wash *her* underwear and another woman would come in to clean *her* room. What kind of feminist did that make her? The kind that settled for working in a supermarket rather than pursuing her dream. There was nothing wrong with working in a supermarket, what *was* wrong was that she had managed to convince herself that debts were the obstacle preventing her from becoming a teacher. In truth, she knew she was a coward. It would take courage to pursue her ambitions – not the courage required to set fire to a building and go to prison in the fight for what she believed in, or to work fifteen hours a day just to keep a roof over her head – but courage nonetheless.

When Sally left, Lou opened the curtains. She lay in bed staring up at the stars, sharp as pinpricks in the dark night sky. The courage she would need to find when she woke up and returned to her own life was nothing compared to the courage each member of this family would need to face the next few years. She pulled the blankets up to her chin. If only Captain Mandeville would listen to his mother and leave the army, then the future of his family could be so very different. Couldn't he see that they all needed him to do that one simple thing?

TEN

20TH DECEMBER 1913

'Please Louisa, won't you come with us?' Charlotte begged as a maid helped her button up her coat. 'It will be such fun. Lady Marshall is Mama's oldest friend, and she's a hoot.'

'Charlotte, I would, but I'm so tired, I'd be awful company.'

Even the prospect of a fine tea couldn't convince Lou to make the trip to Leamington Spa with Charlotte, Mrs Hart and Lady Mandeville. She had barely slept. She was exhausted. Fagged out. Bone-tired. Since she seemed stuck in this imaginary world, there seemed little option but to immerse herself in it. Nevertheless, the prospect of making polite conversation for hours on a train was a step too far. As the house was to be empty all day – Sir Charles having taken his sons to a meeting in town – all she wanted was to find an out of the way spot to curl up in. Charlotte tried again to entice Lou, but Mrs Hart took hold of her hand.

'The train won't wait for us, Charlotte,' she said, leading her niece to the front door. 'It's already after eleven. Come along now.'

From the morning room window Lou watched the car disappear into the freezing fog that had descended overnight; a fog so dense and so white that it was impossible to tell where the snow ended and the sky began. She listened to the silence. At last, she was alone.

Wandering out into the hall, she made her way to the library where the shelves lining each wall were densely packed with books of all colours and sizes, from atlases over a foot tall to tiny folios of poetry, no more than six inches high. Lou selected a small, buff-coloured leather-bound volume and sat in the armchair closest to the fire. She opened the book, closed it again and placed it on the arm of the chair. Nestling into the cushions, she was as warm and as snug as a dormouse in a teapot. A log crackled and slipped through the grate. She closed her eyes. Ten minutes . . . that's all she needed . . . ten minutes. . .

After what felt like just two, a voice shattered her peace.

'Hello there.'

'Oh, I'm sorry.' She sat up abruptly. 'I thought I was alone.' Of all the people to catch her unawares, it had to be one half of the tag-team that had teased her at dinner last night and the man partly to blame for her sleepless night. She made to stand.

'Don't get up,' Captain Mandeville said. With a rolled-up newspaper he pointed to an empty chair beside her. 'Do you mind? I like to read the newspaper in here when I'm home. It's such a quiet spot.'

Lou sank back and shook her head; it was his chair, his house, he could do what he wanted. He placed the newspaper on a small side table, sat down and picked up the book she had abandoned.

'Plato?' he said, reading the spine.

'Yes, Plato.' Did he think her female mind too feeble to understand philosophy?

Returning the book to the arm of the chair, Captain Mandeville slipped a silver case from his breast pocket and took out a cigarette. He offered the case to Lou, but she shook her head. 'I'm afraid Shakespeare's about my limit before lunch,' he said, gripping the cigarette between his teeth, patting his pockets. 'The odd sonnet or two, nothing quite as taxing as Latin philosophy.'

'Greek,' Lou said, taking great pleasure in correcting him.

'Ah yes, of course, Greek. "Wise men speak because they have something to say; fools because they have to say something." Wasn't that Plato?'

'Yes,' she said gloomily. He was teasing her again.

Captain Mandeville lit his cigarette and dropped the match into an ashtray on the table. He stared at her, his lips forming a wry grin. 'If you don't mind my saying, you don't seem quite so . . . *effervescent* this morning.'

Effervescent? What did he mean by that?

'If you're at all worried about your debate with my father last night, you needn't be. He enjoys the sport of wordplay. To him people are targets or team-mates, he uses words to attack and parry—'

'Before delivering the killer blow.'

Captain Mandeville laughed. 'Quite.' He drew deeply on his cigarette.

As much as she believed in everything she had said the previous evening, Lou still felt the need to clear the air. 'I hope I didn't offend Sir Charles.'

'Good God, no!' Captain Mandeville laughed again. 'Father is never happier than in the midst of a rip-roaring debate. You should see him go to work on the opposition across the floor of the House.' He tapped the ash from his cigarette. 'And the truth is that he's on your side. When the vote for universal suffrage comes, he'll pin his true colours to the mast. There are plenty of Tory heiresses hereabouts expecting him to do the right thing by them. Father would never risk losing his seat. Or the good lunches they provide him with when he's in the county.' He smiled. Was he attempting to put her at ease? Possibly, but she was more interested in picking up the thread of his suggestion.

'You think there will be a vote?'

'*You* certainly seemed sure of it last night.' He pinched a stray strand of tobacco from his tongue, and she noticed his right eyebrow lift slightly.

'Oh . . . yes.'

'Father respects people who speak up and have the courage of their convictions. As do I. Right!' He stubbed out his cigarette and got to his feet. 'If you're ready we'll start the guided tour.'

'The what?'

'You want to see all the nooks and crannies of Hill House, don't you?'

Lou looked him up and down. He didn't appear to be playing a trick on her. Even so, she could recall enough of his teasing to have second thoughts about wanting to go anywhere with him. But a behind-the-scenes tour of Hill House . . . "I wouldn't want to disturb your plans for the day.'

'Plans! What plans? As you can see, I am yesterday's news. I have been cast aside in favour of the delights of tea with Lady Marshall and lunch with Father's solicitor. You'd be doing me a huge favour if you'd spend a couple of hours with me. I'm damned rotten company for myself.'

Captain Mandeville strode out into the hall. Not wanting to be left behind, Lou followed and almost crashed into him when he stopped suddenly in the centre of the hall.

'Take a look around you,' he said, spreading his arms wide, his voice echoing all the way up to the glass dome high in the ceiling. 'This is the very epicentre of Hill House. From here you can see all of the clues as to why my great-great-grandfather, Thomas Mandeville, came to build Hill House.' He lowered his voice and moved in closer, as though taking Lou into his confidence. 'My family has never been particularly original when it comes to naming sons. Although there was an Algonquin somewhere along the line, so I suppose Edward and I should be

thankful for small mercies.' He grimaced and, almost in spite of
herself, Lou laughed.

'Where were we? Ah yes, great-great-grandfather Tom. He
was a clergyman, which back in the seventeen hundreds was
quite a lucrative profession, providing you had a good parish.
And St Mary's, although rural, was a *very* good parish. Plenty of
wealthy landowners with very deep pockets.' He tapped the
side of his nose. 'Old Tom was from relatively humble begin-
nings so you might assume that he would be perfectly content
with his elevated position to the gentry and his comfortable
income, but you'd be wrong. Every morning, over his toast and
kippers, he had to look out of the window of his small vicarage
in the village, to see a sweeping landscape of virgin hills and
woods. He was an ambitious man, and he coveted that land. To
possess it became something of an obsession. Old Tom was
nothing if not shrewd, he knew that the only way to get his
hands on this land was to marry into the family who owned it,
the family of the Earl of Caxton who lived on the other side of
the valley. So, what do you think clever Old Tom did next?'

Lou shrugged, keen for Captain Mandeville to continue the
story without any interruption from her.

'He did what any right-minded young chap would do and
set his sights on the most beautiful of Lord Caxton's daughters,
Miss Sarah Caxton. By all accounts, Tom was a charismatic
character and soon had Miss Caxton and her family eating out
of the palm of his hand. After a short engagement, they married
and, to Old Tom's delight, Lord Caxton presented his new son-
in-law with this land as a wedding gift. Not a bad gift, eh?' He
winked, making Lou laugh again.

'With the generous allowance, the Earl settled on the happy
couple, Old Tom was able to commission the finest architect in
England to design his fashionable Palladian idyll. As well as the
house, he had a wall constructed to bring all of his property
within its boundary, including the sixteenth-century church

where he remained as vicar. But Old Tom knew not to build his house as grand as Caxton Hall and risk offending his father-in-law – his bankroll. You'll see that the portico outside is barely deep enough for a handful of people to stand beneath, when by rights it should be large enough to drive a horse and carriage up to the door. And for Hill House to qualify as a truly great property there should be half a dozen or so more rooms downstairs and a gatehouse at the end of the drive. Nevertheless, by the time he died, Old Tom had made Hill House into one of the finest houses in the county with acres of farms rented out to tenant farmers. By virtue of his marriage, he also had a baronetcy bestowed on him by the king and, thanks to that and some judicious investments, Old Tom died a very wealthy and respected man.' Captain Mandeville stopped to draw breath.

'You've told this story before,' Lou said.

'Once or twice. When I was a small boy, my father had me give tours to all his visitors because I was so enthusiastic about the story of my namesake.' Captain Mandeville paused briefly. 'But do you know the funny thing? The older I grew, the less I saw Old Tom as a character from an adventure story and more as a rather tragic figure. You see, this house and all the fine furniture and fittings, they were inspired by the Grand Tour. Even the coat of arms he had designed.' Captain Mandeville nodded to the crest carved onto the chimneybreast. 'The two lions holding a globe aloft are supposed to symbolise that he was a man of the world, when the truth is, Old Tom never set foot outside England. Not once. Everything he knew of the Grand Tour, he learned from books or from the knowledge of others. I can't imagine anything worse. I've never felt more alive than waking beneath canvas, pushing back a tent flap to see the sun rise over the desert and feel the fresh air of a new day warm my face.' He paused and scratched his chin. 'Sorry, that isn't a standard part of the tour. Not sure what came over me there . . . Come on then, fellow explorer. Onwards and upwards.'

Captain Mandeville led Lou around the hall, pausing to point out each ancestor in the paintings. He knew them all by name – the men, women, children, even the animals – and was able to offer nuggets of information and the occasional titbit of scandal about each. He took her upstairs and stopped at a portrait on the landing of a young man in breeches, a ruffled shirt, a black full-skirted coat and a grey powdered wig, with a huge Irish hunting hound by his side.

'Say hello to Great-Great-Grandfather Thomas Mandeville,' Captain Mandeville said. The spark of mischief in his eyes reminded Lou of the spark she had seen the day before when he bounced Albert up and down on his shoulders. He turned to the side and stuck out his jaw. 'Do you think I inherited his chin?'

Lou grinned. Should she . . .? Why not? 'I'm sure I've seen a better likeness somewhere else . . . Oh yes, now I remember. There's a painting down in the hall, below the stairs, which you left off your tour. It's of a cavalry officer on a horse. He looks a bit haughty and has a large nose and—'

'Miss Arnold!' Captain Mandeville interrupted, his eyes gleaming. 'You do know that teasing your tour guide attracts a forfeit of an extra guinea, don't you? Remind me to add it to your final bill.' His smile turned into a frown. 'It's truly dreadful, though, isn't it? I can't believe I let my mother talk me into posing for that God-awful portrait. If I had my way, I'd chuck the abomination up into the attic. I ask you, who wants to look at my face every day?'

Lou laughed, lost in the banter with Captain Mandeville. In the space of a single sentence he could go from faux-haughtiness to self-deprecating humour. His face was open, expressive, with fine lines around the eyes. It was a friendly face. When he touched the tip of his nose and asked whether it really was so big, a quite unexpected sinking sensation hit Lou in the pit of her stomach. She lost her footing and fell against the wall.

Captain Mandeville stepped towards her, blocking the top of the stairs. 'Are you all right? Shall I call for a glass of water?'

'It's nothing. Really...' She could have blamed the fainting spell on her tight corset, but thought better of bringing up the subject of her underwear. She wiped a tear that surprised her by running down her cheek.

'Is it your mother?' Captain Mandeville asked awkwardly. 'I hope you don't mind but Aunt Leo told me. I'm sorry if anything I said . . .'

'It's not you. It's just ... sometimes, when I'm enjoying myself, I forget. And then I remember again. Sorry, I'm not making any sense.' How could she even begin to explain that the sudden pang of sadness which had knocked the wind from her had more to do with his future than her own recent past?

'Let's get out of here,' Captain Mandeville said. 'I don't know how you women stand to be cooped up inside for so long. Fresh air is just the tonic you need.'

Lou let Captain Mandeville take her by the elbow and guide her down the stairs. He opened the front door, and an icy chill penetrated the enclosed space of the vestibule.

'I'll send for Bainbridge to bring you a coat?' he said.

'No. Thank you,' she said. She wanted to feel the ice bite her cheeks, let the cold freeze the thoughts in her head.

Outside, the fog had deepened to a solid wall of white, shrouding Hill House as though a cloud had slipped from the sky. The world had shrunk to only that which was visible within two, perhaps three feet. Lou followed Captain Mandeville around the side of the house. She had to take two steps for every one of his strides and, once or twice, sensed him slow his pace allowing her to catch up.

They passed the entrance to the walled garden and Lou peered through the gates. She could just make out the gnarled branches of plants in hibernation and, in the far corner, a welcoming smudge of orange light glowed inside one of the greenhouses.

'Watch your step,' Captain Mandeville said, as they crossed the stable yard. 'The cobbles are swept clear of snow every morning, but they can be treacherously slippy.' Opening the heavy wooden door, he moved aside, letting Lou enter the stables ahead of him.

A wall of warmth hit her, followed by the sweet scent of hay mixed with the tang of leather. She gazed around the stables, taking it all in – the row of stalls running the length of one wall, each decorated with polished brass; the horses tethered loosely to metal hoops in the brickwork; the hand-painted porcelain plaques announcing the names of each horse chomping at the feed in their troughs – *Ambrose, Delilah, Leopold, Horatio*. These stables were so full of life; so full of beating hearts; so unlike the charred shell of her own time.

A man appeared from a room at the end of the stalls, rolling down his shirtsleeves. A black Labrador slipped past his legs. Wagging its tail frantically, it made a beeline for Captain Mandeville.

'Hello Clarence.' Captain Mandeville stooped to ruffle the dog's ears. 'And Elliot, how the devil are you?'

The groom snapped his heels together and saluted Captain Mandeville. 'Can't complain, Sir,' he said in a broad Yorkshire accent.

'Really, there's no need for that.' Captain Mandeville took the man's hand and shook it. 'And the mounts?'

'Ambrose there had a touch of colic in the summer.' With an almost imperceptible twitch of his head, the groom indicated he was talking about a grey and white dappled horse snuffling in his trough. 'Aside from that, they've given me no trouble.'

'Good. Excellent.'

Captain Mandeville introduced Lou to Elliot, before joining him in going from stall to stall so that Elliot could update him on when each horse had been ridden last, how their appetites had been, how much roughage had been added to their feed in this cold weather. Captain Mandeville listened intently, patting the flank of each horse as he paused in its stall. When he reached Ambrose, he gave the horse an extra pat and Ambrose responded by scratching his hoof across the cobbles, letting out a contended-sounding snort.

At the very last stall, which was obscured by a high dividing panel, Elliot stepped aside. Captain Mandeville entered alone.

'I was about to brush him down,' Elliot said. 'But I reckon you'll be wanting to spend some time with him first.'

'I don't want to upset your routine.'

'There's no upset. I'll go and get me tea up at the house, if it pleases you, Sir.'

'Of course. Nothing should come between a man and his tea.'

Elliot took his coat down from a peg. He pulled on his cap, tugging the peak as he passed Lou. With a sharp whistle, he brought the Labrador to heel and closed the door behind them.

The instant they were gone, Captain Mandeville appeared from the stall and beckoned to Lou. 'I want to introduce you to Samson,' he said, 'the finest hunter in the county.'

Lou joined him, hovering in the entrance to the stall. She instantly recognised Samson as the horse in the painting. He was huge – far taller than his stable mates and, as he moved, his muscles undulated beneath a coat of satin black. His size and presence were intimidating but Lou felt compelled to touch him. Stepping forward, she placed her hand on his flank and found him surprisingly soft and warm and muscular, all at once.

'Stunning, isn't he?' Captain Mandeville said proudly.

As though in response to his master's voice, Samson turned from his hay and bent his neck. With the horse's face on a level with his, Captain Mandeville closed his eyes and pressed his forehead to the space between the animal's eyes. Lou watched as they stood together, perfectly peaceful. When Captain Mandeville stepped away, he continued to stroke the horse's face. 'He was my father's gift to me on my twenty-first birthday,' he said.

Lou increased the pressure of her stroke, enjoying the sensation of the soft coat beneath her fingertips. 'Is he the horse you ride in the cavalry?'

'No, he's far too valuable for that. Besides, I would never deny my father, or Samson, the chance to take regular rides around the countryside here.' Captain Mandeville ran his hand down Samson's flank and patted him on the hindquarters. He bent to collect an armful of hay from a sack on the floor. 'I only posed on him in that wretched excuse for a work of art for my mother's benefit.' As he turned to place the hay into the trough, Samson nudged him in the back. Captain Mandeville laughed, his voice quiet and low. 'Sorry old chap, wasn't I paying you enough attention? You see, that's what I admire about horses – drayman, groom or baronet – all men are equal in their eyes.'

For the first time since his arrival the previous day, Captain Mandeville sounded serious.

'Samson is more intelligent than any man,' he said. 'When we ride out, I know that I can trust his instincts implicitly. He predicts every furrow, every low hanging branch, every hidden hole in the ground, better than I ever could. He has saved me more times than I care to count by insisting on going in one direction when I have tried to steer him in the other. Sometimes when I look into his eyes, I feel he even knows what I'm thinking.' He shook his head as though suddenly coming to his senses. 'Sorry, I'm talking absolute rot.'

'I don't think it's rot,' Lou said. She liked being given a glimpse, through the bluff of the cavalry officer – behind the throwaway quips and gentle sarcasm – of the sensitive man below.

Captain Mandeville wiped his hands on his trousers. 'Come

on, then. Onwards fellow traveller.' He led the way out of the stables and round to the far side of the house. Lou crossed her arms and tucked her hands into the warmth of her armpits.

'I'm sorry,' Captain Mandeville said. 'I should have insisted you wear a coat. We'll be back inside in a moment or two.'

'I'm fine, really,' Lou said. As she walked by his side, Lou noticed how the damp air was playing havoc with Captain Mandeville's hair, freeing the waves from the confinement of his hair cream.

They came to a stop and, disorientated by the fog, Lou was surprised to find they were outside an extension attached to the house. She had no recollection of having seen a conservatory before. Captain Mandeville pushed the door open and ushered her out of the cold and into the near tropical heat of the octagonal-shaped room.

Lou's arms dropped to her sides, and she looked around in wonder as they walked in. Ivy trailed up the windows and ferns with fronds like broad parasols met in the space overhead. Every plant in the raised metal flowerbeds was separated from its neighbour by lilac-coloured gravel and each bed exploded with colour – scarlet, orange, purple, and blue. The air was thick with perfume and, with the regularity of a metronome, a single droplet of condensation dripped from the glass ceiling, instantly drying on contact with the heated floor tiles.

'This is my father's contribution to the house,' Captain Mandeville said, stamping the snow from his shoes. 'When he was a young man, he travelled extensively throughout South America and came back with a passion for orchids.' He pointed to a bloom of the softest pink. 'Father keeps a gardener who specialises in the care of these flowers. He cultivated this one – *Beautiful Charlotte*. Apparently, its petals are the same pink as my sister's cheeks.'

Lou touched the tender green stem. 'Captain Mandeville—' she began.

He held up his hand. 'I insist that you call me Tom. And what do your friends call you? I'm sure it's not Miss Arnold.'

Without thinking about whether or not it was appropriate, she said, 'Lou, my friends call me Lou.'

'Lou it is then.' He smiled and there was something about his smile that made Lou smile back at him. 'So, Lou, please continue,' he said.

It sounded so odd for him to use her name that it took a moment to find her voice. 'Your sister . . .' she said finally. 'Edward said something a few nights ago about her—'

Tom let out a laugh. 'I shouldn't take much notice of anything Edward says. He's even more out of sorts than is normal for him.'

'He's often . . . unhappy?'

'Unhappy?' Tom laughed again. It wasn't a mean laugh, more a sign of resignation. 'My brother makes it his business to make life hard for himself. Always has. Aunt Leo would say it's because he's sensitive, artistic. I say it's because he's bloody-minded. In fact, I'd go so far as to say he enjoys being miserable. At school, he absolutely refused to compete in sports, preferring to sulk in his dorm all day. I may have been six years ahead of him but even I had one hell of a job saving him from the other boys' beatings. Not that he ever showed the slightest gratitude.'

With two brothers, Lou knew the sibling relationship was never straightforward to navigate. 'I'm sorry,' she said.

'Why? It's hardly *your* fault that my brother dislikes me. And sorry, you were about to tell me something about Edward before I interrupted you.'

'It's just . . . well, he mentioned something about Charlotte's marriage.'

'Oh, I wasn't aware of an impending engagement.'

'I mean her eventual marriage.'

'Ah, I see, a hypothetical marriage. I shouldn't worry, I'm sure my mother has that all in hand. It wouldn't surprise me if she hasn't already got her eye on a number of eligible chinless wonders with money and titles.'

'Like your cousin?' The words were out of her mouth before Lou knew whether she should say them, especially in light of Charlotte's response to the suggestion of such a marriage.

Tom's expression changed. His smile disappeared and his eyes locked on Lou's. '*Caxton,*' he said as though spitting out a sour grape.

'I must have got it wrong. I thought I heard . . . I'm sorry . . .'

Tom turned away. He clenched his fists and stared out of the window. Unable to see his reflection in the glass, Lou read his mood in the rigid line of his shoulders. After a minute or so of stony silence, which she didn't dare fill, Tom said, 'Let's carry on.'

He led the way from the conservatory through the billiard room and Lou was relegated to watching his back rather than walking beside him. She had gone too far by insulting his family. For all she knew, Tom and George Caxton were best friends. When was she going to learn to keep her big mouth shut and her nose out of other people's business?

Tom was subdued as he continued the tour. He stuck to his promise and took her to parts of Hill House that she would not have seen without him. They went in and out of rooms, Tom explaining the history of ornaments and architectural features. His enthusiasm gradually returned as he pointed out the South American carvings and Asian tapestry wall hangings in his father's office – souvenirs from his travels abroad as a young man and army officer. By the time they reached the top floor, Lou was relieved to find him slipping back to his more good-humoured self.

Leading her through a doorway on the uppermost landing, Tom took her along a narrow corridor beneath slanted eaves. The bare floors and walls up here were in stark contrast to the splendour of the world they'd left behind below. 'These are the rooms of the male staff,' Tom said quietly. 'We shouldn't really be up here.'

At the very end of the corridor, he opened a door to a room stacked from floor to ceiling with luggage – trunks, cases, valises. They passed through to an attic beyond – the lumber room, Tom called it – where old and broken furniture and furniture that had fallen out of fashion was kept. He pulled dustsheets from paintings; from an old pram; from long-forgotten furniture and toys whose home had once been the nursery on the floor below. With his breath clouding the unheated air, he told her the story of how the rocking horse had suffered its battle wound the Christmas Day Sir Charles had given both his sons the gift of a toy sword. He found a box of lead zoo animals, which he handled fondly, remembering how he had favoured them as a child. He unearthed a tiny chair mounted on rockers, which he said Charlotte had regularly managed to squirm out of, much to the frustration of her nanny.

When neither of them could bear the cold any longer, Tom led the way back downstairs, all the way down to the hall where their tour had begun. He stopped at the double doors, which opened into the ballroom; a room Lou now realised she had not seen since her arrival.

'Go on,' Tom said, opening the door.

Lou stepped inside and her breath caught. The day outside was slipping away to grey but inside the little light that lingered glimmered in the crystal pendants suspended from two vast chandeliers. Gold leaf coated the moulded vines decorating the ceiling and light reflected from the gilt-framed mirrors lining the walls.

'This is Thomas Mandeville's crowning glory,' Tom said. 'A room of this scale and grandeur is unheard of in a house of this size.' With his hands in his trouser pockets, he bounced up and down. 'The floor's sprung for dancing. You'll see how useful that is at Mother's Christmas Ball.'

'It's beautiful,' Lou said.

'Old Tom may not have got everything right, but he hit the jackpot with this room. He was a man who understood the true value of beauty.'

Lou looked up at Tom. He was staring at her. He coughed and pulled his watch from his pocket. 'It's almost three, I'm afraid we've missed lunch. I could ring for tea.'

'I'm not hungry,' Lou said, barely hiding a grin.

'No, come to think of it, neither am I.' This time when Tom smiled at her he didn't look away.

A silence hung in the air for a moment before the second footman appeared in the doorway. He handed Tom a note and took his leave.

'My father has telephoned,' Tom said, reading the note. 'He's had word from my mother that the train from Leamington Spa will be delayed by the weather. He and Edward are going to wait in Northampton and if it gets too late, they'll book into The Royal Hotel rather than drive back here tonight.' He folded the paper and tucked it into his pocket. 'I'm afraid it looks like you're stuck with me. What say we have an early supper and give the gramophone a run for its money? I could do with some dance practice before the ball.'

Remembering how she had barely scraped her Country Dancing badge at Brownies, Lou said, 'That's not such a good idea.'

'Oh, oh right, I see . . .' Tom looked crestfallen. 'I didn't think that dinner with me would be so awful.'

'Sorry,' Lou said. 'I didn't mean the dinner, only the dancing. It's just that I've got two left feet, I—'

Tom sighed. 'I'm sure we can muddle along somehow.' He looked at her. She wanted to apologise for speaking out of turn about his cousin – to clear the air – but didn't want the memory of that awful moment to sour this one.

Someone coughed in the doorway and a crease furrowed

Tom's brow. 'What is it now?' he said, a note of undisguised frustration in his voice.

'I'm sorry, Sir,' Bainbridge answered. 'But there seems to be a problem with the telephone line. With your father in town, I thought you ought to know.'

'Yes, thank you. I'll be there in a minute.' He turned back to Lou. 'Shall we say seven o'clock for dinner?'

'All right.'

'I shall look forward to it.'

ELEVEN

Lou had only been back in her room ten minutes – barely enough time to process what had just happened; if anything had happened – when Sally knocked on the door.

'Will you be wanting to dress in something simple tonight?' Sally asked. 'With it being just you and Captain Mandeville dining?'

News certainly travelled quickly here.

Lou wondered what the right response was. 'I'd still like to look presentable. Although not too . . . showy.'

'Very good, Miss.' Sally took a dress from the rail in the wardrobe, frowned and put it back. 'Chef's livid,' she said over her shoulder. 'He's spent all afternoon preparing a meal for the family, which he's now going to feed to the staff. He says it's wasted on us. Ah, this will do perfectly.' She closed the wardrobe and hooked a dress on the door.

Lou hovered beside the bed, waiting for Sally to help her undress. At least Sally now seemed to feel able to talk more openly to her, even if she did still insist on calling her 'Miss'.

After her bath, Lou sat at the dressing table where Sally had arranged a series of bottles and jars. If she had her way, she'd apply her own make up but, as most of the powders and creams remained a mystery, once again she surrendered herself into Sally's capable hands.

'Miss,' Sally said as she rubbed rouge into Lou's cheeks, 'would you happen to have seen your kidskin gloves anywhere?'

Lou shook her head. 'Not since I wore them to church yesterday.'

'That's what's so odd. I'm sure I put them away in the drawer, only when I looked earlier, they weren't there. I'll ask Mrs Moriarty whether they've somehow got muddled with the laundry.'

Lou's mind drifted away from any thought of gloves. Through the open curtains she watched the snow fall outside. Thanks to Mother Nature, Hill House was an island tonight. The hatches battened down. There was no chance of anyone arriving unexpectedly.

'Are you thinking of something nice, Miss?' Sally asked.

'Why?'

'You're smiling.'

'Am I?' Lou looked in the mirror. Sally was right, she was smiling.

Smoothing her dress, Lou made her way downstairs. But halfway down the front door flew open, and Lou's smile dropped as Sir Charles, Lady Mandeville, Edward, Mrs Hart, and Charlotte all rushed inside, chased by a flurry of snow.

'Oh, it's so cold. It really is too much to bear,' Lady Mandeville said as Charlotte ran to the fire and held her hands out to the flames. Mrs Hart removed the pin from her hat, brushing snow from the brim. Edward ruffled his damp hair and Sir Charles rubbed his hands together and stamped his feet. An army of staff appeared and converged on the party, removing coats and taking hats.

'I'm so sorry that Dawson didn't come to meet you, Sir Charles,' Bainbridge said. 'But we weren't expecting you home.'

'Neither were we.' Sir Charles handed his hat to his valet. 'But since the ladies managed to get a train from Leamington Spa, Edward and I decided that we had better find a way to get us all here. We couldn't let them beat us in a test of endurance now, could we? When I was unable to get through on the telephone, I found a man with a car and struck a deal with him to drive us back.'

'I'm so sorry that you were inconvenienced, Sir Charles. The engineers will be out tomorrow to mend the telephone line.'

'Jolly good. And you can stop apologising, we had something of an adventure.'

The door to the billiard room opened. 'And so, the intrepid travellers return,' Tom said. 'And scupper my plans for a quiet evening in.'

He glanced up the stairs and smiled.

'Miss Arnold,' Lady Mandeville said, 'don't you look a picture, and what a pretty dress.'

'Oh, Louisa,' Charlotte sighed exaggeratedly. 'What a day we have had. Come down so that I can tell you *all* about it.'

Lou took the last few steps and Charlotte grabbed her hand while Sir Charles convinced Lady Mandeville that there really was no need to dress for dinner since they were all famished. Relenting, Lady Mandeville asked Bainbridge to have dinner served as soon as it was ready. Lou imagined Monsieur Gotti's delight at decanting his creations into silver serving dishes rather than on to stoneware plates for the staff.

The party made their way through to the drawing room where William poured everyone a warming sherry before they took their places in the dining room.

As they ate, the family shared details of the saga of their

return through the snowy night and around winding treacherous roads.

'You missed a splendid lunch at Franklin's expense,' Sir Charles said to Tom. 'It made a refreshing change for *his* chequebook to see the light of day. Edward and I spent a few hours reading the newspapers in the residents' bar of The Royal Hotel. They had a very passable scotch. You would have enjoyed it.'

'Perhaps,' Tom said. 'But I wanted to spend some time reacquainting myself with the old place.'

'Reacquainting yourself! Why, you know every inch of this house, better even than I do,' his father laughed.

'And you, Louisa,' Mrs Hart asked. 'How did you pass your day?'

'Oh, I read a little. Explored a little. I saw the conservatory for the first time.'

'What did you make of my orchids?' Sir Charles asked. 'Beautiful, aren't they?' He launched into a lecture on the origin of each flower. Lou nodded politely, all the while sensing someone watching her. She glanced along the table and saw her accomplice holding a napkin to his mouth, feigning a small yawn, which was visible only to her. She stifled a laugh before she noticed that Mrs Hart was watching them.

The atmosphere in the room was light, the conversation easy. Even Edward's mood was brighter than the previous evening, which Lou decided went someway to making up for the change in plans. At least the Mandevilles' return saved her from having to explain why she couldn't dance a single step.

After dinner, the women left the men to return to the drawing room and Lady Mandeville called for a restorative brandy for each of them. Charlotte sat on the floor beside the fire with the new glass baubles that had arrived from Selfridges arranged on the hearthrug. She was brimming with excitement at the prospect of trimming the tree the next day.

'Well,' Lady Mandeville said, sitting back in her chair. 'We've all had quite a day, haven't we?'

Mrs Hart nodded her agreement and Charlotte looked up from her ornaments. 'All except Louisa. She's been stuck here all day while we have been having our adventures. How dull it must have been for you.'

Lou swirled the brandy around her glass before taking a sip. Warmth inched down her throat and spread to fill her chest like the petals of a spicy orange orchid unfurling.

She smiled at the memory of Tom looking up the stairs at her and yawning behind his napkin. Lady Mandeville was right. It had been quite a day. And she would gladly stay in a dream if every day played out as this one had.

TWELVE

21ST DECEMBER 1913

'No, Miss,' Sally laughed. 'You go to *your* left and I go to *my* right.'

Lou let her hand slip from Sally's shoulder. 'It's hopeless, isn't it? I really do have two left feet.'

'You need to practice, that's all. Come on.'

Lou placed her hand on Sally's shoulder. 'All right. But don't blame me if you end up with bruised toes.'

Together they set off on a waltz around Lou's bedroom.

'And one. And two. And three. And four.' Sally counted out slowly, but no sooner had she told Lou to look up, than Lou tripped over her own feet and tumbled to the bed, taking Sally with her. Collapsing in a heap, they disintegrated into fits of giggles.

'I'm sorry, Miss,' Sally said, struggling to her feet. 'What would Mrs Moriarty say if she came in and saw me in such a manner?'

'Stuff Mrs Moriarty.'

Sally hid a giggle behind her hand. 'Oh, Miss!'

'Go on, admit it,' Lou said, resting back on her elbows. 'It's hopeless, isn't it? There's absolutely no way I'll be ready to dance with anybody in just three days.'

'We can practice again tomorrow morning after breakfast, if you like.' Sally took hold of Lou's hands and pulled her to her feet. 'You'll be wonderful at Her Ladyship's Ball, just you wait and see.'

'I don't think so. I'm no Darcey Bussell.'

'Who?'

'It doesn't matter,' Lou laughed. 'But if I've learned one thing this morning, it's that I have about as much grace as a fairy elephant.'

Sally gave a subdued laugh. She began to fuss with the straps of her apron. Looking to the floor, she said, 'If *I* had the courage to stand up to Sir Charles, I'm sure I'd feel I could do anything. Sorry, Miss,' she added quickly. 'I've said too much. It's not my place . . .'

'We're friends, Sally,' Lou sighed. 'You can say anything to me, and I won't mind.'

Sally fiddled with the pocket of her apron, twisting the lace through her fingers.

'Was there something else?' Lou asked.

Still concentrating on her pocket, Sally said, 'It's just that . . . well, the men downstairs mightn't agree with what you said to Sir Charles, but they wouldn't, would they? It suits men to keep us women where we are and . . . I suppose I'm fortunate that William is a good husband and our employers are fair because there are plenty of women who aren't so lucky. Us women downstairs were talking and we're . . . that's to say . . . we're grateful that somebody like you should bother enough to stand up for us. I promised that I would thank you when I had the chance.'

Lou felt a little swell of pride, but she was sorry to see that Sally's cheeks had coloured. Patently wanting to get back onto a more familiar footing, Sally shifted her attention to Lou's blouse, fussing over the buttons. 'I don't suppose you've seen your embroidered handkerchief anywhere, have you?' she asked. 'I couldn't find it this morning and I still haven't come across your gloves.'

Lou took hold of Sally's hands. 'Don't worry so much. They're just *things*. People are what matter.' Gently she straightened Sally's white cap, which had been knocked askew when they fell on the bed. Taking a step back, she looked Sally up and down. 'That's better,' she said. 'Now we're equal.'

Still smiling at the look of utter surprise on Sally's face, Lou entered the morning room and had to dodge Charlotte who leapt from her chair and ran to the window.

'Please Charlotte, do sit down,' Lady Mandeville said. 'You're making me quite dizzy. Running to and from the window will not make anybody return any quicker.'

'But I really thought I heard them this time.' Charlotte slunk back to her chair. She picked up her box of baubles and placed it in her lap. The constant jiggling of her legs made the tissue paper protecting them rustle. When her mother let out a loud sigh, she placed the box back on the table.

'It's a lovely tradition,' Lou said, 'to go out into the woods and chose your own Christmas tree.'

Charlotte poured a cup of tea and handed it to her.

'And you will join us this afternoon, won't you, Miss Arnold?' Lady Mandeville said. 'The women gather on the afternoon the tree is erected to decorate the hall and welcome Christmas into the house.'

Lou took a sip of her tea. 'I'd be delighted. It all sounds wonderful.'

'What sounds wonderful?' a man's voice said from the doorway.

'I thought you were helping your father choose the tree,' Lady Mandeville said.

'I was.' Tom entered the room and plucked a biscuit from a plate on the table. 'But I got bored of standing around like a spare part, watching other men cut it down. So, I came back ahead of everyone else.' He popped the biscuit into his mouth, chewing as he paused to warm his hands at the fire, before carrying on past Lou. As he passed, he bent and whispered in her ear. 'Your feet had a lucky escape last night. Don't imagine they'll get off so lightly on Christmas Eve.'

The tea Lou had just sipped shot down her windpipe. She began to choke.

Tom put his hand on her shoulder. 'I'm sorry,' he said. 'Are you all right? I didn't mean to—'

'Thomas!' Lady Mandeville called. 'Whatever have you said to upset Miss Arnold?'

Charlotte rushed to Lou's side, and she felt Tom remove his hand. He retreated to the sofa and sat beside his mother. When Lou stopped coughing, he crossed his legs and said, 'If booking my place on a woman's dance card is enough to send her into a fit of apoplexy, then I stand guilty as charged.'

'In that case, I'm not surprised Louisa is choking,' Charlotte groaned. 'My brother is a terrible dance partner, Louisa. Oh, his foxtrot and waltz are just about passable, but his conversation is so dull! Other men talk about the music and the splendid decorations and the beautiful gowns. Some even touch on politics. But with Tom, it's all horses and motorcycles. If you dance with him then I'm afraid you will die of boredom.' She paused and when she spoke again, it was with a tone of mischief. 'Although I doubt anyone will get a look in with Tom this Christmas Eve, not with Cousin Emma at the ball.'

'Charlotte!' Lady Mandeville shot her daughter a warning glance and changed the subject to the food she had arranged for the upcoming shooting party. But it wasn't quick enough to stop a muscle twitching in Tom's jaw. He collected his newspaper and stood up. 'I'll be in the library if anybody wants me.'

Charlotte leant towards Lou. 'I'm not wrong,' she said quietly after checking that her mother wasn't looking in their direction. 'You'll see that for yourself when cousins George and Emma arrive later today. George is a bore, but Emma is so interesting. She knows everybody and everything. She spends most of the year living in Lord Caxton's house in Belgravia and goes to all the plays and the very best parties and is only ever seen in the very latest fashions. I'm sure you will adore her, everybody does. Which is why I can't understand why she would be at all interested in marrying my silly brother.'

Lou stood up abruptly. 'I should change. I've spilt tea on my blouse.'

'Really? I can't see—'

'There . . . on the sleeve,' Lou said. She hurried from the room before Charlotte had the chance to examine the non-existent stain.

THIRTEEN

Pacing up and down in her room, Lou tried to distract her thoughts by mentally rehearsing the dance steps Sally had taught her. But what was the point when, with Emma Caxton at the ball, no other woman would get a 'look in'? And what did any of it matter when none of this was real? She took a hairpin from a dish on the dressing table. It was just her luck that the doctors had put her into some sort of light coma that allowed her brain to run riot in this hallucination. Hopefully, someone would take pity on her and add a stronger sedative to her drip so she could slip further into sleep and out of Cloud Cuckoo Land.

Lou gripped the hairpin so tight that it sprang from her fingers. Stooping to pick it up, she placed it back in the dish. As she stood up, she glanced at the window and noticed how the fog outside still hung low over the land, although not nearly as dense as the day before. She became aware of a movement amongst the trees. Slowly a form began to take shape. Emerging from the safety of the fog, picking its way gingerly through the snow, was a deer. A deer! She had only ever seen the odd crow on St Mary's spire or a gnarly old grey squirrel scratching in the leaves. Never a deer!

Gathering up her skirt, Lou ran from the room and raced along the corridor.

Down in the hall she had to leap over the branches of the huge fir tree Bainbridge, William, and a groundsman were dragging across the floor. 'Sorry!' she called on her way to the library. She threw the door open, and Tom looked up from his newspaper.

'Where's the fire?' he asked.

'Come on,' she said, gesticulating wildly, trying to catch her breath.

'What are you up to?'

'Please, Tom . . . just come . . . look . . . you have to see.'

'This had better be good.' His eyebrows rose as he smiled. He placed his newspaper on the table and followed her into the now empty morning room where she pointed out of the window.

'See,' she panted, '. . . there. It's a deer.'

'So it is,' Tom said. 'And from the single fork in his antlers, I'd say he's a yearling. Stay perfectly still. If he so much as senses us watching, he'll take fright and hightail it for the trees.'

The deer took a few tentative steps across the white lawn.

'He's so beautiful,' Lou whispered, conscious of Tom's closeness to her. 'Why do you think he's broken cover? Won't he be in danger?'

'He wants something. But he's timid. See how he looks about, checking for any sign of danger. He's taking each step carefully, purposefully . . . Lou, I—' Tom's gentle words disappeared, drowned out by the *honk! honk!* of a horn and a car revving its engine as it sped up the drive.

The deer stood perfectly still for a moment, frozen in shock, before coming abruptly to its senses. It fled to the safety of the woods as the murky yellow light of two headlamps emerged through the frozen fog.

Tom sighed and Lou looked round to see a crease between

his eyebrows. She followed his stony gaze to the post-box red, open-topped car screeching to a stop in front of the house. The driver's door flew open, and a large man squeezed his bulk from the car. In a full-length brown fur coat, driving helmet and a red scarf around his neck, he looked just like Toad of Toad Hall. Lou was about to share the observation with Tom, but the dark look in his eyes told her he was in no mood for jokes.

'It's my cousins, George and Emma Caxton,' he said sullenly. 'We should go and greet them.'

Outside, Lou waited with Tom beneath the portico while Bainbridge, William, and the second footman unloaded luggage from the boot. Bainbridge opened the passenger door, but the driver blocked Lou's view of his travelling companion.

'George,' Tom said flatly, offering his hand to the man.

'*Mandeville*.'

The two cousins shook hands. It was unlike any greeting Lou had ever witnessed. Each man gripped the other's hand so that their tendons stood proud. It looked more like a test of strength than a friendly welcome.

She had been right to think that Tom disliked his cousin. And judging by George Caxton's sneer, the feeling was mutual.

Pulling his hand free, Tom said, 'This is our guest, Miss Arnold. Miss Arnold, this is my cousin, George Caxton.' He spoke flatly, no trace of warmth.

With eyes set slightly too far apart, George Caxton looked Lou up and down. Taking her hand, he kissed it, and she had to fight the urge to wipe it immediately on her skirt.

'Actually, it's The *Honourable* George Caxton,' he said. 'And don't let Mandeville mislead you. It was our ancestors, centuries ago, who were cousins, not us. These things are important to establish upfront, don't you think? Avoids misunderstandings later on.'

Caxton spoke as though Tom's presence was of as little significance to him as that of the staff waiting to do his bidding.

Remembering old Albert's warning about Charlotte's marriage to this man, Lou took a step closer to Tom. But George was too busy lambasting William for his handling of one of the trunks to notice her intentional slight. He stormed back to the car and in doing so, revealed his travelling companion to be a young woman in a fur coat of immaculate white. A wide-brimmed hat covered her dark hair and was held in place by a sheer scarf. Her complexion was pale, her features fine, but it was her lips that Lou found herself transfixed by. Enhanced by scarlet lipstick, they were so full and so plump that Lou couldn't imagine any man not wanting to kiss them or wanting to stop once he had begun.

The woman walked towards the portico, her red lips parting to reveal a dazzling smile.

'Emma,' Tom said, stepping away from Lou.

'Tom, darling.' Emma met Tom in a warm embrace. 'How tanned you are!' she said, a laugh in her voice. 'It suits you. Perhaps next summer I should dispense with the parasol and go *au naturel* on the Riviera.'

'Emma,' Tom said, only half turning to Lou. 'This is Miss Louisa Arnold, my aunt's guest for the week.'

'My aunt's guest'? No longer 'our guest'? How cold that introduction sounded. How distant.

'Miss Arnold,' Miss Caxton said, treating Lou to the warmest of smiles. 'It's delightful to meet you.'

'And you, Miss Caxton,' Lou said.

'Oh, call me, Emma,' she laughed. 'And may I call you Louisa?'

Charlotte ran from the house. 'Emma!' she called and threw her arms around her cousin. 'Come inside,' she said, taking Emma's hand. 'Mama is beside herself waiting to see you. *I* want to hear all about London. Did you go to see the exhibition at The Natural History Museum in the end? Was it marvellous?'

Emma and Charlotte disappeared inside, followed by George Caxton. Tom walked beside Lou, but the look on his face didn't invite conversation.

In the hall, Sir Charles, Lady Mandeville, Mrs Hart, and Edward waited to greet George and Emma. A maid hovered with a tray of mulled wine. She offered a glass to Lou, but she shook her head. Other staff helped the guests with their outdoor clothes. Lou tried not to gawp when Emma unfurled her scarf and removed first her hat and then her coat. Beneath the white fur, she wore a simple dark green dress, shorter in length than any Lou had seen in her time at Hill House; so short that it was possible every now and then to catch a glimpse of Emma's ankles. It was lower cut too, revealing just a hint of the swell of Emma's bust, so perfectly in proportion with her slim waist.

Lou frowned at her tweed skirt and high-necked blouse. She looked like she'd dressed herself in cast offs from an old lady's wardrobe.

Emma chatted easily with everyone, and her eyes brimmed with what appeared to be genuine happiness. She was so unlike her brother, who brooded in the corner, helping himself to a glass of mulled wine. He knocked it back, returned the glass to the maid's tray and immediately took a second. Sir Charles engaged him in a conversation about his car. It was new – apparently – and incredibly expensive. Lou looked from the burly George Caxton to the slight, childlike Charlotte. It was impossible to imagine a day when she would stand by his side at the altar.

'Emma, you look beautiful,' Lady Mandeville said. 'Thomas, doesn't Emma look beautiful?'

Tom took two glasses of wine from the maid's tray and handed one to Emma. 'A true English rose is always in full bloom.'

Emma slipped her arm through his and tapped his hand. 'I suppose I'll have to take that as a compliment since it's the closest thing to one I'm likely to get from you. Why must you always talk in riddles?' She took a sip of her wine and looked up to the bare boughs of the tree. 'What a beautiful fir, I'd say it's the finest yet.'

'We have some lovely new decorations,' Charlotte said. 'Mama ordered them from Selfridges.'

'Oh dear, you haven't done away with the beautiful old decorations, have you?' Emma pouted. 'I do so like those hand-painted globes. The ones decorated with holly and ivy.'

'They belonged to Sir Charles' mother,' Lady Mandeville said. 'They were her favourites. I would find it so reassuring to know that one day I might pass them into the care of someone who treasures them as I do.'

'I'm glad you keep the old traditions going,' Emma said. 'It means I always feel so at home here.'

'And so you should,' Lady Mandeville smiled.

George muttered something under his breath about the tree at Caxton Hall being twice the size. When nobody took any notice, he grabbed a third glass of mulled wine.

'Come,' Lady Mandeville said. 'You must hear all about our adventures yesterday. We were stranded in the snow and had to make our way back through a blizzard! Can you imagine? At one point I was certain I would never see Hill House again.'

Mrs Hart shook her head. 'I have never known so much drama to be made from a mere inconvenience. Anyone would think we had made our way back from Antarctica rather than Leamington Spa.'

'Oh, Aunt Leonora,' Emma said, clearly not sharing her brother's squeamishness about addressing this side of the family as close relatives. 'I'm sure you're underplaying the adventure. I want to hear all about it. It sounds positively thrilling.'

Lady Mandeville directed her guests into the morning room, but Lou hung back. When she was sure that her presence – or rather lack of it – had gone unnoticed, she slipped away through the billiard room and into the conservatory. Amongst the spicy scent and the lush greenery, she sat on one of the wicker chairs. So, Emma Caxton was not only beautiful, but clever and witty too. An equal in every way for Tom.

The door opened. 'Oh,' Edward said when he saw her sitting amongst the plants. 'Sorry. I'll find somewhere else.'

'Don't go,' Lou said.

Edward hesitated before closing the door and taking the seat beside her.

'It's a lovely room,' she said. 'Very tranquil.'

Edward stared at the floor between his feet. 'Yes, I suppose it is.'

Silence.

'You didn't want to join the party?' she asked.

'I despise enforced jollity.' Edward's spectacles slipped down his nose and he pushed them back up. He sat forward in the chair, hands hanging limply between his knees. This close, Lou could see that Edward shared Tom's strong features, although his face was slimmer, his skin paler. The dark circles beneath his eyes were also a giveaway that he hadn't slept well in days.

'Are you looking forward to the shoot?' she asked, hoping for some sign of enthusiasm.

Edward twisted the cufflink around in his sleeve. 'Have you ever seen a pheasant shot?' he said.

'No.'

'After the beaters flush them out, each pheasant soars into the sky, wings outstretched. For a moment they are suspended in the air and are quite, quite beautiful. Until you realise they are flying not for pleasure, but in fear of their lives. Within seconds, each is shot full of lead. Their hearts stop in their chests as they crash to the ground where they meet the final indignity of finding themselves clamped in the lolling jaws of a retriever.'

He turned his attention to the condensation inching down the window. There was such sadness in Edward's expression, and not just for the pheasant. Lou so wanted to ask what troubled him; what had made him weep the other evening.

'Sorry, I'm afraid I'm not much company.' He eased his long, slim limbs up from the chair with the effort it would take a man three times his age. 'The fog's lifting. I think I'll go for a walk.'

Remembering another lost boy, Lou said, 'If you ever want to talk . . . about anything, then I'm a good listener.'

Edward shook his head but gave her the briefest of smiles. 'Thank you, but I'm beyond talking. If you'll excuse me.'

He opened the door to the outside and closed it behind him. Crossing the snow-covered garden, he shrugged his shoulders to his ears and wrapped his arms around his body, heading in the direction of the woods.

FOURTEEN

Following afternoon tea, Lou sat on the stairs, threading red ribbons around evergreens. Lady Mandeville had set her the task of making an arrangement for the mantelshelf in the hall. Along with the other women, she listened to Emma's tale of a rebellious debutante in London.

'It's scandalous!' Emma said as she tied one of her precious old baubles to a branch of the Christmas tree. 'And do you know, her mother had her on the boat to her godmother in Switzerland before she could say "cow bell"!'

Charlotte collapsed in a fit of giggles and Mrs Hart smiled as she placed a small parcel on a branch.

'If Charlotte dares to behave in such a shameful way when she is presented next year, I will have no hesitation in sending her up to my sister in the Highlands,' Lady Mandeville said. 'She would have plenty of time there to reflect on the disgrace she had brought on her family.'

'I shouldn't worry, Mama,' Charlotte said. 'I may just save you the trouble and continue my education. Imagine how much money I could save Father. Three years at university is surely cheaper than a trousseau of new dresses.'

'And much better value,' Mrs Hart added.

Lady Mandeville threw her arms in the air. 'Do you see what I have to withstand, Emma? You were never this much trouble to Lady Caxton, were you? As I remember, you were always such a good girl.'

Obscured by the tree, Emma winked at Charlotte. 'That's right, Aunt. I was the very model of daughterly obedience.' Lowering her voice so that only Charlotte – and Lou – could hear, she added, 'But Mother could only keep her beady eye on me *some* of the time.' She nudged Charlotte and they both giggled like two naughty schoolgirls at the back of the class.

Taking up another length of ribbon, Lou had just tied two stems of holly together when she became aware of someone watching her.

'Fiddly job.' Emma said, pointing to the ribbon and the holly. She had left the decorating party and now stood beside the stairs.

'Yes, I suppose it is,' Lou said.

'I'm afraid I'm so clumsy, I'd be sure to jab myself and draw blood.' Emma gave Lou one of her winning smiles. 'What say you take a break from the perils of garland making and take a turn around the hall?'

Emma began to walk away, leaving Lou no option but to follow. In the short time Emma had been in the house, Lou had learned that she wasn't the kind of woman who would take no for an answer.

Emma stopped at a statue of Pan so Lou stopped too. Emma made a show of pointing out details of the carving before glancing towards the tree. 'Do you know, your name came up in conversation a number of times this afternoon?' she said. 'I do believe you've made quite an impression on the family. Especially Tom.' She watched Lou, obviously waiting for a reaction. 'You needn't look so surprised. Tom considers you to be an

eminently sensible person, with your head on the right way, sort
of thing. And from what I've seen, I'd say he's right. Which
helps me no end.'

Lou stared at the silver particles glittering in the marble of
Pan's pipes. 'Oh, right,' she said. 'I see.'

'Thank goodness.' Emma gave Lou a conspiratorial grin.
'That makes this all much easier. You see, as soon as I laid eyes
on you, I thought to myself, now there's a good bean who knows
what's what. The sort of girl who can be trusted to keep a secret.
I'm not wrong, am I?'

'No,' Lou said. Just where was this conversation heading?

'I'm sure I don't need to tell you that these old houses lap up
money like a cat with the best Jersey cream. And it's just . . .'
Emma glanced towards the tree again. 'Look here, nobody will
have told you this, but I think it's important you know everything. How else are you to understand the urgency of the situation? You see, dear old Uncle Charles – who I adore of course –
well, a few years ago he made a rather misguided investment in
a Polish salt mine. You might have read about it. It's rather gone
belly up and left a few chaps completely on their uppers. But
it's not Uncle Charles' fault at all,' she added quickly. 'My
father's had a word with some his chums and has managed to
keep Uncle Charles' name out of the papers. He wanted to do
something more to help and came up with what he thought was
an excellent plan to rent some of Hill House's land to expand
his stud farm. But Uncle Charles won't hear a word of it. He
can be a stubborn old goat when he wants to be, and he thinks
Father's plan has the whiff of charity about it. I'm afraid that his
pride was dented even though he can't do anything else with the
land because of the dratted issue of entailment. He's insisted
the ball go ahead this Christmas along with the shoot, when he
can ill-afford either. Father's in cahoots with Lady Mandeville
and has been sneaking crates of champagne and brandy into the

cellar here for months now, just to take the edge off the costs. You see the fix poor old Uncle Charles is in, don't you?'

'Somewhat,' Lou said. She understood that entailment meant an inheritance had to remain intact to pass on to an heir. But what this had to do with her, she had no clue.

Emma took hold of Lou's arm and drew her in closer. 'My father has made it clear that when I marry, he'll send me packing with a hefty dowry.' Emma spoke quietly but forcefully, so that Lou was in no doubt of the benefit of a match with a Caxton. 'Old-fashioned, but that's Daddy all over for you. And I know from Lady Mandeville that you are aware of our little . . . arrangement. If it comes off, the family's money worries will be over. Sir Charles could hardly refuse a helping hand from his new daughter-in-law, now, could he?'

Lou couldn't speak. Was this marriage being plotted behind Tom's back some kind of business transaction? Was he being auctioned off to swell the family coffers? She took a step away from Emma so that she could see her eyes. Hoping to read Emma's real thoughts, Lou said, 'You do feel something for him, don't you? For Tom? It isn't all about money, is it?'

'I don't give two figs for money,' Emma said, her eyes wide, a laugh in her words. 'I'd never marry for something as vulgar as that.' She released Lou's arm and took hold of her hand, practically dragging her up the hall and coming to a stop before Tom's portrait. 'I defy any woman to look at that man and not *feel* something.'

Lou dipped her eyes to the floor.

'I have adored him since we were children.' Emma's voice took on a softer tone when she said, 'I can pinpoint the precise moment. Tom was fourteen, I was nine. He hardly knew I existed. He was home from school for the summer holidays and spent almost every day running amok in the grounds of Caxton Hall with George. They were as thick as thieves then. I remember it so well because it was the year that my darling kitten, Sissy, went missing. Tom dropped everything and spent hours scouring the house and grounds, helping me look for her. George was furious. He wanted Tom to go fishing with him.' Emma's voice drifted away as she gazed up at the portrait. 'I've never forgotten how Tom comforted me when I cried, promising to buy me another kitten one day. He was so kind, so gentle, so gallant . . . Have you noticed that when he looks at you, he seems to be looking inside you? Sort of rummaging around in your thoughts?' She turned to Lou. 'And there's my problem. You and I both know that men like Tom don't marry women whose lives are played out in the pages of *Tatler*. Which is where you come in.'

Emma still had hold of Lou's hand and Lou felt it given a hard squeeze. 'Me?' Lou said.

Emma pressed closer to her so that their shoulders touched. 'He clearly respects your opinion,' Emma said. 'So, I need you to plead my case. I need you to show him that I'm a serious person, that the person filling the gossip columns isn't the *real* Emma Caxton. If I miss the chance to convince him this week, it might be months, years even, before I get another opportunity. Hill House can't wait that long. *I* can't wait that long.'

'Does your brother approve of Tom?' Lou asked, surprising even herself. Why was she trying to put obstacles in Emma's path? Why couldn't she just say yes, she would be happy to help?

Laughing gently, Emma said, 'It's lucky for me that we don't live in the Dark Ages. If I needed George's approval to marry, I should die an old maid.' She looked up at the portrait again. 'Do you know, I think he's even more handsome now with all of those freckles? It may not be fashionable to appear as though one has spent time out in the sun, but on him . . . well, they look just adorable.'

Lou followed Emma back to the other women. As Emma took up a decoration to place on the tree, Lou summoned up

Tom's face, remembering how, at a distance, his freckles mingled to a single tanned mass but up close, they were distinct smudges. At times, she had been so close to Tom that, had she wanted to, she could have counted those freckles. Every single one.

FIFTEEN

Following dinner that evening and after the other women had retired, Lou sat with Mrs Hart in the drawing room. She held a book but hadn't managed to read a single word. She had spent all evening searching her brain, trying to remember anything she'd learnt about Sir Charles Mandeville's investments. There was nothing to be found. Her schoolteachers hadn't gone into that level of detail. It must be all in her mind; just one more example of her imagination overlaying another level of complication to this dream.

Mrs Hart yawned and got up from her chair. 'You look done in,' she said, touching Lou's shoulder. 'You should get some sleep. You'll need it to brave the whirlwind of parties ahead.'

'I will,' Lou promised. 'Once I've finished this page.'

Finally alone, Lou placed the copy of Plato's collected philosophy aside. She gazed into the fire. If this was all a dream, why did it feel so real? Why was she starting to care about these people? Around her, the house made small creaking noises, settling down for the night. She collected her wrap and headed out into the hall.

She paused at the bottom of the stairs. Inside the billiard

room, Edward sat beside the fire, staring into the flames. George Caxton had fallen asleep in the chair beside him, snoring, a glass clasped proprietarily to his chest. Beyond them, Sir Charles was seated at a small table, smoking a cigar. Across from him was Tom. Lou studied his face in profile, his nose turning up at the tip. It was a retroussé nose, sweet like a child's. He placed a cigarette between his lips and drew the smoke into his lungs before throwing back his head, exhaling, laughing at something his father said.

Just looking at him made Lou feel like a traitor. Emma had taken her into her confidence and here she was, stealing a secret look at Tom. Emma's Tom.

Holly berries on the garlands over the mantelshelf crackled in the heat of the fire. A wave of nerves rippled through Lou's stomach. Turning away, she began to cross the hall but, too late, became aware of rapid footsteps approaching from behind.

'Where have you been tonight?' Tom asked from just over her shoulder.

Lou watched candlelight glint in the tiles of the floor. 'At dinner. Didn't you see me?'

'In body, yes,' Tom said. 'But your mind, well, I suspect that was elsewhere. I lost count of the number of times I tried to catch your attention. Once or twice I could have sworn you avoided looking at me, just as you are now.'

'I'm not avoiding you,' she lied.

'Lou,' he sighed. 'I'm a dumb man. If you're playing some sort of game, then I'm afraid you'll have to let me in on the rules.'

She turned to look at him. He smiled at her. Waiting for a response.

Lou's heart leapt into her throat. Why did every encounter with Tom result in a reconfiguration of her insides? 'I would never play games with you,' she said. 'Ever.'

SIXTEEN

22ND DECEMBER 1913

'Here you are, Miss. Just what you need, a nice boiled egg. It's the breakfast of kings, or so my mother says.' Sally placed a tray on the dressing table.

'Thank you,' Lou said, although she had no intention of touching the food Sally had insisted on bringing her. Her mind too full to sleep, she had left her bed in the small hours and had sat in the chair in the window until the sun rose, pink on the horizon.

'Would you like me to help you dress?' Sally asked, straightening out the bedclothes.

'Not yet. I'd like to sit here awhile.'

'Are you feeling poorly, Miss? You're very pale this morning.'

Lou tightened the knot in the belt of her robe. 'A little off-colour, perhaps.'

'No dancing practice today then?'

'No.' Lou forced a smile. 'No dancing practice today.'

Sally excused herself but returned at regular intervals until Lou relented and allowed herself to be dressed. It was almost midday when Sally left, taking the breakfast tray with her.

Knowing that by now, most guests would be elsewhere, going about their daily business, Lou crept down the stairs and let herself into the morning room.

She stood in the window, watching two groundsmen go about the unrelenting task of clearing the drive. As quickly as they could shovel away the snow, more fat flakes fell from the heavy clouds. A movement off to one side caught Lou's attention. She pulled back the curtain and saw Elliot come from the side of the house, leading Ambrose on a short rein. They came to a stop before the front door where they waited. And waited. Elliot stroked Ambrose's neck as the horse placidly chewed at his bit, steam rising from his warm body.

Eventually a man dressed in a black jacket and jodhpurs emerged from beneath the portico. Lou couldn't help curling her lip as, ignoring Elliot, George Caxton placed his foot into the stirrup dangling at Ambrose's flank. When he failed to mount from a standing start, he snapped his fingers. Dutifully, Elliot took up position beside the horse, knitting his fingers together to create a cup for George's boot. The groom bore the weight of the much heavier man with no outward sign of strain, but as George swung his leg over the horse's back, Ambrose shifted, causing him to fall backwards. Somehow George managed to land with both feet on the ground but clearly furious, waved his whip and barked a few words at Elliot who knitted his fingers together for a second time. Again, George placed his boot in Elliot's hands but this time he pulled savagely on the reins, yanking Ambrose's head to one side. As he finally got into the saddle, Ambrose reared on to his hind legs. Through the closed window, Lou heard his pained neigh. Elliot grabbed for the bridle, trying to bring the startled Ambrose under control. Ambrose reared again and this time George lost his grip on the reins. He freed his boot from the stirrup and landed heavily, but still upright, on the ground. His face red, his features contorted, he raised the whip and brought it down with a crack on Ambrose's behind. Ambrose's nostrils flared, his front hooves swept at the air. Elliot struggled to keep a grip of the bridle. George raised the whip again. Lou slid the window up, intending to shout at him to stop. She was beaten to it.

'What in hell's name are you doing?' Tom ran from beneath the portico. He grabbed George's arm, saving poor Ambrose from another vicious blow. Yanking the whip from George's grasp, Tom threw it to the ground and, with no apparent consideration for his own safety, approached Ambrose's flailing hooves.

'Whoa boy,' he said, his voice calm. He held his palms out flat, talking to Ambrose until the horse, responding to his voice, began to calm. When all four hooves were down on the ground, his head no longer tossing, Tom was able to take hold of the reins. He rested his forehead against Ambrose's neck and ran his hand down the horse's face.

'I'm sorry, Sir,' Elliot said. 'Mr Caxton wanted a ride. Ambrose will normally take anyone on his back. I wouldn't have brought him round the front only Mr Caxton asked in particular—'

'You've done nothing wrong,' Tom said. Stepping away from Ambrose, he handed the reins to Elliot. 'Please take Ambrose back to his stable. Be sure to stay with him until he has calmed.'

Elliot touched his cap and led Ambrose away. With his back to the house, Tom stood and watched them go.

'"Stay with him until he has calmed,"' George mocked. 'It's a bloody horse, Mandeville. You're soft, just like the rest of your shower. There's not a backbone between you.'

Lou stared at Tom's shoulders, at his hands balled into fists.

'If that sorry excuse for an animal were mine, I'd see to it that it was properly broken.' George stooped to pick up his whip and lashed at the air. 'I've a mind to go and teach it a lesson now.'

Tom spun around, his face set in anger. 'Touch that horse again and I'll break that whip on you.'

'Well, well, well, what have we here? Maybe a few years in the service of His Majesty has finally turned Little Boy Blue from a snitching coward into something that resembles a man. Of sorts.' George grasped the end of the whip and bent it so that it bowed in the middle, mirroring the shape of his ugly frown.

Tom made to move away.

'Surely you've heard what's been going on here in your absence?' George said. 'That brother of yours sniffing around the help.'

Tom stopped. His brow creased. *Don't*, Lou thought. *Don't let him see you react.* Too late.

George grinned. 'I suppose it was only a matter of time before a Mandeville sank back to the level from where you came. But taking up with a servant.' He tutted exaggeratedly. 'Even I didn't think one of you would stoop quite *that* low. Oh sorry, we mustn't call them servants here, must we? *Staff*, isn't that what we say?'

Tom's fists tightened. Lou knew it was taking all his willpower to hold back. But his lack of response gave George the chance to press his advantage.

'Good old Edward, finally dipping his wick,' he laughed. 'Mind, it doesn't say much for his prowess that the little floozy came to her senses and went screaming off into the sunset. And who is that woman you have staying here? I've never heard of her people. What is she? Some waif you've dragged in to keep your own wick wet?'

Like a clockwork toy wound one too many times, Tom snapped. He grabbed George by his collar. 'If I were less of a gentleman I would whip you,' he seethed.

George allowed himself to be manhandled. But it was more than that, Lou thought. He actually appeared to be enjoying it; to be feeding off Tom's anger.

'If you were *more* of a gentleman, you would have better control over the household that is to be yours,' George said. 'And if you think you can engineer a marriage to my sister to save your pointless family, then you can think again. I'll make it my life's work to wipe the name of Mandeville from the history of my family. Forever.'

'I'd be cold in my grave before I let that happen.'

'All in good time, Mandeville. All in good time.'

Tom pulled back his arm and raised his fist.

'Go on.' George offered up his cheek. 'Show the world that you are the powerful man in that laughable portrait. What are you waiting for? Be sure to leave a nice big bruise. You never know, you might still be in the police cells on the night of your mother's ridiculous party. Don't worry, you can thank me for that later.'

Tom's fist began to shake. Lou willed him to hit his cousin, to beat him until he couldn't stand. Instead, he pushed George away with such force that he landed on his backside on the ground.

He stayed down, looking up at Tom. 'Trust a Mandeville not to have the balls for a real man's fight. You prefer to sneak around, telling tales like a schoolgirl, don't you?'

Tom marched towards the stable yard.

George pulled himself to his feet and brushed the snow from the seat of his trousers. 'That's it!' he called after Tom, 'Run away and play with your horses, *soldier boy.*'

Before Tom had turned the corner, Lou was out of the morning room. She flew out of the front door. Without waiting to see whether George was still there, she ran around the side of the house, past the walled gardens and into the stable yard. She slipped, losing her footing, but didn't stop. Why she was racing to Tom, she had no idea. All she knew was that she had to.

SEVENTEEN

In the yard, Lou met Elliot on his way out of the stables. He raised his cap and closed the door behind her. She found Tom in Ambrose's stall. He was running his hands slowly and methodically over the horse's flank and back, whispering gently as he presumably checked for injuries. For a few moments she watched in silence, not wanting to disturb Tom's peace. But it would be worse if he looked up to find her staring at him. 'Tom,' she said quietly.

He stopped stroking Ambrose. 'Lou, please go back to the house,' he said, without turning to look at her.

'I saw you,' she said. 'With George. Outside. I saw what he did to Ambrose.'

Tom braced himself against the side of the horse. 'What did you hear?'

'Nothing.' She fibbed.

Tom's shoulders relaxed, but only slightly. 'Please go back to the house, Louisa. I'm in no mood for conversation.'

As much as his use of her full name stung, she wouldn't back down. 'I won't leave you like this.'

'What *exactly* do you want from me?'

'To see that you're all right. You're clearly upset—'

'Upset?' His arms snapped to his sides. His hands balled into fists. 'How dare Caxton stand on Mandeville land and abuse me? We're at his mercy and by God, doesn't he know it. I can do nothing to stop him. *Nothing.* I'm neutered. A bloody gelding.'

Lou chose her next words carefully. 'Why does your cousin dislike you so?'

Tom laughed harshly. Finally, he turned to face her. '*Hate,* Louisa, my cousin *hates* me. Don't mince your words.'

'All right, hates then. Why does he hate you?'

Tom seemed on the verge of saying something but stopped. 'It's not important.' He walked away, heading for the storeroom, his shoes crunching on the straw underfoot.

'George Caxton is not a nice person, is he?' Lou called after him. 'Definitely not the kind of man you would want your sister to marry?'

Tom came to an abrupt halt and spun around. 'For Christ's sake, Lou. Why do you insist on raising that subject? I'd kill before I let Caxton within an inch of my sister.'

'I'm sorry, Tom. I didn't mean . . . It's just that Charlotte is a wonderful, intelligent young woman who deserves more than a marriage to a—'

'Good God! Is marriage all that you women think about?' Tom's usual smile was replaced by an angry frown. 'You disappoint me, Lou, it seems that I misjudged you. You are just like the rest of your sex, after all.'

'*You disappoint me.*' The words rang in her ears. At the same time, her hackles rose. This was turning into an argument. Tom was backing her into a corner, her least favourite place. 'That's not all I think about. Why are you determined to misunderstand me?'

'Oh, I understand you perfectly well.' He disappeared into the storeroom and emerged carrying a sack of hay, which he took to Ambrose's stall. He began to shove fistfuls into the trough. 'I suppose I should be grateful that, for a change, it's my sister who is the subject of conjecture. If you all had your way, I'd resign my commission today. You'd have me leave the real world behind and return to this . . . this . . . well whatever this is.'

'Don't put words in my mouth,' she said. Tom seemed not to hear. That, or he chose to ignore her.

'You'd have me spend my life in the company of men like my cousin. Men who have never done an honest day's work in their lives. Who spend their time in idle pursuits at their clubs, drinking and gossiping like a bunch of Bloomsbury housewives.' He paused, a handful of hay in his fist. 'The men in my command, now they are real men. There's one lance corporal, Hughes, the son of a dead cabinetmaker. He's had nothing in the way of opportunities yet has learned to ride and carry a lance and fight as well as any man born into the saddle. No, better! That boy has more honour in his little finger than a man like Caxton will ever have.' He shoved the hay into Ambrose's trough. 'The men in my regiment don't have the luxury of believing in the conflicts they fight in, but by God, they will fight. For pride, duty, honour – yes. But for more than that. Hughes has a widowed mother and siblings to support. Other men fight for wives, children, sweethearts. They fight with passion because they have a *reason* to. I'm just biding my time, filling the hours before I am called on to fill a dead man's shoes.'

'Tom, don't.' Lou could hardly bear it. 'You're honest and dutiful—'

'Am I? *Really*? Oh, I love this place – every tree, every blade of grass, every brick – of course I do. And when the time comes, I'll return to sit on the family seat. I'll even become the MP if the locals will have me. But for what? What point is there to any of it? What is *my* reason?' He dropped the bag to the floor. His shoulders slumped. The fight had gone out of him. 'Perhaps I should accept defeat and abandon a life where I have purpose to come back here and slip into the tedium of becoming my father's estate manager. I'll hide away in that office with maps and rent ledgers and settle for a marriage to Emma Caxton. Perhaps the price I must pay for the privileges I have enjoyed is to spend the rest of my days living a half-life, but ensuring that this house is preserved for another generation.'

'You make marriage sound like death.'

'To the wrong person, it would be.' Tom's voice had lost its harsh edge. He took a step towards Lou. 'I would rather love passionately for one hour than benignly for a lifetime. What about you, Lou? What do you think?'

'About what?'

'Should I resign my commission and marry my cousin?'

He stared at her intently, waiting. She could hardly breathe. Did he really want a truthful answer? Did he want to hear her say that marriage to Emma was the only way to save his home and his family? *Tell him to marry Emma. Tell him now!* Her mouth refused to form the words.

Tom continued to look at her. His expression didn't alter as he waited for a reply. Finally, giving up on her, he shook his head, turned and left Ambrose's stall. He grabbed a saddle from a bench and Lou followed him into the very last stall. He placed the saddle on Samson's back and tightened the straps around the horse's belly. Lou looked from his leather brogues to his suit. 'Are you sure it's safe to ride in the snow?'

Tom placed the bit between Samson's teeth. 'I ride for a living. It's the single thing I know I am good at.' He pulled gently on the reins and led Samson out into the yard, the horse's hooves clomping on the freshly cleared cobbles. After checking the straps again, Tom placed his foot in the stirrup and threw his leg over Samson's back. From his lofty position in the saddle, he looked down at Lou. 'I have things to think through and I think more clearly when I ride.'

Taking up the slack in the reins, he squeezed Samson with his heels. They crossed the yard at a walking pace but as soon as they were free of the gates and on to the soft snow, Tom stood in the saddle and shouted a command. Samson responded instantly and sped to a gallop, kicking up the snow.

EIGHTEEN

With her arms wrapped around her body, Lou made her way to the front of the house and back inside. She stopped before the fireplace in the hall to warm her hands. Why hadn't she been able to tell Tom to marry Emma? She kicked the hearth. What did any of this matter when this house, these people, that Christmas tree, even this sensation of being chilled to the bone, were nothing but fantasies? She wandered through to the morning room.

Bertie looked up from the dolls' house.

'Oh,' Lou said. 'I wasn't expecting to find anybody in here.'

'My granny's helping with some cooking,' Bertie said. 'I'm very lucky that Lady Mandeville has let me play and I must stay right here, be quiet as a mouse and definitely not be a bother to anybody.'

Hearing Sally's voice in her son's words, Lou smiled. 'May I join you?'

Bertie nodded and returned to rearranging the miniature furniture inside the house. He took a small Christmas tree from his cigar box and placed it at the bottom of the staircase. The dining room was crammed with dolls, and he laid some tiny silver plates on the table.

Lou knelt on the rug. 'Are they having their Christmas Ball?'

Bertie nodded.

'Oh dear, you seem to have forgotten someone.' Lou took the only figure remaining in the box – the figure of the maid with red hair – and placed her in the kitchen. Immediately, Bertie reached inside, removed the doll and placed her back in the box.

'Won't she be lonely with everybody else at the party?' Lou asked.

Bertie closed the lid and moved the box out of her reach. 'Hill House decides who will come to stay. Not us. One in, one out.' His sweet little face was so stern that Lou had to stifle a laugh

'I see,' she said. 'And who exactly told you about this one in, one out rule?'

Bertie screwed up his nose. 'I don't remember. But I knew that you were coming, and I knew that she was leaving.' He opened the box and removed the maid. Holding her, he ran his little thumb over her red hair. 'She was nice. I liked it when she used to stick her tongue out at me when nobody was looking. I was sad when she went but I was glad that you came.' He took an elegantly dressed doll from the ballroom. Lou gasped as she recognised it as herself in miniature. Holding a doll in each hand, Bertie closed his eyes and moved his hands up and down as though weighing them. 'Who will stay?' he whispered.

As he spoke, his cheeks grew pinker, and his eyelashes began to flutter as though in the midst of a dream.

'Bertie?' Lou said.

He didn't respond.

'Bertie?' she tried again. Worried that he was sitting too

close to the fire and overheating, she tried to move him. He resisted; his small body becoming a deadweight.

'The house wants to help,' he said quietly. He was speaking in his own voice although it sounded different. Somehow older. 'It saw your pain and wished for you to come. You were so sad. So very sad. Your mama, she left you. Oh, my poor darling. My poor, poor, darling.'

Bertie opened his eyes. The look in them was distant, as though Bertie was no longer there. He put the dolls aside, got to his feet and cupped Lou's face in his warm chubby palms. He looked directly into her eyes and without blinking, said, 'You need to be loved.' He slipped his arms around her neck, rested his head on her shoulder and patted her gently, his hair soft against her cheek.

This little boy, using vocabulary well beyond his years, could have no idea that he was reaching inside Lou, plucking the strings of her pain. 'It's all a dream,' she said. 'I'm ill, I'm hallucinating.'

'No, my darling,' Bertie said, 'you are very well. And you are as real as I am.' He took her hand and placed it over his chest. She could feel his little heart beating rapidly beneath his woollen sweater.

'You're making this up aren't you, Bertie? It's not real. It's all part of a game.'

'The truth can be frightening, the house knows that. But you must believe me if you are to accept what is happening. Hill House brought you here. It needs you.' He kissed her softly on the cheek. 'So now you know.'

He shook his head, blinked and then once again knelt on the rug. He began to rearrange the furniture in the dolls' house, as Lou watched him, bewildered. He seemed oblivious to what had just passed. Taking up the doll of the finely dressed lady, he placed her in the ballroom and positioned the hands of a man around her in a stiff sort of dance. He returned the maid to the box but this time he didn't close the lid.

'Aren't you going to play?' he asked, looking up at Lou.

'No . . . I . . . you carry on without me. I need some air.'

NINETEEN

Out in the hall, Lou rubbed her hand across her forehead. It was clammy. She touched her face; warm. Ran her fingers through her hair; soft. She breathed in deeply, filling her lungs with air and her nostrils with the scent of pine, oily floor polish, and beeswax. She stared at one of the tiny candles in the branches of the Christmas tree until the flame flashed before her eyes each time she blinked. Hitching up her skirt, she felt the breeze sneaking beneath the front door whistle around her ankles. How could this be? How could any of this *be*? She spun around beneath the glass dome high up in the ceiling. In the pale winter sunlight, she gave in to the overwhelming urge to laugh.

A maid appeared from the dining room, dustpan and brush in hand. When she saw Lou, she took a step back.

'It's all right,' Lou laughed. 'I'm not mad. At least I don't think I am. You can see me, can't you? So, I must be real!'

The maid curtseyed. 'Yes, Miss. Very good, Miss.' She hurried to the basement door, rushing to get away. But Lou didn't care. She circled the hall, running her fingers along the walls, moving from statue to vase, pillar to sculpture; wanting to feel everything. Lou Arnold – Time Traveller – at the behest of a building, for God's sake! Hill House had brought her here. Hill House had a spirit, an unknowable force all of its own – it was mad, crazy, unbelievable, and yet this most ridiculous, farfetched, impossible explanation for her presence here was the only one that made any sense. Giddy and dizzy from circling the hall, she came to a sudden halt. But as she stopped, she caught sight of a pair of eyes watching her every move. Eyes that looked inside her and rummaged around in her thoughts.

If her time here was real then that man in the portrait was no longer a shadow, a ghost summoned up from the crumbs of knowledge she had collected at school. He was a living, breathing man. Flesh and blood. But not for much longer. In less than eight months . . . ashes to ashes, dust-to-dust . . .

Tom's death and her mum's death tangled into a single knot of grief in Lou's stomach. She remembered the police cordon, the officers who had seemed so big and out of place in their living room as the memory of them seemed now in this fine hallway. But scouring the corners of her brain, she could find no image to align to Tom's death. With no specific knowledge of the circumstances, her brain summoned up the most horrific images of war it could find – carnage, shrill whistles, screeching, red-hot lead, mud, explosions – until she could no longer bear it.

If Tom resigned his commission, he wouldn't go to France. If he didn't go to France, he wouldn't die. But hadn't he made it plain that he would never resign from the life he loved without good reason? What better reason could there be than marriage? Lou had to take every opportunity to drip honey into his ear; to plead Emma's case. Emma would make any man a good wife. Tom would learn to love her. How could he not? But what about George Caxton? Would George let his sister marry a man he hated? If there were any truth in the rumour of Edward's relationship with the missing maid, George would be sure to find it out. And if George got his hands on any evidence, he would waste no time in sharing it and unleashing such a scandal that the reputation of the Mandeville's would be ruined. No decent parent would allow their daughter to marry into such a family, even if they were related. The rumour had to be quashed. And there was only one way to get the upper hand over a man like Caxton. Lou had to play him at his own game, to find the truth before he could.

There wasn't a second to lose – since she had no idea how she had come to be here, she had no idea when or how she would leave. At any moment, she could turn a corner and find herself plunged back into the darkness of the derelict Hill House.

She ran up the stairs, rushing from room to room until she found Sally in a bedroom along the corridor from her own.

'The maid who left after I arrived,' she said, hardly able to catch her breath. 'Where did she go?'

Sally's feather duster hovered over a silver trophy shaped like a dog on the mantelshelf. 'I'm sure I don't know.' Her eyelid twitched. She was a terrible liar.

'Please Sally,' Lou said, 'it's important that you tell me everything you know about Alice.'

'There's nothing to tell. She was here a month, hardly enough time to get to know anybody when you're as busy as we are.'

'But she had access to the family?'

'To clean their rooms and serve tea.'

'Why did she leave?'

Sally returned to her work, vigorously dusting the silver dog. 'Mrs Moriarty is hardly likely to share the contents of a resignation letter with me now, is she?'

'Was there any suggestion of a . . . well, of a man?' Lou pressed.

The feather duster stopped again. This time Sally didn't look up, focusing instead on the chimneybreast. 'If I knew anything about why Alice left – which I'm not saying I do – then it's only the tittle-tattle of the other staff.'

This was impossible. There was no time to pull punches, not even with Sally. 'Aren't you supposed to do what I say?' Lou asked. 'Tell me everything you know about Alice, this instant.' She shocked herself with how harsh her words sounded. She was about to apologise but she hadn't counted on Sally's ability to stand up for herself.

Sally spun around. 'Like I said. I *know* nothing.' There was a challenge in her eyes that Lou had not seen before.

'If I said somebody's life depended on you telling me, would you?'

'If I said that my livelihood and my family's home depended on me *not* telling you, would you leave me be?'

An awkward silence descended, filled only by the rustle of Sally's apron as she picked up a paperweight from the desk, dusted it and slammed it back down. Lou took in other details of the room – the handwritten papers scattered across the desk; the bookcase packed with sport and military history titles; a pair of hairbrushes and a porcelain bowl on the washstand; an armchair beside the fire with an ashtray on the arm; a pair of riding boots beside the door; a small, battered leather case lying on the bed bearing the monogram *TM*. 'Whose room is this?' Lou asked, as though any confirmation were needed.

'Captain Mandeville's. What of it?' Sally snapped.

'Nothing . . . nothing at all.'

The hall downstairs was empty. Lou held her hands out to the flames in the hearth and moved in closer, closer still, until the heat forced her to recoil. What had just happened? Any normal person on finding out that this experience was real – real! – would have gone off to explore and marvel at the house, the furniture, the people. But not her. Oh no, she had to roll up her sleeves and interfere in a situation that was none of her business. When would she ever learn to keep her nose out of what didn't concern her? She should go upstairs to apologise and reassure Sally that she had no intention of shattering the peace of her life. And she would have, if only the very thought hadn't made her guts churn. Because in imagining Sally, she placed her in the room with the shelves of books, riding boots and battered suitcase.

As though reeled in by an invisible thread, Lou was drawn away from the fire, towards the portrait below the stairs. Not twenty minutes since, she had seen those blue eyes cloud over. George's treatment of Ambrose may have started the process, but it was her uninvited presence and unwanted questioning of Tom's feelings that had seen him run from the stables just to escape her.

She wrapped her arms around her waist and held herself.

She should leave this place. She should return to her own life before she did or said something to put an obstacle in the way of Tom's marriage. With any luck, their conversation had been enough to convince him to rethink his plans. Why wouldn't he come to his senses and marry the beautiful, witty, wealthy Emma Caxton?

Hurrying down the hall, she made a beeline for the front door. As she passed the morning room Bertie looked up. She stopped and blew him a kiss. 'Goodbye, Bertie,' she said. 'I'll miss you.'

He smiled and humming a tune, opened the door of the miniature ballroom. Lou slipped away, made her way through the vestibule and let herself out of Hill House.

Trying to ignore the cold leeching through her thin blouse, Lou froze all thoughts from her mind and walked as fast as she could through the deep snow, keeping her eyes on the ground.

Reaching the end of the drive, she paused to look up at the golden lions atop the gates. She closed her eyes, took a deep breath, and stepped through.

The moment she began to cross the boundary, she stopped dead, staring in utter disbelief at her feet. Of all the bizarre events of the last few days, this was the most surreal of all. Her foot out on the pavement wore a battered shoe while her foot still on Hill House land wore a pristine brown leather boot. She hesitated. It would be just as easy to take a step back as to go forward. No! She didn't belong in that world of fancy boots. She belonged in the world of battered old shoes where her brothers must be going out of their minds with worry that she had vanished for – how many days had it been . . .? Four days. *Go now. Go now and don't look back.*

Lou's back leg felt leaden as she forced it to join her other leg out on the pavement. Gone were the fine boots, the serge skirt and blue blouse, replaced by battered shoes, jeans and a parka. The natural order of things had been restored. And it was a natural order that made her want to turn and run. To escape to another place. And another time. She stamped on an empty beer can and kicked it towards the abandoned mattress and bags of rubbish.

TWENTY

22ND DECEMBER 2013

A mass of cars and vans flashed along the motorway, choking the air with exhaust fumes. The roar, once the soundtrack to Lou's life, was so at odds with the peace of the world she had left behind. Although it hadn't all been peace and gentility: scratch the surface of the early twentieth century and it was as riven with emotional turmoil as the century that followed it. In her mind she saw a pair of blue eyes. *Stop it, Lou. For God's sake stop it!* Without looking back, she crossed the footbridge, freezing drizzle soaking her hair.

At the end of the alley, she turned left and passed the snowman on the green that had melted to a compacted nub of ice. She arrived at the only house still not decorated for Christmas, found her keys in her pocket and let herself in.

The sight that greeted her made her shoulders slump. She hadn't been expecting Stephen and Dean to welcome her home with banners and bunting but neither had she been expecting to find dirty, limp items of clothing lying on the floor, and shoes and boots discarded at the bottom of the stairs. 'Hello?' she called. No response. Through the open kitchen door, she could see the sink piled high with dirty crockery and the table strewn with wrappers and cartons – the remains of four days' worth of kebabs and pizzas. Had her brothers been waiting for her to come back to clean up their mess? Had they even noticed she had gone?

Fighting the instinct to leave everything as it was and let them fester in their own filth, Lou scooped up the bills and takeaway flyers piled up around the doormat. Amongst the brown envelopes and junk mail was a white envelope addressed to 'The Arnolds'. She dumped the rest of the post on the hallstand, slid her finger under the flap, and pulled out a card decorated with a plump glittery robin.

> To Maureen, Stephen, Lou & Dean,
> Hope this little chap finds you all well.
> Sorry not to have been in touch. Must catch up in the New Year.
> Have a Happy Crimbo!
> Lots of love, John, Laura, Finley & Liam xx

In the chaos surrounding Mum's funeral, they had been unable to find the new address for their old neighbours, the Barkers, who had moved up to Durham earlier in the year. As far as John and Laura were concerned, good old Maureen from next door, who had always been on hand for a spot of babysitting, was alive and well. In their world, there had been no trip to the takeaway, no police family liaison officer, no reporters, no undertakers.

Lou dropped the card on the hallstand, turned her back on the mess, and left the house, slamming the front door behind her. She hurried down the path and up the road, replaying in her mind the scene from Stephen's favourite childhood film where Superman, driven by grief, reversed the world on its axis to alter history and bring Lois Lane back to life. Lou had no powers – super or otherwise – to travel back just a few weeks in her own world to perform that same miracle. How then had she travelled back one hundred years? She shook the thoughts from her head and pulled up her hood, shoving her hands deep into her pockets and walking quickly away from the estate, towards the familiarity of town.

Halfway up the High Street, the rain began to come down harder. Lou dipped into The Arc to take shelter. Posters plastered to the shutters of closed shops whipped back and forth in the wind, as though yanked by unseen hands. Out in the open air of the central plaza, she cowered beneath the overhanging canopy, the drizzle dripping into her eyes. At least the management had made the effort to drag out their perennial decorations – a handful of plastic snowmen tied to the lampposts, their once white bellies long-since stained to a nicotine-yellow – and the remaining shopkeepers had decorated their windows with tinsel. The whole scene was reflected in the deep puddles around the courtyard, a shimmering, waving version of the world in reverse. Lou stamped in a puddle. One version of that world was one too many.

The doors of Freezerfayre opened and a woman came out, pursued by the synthesised saxophone of Christmas muzak. She was laden with carrier bags and struggled to open an umbrella. Through the window, Lou saw that the aisles were busy with seasonal shoppers pushing full trolleys. Mel was behind her till, chatting to a couple as she manhandled their bulbous frozen butterball turkey over the scanner. She laughed at something the customers said and the little Christmas puddings attached to her hair band jiggled. The supervisor joined her. Lou shrunk further beneath the canopy. What would she say if Mel or the supervisor saw her and demanded to know where the hell she had been for the last few days? If she told the truth, they would have her carted off in a straitjacket.

Keeping to the shadows of the deserted boulevards, Lou left The Arc and headed along the High Street. When she came to a familiar landmark, she checked that her purse was in her pocket before entering.

The sudden hot mass of people, the noise and the light inside The Hill House Arms, made her stop. She only managed one more step inside when she stopped again. A group of men dressed in green polo shirts, black cargo trousers and steel toe-capped boots stood at the bar. They picked up their drinks and downed at least half a pint in their first gulp. She spotted Stephen among them; he wiped his mouth on the back of his hand and smiled. In the midst of his workmates, and for the first time in weeks, he looked . . . happy, not at all like a man driven to distraction by the disappearance of his sister. One of his mates patted him on the shoulder and Lou backed away, timing her exit with a lone smoker huddled in the doorway, blowing out a stream of smoke. He apologised and tried to waft it away. But Lou was too distracted to respond. She was no longer in the pub car park. She was sitting beside an open fire. The man beside her tapped his cigarette on a silver case. He struck a match, lit his cigarette and gently laughed, exhaling a cloud of smoke as he made a quip about Shakespeare at her expense.

A thread inside Lou gave a hard yank. She imagined the blue eyes and it yanked again. Was this a dream? Or was she actually going mad? With every ounce of determination, she forced herself to focus on the twenty-first century. She took her phone from her pocket and scrolled through the call list. No missed calls. No messages, not even from work. No credit to make a call. She resorted to a text.

Haven't seen you for a few days. You ok? xx

She waited for a few moments. A reply flashed up.

> At a mates. Stayin here tonite. Why?

That was it. No '*Where have you been? I've been worried sick*'. No kisses.

> No reason. C U Soon xx

Even Dean had found his comfort elsewhere.

Lou had been gone for days and neither of her brothers had missed her. Katie and her workmates had been too busy living their own lives to notice that she had disappeared from hers. Standing in the rain on the High Street, the very thought that she had spent the last few days in Hill House was incongruous.

She had to find out if she had helped Tom and the rest of the Mandevilles. And there was only one way she could think of to do that.

Ignoring the freezing rain, Lou retraced her steps, heading away from town. At the parade of shops on the estate and just past a sign advertising the lead story in the local newspaper – *Police hunt for metal thieves continues* – she ducked into an alleyway, dodging rubbish bins, and came to the exit giving out on to the pavement. Instead of turning on to her street, she crossed the road, rejoining the alley until it came to an end on the road behind her house.

It was growing darker, but a security lamp bolted to the ancient brickwork guided her past the porch of St Mary's. She crossed the churchyard and made her way through the crooked, moss-covered gravestones to the statue of a soldier. His head was bent, his hands rested on the butt of a rifle, a century of filth and pollution had collected in the folds of his stone uniform. Lou wiped away the beads of rain from the brass plaques mounted on each side of the plinth on which the soldier stood.

With the light from her phone, she illuminated the regimented list of engraved names. Coming to the end of the L's, she paused, bargaining with every power and every god she had ever heard of. *Let him have lived. Please, let him have lived.* Just two names into the M's, the beam of light began to shake.

She steadied herself against the memorial. She'd left Tom and the Mandevilles behind and for what? To spend an afternoon in a world where she was not missed and not wanted. Her departure hadn't saved him. The evidence was there before her eyes: the name Thomas Mandeville, engraved in perpetuity, along with the other names of 'Our Glorious Dead of the Great War 1914-1918'.

Twenty-five years after Tom's death, Edward had abandoned Hill House forever. What horrors had befallen the Mandevilles in those years between the First and Second World Wars? Had Charlotte married Caxton? Had he destroyed the Mandevilles as he had promised Tom he would?

What had been the point of her visit? Something shifted inside Lou. She was behaving as though she had just returned from a rainy weekend in Scarborough when she had actually travelled to the past and back again. Travelled to the past and back! How had that even happened? People don't defy the laws of physics for no reason. They can't go into a travel agent and book a ticket to go bouncing around through time because they need a holiday from their mundane or awful life.

If time travel was beyond the understanding of scientists, there was little point in Lou with a GCSE in physics trying to work out how it was possible. The only question she could hope to answer was *why*. Why had she, of all people, been allowed to travel back in time? Whatever force had taken her back must have had a purpose for her. She couldn't repay that force by sloping home to clear away a week's worth of takeaway cartons and junk mail.

Lou snapped off the light on her phone. She left the churchyard and headed quickly back to town, navigating the afternoon rush hour traffic. After calling into a newsagent to buy a notebook and pencil, she stopped at another relic from the nineteen-sixties town-planning boom.

The closest she had been to this building since leaving for Sheffield was walking along the opposite side of the road on her way to work. A few months back she'd toyed with joining the book group that met here, but in the end, she hadn't bothered. Not because she thought herself above spending every other Tuesday evening in the company of a group of locals, dissecting the latest Zadie Smith or Kate Atkinson, over a cup of weak tea and a chocolate digestive. If only the decision had been that considered. It hadn't really been a decision at all. It was simply that it had been easier to spend evenings in the pub or slumped in front of the telly rather than doing something that required effort.

Lou's ghostly reflection stared back from the library window. Growing up, she had spent entire days here, her nose stuck in a book, studying, keeping clear of her noisy brothers.

Christ, she was beginning to sound like a stuck record. She had always criticised anybody who moaned about their lives and did nothing about it. And here she was; one of those people. Well, no more. For the first time in years, she would *do* something.

The vent above the door blew warm air on to Lou's hair and the musk of paper wrapped around her like an old comfort blanket. The librarian stopped arranging books on a trolley and looked up. Lou prepared herself for a sharp look, or a warning against any transgression of the strict policy of silence. When Mrs Rogers simply peered over the rim of her glasses, an inkling of recognition resulting in the briefest of smiles, Lou's muscles softened like dough in the hands of an experienced pastry cook. The years fell away. She was back, in a world where a library card was the passport to realms beyond her grey hometown.

Lou strode to the bank of computers and took a seat. A man and two old ladies already seated there took no notice when she shrugged off her parka and draped it over the back of the chair. Flipping open the notepad, she placed it on the desk, its perfect blankness like a field of virgin snow. She placed her fingers on the keyboard and began to type, calling up the archive of the old local newspaper, *The Courier*. On the search page, she punched in a date range between 1915 and 1930 and entered 'Caxton' as a key word.

A wave of nausea rose from her gut. *An historian needs dispassion, remember? Remember, facts are facts.*

She took a deep breath. Okay, so if old Bertie's memory of events was to be trusted then Charlotte had committed suicide while pregnant with George's child. Knowing Charlotte as Lou now did, it was impossible to imagine that she was capable of taking her own life. She needed to find out how that had happened, starting with what hold George had had over the Mandevilles that allowed such a marriage to take place.

Lou scrolled through a list of articles about business deals, munitions factories and social calendars, until she saw the words *Coroner's Inquest into the Tragic Death of a Lady*. It was an article dated April 24 1920 and there was a name beside it. Lady Charlotte Caxton.

Lou picked up her pencil, aware of her hand shaking. Just last night she had helped the young girl thread ribbons around the branches of a Christmas tree and now here she was, about to read a report into her death.

Dispassion, Lou. You're an historian. Imagine you're researching a stranger.

She took a steadying breath and clicked on the link. A scanned article appeared, the headline blazing across the screen in an antiquated typeface. Lou began to read the report of an inquest held in Northampton, making notes as she went.

The reporter recalled the scene in the coroner's court. The

public gallery had been filled to capacity, with standing room only, to hear the facts and evidence surrounding a death that had shocked the community. In the sixth month of her pregnancy, Lady Charlotte Caxton had been discovered at the bottom of a little-used staircase at her husband's ancestral home, Caxton Hall. Her husband, Lord Caxton, had been at home at the time of the unfortunate event but, having spent the best part of the morning in his orangery before leaving to pay a visit to his mother, the Dowager Vicountess Caxton, he had been unaware of anything untoward. He was alerted to his wife's accident by a messenger dispatched to the dower house, at which point Lord Caxton returned to Caxton Hall. Various servants had been called to give evidence to the coroner and the jury. A picture was painted of the shock they all experienced on discovering Lady Caxton, who was presumed to have lain where she had fallen for up to an hour, on account of her maid having last seen her on taking up her breakfast. The doctor and police who had attended all confirmed that there was nothing to be done for the poor young woman. Lady Caxton had been removed to her bedroom where she miscarried her baby and herself passed away within the hour. The butler gave evidence, as did the two footmen who carried Lady Caxton to her room. Her lady's maid had to be excused from the witness stand three times before she was able to finish giving her testimony. The final witness to be called was Lord George Caxton. He confirmed the details that had been given as to the events surrounding his wife's death. A hush had fallen over the court when he further stated that he was sorry to report that his wife had been of troubled mind for some time, suggesting that it was due to an infirmity that ran in her family. He had hoped that marriage would quiet her mind but had privately been concerned about what this inherited infirmity might make his wife capable of, especially in light of the events surrounding her father's death the previous year.

Lou stopped reading. Sir Charles had died too. She fought

the instinct to search *The Courier* for an obituary. She mustn't get side-tracked. Only once she had finished researching Charlotte should she move on to Sir Charles. With a heavy heart, she made a note that he must have died in 1919. She read the report again, focusing on George's assertion that there had been some sort of inherited mental illness in the Mandeville family. What evil game was he playing? It was a lie. Even so, she dutifully made a note in her pad before scrolling through the articles and locating a report in the following week's edition of *The Courier*. It recorded the verdict. Accidental death. The coroner and jury had come to the conclusion that the most likely explanation for Lady Caxton's death was a fainting episode brought about by her advanced state of pregnancy, as a result of which she had tripped and fallen down the stairs.

Lou sat back. Poor Charlotte. Poor, lovely Charlotte. All that life and promise snuffed out. And nowhere, in any of the reporting, was there the remotest suggestion that George's treatment of her had any bearing on her death. George would have been too clever – no, too devious – to get caught. But what had gone on behind closed doors at Caxton Hall? If the staff had seen or heard anything, they would have been too afraid to implicate their powerful employer. Had George snuck up behind Charlotte and shoved her down the rarely used stairs, knowing she wouldn't be found? Or, as Bertie had suggested, had Charlotte thrown herself down the stairs, committing suicide to spare her unborn child the horror of having George Caxton for a father?

A grainy black and white photograph accompanied the article. George Caxton held a handkerchief to his face, mopping up crocodile tears. Lou had to fight the urge to punch the screen. She was sure of one thing. Directly or indirectly, George Caxton had Charlotte Mandeville's blood on his hands. He may have failed to convince the coroner that Charlotte had taken her own life, but his suggestion that she had been mentally impaired would have planted a seed of doubt in the mind of every person in that packed courtroom and every reader of *The Courier*. Even in death he had been determined to besmirch Charlotte. Were there no depths to which George Caxton would not plunge to destroy the Mandevilles?

Lou forced herself to read on, but just a paragraph in, had to stop. Her anger turned to gut-wrenching sadness. The reporter described the 'deceased's family listening in silence and with immense dignity to the coroner's verdict'. He described Lady Caxton's brother, Sir Edward Mandeville; his recently widowed mother, Lady Mandeville; and the deceased's aunt, Mrs Hart, all of whom had attended every day of the inquest and had sat through every awful detail. Lou pictured them as vividly as if she were sitting on the bench beside them. Edward pale, cheeks gaunt. Lady Mandeville and Mrs Hart, their faces obscured by veils to hide the ocean of tears they would have shed for their darling girl.

Lou's thoughts shifted away from the Mandevilles and to another day in a different coroner's court. There had been no veils, no packed galleries and no jury when Lou and her brothers sat before the coroner. They didn't have to attend. The family liaison officer explained the purpose of the inquest was to establish the facts of an unexplained death, not guilt. There would be witnesses but it was not a trial. They may prefer not to hear the specific details. Only a few bored-looking officials had been present to bear witness to the coroner opening and then adjourning the inquest until the New Year, pending further evidence- gathering.

Lou gripped her pencil. What more evidence did the coroner need? Someone had stolen a car and driven it into her mum, causing catastrophic internal injuries. They had driven off and left her for dead. Had a similar anger to that which now blazed in her heart filled the hearts of the Mandevilles? Had Edward, Lady Mandeville and Mrs Hart contained their rage as they listened to the details of Charlotte's death? If Bertie, a boy of only ten years of age at the time, had known that George's brutality had driven Charlotte to her death, then surely the adults must have done. George had been free to marry and terrorise Charlotte. There had been nobody to stop him. There had been no Tom.

'Old newspapers. That looks interesting,' a voice came from behind her.

Lou spun around. A young man was looking over her shoulder at the screen.

'What is it?' he asked 'A report into an inquest? Makes a change from *The Daily Mail* and online sudoku.' He glanced at the old man and two old ladies as he struggled to tuck a file beneath his arm, freeing a hand to shake Lou's. 'Will,' he said. 'Trainee archivist and full-time nosey parker.'

'Lou Arnold,' Lou said quietly, conscious they had come under the beady eye of Mrs Rogers.

'Family research?' Will asked.

'Not quite. I live over by Hill House. I was just . . . I was just interested in the history of the family that used to live there.'

'Ah, a budding local historian. Do you need any help?' His response was a little too animated and drew a frown from Mrs Rogers. He nodded towards a door at the back of the library and mouthed to her to follow him. Lou collected her notepad and pencil. If this Will person knew the records, he might be able to fast track her research.

Will unlocked the door and they entered a cramped room with just enough space for a desk and a row of shelves packed with ledgers and archive boxes. Closing the door behind them, he dumped his file on a desk crowded with boxes of index cards and a laptop. Lou took in his faded jeans and oversized knitted sweater. With a pang of nostalgia, she remembered her fellow history students from Sheffield who she hadn't seen or contacted in years.

Will pulled out one of the two chairs and Lou took a seat.

'It's a bit pokey, I'm afraid,' Will said. He puffed out a breath of air, disturbing his long fringe. 'But at least we're free to talk in here.' He took a seat at the desk opposite Lou. 'I'm cataloguing the records of an old shoe factory out by the industrial estate as part of my training. Do you know it?'

Lou nodded. Everybody knew the shoe factory. Along with the sorting office, it had been the main source of employment for the town until it closed down.

'It's due to be demolished in the New Year,' Will continued, 'so the library took on the records to catalogue them before they're transferred to the archives in Northampton. Industrial heritage and all that. Sorry, is this boring?' he asked, wrinkling his nose.

'Not at all,' Lou said.

Will smiled. 'That's where I work, the archives in Northampton. Well, sort of work. I'm doing a placement for my Masters. Sorry, I'm talking too much. I do that rather a lot after spending the day on my own in here. Occupational hazard. So, what's this research you're undertaking?'

Lou smiled back. 'It's okay, But I don't want to keep you from your work.'

'Oh, don't worry about that. There are only so many shoe patterns a man can catalogue in a day. So, why are you digging around in the history of an old family? Is it some kind of project?'

'It's just an interest. I've lived behind Hill House all my life and I'm curious to find out a bit about the family that lived there. The Mandevilles. They were there for generations before they left and the house fell into disrepair. At least that's what I remember from a school project I did years ago,' she was quick to add.

'I see.' Will tapped his teeth with a pencil. 'I'm not a local so don't know much myself, but I do have a colleague, Jem, who's been researching the old families of the area for a project she's working on for the First World War Centenary. You know, the lost generation of sons sort of thing.'

Lou closed her eyes and saw Tom's name etched into the brass of the war memorial. She swallowed hard. 'I was reading about the inquest into the death of the daughter of the family. Her name was . . .' Lou stumbled. 'Her name was Charlotte and around 1920 she married George Caxton – Lord Caxton.'

'A Caxton? You won't have any trouble finding information about them. They've got records coming out of their ears over at Caxton Hall. They practically kept the War Office in shells and munitions. Made a fortune. I'm pretty sure most of their archives have been digitized.'

The thought of the Caxtons revelling in success while the Mandeville's fortunes plummeted, made Lou's stomach churn. But she also tuned in to Will's revelation that the Caxton records might be available online. 'Would there be anything about the death of Sir Charles Mandeville in any records?' she asked. 'He was the last baronet's father. And Charlotte's father. He died around 1919. He was mentioned in the inquest.'

'Probably. Let's see if there's anything in the press.' Will typed Sir Charles' name into his laptop. Lou let him get on with it and kept her mouth shut. If he knew that she had a degree in history, he might not be so inclined to help. And she would need his help if he could gain access to a private digitized archive.

'Bingo!' Will opened an article from *The Courier* reporting the inquest into Sir Charles Mandeville's death. 'Oh dear, it looks like he came to a bit of a sticky end.' Will scanned the article, relaying the keys points. 'Sir Charles was killed when he went out shooting alone in the woods on his land – something he had never done before. It was a freezing day. Early January.

A dense fog. Evidence that Sir Charles stumbled on a patch of ice and the gun went off as he fell. His groom heard the shot and ran into the woods where he discovered Sir Charles. He was ex-military and knew time was of the imperative, so carried Sir Charles back to the house. By the time the doctor arrived, there was nothing to be done. Sir Charles died of a gunshot wound to the head. The coroner recorded a verdict of accidental death.'

'What was the name of the groom?' Lou asked.

Will scanned the article. 'Elliot. It says here that he was Sir Charles' batman when he was in the military. The coroner commended Elliot for his efforts and warned that Sir Charles' behaviour be a salutary lesson for any man tempted to venture abroad with a loaded gun on his own. He delivered his verdict of accidental death in spite of evidence presented by a number of witnesses that Sir Charles had been in a troubled state of mind following reports of a business deal that had gone sour. The resulting scandal caused him to resign from his seat in the Commons. The coroner said he had taken this factor into account but had concluded that it had no bearing on Sir Charles' death. Looks like the Mandevilles had a lucky escape.'

Lou frowned. 'How's that lucky?'

'It's obvious, isn't it? It was a cover up. If the coroner had delivered a verdict of suicide – which this clearly was – the stigma would have crucified the Mandevilles. There's no way the coroner would have wanted to subject a titled family to that, even if this Sir Charles was a discredited MP.' Will tapped his teeth with his pencil again. 'I wonder what this dodgy business deal was that Sir Charles was involved in?'

A creeping dread spread through Lou. 'Is George Caxton mentioned as one of the witnesses?'

'No. Should he be?'

'I just wondered. He married Sir Charles' daughter later that year, so I thought . . . Actually, I don't know what I thought.' She shook her head and asked, 'Does it have any detail about the business deal that went wrong?'

Will scanned the article again. 'Nope. Your best bet is the national press. The local press were less likely to report a scandal in their backyard. A juicy story of the resignation of an MP would have shifted plenty of copies for the nationals though.'

Will navigated to the website of *The Times* but before he could go any further, there was a knock at the door. Mrs Rogers stood at the small window and tapped her watch.

'Time waits for no man,' Will said. 'Listen, I'm here again tomorrow. Come back and we'll see what else we can dig up on your Mandevilles. I might even be able to get access to the Caxton archive. I'm pretty sure Jem can help with that.'

Lou stood outside the library, looking into the dark window. It seemed impossible that she had spent the last hour researching the Mandevilles as though they were part of an assignment on a family from the dusty, distant past, when that morning she had seen them. She had eaten breakfast with them and talked to them. They were as real and as present as the drizzle now soaking her hair.

Lou focused on her reflection, now split by vertical security bars. She may be powerless to change the course of events in her own life but what if she could influence the outcome of that distant past? If events in 1913 played out unchanged, George Caxton would destroy the Mandevilles so completely that their history would be scattered in a few forgotten newspaper columns. And with no heirs to remember them, there was nobody to care.

If she had it in her power to save a man's life, and in turn, that of his family, shouldn't she at least try? Stephen and Dean wouldn't miss her if she stayed away for a few more days. The people that needed her now were a mile from here and one hundred years away.

She pulled up her hood and headed away from town. The closer she got to Hill House the more she picked up her pace. By the time she reached St Mary's, its weathervane creaking in the wind, she was running. She didn't hesitate at the broken gates but put her trust in blind faith and ran straight through.

Momentarily blinded by snow, Lou laughed. The hazy, artificial light of the town had given way to a black night sky with an ocean of sharp white stars. The only sound was the squeak of her leather boots in the thick snow as she spun around.

'I'm back!' she called into the silence. 'You let me back in!'

So what if the cold bit her cheeks and froze her hair. Let it! So what if she didn't understand how any of this was happening. She had come back, that's all that mattered, and she would help the Mandevilles. Hitching up her skirt, she sprinted across the lawn towards the beacon of Hill House and the warm glow of light radiating from every room.

TWENTY-ONE

22ND DECEMBER 1913

Despite her best efforts, by the time Lou reached the front door, the hem of her skirt was sodden. Since nobody was expecting her, she managed to slip into the entrance vestibule unnoticed. A welcoming fire blazed in the hearth in the hall. She winked at the lions on the stone chimneybreast and checked her reflection in the mirror, grinning inanely at her cheeks, flushed to a bright pink, and her wet hair only vaguely held in place by a silver clip. She would have pinched herself had she not known that it would now hurt for real! The long-cased clock chimed six. It was late to be dressing for dinner, very late. She grinned at her reflection again before taking hold of her long skirt and running up the stairs.

She found Sally waiting in her room, a towel over her arm.

'Am I glad to see you,' Lou said. 'Don't worry with a bath, there's no time.'

'Very good, Miss,' Sally said brusquely. Lou could see she was still cross about their argument, but an apology would have to wait until tomorrow. Lou's brain was too busy buzzing with next steps to be distracted by anything else. The extra time would give her the opportunity to come up with an explanation for her behaviour that didn't make her sound like a lunatic.

Wordlessly Sally peeled away the layers of wet clothes and dressed Lou for dinner. Lou sat silently at the dressing table, allowing Sally to get to grips with her dishevelled hair. When Sally pinched a damp strand, she tutted as though she were about to plait the mane of a horse that had been left out in a field. Sally didn't ask how Lou had managed to get into such a state, but Lou was sure Sally was rougher than usual – her hair brushing harsher, the twists and pinning more severe. When she pushed a black feather into Lou's hair to compliment the black lace decorating her jade green dress, it dug into Lou's scalp. But Lou didn't complain. She deserved it. Sally had a job to do, and she had left her little time to do it in. Anyway nothing, not even Sally's scowl, could dent Lou's good mood. Because tonight she was going to begin helping the Mandevilles for real.

Sally carried away a pile of wet clothes at arm's length, leaving Lou to pace up and down, ploughing her way through the field of facts she had learned. The coroner may have returned verdicts of accidental death to spare the Mandevilles the scandal of two suicides in the space of a year, but all the evidence pointed to the deaths of Sir Charles and Charlotte being anything but accidental. Surely the only reason Charlotte married the cousin she loathed was because the Caxton wealth provided a lifeline for the Mandevilles after the death of Sir Charles?

Lou stopped pacing and pressed her forehead to the cold glass of the windowpane. What disastrous business deal could possibly have made Sir Charles throw away his life? The full story behind his suicide was the missing piece of the puzzle. Not that she needed proof; her gut told her that the missing piece was the exact shape and size of George Caxton.

Sir Charles and Charlotte were the most positive members

of their family and the least likely to do anything as awful as taking their own lives. Neither of them would have considered leaving the Mandevilles at George's mercy had they not been absolutely desperate. There had to be a link between their deaths, it was just waiting somewhere in the archives for her to find. There was nothing for it; when the opportunity presented itself tomorrow, she would slip away and go back to the library to dig up a barrow load of dirt on George.

The dinner gong rang, and Lou was the first to arrive in the drawing room. She accepted a glass of sherry from William's tray as Charlotte entered the room along with Mrs Hart and Edward.

'Louisa!' Charlotte exclaimed, rushing to her. 'Where have you been? We waited for you at tea this afternoon. Nobody knew where you were, and I had begun to worry about you.'

'You mustn't mind Charlotte, Louisa,' Mrs Hart said, thanking William as she accepted a glass of sherry. She took a seat beside the fire, next to Edward. 'Charlotte, dear, there is no call for high drama. You must understand that there are times when some of us prefer to pass an afternoon in our own company without the intrusion of others.'

'But where on Earth were you?' Charlotte pressed, her aunt's words having no effect. 'I looked everywhere and asked everybody, but nobody had seen you.'

Lou tried to smile, but the muscles in her face refused to work. She wanted to grab Charlotte and warn her about George Caxton. 'I went for a long walk,' she said. 'That's all.'

'Where to? Timbuktu?'

Lou spun around with such haste that a wave of sherry spilled from her glass.

'Tom,' Charlotte said, taking her brother's hand, 'Louisa is here. I told you she would come back. She only went for a walk. So, you see, there was nothing to worry about after all.'

'Who was worried?' Tom said. He offered his handkerchief

to Lou to dry her wet hands. She accepted the cloth offered by William instead. Tom's eyes locked on hers. When William retreated and Charlotte joined her aunt on the sofa, Tom asked, 'How are you, Lou?'

It was a simple question, but she couldn't respond. In all of her grandiose plans of swooping in like a guardian angel to save the Mandevilles, she hadn't stopped to consider how she would feel when standing in the presence of people made of flesh and blood, not dreams and fantasies. People who had become a reality once again. A muscle twitched in Tom's cheek. He took a step towards Lou. Those blue eyes that had pursued her into her own time searched hers. She would have stepped away, but her feet were rooted to the spot, as though the woven branches of the rosebushes decorating the rug had reached up to take hold of her ankles.

'I had hoped to speak to you,' Tom said, a furrow in his brow, 'about our conversation earlier in the stables. I—'

He was interrupted by the arrival of Sir Charles and Lady Mandeville. After a round of 'Good evenings' and asking how each other had passed the afternoon, Sir Charles called him over to make arrangements for the next day's shoot.

'I'm sorry,' Tom said, still frowning. 'I should go and speak to my father. Perhaps we can find an opportunity to talk later.'

Lou watched him go. She watched the various groups of Mandevilles talk while they sipped their sherry. The sight of Charlotte taking her father's arm, smiling up at him, pierced Lou's heart. She could have joined them, made small talk. But what would she say if they asked about her day? She took a swig of sherry. It sloshed in her empty stomach.

Emma arrived and leant in for Tom to kiss her cheek. Her slender neck elongated gracefully, and her white-gloved hand rested on his shoulder. Lou stared at the 'v' of hair that dipped into the nape of Tom's neck, just above his collar. She took another slug of sherry. How had she ever imagined that she

could be the saviour of this man and his family? If only the
thorns from the rosebushes would dig into her flesh and pull her
down so that she might disappear.

Lady Mandeville had already begun pairing the women
with the men to escort them in to dinner when George Caxton
lumbered into the drawing room. Lou knocked back the
remainder of her sherry and placed the empty glass shakily on
William's tray. Edward offered her his arm and George grudg-
ingly held his out to Charlotte. Lou wanted to scream at him to
take his hands off her. *Calm Lou, calm.* If she began to talk
about future events, they'd have her carted away in the blink of
an eye. She had to bide her time and keep her mouth shut until
she had some real and current evidence to use against Caxton.
Slipping her arm through Edward's, she walked into dinner by
his side.

The first course of the meal came, and Lou took a few
mouthfuls without noticing what it was. She drank her wine.
When the fish course was placed before her, she recoiled. A
trout lay on a bed of wilted spinach, dead eyes fixed on her, its
silver skin pulled back to reveal tender pink flesh beneath.
Beside her, George tore into the poor fish on his plate, exposing
its tiny, fragile skeleton. Lou fingered the prongs of her fork. A
well-placed thrust into George Caxton's side now and this
could all be over. Her plate was removed to make way for the
main course. She drank more wine.

'As well as constructing his new stable block, Father has
commissioned an architect to design a conservatory to house his
pineapples,' George said, directing his words towards the head
of the table. 'It's his latest fancy, don't you know.'

Sir Charles chewed his food slowly, hooking his index finger
over his top lip. 'That sounds like a splendid idea. A man must
be allowed to indulge his passions, as far as he is able.'

'Father's never been shy of indulging his passions,' George
scoffed. 'This conservatory business is costing a king's ransom,

but it all adds to the value of the estate. It's a sound investment for the future.'

Lou fixed her gaze on the little white caps, like chefs' hats, obscuring the bones protruding from the lamb cutlets on her plate. She wanted to stick her fingers in her ears to block out George rubbing Sir Charles' nose in the Caxton wealth. All of Sir Charles' responses were suitably diplomatic, but it had to smart.

George carved a chunk of meat and shovelled it into his mouth. 'From the plans I've seen,' he said, talking as he chewed, 'I dare say it will be larger than this whole wing of Hill House.' He waved his knife in the air as though to indicate size. 'Possibly even the whole of your ground floor.'

'Oh George, you do exaggerate,' Emma interrupted, laughing. 'It's nowhere near as large. Besides, not all of us want to live in a house with so many vast rooms that one couldn't possibly ever use them all. Some of us prefer a more intimate home.'

At the far end of the table, Tom sat mutely beside his father. Why wasn't he standing up to George as he had earlier in the day with Ambrose? How could he and the rest of the Mandevilles bear to sit around their exquisitely laid table while George filled his face with their food, repaying their generosity with insults? If Lou had her way, she would have taken one of the strands of ivy decorating the tablecloth and strangled him with it. Didn't they know, couldn't they see, what he had planned for them? She slumped back in her chair. Of course, they couldn't.

'At any rate,' Lady Mandeville interjected, smiling a little too sweetly, 'Hill House will more than serve for the ball, I'm sure.'

'I daresay it will suffice,' George said.

'It must be nice for you.'

'What?' George turned to Lou, fork midway to his mouth, a note of surprise in his voice.

She could hold her tongue no longer. 'I said it must be nice for you. You know, having all that space. All those magnificent rooms in a splendid house.'

George frowned. 'What the devil are you getting at?'

'Me? Oh, nothing.' She twisted her glass this way and that, watching the candlelight refract in the precision cuts in its crystal surface. 'It's just that it must make you feel very special to live in such a house.'

'Now listen here,' George said. 'Who are you to—'

'Me? I'm nobody.' She didn't have to look at George to know that, at that moment, he resembled a snorting bull. Twenty-eight years of waging war with Stephen had taught her how to get under a person's skin. She could manipulate with the best of them. The only difference between her and George was she used words rather than fists. 'I was simply saying that it must be nice to have power and influence, that's all. You can truly say that you *lord* it over everybody. I wonder, what do you think of the current German expansionist plans? Are you concerned that they will have an effect on your estate and businesses?'

George slammed his fist down on table, rattling the cutlery around his plate. 'What are you talking about?' he grunted.

'Come come, Miss Arnold,' Sir Charles said from along the table, his tone light. 'You are toying with George. He does not concern himself with continental politics. And George, you must understand that Miss Arnold's wit comes from her penchant for the egalitarian. Isn't that correct, Miss Arnold?'

'Egalitarian?' Lou smiled at Sir Charles. 'I don't recall saying as much.'

'Perhaps,' Sir Charles said. 'But if this old nose can't sniff out a social reformer, then it's no longer of any use to me. Miss Arnold's tastes extend not just to suffrage for women but universal suffrage.'

'A suffragette in our midst,' Emma trilled. 'How thrilling. I've met Mrs Pankhurst and her daughters on a number of occasions. They are rather stern, but one has to admire their tenacity. Just think, George, if they have their way, perhaps it will be me who will inherit Caxton Hall and father's wealth and not you. Imagine!'

'Social reform. Suffragettes. Fools the lot of them.' Returning to his dinner, George forced an overly large piece of potato into his mouth.

'Emma, dear,' Sir Charles said, 'Miss Arnold is not the only suffragette in our midst. Only last night my sister and daughter made it clear that they have pinned their colours to that particular mast. I shouldn't wonder if they're not card-carrying members of the WSPU, along with Miss Arnold.'

'Aunt Leo and cousin Charlotte! Members of the Women's Social and Political Union?' Emma exclaimed. She leant forward as if seeing them in a new and exciting light. 'How absolutely *revolutionary* of you. I would never have thought it.'

Mrs Hart placed her cutlery down and wiped her lips on her napkin. 'The WSPU are not revolutionaries. They are socialists.'

'Listen to how my sister emphasises the word 'they' in favour of the word 'we',' Sir Charles said, with a laugh. 'I find that the truth is invariably to be found in what we do not say rather than what we do.'

'Once again, Charles,' Mrs Hart said, colour rising like wine stains in her cheeks, 'you make sport from misunderstanding me, imagining that you know my thoughts better than I myself know them.'

'Come, Leonora,' Sir Charles said, his tone now conciliatory. 'You know I mean no harm. You know I consider you to be the most intelligent woman of my acquaintance. If I've offended you then I am truly sorry. Bainbridge, please fill Mrs Hart's glass and we will say no more on the subject.'

Bainbridge stepped forward and Mrs Hart nodded her thanks. It seemed, for a moment at least, that the ripple, which had disturbed the millpond of the meal, was at an end.

'I wouldn't give houseroom to a single one of those blasted women,' George seethed. 'If I found one in my household, I'd knock those ideas out of her head.'

Before Lou could react, a voice that had been quiet until now spoke up. 'I admire anybody who has the courage of their convictions,' Tom said, his voice low and tight. 'I'd rather a lion that roared, than a mouse that stayed silent.'

'You would. Spineless idiot.' George spoke these venomous words so quietly that Lou was sure nobody but she had heard. Perhaps he wasn't such a fool after all.

'I do hope you manage to shoot a brace of pheasant tomorrow,' Lady Mandeville chimed. 'I've asked chef to prepare liver pâté for the ball.'

Everyone seized on the change in subject, throwing themselves into plans for the next day's shoot. Lou was too busy basking in George's fury to be irked by Lady Mandeville's insistence on once again turning conversation away from the important and expansive issue of women's politics to the narrow confines of the domestic. Beside Lou, George's rage boiled like a kettle about to explode. She had tested his temper and found that it lay only a hairsbreadth beneath the surface. Knowing an enemy's weak spot was key to knowing how to deal with them. George wanted to control every situation so he could manipulate it to satisfy his own ends. He wouldn't be happy if he knew she had heard his exchange that morning with Tom.

The glow of Lou's success came to an abrupt end when conversation turned to clothes and dancing, with the arrangements for the ball taking on the proportions of a biblical saga. *None of it matters*, Lou wanted to shout. *Your parties are all coming to an end.* But how were they to know that Kaiser Wilhelm was unwittingly in league with George Caxton and that together, they would rip the heart from this family?

Lou drained the wine from her glass, doubt of her ability to help them creeping in like a spectre at the feast. William stepped forward to refill her glass. His presence reminded her of the awkward silence in which Sally had dressed her for dinner. She'd got that wrong too, hadn't she? Crossed the unseen barrier that should have separated them. By being over-friendly, feeling that she could say what she wanted, she had placed Sally in an impossible position. She washed away the nasty taste in her mouth with another mouthful of wine. Again, her glass was refilled. Her untouched meat was taken away and a choux pastry swan appeared. She stared at it gliding serenely on a slick chocolate lake. Taking her fork, she pushed it across the plate towards the gilded edge, wondering whether beneath the surface, it was paddling desperately to stay afloat.

When the meal came to an end, Sir Charles got to his feet. 'Come along, my dear,' he said to Lady Mandeville. 'And you too, sister.'

Lou was about to rise from her chair but, seeing that neither Charlotte nor Emma had moved, she hesitated.

'Mother and Father and Aunt Lenora always leave us to our own amusement on the evening before the shoot,' Charlotte explained.

'There's nothing like old bores to pour cold water on the fun of a party,' Sir Charles said, offering his arm to his wife.

'Speak for yourself,' Mrs Hart laughed, her earlier frustration at her brother forgotten. Unlike Lou, Mrs Hart knew how to behave in this world.

Following the others into the billiard room, Lou slumped into a seat by the window and away from the heat of the fire. The room was dimly lit by candles in sconces lining the walls. The only electric light came from a large lamp over the billiard table. She didn't care that it was dark. Sitting in the shadows suited her. Her face burned. Her vision swam. She accepted a brandy

Edward offered. After handing the glass to her, he took a seat closer to the fire, beside Tom.

Lou nursed her drink and watched Charlotte and Emma take up cues.

'Join us, Louisa,' Charlotte called.

Lou held up her glass, indicating that she was busy with her drink.

George joined his cousin and sister, a fat cigar clenched between his teeth. He balanced an ashtray on the edge of the billiard table and took aim through a fug of smoke. The sound of balls cracking smashed inside Lou's head. The game was loud and animated, Charlotte squealing and clapping, Emma laughing, and George telling them off for putting him off his shot. Lou watched as, in every break in play, he replenished his glass from a decanter of whisky. *Bastard.*

Tom and Edward sat silently drinking. Every so often Tom glanced at his brother. Was he wondering how Edward could have been so stupid as to get involved with a maid? Or rather, that he had been careless enough to get caught. Eventually Edward got up and sat at the piano in the corner of the room. Lifting the lid, he began to play a melancholy sort of tune. His departure gave Emma the opportunity to make her move. Balancing her cue against the wall, she sat on the arm of Tom's chair, the blue silk of her dress rippling down her curves. Hidden as Lou was in the shadows, Emma didn't appear to notice her presence nearby.

'Oh dear,' Emma said, her lips close to Tom's ear. 'Somebody doesn't look very happy tonight. Won't you come and play?'

'Thank you, no.' Tom said.

'Is there nothing I can do to improve your temper?' Emma placed her bare arm around his shoulders. 'You haven't told me how beautiful I look this evening. Before you say anything, I know how terribly shallow that is, but nevertheless, I shall get a complex if I don't hear somebody say it at least once tonight.'

'Surely my mother has told you.'

'You absolute tease!' She tapped him on the arm. 'Your mother would proclaim me beautiful if I wore nothing but a potato sack. What about you, Tom? What do *you* think?'

Tell her, you idiot, Lou mentally screamed.

Tom scratched the side of his nose. 'If it pleases you to hear it, then you have never looked more beautiful.'

Lou felt something like a jolt inside her. Emma threw back her head and laughed. 'Now I know you're teasing. This old frock is on its final outing before meeting its fate with the second-hand man. But I had hoped you might like it. You once told me that I should always wear blue, as it's your favourite colour. But we were small children then. You were always so kind, so gallant, so—'

'For Christ's sake, Edward! What is that infernal racket?' Tom sprang from his chair and Emma's arm slipped from his neck. 'Play something less dreary, can't you?'

Edward slammed the lid of the piano shut.

'I know!' Charlotte squealed. 'Let's get the gramophone out and play something jolly. Oh please, Tom, let's.'

Tom abandoned Emma to help Charlotte set up the gramophone. 'What a good idea, Tom,' Emma purred, rising from the arm of the chair. Tom's rebuff fell away like rain down oilskin. 'Why don't we have a game of cards too? I feel good fortune is smiling on me this evening.'

Edward unfolded a green baize card table and placed it beside the billiard table. Tom helped Charlotte set up the gramophone. Music – a sort of scratchy dance – came from the trumpet. Lou watched as Emma swayed around the room; every movement, every stride, every brush of fingertips along furniture, carefully designed to seduce. So accomplished was she at the art of flirting, Lou felt sure Emma could move the balls on the billiard table through the power of her charm alone.

Tom, George, Charlotte, and Emma, all took seats around the card table. Tom glanced at Lou, and she looked away. Like Edward, she refused the invitation to join in. The game commenced and Edward stood beside Lou, staring at the group, his expression impassive.

Talk to your brother, Lou wanted to say. *He knows your secret about the maid. Let him help you work out how to handle it, before it's too late. You might not get another chance.* She didn't want to think that her plan to somehow stop Tom going to fight in France might fail, but there was no harm in having a back-up plan. Edward must understand his position. She bit her lip. All the while the game progressed across the room, Charlotte delighting in her success and Emma cheering her on.

'It's fortunate for our family that Tom was born first,' Edward said to Lou. 'I have neither the skills in diplomacy nor the temperament required to be him. Goodnight, Miss Arnold.'

Lou helped herself to more brandy and a cigarette from a box on the table. After a couple of attempts, she managed to connect the flame from a match with the tip of the cigarette. When the smoke reached her lungs, she coughed.

'Why are we sitting in near darkness when we have electric lights?' Tom said.

'Because candlelight is more . . . romantic.' Charlotte smiled and placed a card on the table.

'I have to agree with Tom,' Emma said, 'I much prefer a bright room.' Taking a cigarette from Tom's silver case on the card table, she leant in for him to light it. She drew the smoke into her lungs, and it escaped from her mouth slowly, swirling in the light above the billiard table. 'I spent a fortnight with a friend of mine in Paris last spring. She has a charming apartment just off the Rue de Passy. The building really is quite stunning. The exterior is designed to take on the appearance of a huge jardinière with ceramic thistles winding around the balconies. The windows are vast and let in so much light that it feels as though the outside is almost inside. When I'm mistress of my own home, I shall take a broom to sweep out the old fustiness and bring in the new and modern.'

'You would approve of that, wouldn't you, Tom?' Charlotte said. 'With your love of all things natural.'

Without looking up from his cards, Tom said, 'The outside is outside. The inside, inside. I see no good reason to confuse the two.'

Lou stared at him in disbelief. What did Emma have to do to elicit a positive response from him? Strip naked and drape herself across the billiard table? Even that might only be enough to receive an arched eyebrow by way of reaction.

'Is anyone going to play this bloody hand?' George slammed his cards down on the table. 'I thought we were here to play cards, not discuss blasted nature and candles.'

Lou had had enough. She got to her feet, crashing into a side table, almost knocking it over, as she made to leave the room.

The cool air in the hall caught her off guard. She grabbed the banisters. She should go up to bed. No. The room would spin and she would be sick. Stumbling into the library, she caught sight of her reflection in the mirror above the fireplace. She was swaying from side to side, eyes swimming, unfocused. She yanked the ridiculous black feather from her hair and threw it to the floor.

'I didn't know you smoked.'

Oh God . . . She turned around. 'I don't. I gave up two years ago.'

Tom stooped, picked up the feather and handed it to her. 'I'd hoped to find you alone. I still owe you an apology for my behaviour earlier today. I acted appallingly when you were so kind. I really am very sorry.'

Why was he apologising to her? Why did he have to be so bloody honourable? Lou threw the feather to the floor again. If she annoyed him, perhaps he would leave her alone. 'I don't know how you can bear to sit at the same table as that *man* after what he did to poor Ambrose today.' *And he's going to murder your sister! Careful, Lou.* 'How can you do it after everything you said about him in the stable?'

Tom picked the feather up again and placed it on a side table. 'What choice do I have? George is family. I'd rather he wasn't but he is. I'm sure you understand the need for the careful management of one's relationships with one's relatives.'

'I'd smack him in the mouth if I were you.' Lou hiccoughed and briefly lost her footing. The floor seemed to be moving, the pattern in the rug coming into and out of focus. 'Am I shocking you?'

'No.' Tom smiled in that way he seemed to when he was amused by something she did or said.

'No?' Lou challenged.

'I have a suspicion that the wine is speaking for you. And perhaps the brandy.'

Lou could hear the laugh in Tom's voice. 'Are you making fun of me?'

'A little.'

Lou stumbled. Tom reached out to help her, but she drew away from him, steadying herself against the back of the sofa.

'May I ask you a question?' Tom said, watching her closely.

'It's your house, you can do what you want.'

'Where did you go today?'

She was drunk but not that drunk. 'Stop wasting your time asking me stupid questions and go back to Emma.' She grabbed the feather from the table and threw it to the floor. Once again, Tom stooped to pick it up. But this time, instead of handing it to her, he held it, running his thumb along the soft plume. Lou's brain swirled around the vision of him, quiet and calm when she felt so hysterical. And those eyes. Those wretched blue eyes that were staring at her so earnestly. Was he having a rummage around in her thoughts? What would he find if he was? Nothing good. Nothing worthy. She turned away so that he wouldn't see the tears that came on so quickly and with such force that she had to gasp just to take in breath.

'Lou?'

She hid her face in the crook of her arm. Tom touched her shoulder, and she shrugged him away. She should make him hate her now. At some point, just like everyone else, he would come to despise her. There was little point in delaying the inevitable. 'My father's not dead,' she blurted. 'He left us when my brother was a baby. So, you see, I'm nothing but a dirty liar. I've lied to you and your family.'

Tom's voice was quiet and close to her ear when he said, 'Do you think we don't all have secrets we would rather keep hidden? I'm certainly in no position to judge anybody, least of all you.'

'I'm not normal, can't you see that? I destroy everything . . . I should have died. It should have been me, not my mum . . . not my mum . . .' she sobbed and Tom placed his hand on her shoulder. This time she didn't shrug him off.

'Don't ever say that,' he said softly. He applied gentle pressure, turning her to face him. Her eyes were on a level with the front of his white shirt.

'Even my brother hates me. He said a man would have to be mad to love me.'

'Then your brother's a fool.'

Tom's arms were around her, pulling her to him. She should push him away: send him back to the billiard room. She certainly shouldn't be talking about her family and definitely not about love. She buried her face in his shirt. He smelled of cologne. Woody and spicy. How easy it was to accept his strength rather than rely on her unsteady legs. She could stay smothered by the comfort of his warmth forever.

'Is this a private conversation, or can anyone join in?'

Lou tensed. Tom pulled away, although his hand stayed on the small of her back. 'Louisa is feeling unwell,' he said. He removed his handkerchief from his pocket and pressed it into Lou's hand.

'Oh, you poor dear.' Emma rushed to Lou's side. 'Tom, be a sweetheart and leave us alone, won't you? Us girls don't need chaps around when we're feeling under par. And you might arrange for some coffee while you're at it. Strong and black.'

Lou felt Tom's hand slip from her back as he left. She tried to object when Emma encouraged her to sit on the sofa, her words sounding like gobbledegook. She didn't notice anybody enter the room, but a coffee pot and cups appeared. She tried to refuse the cup held to her mouth, but Emma was insistent, so she gave in and took a sip of the black liquid.

Emma forced her to take another mouthful. 'You are a dark horse, Louisa.'

'What do you mean?' Lou slurred. Had Emma read more into Tom's hug than an act of sympathy? Did she think Lou had designs on him?

'A suffragette and a drinker,' Emma smiled. She nudged Lou and laughed. 'I suppose I should have guessed. You are slightly . . . unconventional. You intrigue me.'

'Do I? I don't know why. But I promise to help you marry Tom, really, I do. It's important. Very, very important.'

'I don't doubt it,' Emma said. She encouraged Lou to lift the cup to her mouth. 'Now come along and have another sip of this coffee. I confess I've been in your position enough times to know what you need.'

'Have you?' Lou laughed and hiccoughed in the same breath. 'I don't think so. You see, I'm a traveller. Did you know that? I'm on a journey.' She put her finger to her lips. 'But it's a secret, shhh.' She tried to focus on Emma's face. 'Why have you got four eyes?'

Emma's two mouths smiled. 'Because, my dear Louisa, you are sozzled. And the only journey you're going on tonight is up the stairs to bed.' Putting the coffee cup aside, Emma held out her hand. 'Come on then, let's sort you out. There's no need to involve anybody else.'

TWENTY-TWO

23RD DECEMBER 1913

Lou slipped in and out of a fitful sleep, disturbed by vivid dreams that jerked her awake but that she forgot the instant she drifted back into unconsciousness. When the clocks around the house tolled one o'clock, she woke suddenly. The chimes were joined by a knocking sound, like water banging through a cooling pipe. It fell in time with the throbbing in her head. She had drunk too much wine with dinner. Too much brandy after. She lay motionless in bed, fragments of her behaviour the previous evening beginning to take shape through the alcohol-induced fug.

She pulled the covers up over her head, but the images refused to budge. All the while, the knocking sound grew louder, more rhythmic, and increasingly insistent. It seemed to be coming from the ceiling above her bed. Letting her mind retrace the journey she had made to the upper floor with Tom – *oh no, Tom, what the hell did you say to him last night? Quick, bury that thought* – she judged the room above hers to be the lumber room. Had someone been up there during the day and left a window open, which was now banging in the breeze? She fumbled for the cord beside her bed but stopped. It wouldn't be fair to drag a poor unfortunate maid from their bed in the middle of the night to close a window just so she could sleep. She pulled a pillow over her face, but the duck feather buffer failed to muffle the knocking. There must be one hell of a storm whipping outside to make the window bang so violently.

Lou dragged the pillow from her face and peered at the fire. It had burned to embers, leaving no flames to indicate that so much as a whisper of a breeze was whistling down the chimney. Letting out a long sigh, she threw back the covers, slipped from the warm cocoon of sheets and blankets, and stumbled while pulling on her robe. Still half asleep, she shoved her feet into her slippers, felt her way along the wall, and let herself out of the room.

The lamps were out. All was dark except for pale fingers of winter moonlight filtering through the glass dome along the landing. The moonlight inched across the walls, casting strange shadows and sapping familiarity from the features of the corridor. There were no fires lit to warm the air; no voices rang out from rooms; there was no bustle of staff going about their business. Drained of colour and life, Hill House took on an eerie, otherworldly quality. Lou's mind took her back to that first, forbidden foray inside this house. The dark, the desolation, the destruction. Tying the belt of her robe tighter, she increased her pace and let herself into the secret door on the landing.

Stepping into the hidden stairwell, with its stone steps, felt like walking into a refrigerator. Even the wooden handrail was cool to the touch. Lou carefully picked her way up in the dark. The booze flowing around her system made her legs wobble and she was so busy trying not to trip that she only realised where she was when she emerged from the stairwell at attic level.

Milky moonlight from a single window in the slanted eaves vaguely lit the bare walls and floors. How would she explain her presence if she was caught snooping around the quarters of the male staff in the dead of night? Picturing the faces of Bainbridge

and Mrs Moriarty, she was on the verge of heading back down
the stairs when the knocking grew louder. How could the
footmen and kitchen porters behind the closed doors sleep
through that racket? They were no doubt dog-tired after a hard
day's graft. And here she was, about to make the floorboards
creak as she crept through their world. *You're doing this for
them*, she told herself. *So they can get a good night's sleep.*
Passing the window in the eaves, she noticed wisps of cloud
hanging motionless in the still night sky. If there was no storm
brewing outside, why was that bloody window knocking so
fiercely in the room at the end of the corridor? A chill – which
had nothing to do with the temperature of the air – raced down
Lou's spine. She tried, and failed, to shake it off. This was
stupid. She should go down to her room, bury her head under
the pillow and wait until morning.

    She turned around. Her long shadow was there on the wall
to meet her. She jumped and her heart felt like it was about to
explode out of her throat. The knocking grew in pace. It seemed
to be demanding her attention. *Okay. Get a grip, Lou. This is
stupid. It's a window knocking, that's all.* She turned back
towards the lumber room to find that the door now stood open.
A light shone from within. A shadow moved back and forth,
back and forth, lengthening and shortening on the bare floorboards. Lou backed away. The shadow began to move more
quickly and with each step she took away from the lumber
room, the noise grew louder. She looked along the corridor. It
was further to go back than she had come, and it would take just
one of the men to stick his head out of his room and she would
have some serious explaining to do. There was no choice. She
made her way more quickly than she wanted to towards the
light, all the while telling herself that there was a perfectly
logical explanation for a door opening on its own – *it's the wind,
it has to be the wind. But what wind?*

    She reached the open door. She stood absolutely still, her

eyes fixed on the floor, her heart battering her insides while the shadow swung like a pendulum across the floorboards. *Okay, now.* She looked up. And in that instant, her fear evaporated.

In the centre of the room stuffed with abandoned treasures and beneath the glow of a single, un-shaded light bulb, was the source of the noise. The rocking horse rocked back and forth and on it sat Bertie. His eyes were closed and his fingers grasped the woollen mane.

Lou ran to him. 'Bertie?' she said, her breath a cloud in the ice-cold air.

Bertie seemed not to hear her. He continued to move in the saddle, keeping up the momentum. Using the weight of her body, Lou stopped the horse and took hold of Bertie's hands. His skin was warm although he wore nothing but a pair of thin cotton pyjamas. She felt his forehead; his face burned and his fringe was damp.

'Bertie?' Lou whispered. 'What are you doing here, sweetheart?'

Bertie's eyelids flickered just as they had when he played with the doll's house, but he didn't respond. He was in the grip of some kind of trance again. Lou was so concerned that she didn't hear the footsteps until they were behind her. She turned with a start.

Mrs Hart swept into the room, her hair loose about her shoulders, her colourful robe floating behind her. 'Don't be alarmed,' she said to Lou, briefly touching her arm before hurrying to Bertie. 'There, there, darling,' she cooed. 'You are quite all right now.'

'I think he's ill.' Lou said. 'He's running a temperature.'

'Bertie's not unwell, are you, my little one?' Mrs Hart wiped Bertie's fringe from his face. Gently she eased him from the saddle and carried him to an old wooden chair where she took a seat amidst the objects hidden beneath sheets. Cradling Bertie, she said, 'Close the door, won't you? We don't want to disturb anybody else. You'll find a blanket in there, if you wouldn't mind.' She nodded towards an old chest.

Lou closed the door. She opened the chest and the rusty hinges creaked as she removed a blanket. She handed it to Mrs Hart, who wrapped it around Bertie.

Mrs Hart wore no slippers and Lou watched the tendons in her feet contract beneath her skin. Unnerved by Mrs Hart's state of undress, Lou said, 'I heard a noise, so I came up. Do you think he came all the way from his parents' cottage on his own?'

'He walks in his sleep sometimes,' Mrs Hart said. 'You go for little adventures in the night, that's all, isn't it, my darling?' She kissed Bertie's forehead and held him closer.

'Should I get someone to fetch Sally and William?' Lou imagined making her way in the darkness to the cottage and shuddered. If the prospect of that short journey down the drive terrified her, how in heaven's name had a little scrap of a boy made his way all alone?

'There's no call to alarm them unnecessarily,' Mrs Hart said.

'Unnecessarily? Their son is wandering around in the dark. Shouldn't they be told?'

'Don't worry yourself, Louisa. This little lamb is so dear, so precious to us. We will make sure that no harm ever comes to him. You see,' Mrs Hart said, 'other people wouldn't understand. Not like us.' She looked up and fixed Lou in what she felt was a challenging stare. Did Mrs Hart suspect something? Lou's guard slammed up. She was glad when Mrs Hart turned her attention back to the rocking horse.

'Bertie loves that old thing as much as I once did,' Mrs Hart said. 'He has a name, you know. Pegasus. He was my dearest friend when I was barely this chap's age.' She tucked the edge of the blanket beneath Bertie's back where his pyjama top had ridden up. 'Charles had already been sent away to school and as a girl I, of course, was kept at home, passing from the care of my nanny into the hands of a governess. I only saw my mother for an hour before tea each afternoon and on special occasions. My father, I saw even less as he was always in London. My mother had children brought from the village once a month to play with me but when they went home, I was once again left alone in the company of adults. I was better acquainted with the staff who were paid to take care of me than I was with my own family. They were all very kind, but it wasn't enough. Many was the day that I sat in Pegasus' saddle and dreamt that he would sprout wings like his namesake and fly me away to a land where I would find somebody to play with. No child should ever feel that lonely.'

She kissed Bertie's forehead. As she stared into his sleeping face, she began to smile. 'Then one day, my mother announced over breakfast that we should expect the daughter of a distant relative to come to stay. I was twelve years old by then so was allowed to take breakfast, as well as tea, with Mother. This relative was to become my mother's ward as her own parents had tragically died in an accident. Mother was vague about the girl's relationship to us, which was immensely odd as Mother was never anything but specific about everything. When I pressed her, she said that the girl was the niece of a second cousin who I would not have heard of. Later that day the girl arrived, alone, at the front door. She carried a small suitcase containing only a very odd dress and she gripped the paw of a stuffed bear. They were her only possessions. Odder than that was the luggage label pinned to her overcoat with her name written on it: *Elizabeth Goodwill*. I wanted to ask why someone would need a tag; did she not know her own name? But Mother said I was not to pry, as it would only upset Elizabeth. It's hard to imagine now but I was an obedient child, so I did as Mother said, besides, I cared nothing for Elizabeth's strange appearance. I was simply thrilled that my prayers had been answered and at last I had a friend.

'Elizabeth was shy and rather sad to begin with, but I made it my business to be so very kind to her and make her smile. We soon became the best of friends. As she cried at nights, Mother arranged for her bed to be brought into my bedroom. Most nights she crept into my bed and we spent half of every night chattering away like birds. Elizabeth shared my lessons with my governess. We played in the grounds and took trips into the village. She was as close to me as a sister would be. But you see, I knew that she was different. I was the only one who knew her secret.' Mrs Hart looked up from Bertie. She spoke her next words slowly and precisely, giving weight to each. 'One in, one out.'

Lou's attention had drifted during Mrs Hart's story, but at the sound of the familiar words, it snapped back to the cold attic. She wrapped her arms around her waist. Mrs Hart couldn't possibly know how she had come to be here. Could she?

'One in, one out?' Lou said, reflecting Mrs Hart's words back at her, hoping at the same time to sound innocent.

Mrs Hart smiled. 'Elizabeth was a visitor like no other,' she said. 'She stayed with us for five years until the day she went out and never returned. A telegram arrived to notify us that she had met an old friend and on the spur of the moment had gone to stay with her. I should have been frantic with worry as Elizabeth had no friends that I was aware of. But I felt something. A shift is the only way I can describe it, as though a piece of the world had fallen into place. A telegram arrived just weeks later saying that she had met a military man who had swept her off her feet. They were travelling to India where her future husband was stationed and where they would marry and settle. I knew that it simply wasn't true. I knew that it was simply a way of accounting for Elizabeth's return to wherever it was that she had come from, and that the house was responsible some-how. But that didn't stop me from being distraught at the loss of my friend. My mother, on the other hand, was quite satisfied, as marriage for Elizabeth was to be celebrated and she had got it on good authority that Elizabeth's husband was a respectable match. When I pushed her as to whose authority this was, she seemed unable to remember. The fact that I knew more than my mother did helped me to accept my special connection to this house. Just as you must accept yours.'

Mrs Hart's eyes had wandered from Lou as she spoke, but now she caught her in her direct gaze again. Lou stared back, unable to speak.

'When the telegram came announcing your arrival, Louisa, and it was from Elizabeth, I knew that you, just like her, were to be a special type of visitor.'

Cold seeped through the thin soles of Lou's slippers. 'I don't know what to say . . . I'm . . . I . . .'

'Take a breath, Louisa. Calm yourself. You can ask me anything and I will try my best to answer you truthfully.'

'But how? I don't understand how this can be happening.'

'That's because you are looking for a logical explanation when there is none to be found. You must look more to the . . . spiritual.' Mrs Hart laughed softly. 'You can imagine how ridiculous I feel saying that. My whole life has been driven by reality and logic, yet here I am advising you to find an intangible answer in the ether. But there we are. It's only fair that I talk plainly so you understand your position.'

'Understand? I'm not sure that I do. I'm not sure of anything.'

'Well, there is one thing you can be sure of. And it's that this dear little chap is looking after you. Bertie is your connection with this house. I lost that connection, that ability – if that's what you would call it – when Elizabeth left. I'm rather glad. I couldn't have borne to see anybody else leave so abruptly. But now you are here, our first special guest since Elizabeth, and that is to be celebrated.'

'But I'm not the first. There was another girl. She left the day I arrived. Bertie told me—'

'Don't continue, Louisa!' Mrs Hart interrupted suddenly. 'I can't know where you came from or anything about you. Or anyone else who might be a special guest. It's part of the rules, if you like. When Bertie talks to you, he's asleep. He has no awareness of what has passed between you. He will sometimes recall the residue of what has been said as though it were a dream, but you mustn't let him know you are aware. I'm only talking candidly so that you understand your situation. I don't pretend to know the rules. I can only act on what I sense.'

'But if it's one in, one out, how can we both have been here at the same—'

'Louisa, please!' Mrs Hart snapped. She paused and looked down at Bertie's face. Her voice regained its normal, measured tone when she continued. 'Elizabeth confided that, while asleep, I sometimes spoke to her about something called "one in, one out" and told her that she had come to stay because we needed her, and she needed us. It was then that she revealed that we weren't actually related. From that day, I sensed that we shouldn't be speaking about how or why she had come to be at Hill House, so we only ever talked in whispers and away from the house. She told me that her family had all been killed in a war. She said that terrible flying machines had dropped bombs from the sky killing thousands and thousands of people. I didn't believe it. I thought it must have been in a dream that these fantastical notions came to her, even though she believed that they were real memories. It was less than a month later that she left and never returned. To this day I don't know if it was because we talked about her past that she was taken from me. I would rather believe that it was because it was her time to go. That she had got what she needed from Hill House and it was time for her to return to her own life. I just wish that I'd had the chance to say goodbye.'

Mrs Hart brushed Bertie's fringe from his eyes. 'It was such an abrupt and cruel separation. More than anything, I hope that, wherever she went, her life was a happy one. She was the dearest friend I ever had.' She pulled Bertie closer and kissed his hair. 'It was Elizabeth who introduced me to the concept that a woman could be more than a daughter and then a wife and mother. That she could be someone and do something worthwhile with her life. Elizabeth was a passionate advocate for the rights of women. You would have liked her, I'm sure.'

'I'm sorry you lost her.'

'It was difficult to accept at first. But the passing years have worn away the sharp edge I felt at Elizabeth's departure. With the benefit of hindsight, I can now appreciate the time I had with her. She taught me so much and shaped so much of the person you see before you today. Although I'm sure some would say that's not a good thing.' Mrs Hart smiled but it was hollow, with no real happiness. 'Why is it that the people who mean most to us are taken too soon?' As the words left her mouth, a look of horror crossed her face. 'Oh, Louisa, I'm so sorry. Your mother—'

'It's all right, really.'

Bertie squirmed. He rubbed his eyes and blinked up at Mrs Hart. 'Hello sleepyhead, you've been for a little adventure again.' Mrs Hart clutched Bertie to her. 'Go,' she whispered to Lou. 'Before he wakes and sees that you are here and wonders why. Remember, he mustn't know that you are anything but a normal guest. I'll see him home safely. And Louisa, remember there is a reason that Hill House brought you here. Find out what it is.'

Lou wanted to hear more, to know more. At last, somebody knew her secret.

But Bertie squirmed again and Mrs Hart gestured Lou away with her hand. Lou carefully backed out of the room.

'Good night, God bless, dear Louisa,' Mrs Hart whispered.

'Oh, and Louisa, remember that sometimes we must cross the path of another in an unexpected way in order to find our own path.'

Lou returned to her room and collapsed into bed. There was nothing like finding out you were a pawn in some mystical game of chess to make you sober up quick smart. She crawled under the covers.

So, Hill House had opened its doors to her, just like it had opened its doors to Mrs Hart's friend and Edward's maid. Was she really lying in this bed, accepting time travel in the same casual way she might accept hopping on a bus? Her mind conjured up an image of a long queue of people at a bus stop, all waiting for their turn to board the Hill House charabanc. Amongst them was Mrs Hart's friend, Elizabeth. With her luggage tag pinned to her coat, her little suitcase and sad eyes telling the story of the loss of her family in what sounded like an air raid, she looked for all the world like an evacuee from the Second World War. Edward's maid was there too. Lou's mind dressed her as an Edwardian maid with a black dress and auburn hair tucked beneath a white cap. There was no telling where she had really come from. The Georgian era? Tudor times? It could even be a future beyond Lou's own. Every sane and rational thought told Lou these people couldn't possibly slip through time. But what had Mrs Hart said? There was no logical explanation, only spiritual.

The image of the bus queue began to fade as snippets of the previous evening elbowed their way through the mist. Any truly lucid memories stopped midway through dinner, although Lou did have a vague recollection of music and of people playing billiards and cards and strangely, of a swan gliding across a lake. She curled into a ball inside her nightdress. At least she had managed to undress herself. Or had she? Her skin recalled the sensation of unfamiliar hands unlacing her corset, rolling down her stockings. There had been lots of lips and eyes . . . Emma! Had Emma undressed her and put her to bed? And what had happened before that . . . ? A feather . . . something about Mum and Stephen and guilt . . . and crying . . . there had definitely been crying . . . She had cried on Tom's shoulder. Lou let out a long groan and buried her face in the pillow. What turns had their conversation taken to arrive at that point? She could have done anything. Said anything. She pulled the pillow tight around her face and groaned again.

Lou spent what was left of the early hours of the morning drifting in and out of sleep. In the midst of a dream, where she watched someone fondle a feather, she sat bolt upright. The room was still dark. She tried to settle down but an unfamiliar creak across the room made her sit up again. Fumbling for the lamp, she squinted in the unwelcome light and saw a girl standing before the open wardrobe door.

'Mary! You gave me a fright.' Lou laughed nervously. It took her a few moments to realise that something was amiss. Mary should be kneeling at the hearth, not standing frozen to the spot like a mouse desperate to avoid the attention of a kestrel hovering overhead. And she certainly shouldn't have a pink scarf in her hands. Lou kicked back the covers and fighting a pounding in her head, crept across the room. She took the scarf from Mary and draped it over the wardrobe door. But when she tried to put her arm around Mary, she flinched.

'I'm not going to hurt you,' Lou said. She guided Mary to the bed and encouraged her to sit down. 'Sally's noticed things have been going missing from my wardrobe,' she said carefully and sat beside Mary. 'You do know that if someone is caught stealing, they'll get into awful trouble.'

Mary began to tremble. A tear ran down her cheek. It

cleared a track through the grime. She was a shadow of the girl Lou remembered from her first day, creeping around outside Mrs Moriarty's room, gossiping with Monsieur Gotti about the mysterious visitor. Lou took a handkerchief that had been left folded on the nightstand and pressed it into Mary's hands. 'You must have had a very good reason to take such a risk, especially with me in the room. Won't you tell me why?'

Mary stared at her apron and shook her head.

'I can't help if you won't tell me,' Lou said. 'And I'd like to help if I can.'

Mary shifted. She twisted the handkerchief through her fingers, turning the white cotton grey with coal dust. 'It's my mother,' she said quietly. 'She's poorly. Terribly poorly. Father hasn't been able to find work in months. And . . . and . . .'

'Go on,' Lou coaxed.

'I'm the oldest so he had to take me out of school to work. But my wages aren't enough, not with the doctor's bills and having to feed my brothers and sisters. Father thinks the things I take home are gifts for good work. He sells them for what he can get. He'll be so ashamed when he finds out I'm a thief.' Mary's chin crumpled. She let out a sob and hid her face in the handkerchief.

Lou's heart went out to this painfully young girl who was shouldering the burden of responsibility for her entire family. 'Please don't cry, Mary. I won't tell anybody. How old are you?'

'Thirteen,' Mary answered, another sob catching in her throat.

'And did you like school?'

'More than anything.'

In spite of her burgeoning hangover, Lou's brain dredged up an idea. 'Mary, if I help your family, will you promise to go back to school and work as hard as you can?'

Mary let the handkerchief drop. 'Father's a proud man. He would never accept charity.'

'Then let's not call it charity. When's your next afternoon off?'

'Today, m'lady.'

Lou smiled. She was nobody's m'lady. 'In that case there's no time to lose. Meet me behind the stable block at noon. Nobody will see us there. I'll have something for you.'

'I couldn't accept. It's not right, not after . . .' Mary glanced at the open wardrobe door.

'Mary, your mother needs medicine more than I need a few silly feathers for my hair. Besides, I always think they look better on birds. And I'm certain that the last time I looked in the mirror I had a nose, not a beak.'

A small smile creased the dirt around Mary's eyes. Obviously feeling a little braver, she made eye contact with Lou. 'Why are you being so kind? You don't even know me.'

'We all need a helping hand from time to time.' Lou took the handkerchief and wiped Mary's cheeks. 'Now, you should go before anybody notices you're missing.' She got up and opened the door. Finding the corridor clear, she beckoned. Mary collected her coalscuttle from the hearth and crept out.

'Thank you, m'lady,' she mouthed and bobbed a curtsey before disappearing into the darkness, struggling with the weight of the scuttle.

Alone again, Lou crawled beneath the covers, her head thumping with a vengeance. She picked up the handkerchief and was about to place it with the laundry when her thumbnail snagged the stitches of a monogram sewn in blue thread into one corner – *TM*. A memory rushed from the deepest coils of her brain. She was pressing her face into Tom's shirt, his woody cologne, his warmth . . . *Oh God* . . . She switched off the lamp and pulled the covers over her head, still clutching the grubby square of cotton.

TWENTY-THREE

When the first hint of daylight crept beneath the curtains, Lou finally gave up on sleep. She sloped from her bed and headed for the bathroom, carefully tucking Tom's handkerchief into the pocket of her robe. Running a bath, she sank neck-deep into the hot water, and pressed a cold flannel to her forehead. When the clocks around the house chimed eight, she heard the bedroom door open.

'I'll leave your tea and toast here, Miss,' Sally called from the other side of the door.

Lou sat up, water cascading down her body. In all of her night-time adventures she had almost forgotten that she still had to make amends with Sally. 'Please, Sally, come in.'

There was a pause before Sally stepped inside, hands clasped in front of her. Head dipped, she curtseyed, a model of subservience.

'You're punishing me, and I deserve it,' Lou said. 'I expected too much yesterday. I'm so sorry.'

Sally's gaze remained resolutely fixed to the floor. 'It's me who should apologise. I had no business speaking to you as I did.'

'Can't we put it behind us and be friends again? I'll never forgive myself if you don't agree.'

Sally's shoulders relaxed. She curtseyed again. 'As you like, Miss.'

'And we'll have less of the curtseying, thank you.'

Plainly as relieved as Lou to have their relationship back on familiar ground, Sally smiled. 'Will I lay out a dress for the shoot today?'

The shoot. Lou had forgotten that she was supposed to join the rest of the women to meet the men for lunch after their morning's shooting. She couldn't possibly go now she had arranged to meet Mary. Not to mention that she would rather take a bite from the bar of soap on the side of the bath than face Tom or Emma anytime soon.

'I think I might take a walk instead,' she said. 'Will you choose me something comfortable to wear. Something loose that doesn't need a corset, please?'

Sally's eyes widened. 'No corset?'

'Mrs Hart manages without one, doesn't she?'

'Well, yes but she's . . . Mrs Hart.'

'And I'll dress myself.' It was time to take back control.

'Dress yourself!'

Lou laughed. 'Is there an echo in here?'

Sally shrugged. 'I suppose you know your own mind, Miss.' She made to leave but Lou called her back.

'I was just wondering . . . not that it matters at all, but did you help me undress last night?'

Sally shook her head and straightened a towel on the rail. 'I came up, but you were already sound asleep. I was impressed that you'd managed by yourself.'

'And I don't suppose anyone on the staff has said anything about me last night either?'

'No. Should they have?'

'Not at all.' Lou brushed her own comment aside. 'I

wouldn't mind a glass of water, if it's not too much trouble. Actually, a jug would be good. And something for a headache.'

Sally left and Lou slumped back in the bath. She clutched the flannel to her head. So, it really was Emma who'd undressed her and put her to bed, saving her the shame of any of the family or staff seeing her worse for wear. She should never have got drunk and let her guard down. She was supposed to be pushing Tom into Emma's arms, not slipping into them herself. Never mind crying onto his shirtfront. To add insult to injury, she had accepted Emma's sympathy. For the rest of her time here – however long that might be – she would have to keep both Tom and Emma at arm's length – literally as well as metaphorically – and help them from a distance. The last thing they needed was her getting drunk again and falling into Tom's arms, taking advantage of his kind nature. Emma might get the wrong idea.

After dressing in a loose skirt and a blouse and washing down two pills with three glasses of water, Lou began to feel vaguely human. With a slice of cold toast clenched between her teeth, she wandered to the window. A fleet of cars had converged down on the drive and a swarm of men in tweeds milled around in small groups, drinking steaming liquid from tiny metal tumblers, their breath white in the morning mist. Other men, dressed in plain breeches, loaded shotguns and boxes onto an open-backed truck while a pack of dogs sniffed around the snow.

Lou spotted Sir Charles and Edward in a group of men along with George Caxton and a man of a similar build but with a shock of white hair. He bore enough of a resemblance for Lou to realise that he must be George's father, Lord Caxton. Another man emerged from beneath the portico to join Sir Charles' group. Lou ducked behind the curtains. This was ridiculous: there was no way anybody could see her all the way up here. She peered down at the top of the new arrival's head, noticing how the damp air had caused his hair to wave.

She sat down on the edge of the bed and gripped the bedspread. Only once she heard the sound of the cars pulling away did she allow herself to get up and look out of the window. The men, the dogs and the cars were gone, leaving just footprints, paw prints and tyre tracks in the snow. She stared at the spot where Tom had stood, trying to pinpoint which of the footprints were his. For crying out loud! She couldn't even look at Tom without noticing his wavy hair and now here she was staring at an empty space, picturing him still there, like some crazed madwoman in the attic. She had allowed herself to get too close to him, blurring the lines between friendship and . . . well, friendship and something else that wasn't there at all. Something that was playing a trick on her because she was grateful for his kindness. Her mind was made up. She would avoid Tom completely. If she allowed her thoughts to get carried away when they were separated by glass, what would she do if she were ever alone with him again?

Channelling her energy into the task at hand, she threw open the wardrobe door and ran her hand along the dresses. Opening drawers, she rifled through neatly arranged underwear, evening gloves, stockings, and cushioned boxes full of gold and gems. Who needed so many *things*? She certainly didn't. Spreading a tasselled shawl on the bed, she began to fill it with small items – costume jewellery, gloves, scarves – anything that looked like it might bring modest sums at a pawnbroker without raising suspicion. She threw herself into the task, feeling like Father Christmas, the Tooth Fairy and the Easter Bunny, all rolled into one. When she was satisfied that there was enough, she secured the ends of the shawl in a bow. If Sally asked where everything had gone, she could say in all honesty that she had made a donation to a worthy cause.

She pulled on her coat and grabbed the bundle. After checking that the corridor was clear, she closed the door behind her and crept down the stairs into the hall.

The morning room was full of wives of the shooting party, noisily taking tea with Lady Mandeville. Giving it a wide berth, Lou let herself into the billiard room and slipped out through the conservatory.

Behind the stable block, Lou paced up and down to keep warm, her boots squeaking in the fresh snow. A few minutes after the church clock chimed twelve, she heard footsteps approaching. Mary appeared around the side of the stable, dressed in a sombre brown coat and felt hat, carrying a wicker basket. She looked like a little girl dressed in her grandmother's clothes. When she saw the bundle in Lou's arms, she put her hand to her mouth. 'That's never all for me?'

'It most certainly is.' Lou forced the unwieldy bundle into Mary's basket. 'Be sure to tell your father to expect good prices. It's all top quality. And you can tell him honestly now that these things are gifts to show appreciation for how hard you work.' She pulled the pink scarf from her pocket and placed it around Mary's neck. 'But this is not for sale. This is for you.'

Mary touched the silk with fingers scrubbed clean except for a semicircle of dirt engrained beneath each nail. 'Oh m'lady, I've never had anything so beautiful in my whole life.' She smiled but in an instant, her pleasure vanished.

'What's wrong?' Lou asked.

'I just wish there was something I could do to thank you for all that you're doing for me. Only, there's nothing a person like me can do for a lady such as you.'

Lou tied the scarf into a bow. 'You don't owe me anything.' But as she tucked the ends of the scarf into the collar of Mary's coat, a thought began to take shape. No, she couldn't . . . could she? 'There is one thing,' she started. But when she looked into Mary's innocent eyes, she was reminded of a trusting puppy. 'No, it wouldn't be fair.'

'What is it? Please tell me.'

One good turn, Lou thought. 'You can say no. In fact, I expect you to refuse. And I want you to understand that my helping your family in no way depends on you agreeing to do anything for me.' She took a moment to work out how best to phrase what she was about to say. 'The Mandevilles have been good to you, haven't they? Giving you a job and putting a roof over your head.'

'Yes, m'lady.'

'And if you knew that somebody wanted to do them harm, you would do your utmost to stop them?'

'Of course,' Mary said, unwittingly playing into Lou's hands.

'There's somebody staying here, Mary,' Lou said. 'Somebody who means to do the Mandevilles great harm. Very great harm indeed. If I could find any information that may show that person in a bad light, I might be able to put a stop to his plans. Before I go on, I need to know that you can keep a secret.'

Mary drew a cross over her chest. 'I swear, m'lady. On my mother's life, I swear it.'

Lou winced. But she knew that such a vow meant she could put her trust in Mary. 'The person I am talking about is George Caxton.'

She didn't have time to think how Mary might react. But she wasn't expecting her to nod, lean in conspiratorially and, without hesitation, say, 'Mr Caxton's fire is the only one I don't make up. Mrs Moriarty says I'm never to go into his room alone. When I asked why not, she wouldn't say.' Mary looked around, checking to see that they were still alone. 'Bertha, one of the maids from Caxton Hall, is sharing my bedroom. She told me that Mr Caxton says things – does things – to maids, that he oughtn't.' She moved in closer still. 'I heard something else last night when I was in the corridor outside the servants' hall. I wasn't eavesdropping, m'lady. I wouldn't want you to think that.'

Remembering the gossipy girl she had encountered on her first day, Lou smiled. 'I'm sure you weren't.'

'There were men talking,' Mary continued. 'I heard William saying how Mr Caxton had mistreated one of Captain Mandeville's favourite horses. That's when Reg said that Mr Caxton is well known for his brutal temper.'

'Reg?'

'He's one of the footmen from Caxton Hall who's come to help. He called Mr Caxton a . . . well, it's a name I can't repeat. Elliot – he's the groom and he never usually says much of anything, really – he burst out all of a sudden. He said that the kind of man who can beat a poor creature is the same kind of man who gambles in the back room of The White Lion with no intention of ever making good on what he owes to men who can ill afford to lose money. And he borrows from men that don't take kindly to bad debts. Reg said that Lord Caxton would be furious if he finds out his son has been gambling. Apparently, Lord Caxton has been heard to say he'd rather see his son in prison than pay off his debts again.'

Lou slowly processed Mary's words and as each one sank in, the green shoots of a plan began to sprout.

'I don't think Mr Caxton is a very nice man, is he?' Mary said. 'He doesn't seem to have many friends. Will I let you know if I hear anything else about him?

'I don't want you to raise suspicion amongst the other staff.'

'Oh, it's all right, m'lady. They're always talking about what goes on upstairs. I'll only be joining in the conversations that are already happening.'

Lou laughed internally at Mary's innocence. She was completely oblivious to the fact that it was indiscreet to discuss one's employers and even more indiscreet to confess to it. 'Thank you,' Lou said. 'But don't give yourself away to anyone. Now,' she touched Mary's hand, 'you should go home. I'm sure your family are desperate to see you.'

After yet more thanks for the bundle and reassuring Lou that her father was meeting her at the end of the lane, Mary left. Lou waited for her to make her way along the path into the wood. As soon as she was out of sight, Lou rushed around to the yard. Pushing open the stable door, she found Elliot, shirt-sleeves rolled to his elbows, cleaning out a stall. He rested his broom against the wall and made to remove his cap.

'Please,' Lou said, 'there's no need to stand on ceremony for me.'

He removed his cap anyway and stood bareheaded before her.

'Do you have somewhere warm where we can talk?' she asked. 'It's perishing out there.'

Elliot led her to a small storeroom at the far end of the stable block, where Lou sat at a table, surrounded by saddles and stirrups, blankets and straps. The scent of horse and leather mixed with the aroma of the tea Elliot prepared in a teapot on a trivet at the fireplace. His dog, Clarence, who was curled up on a rag rug at the fire, lifted his head every now and then to watch them, flicking his tail. When the tea was ready, Elliot placed a mug before Lou and took a seat opposite her. He didn't apologise for the chipped mug and didn't offer any sugar.

Lou raised the steaming brew to her lips, enjoying its warmth and Elliot's brusque, honest hospitality. 'Thank you,' she said and, having broken the silence, Elliot was at liberty to speak.

'Were there summat particular you wanted?' he asked.

Straight to the point, no-nonsense Yorkshire. She liked that. She placed the mug on the table. *Here goes nothing.* 'I won't offend you by beating about the bush. You know George Caxton, don't you?'

Elliot's top lip twitched, revealing his eye tooth. 'Aye,' he said, 'I know of him.'

'And you drink at The White Lion where he gambles?'

Elliot raised an eyebrow.

'I said I wouldn't beat about the bush. I saw what he did to Ambrose yesterday. I'm here to ask for your help. If you don't like what I have to say, then I'll go and won't trouble you again.'

Elliot rolled and lit a cigarette and listened without a hint of emotion to Lou's explanation of her need for evidence of George Caxton's gambling debts.

'Do you know someone who could supply such a thing?' she asked.

Elliot took a sip of his tea. For a moment Lou thought he was about to refuse. Had she been wrong to bank on his loyalty to Tom? He ground his cigarette out in the ashtray and looked at her so that she felt her integrity come under scrutiny.

'Of course, I'd be happy to make it worth their while,' she said. In rummaging around the wardrobe, she had come across a purse containing a few banknotes and couldn't think of a better way to spend them than on buying some scandal on George Caxton.

Elliot sat back in his chair. 'I know someone who might help. But there'll be no payment required.'

Lou let out a sigh. She had clearly passed whatever test Elliot had set and he hadn't even asked what she needed the evidence for.

Finishing their tea, they made arrangements for her to return at lunchtime the next day to see what Elliot had been able to find out. He drained his mug and offered to hitch up a carriage to take her out to the shoot. 'They'll be starting lunch soon.'

'Thank you, but I'm not hungry.'

'As you wish.'

On her way out of the stables, Lou paused at Ambrose's stall to scratch him between the ears.

'He's not so bad now,' Elliot said, 'in case you were worried, like. Horses don't hold a grudge.'

TWENTY-FOUR

Outside, the mist had burned away, and Lou emerged from the stable block to a crisp winter's day. With a free afternoon, she had time to go back to the library. But not before taking a turn around the grounds in the glorious weather. What she was going to do with any incriminating information on George Caxton, she wasn't sure, but it was enough for now to know that she might find something to use against him.

Keeping the church to her right, she walked at a fast pace, the sun shining on her face, the icy air chilling her nose and cheeks. She followed a set of rabbit tracks, venturing into the woods and the darkness of the snow-covered canopy. The tracks eventually disappeared into a tangle of branches. Where did they come out? Over by the church wall? Down by the frozen fishing lake? Among the neat vegetable patches in the walled garden? Somewhere across the vast expanse of fields?

Shivering, she pulled her collar around her neck and pressed on, wanting to escape an unwelcome image of this forest floor buried beneath six lanes of tarmac with a footbridge replacing the oaks and a dismal concrete housing estate sprawling across the countryside.

With no discernible path, she beat her own, squeezing between tree trunks, ducking beneath low-hanging branches. In some places, the snowdrifts were so deep that snow spilled over the top of her boots. But she didn't care; she was determined to feel everything this world had to offer. Even soggy stockings.

For ten minutes, perhaps longer, she pushed further into the wood until she became aware of a noise other than that of her boots breaking the crust of the snow. It began as a distant murmur but soon became recognisable as voices. She followed them to a clearing in the woods. Still sheltered by the trees, she looked at the fleet of vehicles parked up beside a marquee. Through an open flap she caught a glimpse of the table laden with food and crystal and china, as though it were a dining room. A rug had been laid over the snow and there was even a heater in the corner with a chimney belching smoke from the top of the tent to warm the members of the shooting party and their wives who sat at the table, served by a small army of staff. The only concession to this al fresco dining experience was the addition of overcoats and hats to the guests' outfits.

A little way off, a group of men sat on upturned logs, huddled around an open fire, eating slabs of pie wrapped in waxy paper. The dogs looked up longingly; their wagging tails flicking up puffs of snow as they waited for crumbs of pastry to drop their way.

Laughter from the marquee mixed with the low rumble of the voices outside, but Lou was too far away to hear the conversation of either party distinctly. Suddenly one voice rose above all the others. 'Oi! What do you think you're doin' there?'

It was only when a large man jumped up and lumbered in the direction of the wood, that she realised with shock that he was shouting at her. She turned and ran, hiding behind the trunk of a large oak. Why was she hiding? She could have gone into the marquee to join the party for lunch if she wanted to. But she didn't want to.

She heard the man's laboured breathing. 'Where are you?' he shouted.

'What's going on?' another man's voice called.

Lou slammed her hand across her mouth, afraid that breathing alone might give her away. There was no time for a confrontation; she had to get to the library. If someone saw her, at best she would get dragged into the marquee. At worst, she would have to explain her behaviour the previous evening.

'I saw someone, Sir,' the man wheezed. 'A woman sneaking around in the trees. Some of 'em caused a scene at the Huntingdean shoot last week, so their gamekeeper told me.'

'Quite.'

'Will I get one of the dogs to hunt her down? She can't have got far. We'll flush her out.'

'What? No. There's no need for that. Go back and finish your lunch, Campbell.'

'The beaters'll be ready to start again in five minutes, Sir. P'raps getting caught in the firing line'll teach her a thing or two. Won't look so clever then.'

'Tell the beaters to be ready to start again in ten minutes.'

'But that'll give her a head start—'

'Ten minutes, I said.'

There was a note of disappointment in the man's voice when he said, 'Very good, Captain Mandeville.'

After a few moments of silence, Lou peered around the trunk. Tom was standing on the edge of the clearing, hands on hips, scanning the line of trees. Lou didn't hear the noise until it was too late. A drift of snow fell through the branches above her head and crashed on to the ground below. She retreated behind the tree but not before Tom spun around. For a fleeting moment, she was sure he caught her eye.

Lou waited. When Tom didn't appear, she peered around the truck and saw him heading towards the marquee.

She ran back through the woods and didn't stop until she

reached St Mary's. The first crack of the afternoon's gunfire echoed around the countryside, and Lou stumbled over a hidden root, tripping and falling heavily to her knees. She got up and ran again, her lungs burning, her heart pounding. Once she was clear of the woods, she turned and ran down the drive.

It was only once she was out on the rubbish-strewn pavement that Lou regained the presence of mind to take a step back through the gates. Her shoe changed back to a pristine brown boot in the snow. She breathed a sigh of relief and couldn't help letting out a laugh. She hadn't outstayed her welcome. Not yet anyway.

At the library, Mrs Rogers glanced up when Lou passed her on the way to the office at the back. She knocked on the door and Will beckoned to her through the window.

'You came back.' He smiled.

'Is this a bad time?' she asked, taking in the sandwich box on the desk.

'Couldn't be more perfect.' Will screwed up an empty crisp bag and dropped it in the wastepaper basket. He patted the chair beside him. 'I hoped you'd come. Our chat yesterday got my research antennae twitching. I was up half the night looking into those Mandevilles and Caxtons of yours.'

'Sorry.'

'Don't be. Jem gave me access to the digitized archive too. I've been itching to share this with you.' He pulled a lever arch file from an oversized satchel on the floor and pushed it across the desk. Lou stared in awe at the hefty brick of paper between the black covers of the file.

'You'll have to let me pay you for the paper and ink,' she said.

Will looked at her from beneath his fringe. 'I wouldn't hear of it. If I'm honest, you did me a favour. I'm staying with my

cousin while I'm on my placement and this gave me an excuse
to stay in my room and steer clear of her kids. I'm not sure how
much more *In the Night Garden* I can take.'

Lou smiled.

'I digress.' Will patted the file. 'The Mandevilles and
Caxtons are fascinating. They had a ridiculously tangled past.
This isn't even the half of it. I could have gone on searching all
night. But you know, I need my beauty sleep.' He waggled his
eyebrows, but Lou was too fixated on the contents of the file to
respond.

Will coughed. 'Anyway, I've been doing my best to unpick
what I can. You said you were interested in the First World War
period, so I used that as my starting point. It was like reading a
blockbuster, but better than the *Da Vinci Code* any day.' Lou
looked at him; his eyes shone with what she recognised as the
thrill of the research chase; the joy of unearthing disparate facts
and documents that had lain unread for decades or centuries
and joining the dots to get to the truth of the story. She had to
fight the instinct to tear into Will's carefully prepared file. He
should be allowed the satisfaction of the reveal. And he might
think it odd if she seemed too keen. She wasn't supposed to
know anything about the history of the Mandevilles and
Caxtons.

At last, and with the reverence of an archaeologist opening
a long-sealed tomb, Will opened the file. Lou didn't need a
dusty old sarcophagus or a room full of gold and gems to experience a rush of delight. All it took was Will's colourful dividers
splitting the pages into meticulous sections with the tabs neatly
marked as *Sir Charles Mandeville, Sir Edward Mandeville, Sale
of Hill House, Lord George Caxton*. She sat on her hands.

'We may as well start at the beginning,' Will said, opening
the first tab. 'Sir Charles Mandeville. You remember him don't
you, the father of the young woman you were researching
yesterday? You read the newspaper report on the inquest into

her death, and we found that her father, Sir Charles, had come to a sticky end too. Stop me if I go too fast or you don't understand anything.' He smiled and Lou smiled back, all the while willing him to get a move on.

'So,' Will said, 'I found evidence that it was under Sir Charles' watch that things took a nasty turn for the Mandevilles. Before his tenure they had been a reasonably successful family with a history stretching back a couple of hundred years, making money from the rents of tenant farmers and other businesses. Sir Charles inherited the baronetcy when his father died in 1890 and in the same year Sir Charles was voted in as MP to represent the seat left vacant by his father's death.'

Yes, yes, yes! I know. 'Oh really,' Lou said sweetly. 'Is that so?'

'Yes. And from what I've read, it's clear that Sir Charles was liked and respected by his political colleagues and constituents, even his adversaries. I read some of his speeches, he was a fantastic orator and had some quite fiery debates across the despatch box! He had forward-thinking views on the rights of the working man – and woman – and was as close to being a socialist as was possible for a Tory. It seems the only criticism that could be levelled against him was that he was a bit too liberal for those on the right of his own party. Are you following?'

YES! Lou nodded politely.

'It was in 1919 that things took a nosedive for Sir Charles,' Will said. 'It would be unfair to lay all the blame at his door – the early twentieth century wasn't an easy time for any titled family. It's a popular misconception that the landed gentry were rolling in pots of cash but that simply wasn't so – unless your name was Caxton, in which case, money sprouted money while you slept! The Mandevilles were on the very lowest rung of the gentry ladder,' Will said. 'It was hardly a hand to mouth existence, but it was hard work to make money from land and keep

it. Many landowners, including Sir Charles, relied on investments. And it was with one of these investments that he made
an epic error of judgement.'

Will took a slug of water. Lou knew what he was about to
say before the cap was back on the bottle. The Polish salt mine.

'You see there was a Polish salt mine scheme that turned
into a huge scandal.' Will wiped his mouth on the back of his
hand. 'Much of what I found out comes from reports in *The
Times* in 1919. Unfortunately for Sir Charles, back in 1912 he
invested in a new salt mine on the recommendation of a friend.
From what I've read about Sir Charles, I'd put money on the
fact that he wasn't a man to gamble on a speculative or risky
business. I'm filling in a gap here but I'm guessing that he
trusted this 'friend'. That's where it went wrong. Sir Charles
was duped. The exact details are a little sketchy in the articles,
but it seems that the friend kept tapping him for more cash,
saying that the mine needed more investment. I suppose once
you're in for a huge sum, you can't back out easily. Once the
friend had drained the coffers, he upped and left, taking all of
the money with him. Sir Charles managed to keep the story out
of the press at the time. An MP implicated in a scam would
have been compromised and at the very least would have been
subjected to a parliamentary enquiry. Over the course of the
next few years Sir Charles managed to claw his way back from
the brink of ruin with some judicious investments. He could
have been forgiven for thinking he had put a lid on the whole
sorry episode. Until this.'

Will flicked through the sheets and stopped at an article. 'In
1919 someone leaked the story of the salt mine investment to
the press. The *Express* broke the story, and took great delight in
twisting the knife, accusing Sir Charles of a hush up, insinu-
ating that he was involved not only in the mine but that he had
his finger in lots of dodgy pies. There was even some suggestion
that he was involved in a scam to fleece the War Office, making

huge profits from investment in a munitions manufacturer. The *Express* steadfastly refused to reveal the identity of their informant, saying only that it was a 'secret source'. They ripped Sir Charles apart. A juicy scandal, especially at the expense of the great and good, sold newspapers back then just as it does now. It was only a few months after the story broke and he resigned as an MP, that Sir Charles committed suicide. The scandal must have rocked an honourable man like him to the core. The truth eventually came out that he had been conned by his so-called friend, and that the accusation of involvement in the munitions scam was false, but it was too late for poor Sir Charles.'

Will sat back and tapped his teeth with his pencil. 'You have to feel sorry for him. He had no idea that the person who engineered his ruin from beginning to end was an enemy within.'

Lou felt the blood drain from her face. 'Who?' she asked, more for Will's benefit than hers.

'George, Lord Caxton. When George's father died at the beginning of 1919, George stepped into his shoes and went on the rampage. As you know he even married Sir Charles' daughter. What was her name again?' Will consulted a notepad.

'Charlotte, her name's Charlotte,' Lou said. 'But I don't understand. How do you know all this about George Caxton?'

Will traced a fingertip down his notes. 'It was the link between the Mandevilles and the Caxtons through Charlotte's marriage that was the key I needed. I went forward in the newspapers to see what I could find out about both families after the deaths of Sir Charles and his daughter.'

He flicked to an article in the file and Lou glanced at it, trying to see what it said. The typeface was different from the others, modern. 'You have to jump forward decades, but this article explains everything. It wasn't published until the nineteen eighties, but it's based on an investigation by a young journalist straight out of college in the nineteen sixties. He wanted to make a name for himself as an investigative journalist and started digging into George Caxton's history. There had been rumours surrounding Caxton for decades with his dubious deals and less than salubrious associations. The young journalist began by looking into a fraud involving land deals in Africa. Once he started digging, he amassed a mountain of evidence linking Caxton to a whole host of dodgy deals. But where other men went to jail, Caxton always managed to wriggle off the hook. The journalist even found witnesses who implicated Caxton in the death of a fellow student way back in his days studying at Cambridge. The journalist had been on the cusp of revealing all in a massive scoop in the sixties when the editor, who'd promised to publish the story, got cold feet and pulled the plug. The journo went to other papers, but no editor would touch the story. Even in the sixties, the aristocracy had real power. It wouldn't surprise me if the Caxtons didn't have a stake in some of the papers or dirt on the editors. It wasn't until the nineteen eighties, after George Caxton died, that the journalist finally found an editor willing to break the story. By then the papers were so full of corruption and scandal that the sting had gone out of the story of a crooked old Lord. It barely caused a ripple.'

Lou tried to piece together everything that Will was telling her, but something was missing. 'What has this got to do with Sir Charles?' she asked.

'Isn't it obvious? Can't you guess who the secret source for the story was? I'll give you a clue; it begins with a 'C''

'Not George Caxton?'

'Got it in one. He was the secret source who went to The *Express* to discredit Sir Charles way back in 1919. The young journalist doesn't say how he found out. I suppose he had a source of his own. It looks like George waited until his father died before going to the press to blow the lid on Sir Charles' Polish salt mine, throwing in the lie about the munitions investment for good measure. There's some suggestion that George's father – the previous Lord Caxton – had coerced certain quarters of the press *not* to print stories about Sir Charles' investment back in 1914. They were distant relatives and in protecting the Mandevilles, he was protecting his own name, not that George seemed to give two hoots about that. He threw poor Sir Charles to the lions and let them tear him apart. Then he had the gall to marry the man's daughter, knowing all the while that it was him who had brought that family to their knees! There's nothing here to explain why he did it, whether he had a grudge or whether Sir Charles was a poor misfortunate caught up in Caxton's twisted power games.'

Will pulled out some more articles to demonstrate how the history of the Mandevilles went quiet after Sir Charles' death – a few reports in the local press about Edward's gradual sale of Hill House land following its use as a hospital in the Second World War and a brief obituary in *The Times* announcing Edward's death.

'Sir Charles' heir, Sir Edward Mandeville, died a sad and lonely recluse in a flat in London, saddled with a financial albatross. After the First World War, income tax skyrocketed and men like Edward Mandeville were just not able to manage that increase. Add to that inheritance taxes and Edward stood no chance.'

'Edward buckled while George Caxton, and men like him, lived the high life,' Lou said.

'Spot on. It's a miracle Hill House wasn't demolished years ago. Not much to show for the end of a dynasty, is it?' Will paused. 'Are you okay?'

'Sorry, what? Yes, I'm fine.' Lou pulled the cuff of her jumper over her hand and wiped her eyes. 'I've got a cold coming, that's all.'

'There's a lot of it going around,' Will smiled sympathetically. 'So, how did I do?'

'What? Oh, it's a lot to take in,' Lou said. 'Fascinating though.'

'Isn't it. Are you sure you're okay? Why don't I pop out and get you a hot drink?' Will grabbed his coat and headed for the door. 'I'll be back in ten. You've got that lot to keep you entertained while I'm gone.'

The moment she was alone, Lou wiped her eyes and grabbed the file. She turned to the section containing the information on George and made straight for the article from the eighties. '*THE TEFLON LORD*', the headline screamed. Lou read quickly, taking in the details of the shady associates of George, who had been only too keen to roll over and reveal all of his secrets to the journalist back in the sixties. His criminal activities had extended to property fraud and embezzlement and had seen many men end up in jail. He had hung his various partners-in-crime out to dry. After a brief first marriage to the unnamed daughter of a minor peer – Lou bit her lip and continued to read – George had been linked to a string of society women and actresses in London until he finally married an heiress in the nineteen forties. He had bolstered the Caxton coffers through lucrative munitions contracts in the Second World War; contracts that the journalist claimed were secured by coercion and bribery.

There was information on the man George had blackmailed into fleecing Sir Charles over the Polish salt mine – an old school friend of Sir Charles'. But it was the details of the death of the student at Cambridge that Lou was drawn to.

The young man – Harry Riley – had spent an evening drinking heavily and playing cards with George and another student. It was while the third student went out to buy more whisky that a gunshot rang out from Riley's room. At the time, it had been reported that without any kind of warning, Riley had taken a gun and shot himself in the head, dying instantly. There had been no suicide note.

A cutting reported the coroner's inquest where George gave evidence. He said he had left Riley's room for a few minutes to answer the call of nature. At the sound of the gunshot, he ran back to find Riley slumped over the table. He said that Riley had been behaving strangely for a number of weeks and while he had been concerned by his friend's behaviour, he had never imagined that he intended to take his own life. It was such a terrible shock, and he had been deeply traumatised by finding his friend in such a manner. The other man who had been playing cards – Ernest Simpson – corroborated George's version of events and the fact that Riley had been behaving strangely.

The coroner recorded a verdict of suicide and with that the sad case had been concluded – until the journalist started digging around decades later. He had tracked down the third man, Ernest Simpson. By then in his seventies and with terminal prostate cancer, Simpson was happy to finally unburden himself of the truth he had carried since his teenage years. His new version of the events of that night were in stark contrast to George's story, and the original evidence given to the coroner. It was true that there had been a game of cards, but George was no friend of Riley's. According to Simpson, George Caxton owed Riley a considerable sum of money in gambling debts. It had been an ill-tempered evening with all three men drinking heavily, George more than the others. An argument had broken out when Riley threatened to go directly to George's father to have him settle his son's debts. It was shortly after that when George had sent Simpson out to buy more alcohol.

'For all these years, I have known the truth about that night. Caxton shot poor Riley,' Simpson was reported as having said to the journalist. 'Caxton came to my room after the police left and warned me off. He said if I didn't want to end up like Riley, then I'd forget everything I'd seen and heard. I was more terrified of Caxton than I was of the law. I knew the likelihood was that if I went to the police and told them the truth, Caxton would go scot-

free, and I would be left to face his retribution. You have no idea what that man is capable of. If I were not dying, I would never have dared tell you the truth, even now.'

There was another article from the eighties in which George's son rebuffed the allegations, saying they were the word of one disgruntled former friend of his father's. The case had been closed a lifetime before and he dismissed the allegations as nothing more than a fantastical, far-fetched vendetta conducted by a left-wing press, hell bent on a discrediting an aristocratic family.

A fuzzy black and white photograph of a fair young man accompanied the story. Poor Riley. By the time Simpson's accusations had been reported – seventy years after that fateful game of cards – Riley had slipped out of living memory. He was yet another forgotten victim of George's tyranny. Just like every member of the Mandeville family.

Another photograph of an old man in a ceremonial gown accompanied the article. With his piggy eyes in a wide, flabby face, there was no mistaking who it was. Lou closed her eyes and saw the eyes of a different man looking back at her through the snow-covered trees that morning. How could a man like George Caxton be allowed to make old bones when a man a million times better than him had been left to rot in a grave on a battlefield across the Channel? She gripped the page, pulled it free of the rings, and screwed it into a ball.

'Crikey,' Will said. He closed the door behind him with his foot and placed two cardboard cups on the desk. Biting the fingers of his gloves, he pulled them free of his hands. 'I leave you alone for a few minutes and you trash my file.' He smiled and Lou released the sheet of paper.

'Sorry, I don't know what came over me.'

Will looked at the page. 'Can't say I blame you. He was a right royal bastard, wasn't he? Oh, and I got this for you. A hot chocolate's too wet without one.'

He pulled a paper bag from his pocket and placed it before Lou. She peered inside and saw a gingerbread man. A sob caught in her throat.

'Oh dear,' Will said. 'I'm sorry. I—'

'It's okay. It's just . . .' He wasn't to know that her mum made gingerbread men every Christmas. She had been so wrapped up in the Mandevilles that she had barely thought about her mum recently. 'I've got to go,' she said, getting up too quickly and bashing into the desk.

'But your hot chocolate,' Will said, steadying the cups.

'I'm sorry.'

'Was it something I said?'

'No. It's not you. I just . . . I'm needed . . .'

'Will you come back tomorrow? We could do more research.'

'I don't think so.'

'After Christmas, then?'

'I don't know.'

Will tried to force the file on Lou, saying he had printed it for her.

'I'm not going straight home,' she said. Unlike the pad and pencil, she couldn't shove the file in her pocket. Who knew what would happen to it when she re-crossed the threshold of Hill House.

Will scribbled something on a scrap of paper and handed it to her. 'It's my number. The library's shut on the 25th and 26th but I'm here between Christmas and the New Year. Or we could meet over a drink to talk about your research. Two heads and all that.'

Lou shoved his number into her pocket. 'Thank you. And thanks for the hot chocolate . . . sorry, I . . .' She ran from the room, passed Mrs Rogers and pushed out through the doors into the dark evening.

Dodging puddles, she rushed down the High Street. The

truth was worse than she had imagined. George Caxton had destroyed the lives of so many people. The coroner should have installed a revolving door just for him; he had spent so much time in the court, playing the grief-stricken husband or friend.

Had the evidence of George's actions not been so overwhelming, she wouldn't have believed anybody capable of such evil. Surely nobody in their right mind would murder a friend for something as ridiculous as the threat of revealing his debts to his father. Especially when the Caxtons were rolling in cash. The information she had gleaned from Mary made it sound like George's father had paid off plenty of George's gambling debts in the past, so why not that one? What made poor Riley so different to everybody else George had owed money to? What had singled Riley out?

Arriving at Hill House, Lou stood before the rusty, twisted gates. She stepped through, the heat in her blood burning just beneath the surface of her flesh. This time when she witnessed Hill House morph into a welcoming stately home, the experience was flooded with sadness. George Caxton wanted to take a sledgehammer to this place and demolish it brick by brick and destroy everyone inside. But why did he hate the Mandevilles so much that he wanted to wipe them from the face of the Earth?

The icy breeze nipped Lou's hands and chilled her legs through the woollen tights that replaced her jeans. Greedily, she soaked up the cold. She had to take her rage off the boil. Fate, karma, chance, divine intervention, whatever it was that had brought her here and put her on a collision course with the Mandevilles, had finally revealed its purpose for her. It had presented her with evidence of George's intentions and the brutality he would commit in the future if events remained unchanged. Tom was the only person who could stand in the way of George. Tom would never allow George to tear his family apart. He would never let George discredit the Mandeville name with his false accusations. Free of scandal, Sir Charles could live a full life and when he died a natural death, it would be Tom, not Edward, who inherited the baronetcy. With Tom in his rightful position as the head of his household, Charlotte wouldn't be forced into a marriage with George. Whatever it took, Lou would make Tom marry Emma; it was the only way to ensure he would resign his commission and return home to take up the vacant job Lady Mandeville had suggested. It wouldn't be the half-life he feared. It would be a good life. He would be happy.

Lou stored the details of Riley's death in a mental file. Finally, she had proof of a crime that George had already committed in this time. Backed up by whatever Elliot was able to provide on his gambling debts, and she should have enough ammunition to use against George. The threat of revealing his crimes would surely bring a man – even one like George Caxton – to his knees.

Lou collected up her skirts and walked slowly up the drive. She had to calm down, gather her thoughts, and formulate a plan for how exactly to use this evidence against George. If saving the Mandevilles was so important that it had allowed her to put aside thoughts of her mum's death for a while, then they were worth fighting for. She could almost hear her mum cheering her on to give the Mandevilles the best Christmas present they had ever had – George Caxton all wrapped up in a huge bow. A bow that would bind him, gag him, and put an end to his plans.

TWENTY-FIVE

That evening the house was full, swelled by the shooting party guests. Gone was the relative informality of the previous evenings, and Lou sat in the drawing room amongst men in tails and bow ties and women draped in silk, dripping with precious stones. Lady Mandeville and Lady Caxton wore tiaras and held joint court of the ladies seated on the sofas and chairs around the fireplace. Mrs Hart blocked Lou's view of the men at the end of the room. Charlotte sat beside her aunt, looking so pretty in a coral-coloured dress with leaves embroidered along the neckline. The only woman unseated was Emma. She circled the room, perching on the arms of chairs and sofas, refusing the canapés the footmen offered.

'Asparagus en croute and caviar on toast,' Lady Mandeville announced when William offered the silver salver to the ladies.

'Your chef is a miracle worker,' Lady Caxton said. 'Asparagus in December, what a triumph. But I'm not so sure about this?' She examined the liquid in her glass. 'Has my daughter been at work with your drinks tray, Lady Mandeville?'

'It's gin and grapefruit juice, Mother.' Emma sat on the arm of the sofa beside Lady Caxton. She shimmered in a black dress, the bodice and thin straps decorated with crystal beads. Her hair was piled high and secured in a Grecian style with a length of silver thread.

'Emma tells me that these *cocktails* are quite the thing in London these days.' Lady Mandeville held the glass away from her face to survey the cloudy liquid.

'And we mustn't be outdone by the Capital,' Mrs Hart added with good-humoured sarcasm.

'Indeed,' Emma smiled. 'Although I must say, I am feeling increasingly enamoured with Northamptonshire on this visit. I could possibly consider making my permanent home here. One can only take so many London parties before they become rather old hat.'

Charlotte glanced towards the group where Tom stood. 'Is that because boring old Northamptonshire has special charms for you now, Emma?'

'Charlotte!' Lady Mandeville snapped. But before she could chastise her daughter further, Lady Caxton placed her hand on Lady Mandeville's arm.

'We are amongst friends here,' she said.

The visiting ladies smiled, and all eyes turned to Tom.

'Stop it, please,' Emma whispered through a smile. 'If he sees you all staring, he'll bolt, just like one of those horses he loves so much.'

'How well you know my son,' Lady Mandeville said. 'Do you know, I'm certain I have seen something new in Thomas' eyes these last few days. A softness and, dare I say it, happiness. Look how he steals glances in this direction when he thinks nobody is watching.'

Lou stared into the flames of the fire. Mrs Hart shifted beside her. 'We must be mindful that Tom is his own man,' Mrs Hart said. 'As his aunt, I hope that any decision on his future is left for him to make.'

'Of course,' Lady Mandeville said, a frosty edge in her

voice. 'As his *mother*, I credit myself with knowing what is good for him. I see no harm in . . . encouraging him in the right direction.'

'Encouraging, yes, but not pushing him. If I know Tom then any hint of conspiracy, any overt sign of meddling, is likely to have the opposite effect to that which you desire.'

It was left to Lady Caxton to intervene in the tug-of-war between mother and aunt. 'It goes without saying that we *all* want what is best for Thomas. We all love and admire him very much. Now that asparagus.' She turned to Lady Mandeville. 'Where on Earth *did* your chef manage to find it at this time of the year?'

While the women struck up a discussion on the importation of vegetables, Lou placed her glass of cloudy, pithy liquid down on the table. She zoned into the men's conversation about something called the day's 'Game Book'.

'There's no question that Edward was on excellent form today,' Lord Caxton said. 'But the figures don't lie. It's *this* fellow who is the crack shot.' From the corner of her eye, Lou saw him place his hand on Tom's shoulder.

'And George wasn't far behind,' Sir Charles added. The other men murmured their agreement.

'George!' Lord Caxton laughed. 'He was fortunate to have the wind as an ally today. Just look at his hands, they're as soft as his mother's. If I'd had my way, he'd have been enrolled at Sandhurst the minute he was sent down from Cambridge. That's where they make men out of boys. Now, Tom, have I ever told you about the time we rescued a Swiss prince from the hands of the Dervishes when I was in the Camel Regiment out in the Sudan?'

George knocked back his drink and took another from the second footman's tray. Lou would have felt sorry for any other man whose father so publicly maligned him, but she had no sympathy for George. He deserved everything his father said, every criticism, every barbed comment. And so much more. Right now, Sir Charles was in the midst of the spiral of debt and scandal that his ill-advised investment had caused. Yet he carried himself with such dignity that not a soul in the room could have guessed at the torment that must be raging inside him. He was a real gentleman. He could have no clue that the man standing just inches away, knocking back his booze, was already plotting his downfall.

It was this thought that occupied Lou throughout the grand meal while everyone but she tucked into Chef Gotti's pheasant liver pâté, roast goose and fine patisserie. An air of conviviality floated across the table, above the crystal and silver, and around the stunning arrangement of Sir Charles' hothouse blooms. But for Lou, it was tainted with the burden of secrets. She sat in a void, unable to stomach a morsel. With so many other guests, her opinions weren't sought. She sipped a glass of water; not a mouthful of wine passed her lips. She needed to keep a clear, unmuddled head.

After the meal, rather than retreating to the library or billiard room, the men joined the women for coffee. The drawing room was thick with the sweet smell of cigar smoke and the floral scent of perfumed oils. A programme of musical entertainment had been arranged and one of the male guests sat at the grand piano in the corner, the enthralled audience tapping their feet to the lively tune he played.

Lou sat before the fire. Swirling her brandy, she watched the thick amber liquid stick to the inside of the glass. Conversation bubbled in the groups around her; the tinkle of laughter and the rounded sound of voices raised in high spirits. Across the room Tom stood amongst a small group, Emma beside him. He said something that caused his entourage to laugh. Emma smiled beautifully and touched his elbow. Lou slammed her glass down on the table.

'Are you quite well, Louisa?'

Mrs Hart took a seat beside her.

'Yes . . . yes, of course. Thank you,' Lou said.

'You barely ate enough dinner to sustain a sparrow.'

Emma laughed again. Lou looked towards her and Tom and experienced an unwelcome sensation; like the walls of the drawing room falling in and crushing the air from her chest.

She turned back and found that she had come under Mrs Hart's scrutiny.

'Oh, Louisa,' Mrs Hart said.

'It's not what you think.' Lou protested but the look on Mrs Hart's face showed she had read her innermost thoughts like an open book.

'Please don't say anything,' Lou begged.

'I hope you know me better than to think I would betray you, Louisa,' Mrs Hart said quietly. 'You know that I will not interfere with whatever it is that you must do while you are here. But it wouldn't be fair if I didn't warn you about Emma. I adore her but you should know that you must be on your guard. When she is your friend, she is your very best friend. There's not a thing she wouldn't do for you, not a kindness she wouldn't bestow. But cross her and . . .' Mrs Hart glanced towards George, who was slumped in a chair. 'Never forget that Emma Caxton is her brother's sister. Her temper may be better hidden, but she can turn in an instant. If she thought for one moment that any woman had designs on—'

'I'm not sure that I do. I don't know what's real and what isn't anymore.'

'We are *all* real, Louisa. You, me, Tom, Emma, here and now, this is the reality that we share.'

Drawn to them as she was, Lou refused to look at Tom and Emma again. 'I'm sorry, I don't feel very well.'

Mrs Hart took Lou's hand. This small act of kindness made Lou swallow hard.

'Go up to your room,' Mrs Hart said. 'I'll smooth your exit

with Lady Mandeville. But please, don't be so harsh on yourself. Whatever happens will be for the best, for you and for us. I'm sure of it. You are more than equal to whatever task has been set for you.'

Lying in the darkness, Lou stared up at the ceiling and listened to the sounds of the house. After what felt like hours, she heard footsteps in the corridor; people gradually winding their way up to bed. The women came first – their footsteps light, their voices hushed – the men later, louder, heavy-footed, some laughing, having had their fill of Sir Charles' cellar. When it all subsided, Lou was left with only her confusion for company.

She tried to focus on her plans for helping the Mandevilles, but her thoughts were continually dragged back to the room along the corridor. Had the occupant removed his tie? Had he slipped out of his tailcoat and draped it over the chair at the desk? Was he sitting in the armchair beside the fire, top shirt button open, the ice in a nightcap chinking against the glass as he took a drink, the warmth swirling down his throat and into his chest? Finally, she shone a light into the dim recesses of her mind. Lurking in the corner, doing its best to shrink from the light, was the truth. The truth that she had fallen for Tom. Hook. Line. Sinker. It was the worst situation imaginable. It would cloud her judgement when she needed to stay sharp. As Mrs Hart had reminded her, in no uncertain terms, these people were real. And they needed her to help them.

TWENTY-SIX

CHRISTMAS EVE 1913

From beneath the protection of the bedclothes, Lou watched Sally balance her morning tray on the bedside table before leaving to see to some of the other guests.

When Sally returned, over an hour later, to draw the curtains, she raised an eyebrow at the full cup of tea, the congealed butter on the cold toast and at Lou, still cocooned in her blankets.

'Are you sickening for something?' Sally asked.

'Not exactly.'

'Will you be going down to breakfast?'

'Yes,' Lou sighed. 'I'll be going down for breakfast.'

If she failed to make an appearance, suspicions would be raised. People would come to check on her and she didn't want that. She wanted to stay in the background and away from any kind of scrutiny. She still hadn't come up with a plan. The prospect of bringing George to his knees felt as far away as ever. If she sat at the breakfast table and said nothing, she could slip between the cracks in conversation and everyone's attention.

After letting Sally dress her, Lou waited for her to leave before slumping into the chair beside the hearth. She took up a brass poker and prodded the fire, jabbing at a lump of coal. It cracked and spat a shower of sparks up the chimney. She had behaved so foolishly and in front of Mrs Hart. She had let her guard down and revealed her stupid crush on Tom. It was hardly a surprise. He was handsome, kind, funny, and she wasn't made of stone.

Lou headed downstairs, pausing outside the dining room to ready herself. She entered and was surprised to find Edward sitting alone.

'Good morning, Miss Arnold,' he said, looking up from his newspaper. 'Are you feeling better this morning?'

'Yes, thank you.' She took the chair opposite him.

'Aunt Leonora said you had been taken ill. You didn't miss much last night. Same old faces, same old conversations. Apart from this.' He tapped his newspaper. 'The political situation in Europe made for some jolly heated debate over the port and cigars. Would you like me to call for some breakfast? The staff were in a rush to clear away to get on with preparations for this evening. Shall I ring for some bacon, or kidneys, perhaps?'

'Thank you, but this is all I need.' Lou poured a cup of tea. How easily Edward moved from the subject of impending war to breakfast. If he knew what was coming in less than a year, he would not find it so easy to speak of war and offal in the same breath.

He folded the newspaper and pushed it aside. 'If you're looking for Mother, she's squirreled away in the ballroom with Mrs Moriarty, preparing for the big reveal this evening. The other women have gone into town to buy her a gift. It's meant to be a surprise, to thank her for her troubles. Not much of a surprise when they do it every year. The men have ridden out to Caxton Hall – another annual tradition.'

At least she wouldn't have to face Tom. Not yet, anyway. 'You didn't want to go with them?'

'And miss the chance of a spot of peace and quiet before the onslaught of this evening?'

Lou sipped her tea. She might not get another chance to talk to Edward alone again. Preparing her words carefully, she said, 'I overheard Lord Caxton compliment you on your achievements yesterday. I was surprised since you said you didn't care for shooting.'

Edward made a spider of his hand and placed it over the newspaper. Moving it from side to side, he said, 'You must think me a terrible hypocrite. I suppose I am. But even I know that sometimes it makes sense to conform. In any case, I split my haul between the beaters so at least half a dozen families will eat handsomely this Christmas. Those birds did not give up their lives in vain.'

Lou smiled. There was a glimmer of hope yet. As much as he railed against it, Edward was a product of the upbringing he shared with his older brother. She took a slice of cold toast from the rack and buttered it slowly, banking on Edward being too polite to leave her to eat alone. 'I think you're more like your brother than you might care to admit.'

Edward peered at her over the top of his spectacles. 'Really? How so?'

'You seem unable to resist doing what is best for your family.'

A pause. Edward rubbed the side of his nose. 'And there you have found my Achilles' heel, Miss Arnold,' he said. 'If I were less concerned with what my family thought of me, then I might . . .' His words trailed away.

Worried that she was losing him, Lou quickly said, 'There's no shame in wanting to please your family.'

Edward's spectacles slipped down his nose. He pushed them back up. 'I'm afraid if you knew everything about me, you might not be so kind. But then I suppose I conform in at least one respect. As the younger son, it's my job to be a disappointment.'

Lou wanted to place her arms around him and tell him she knew all about the maid and it wasn't so bad. That everything would work out for the best. But would it? 'There's no weakness in asking the people we love for help. Why not speak to Tom? Whatever your troubles, I'm sure he will want to help if you give him the chance. Perhaps I shouldn't be so blunt, but he will be going away soon and if something should happen to him . . .' She managed to stop before she said too much. Not that Edward appeared to notice. He circled the rim of his teacup with his fingertips.

'I appreciate your concern,' he said, 'but there are some things not even my brother can help with. If you'll excuse me.' He rose and picked up his newspaper. As he left, a maid appeared. She had been asked to check whether it would be possible to clear the room so that the staff could start preparations for the party.

With the hall full of activity and staff rushing from the passageways into the ballroom and dining room, carrying boxes and crates, Lou made herself scarce. She roamed the rooms that didn't require decoration, killing the time before her meeting with Elliot at midday. The hands on every clock crept around, making each minute seem like an hour and each hour, a lifetime. Her thoughts were preoccupied with what information Elliot might have for her and with Edward's sad face. In the billiard room, she pushed balls around the table. In the library, she flicked through the newspapers and pulled books from the shelves, returning them without reading a single page – even the Plato, which she had been enjoying. In the morning room, she sat in the window seat. Outside, two gardeners hammered spikes into the ground along the drive, from which they suspended colourful paper lanterns. Lou was so busy concentrating on their work and the drone of staff chatter in the hall, that she didn't notice the two cars pulling into the gates until they came to a stop on the drive.

She jumped to her feet and rushed over to the door. In the hall, she almost bumped into William who was on his way to open the front door. He paused to give her a quizzical look.

'I'm . . . I'm going somewhere. I'm in quite a rush,' she said, not wanting to get caught up in the gaggle of women.

'Very good, Miss.'

She closed the billiard room door behind her and listened to the sound of people entering the house – heels clicking on tiles, voices exclaiming how nice it was to be back in the warm.

'I've never seen Northampton so busy.'

'One fears for one's feet in the midst of such commotion.'

'A positive ocean of people.'

Then came a banging noise. 'Mama, Mama, let us in,' Charlotte called. 'I long to see the decorations. What have you been doing all morning? I must see!'

'Patience, child,' Mrs Hart intervened. 'William, might we have some tea in the morning room, please. I think my niece is in need of something to calm her spirits.'

Lou shrank from the door. After last night, she would rather not bump into Mrs Hart. Slipping out through the conservatory, she made her way down the path along the back of the house.

The stables were almost empty, the horses having been taken on the ride to Caxton Hall. Lou headed for the only occupied stall.

'Hello, boy,' she whispered. She approached Ambrose cautiously and ran her hand along his warm, rough coat. He hardly seemed to notice her presence and carried on pulling hay from a net on the wall, chewing it slowly. She went into the stall so that she was level with his head. She stroked his satiny ears and when he turned his face to her, she ran her hand along his neck. His mane was far shorter than that of any of the other horses and stood in a line of grey tuft down his neck.

'It's called a hog cut.'

Lou spun around.

Elliot pointed to Ambrose. 'His mane's coarse, so we keep it cut short. Not pretty, but it's practical.'

In the storeroom, instead of placing tea on to brew, Elliot produced a bottle of cider, which he poured into a small, battered pan and placed on the trivet in the hearth. He added sugar, stirred the mixture and, just before it came to the boil, shared it between the two chipped and tea-stained mugs. He took a heavy fruitcake from a tin and cut two thick slices. Pushing the cake towards Lou, he sat down. 'A woman in the village makes it for me. It's good.'

Lou took a slice. They ate and drank in silence. The cake washed down with mouthfuls of hot cider was the most satisfying meal she had eaten in days. Elliot's silence and aura of calm was a welcome relief from the chaos in the house. When he held the pan above her cup, she nodded for him to top it up. He lit a cigarette and smoked slowly. Once he was finished, he stubbed it out, reached into the pocket of his jacket and removed an envelope. He pushed it across the table.

'This is what you'll be wanting.'

Lou left the stables and made directly for her room where she sat on the edge of the bed. After handing the envelope to her, Elliot had apprised her of additional, important details. George Caxton was in debt. Huge debt. According to Elliot, he was attempting to gamble his way out of it, playing cards with men who he assumed he could beat. He thought he could outwit the simple men from the pub but hadn't banked on their combined skills and tenacity. Having failed to fleece them, he had borrowed considerable sums of money from men in Northampton, loaned on the strength of anticipated dividends from an investment in a diamond mine in South Africa. As evidence of this investment, George had produced a certificate, which Elliot knew to be falsified, since the mine was entirely fictitious. If the men in Northampton realised they would not see a penny of the money owed to them, they would extract recompense in other ways. There had been no need for Elliot to elaborate. His meaning came across loud and clear. How he knew all this, Lou couldn't be sure, but it was no doubt true. George had form.

Lou eased a sheet of paper from the envelope. It was a statement, written in a neat, careful hand, from a witness prepared to come forward and give any evidence required of George Caxton's behaviour and debts. It was signed *Matthew Elliot*.

She had banked on Elliot's loyalty to the Mandevilles, and it had paid off. Now what? She was playing with Elliot's life. If it went horribly wrong, *he* would be left to face the wrath of George Caxton. *She* had an escape route.

Lou folded the sheet of paper and slipped it back inside the envelope. She had to clear her head and plot her next move. To plot any move. She placed the envelope in the drawer beside the bed, locked it, and slipped the key into the pocket of her skirt.

Creeping down the stairs, Lou passed the morning room, where Mrs Hart was still entertaining the other women over tea, and slipped out through the conservatory. She skirted the drive, taking a detour through the trees to avoid being spotted from the house.

Before she could think about where she was heading, Lou was halfway through the gates. Her leg still on the drive was draped in a burgundy tweed skirt, while her leg out on the pavement wore her old jeans. She managed to smile at the impossibility of it all. She would never tire of the craziness of this awesome sight.

Once wholly across the boundary, Lou slipped into her now familiar routine of pulling up her hood. Heading for the High

Street, she stopped at the newsagent to put some credit on her phone, before retracing her steps back to the privacy of St Mary's. She took the scrap of paper from her pocket and dialled the number.

'Y'hello?'

'Will? Is that you? It's me. Lou.' Had she even given him her name? 'We met at the library. You helped me research the Mand—'

'Lou! Hi. I wondered whether you might call. I just wanted to say . . . was the hot chocolate and biscuit a bit over the top yesterday? I—'

'The what? No. I was just phoning because I wondered whether you could tell me how to research a living person. Actually, they might be dead. But they were alive.'

'I hope so. Otherwise, there won't be much of a paper trail to follow.' Will laughed, but Lou was too focused on her mission to appreciate the joke.

'I think the person might have lived at Hill House as an evacuee during the Second World War,' Lou said. 'Do you think you might be able to help find her?'

'If they were a child in the forties there's a good chance they'll still be alive. What's the interest?'

'She's a friend of a friend. A sort of step-sister of a friend.'

'Why don't you come into the library? We can look her up together.'

'I can't today. I don't have time. If you're too busy—'

'Not at all. Tell me everything you know.'

Lou gave Will the scant details of Elizabeth Goodwill that she possessed – her rough age, the possibility that her parents had died in the War – and he promised to call her back. After hanging up, Lou checked her phone for messages or missed calls. Nothing. She was about to shove her phone back in her pocket when it buzzed. It was a message, from an unknown number.

Your application for extended compassionate
leave has been authorised. Return date set as 2
January. R Turner, HR Officer, Freezerfayre.

Lou read the message for a second time. She hadn't applied
for leave, extended or otherwise. She just hadn't turned up for
work one day. But why was she surprised? If that house beyond
the wall could bounce her around through time, was it beyond
the realms of possibility that it could smooth things over with
her employer so she could resume her life of passing frozen
pasta dishes over a scanner? At least there would be a job to go
back to when she returned for good. *For Good.* It sounded so . . .
final.

The clock of St Mary's chimed two. Lou hovered around
the overgrown gravestones for a few minutes longer. When the
sense of duty finally kicked in, she left the churchyard and
made her way reluctantly down the alley.

Halfway down the road, a large car – a dark people carrier –
passed her and pulled up on the grass verge, in Stephen's parking
spot. The driver's door opened and a man got out. He looked at
their house and seemed to hesitate before walking slowly up the
path. He knocked on the door. Lou ducked behind a neighbour's
overgrown hedge. She could do without making pleasantries with
some stranger today. She peered around the leafless branches. The
man stepped back from the door and tipped his head to look at the
upstairs windows. Everything about him – the jeans and padded
jacket, the stubble, the close-cropped hair, greying at the temples –
reminded Lou of the plain-clothes police officers who had trooped
in and out of their home recently. Was this one making a house call
with news about the inquest? Lou slumped against the fence.

The front door opened, and Dean appeared carrying a
holdall. The man slipped his arm around Dean's shoulders, and
they walked together down the path. When they reached the

car, the man took the holdall and put it in the boot. Dean got in
the passenger side. Lou swallowed down her instinct to call out.
Dean seemed happy enough with this man, happier than he
would be at seeing her.

The car drove away, and Lou experienced a strange, unset-
tling sensation deep in her stomach. This man was clearly one
of Dean's sport coaches giving him a lift to training. Dean had
always been close to his coaches. But there was something about
this man that seemed more familiar than any of the coaches she
could remember meeting. Lou gave herself a mental slap. After
the events of the last few days, she could probably convince
herself that the postman delivering mail up the road was actually Prince William.

Emerging from behind the hedge, Lou leant against the
fence outside her house. She rolled a stone across the pavement
under the sole of her boot. With nobody home, there was no
rush to go inside. She'd only get cross if she saw the mess in the
kitchen again.

A strange hissing sound made her look up. In a garden
further along the road, a giant yellow and red inflatable began to
take shape, rising above the fence as a generator filled it with
compressed air. Within minutes, the giant Homer Simpson
bobbed on his tether.

Lou half-smiled. She couldn't see any character from *The
Simpsons* without being reminded of Stephen. As a kid, he
could watch that programme for hours. He'd even let her watch
it with him as long as she was quiet. One Christmas, he'd squirreled away enough pocket money to buy a decoration of Homer
Simpson, chugging on a festive can of beer. When he'd hung it
on the tree, their dad had joked, asking whether it was supposed
to be him as he took a swig from his own can. Dad had ruffled
Stephen's hair, making him smile. Stephen had always smiled
when he was around their dad; when Dad cheered him on at

junior football, when they were planning one of their all-day fishing trips to the canal.

Lou rolled the stone beneath her sole again. At least Stephen had those memories. For her, any happy memories of their father were confined exclusively to playing games when she was very small. As she had grown, her father's interest in her had waned. When Stephen talked about football, their dad pounced on the conversation. If she talked about school or asked for help with homework, his eyes glazed over, and he told her to ask her mum. 'It's only because you're a girl,' Mum had tried to explain when she helped Lou with her long division. 'Dads always spend more time with their boys.'

Lou's final memory of her dad was the morning he'd left for work with his Tupperware box of ham sandwiches, made by Mum, just like he always did. But that night his Ford Escort didn't pull up on the grass verge outside the house and the Tupperware box didn't appear on the draining board. It was a few weeks later that Lou spotted a familiar shape in the kitchen bin. She fished it out and showed it to Stephen, asking if he wanted it. He snatched it, threw it to the floor and stamped on it, smashing Homer Simpson and his beer can into tiny pieces.

Looking back, it was obvious that had been a sign of things to come. When their dad left, something inside Stephen snapped. Without a man around to keep him in check, and whenever their mum was out, he ruled the house any way he saw fit. Not that their father knew or cared. None of them had seen him since the day he left to set up home somewhere with the receptionist from the garage where he worked. They had a new family. Two kids, if Mum's friends who still kept tabs on him were to be believed. Lou didn't care. Even before he had become a stranger to their family, the man who sat across the kitchen table had become a distant figure in her life. Dean couldn't miss him either, as he'd never known him. But she'd never forgive him for what he had done to Stephen. And Mum.

Lou's phone buzzed. She pulled it from her pocket.

'Got her!' Will said.

'What? Are you sure?' She pushed down all thoughts of her father. He wasn't worth the space in her brain.

'Pretty sure,' Will said. 'Luckily for you, Goodwill is an unusual surname. There's only one Elizabeth Goodwill listed in the register of births in London in 1927. She would have been twelve in nineteen forty, so that puts her at the age you said. Her parents' surnames are listed, and I found the records of their marriage in 1919 and their deaths in 1940. They're recorded as fatalities in an air raid in Kensington. Does that sound about right?'

Lou pictured the mechanical birds bombing London. 'Yes,' she said, 'that sounds right.'

'Good. Well, not quite so good for them, but at least it means I'm barking up the right tree. After 1940, little Elizabeth's trail goes rather cold, no doubt because she was safely ensconced for the duration in the Northamptonshire countryside. I picked her up again in 1948 when an Elizabeth Goodwill married a Montague Elderman. Handily another unusual surname. As far as I can see, they lived in London and had two children. Nothing again for a few decades, but I found a record of a death ten years ago of a Montague Elderman. But nothing like that on Elizabeth, so I think she must still be with us.'

'Elizabeth's alive?'

'And living just a few miles away. When old Monty died, it seems Elizabeth upped sticks and moved to a village just down the road from here. I found her on the electoral role. Perhaps she moved here after husband died because she had happy memories of her time as an evacuee.'

Lou wedged the phone between her chin and shoulder and dug in her pocket for her pad and pencil. In her excitement, she dropped the pencil to the ground and stooped to collect it. 'Could I have her address?'

'Whoa there, tiger,' Will laughed. 'You might want to order up some birth, marriage and death certificates before you go knocking on her door. It's possible I might be barking up the wrong tree, after all.'

'Please, I'd like the address.' Will had found the right tree; she could feel it.

Almost reluctantly Will read it out. 'Are you planning on visiting her today? I could bunk off early. Give you some moral support.'

'No, it's fine. I'd rather go alone. But thank you. Thank you so much.' She began to run through the buses that would take her to the outlying villages and was already on her way towards the High Street when she realised Will was still talking.

'So, you know, after Christmas, we could meet up to go through everything I've found out about the Mandevilles and Caxtons.'

'Okay, if you'd like to.'

'Really? Brilliant. I'll book the carvery up the road. You know, because we'll need a table to spread out all of the papers.'

Oh crap. Had she unwittingly agreed to a date?

'When are you free next?'

Somehow, she had. 'I'll have to let you know. I'm a bit busy at the moment.'

'No problem. You know, whenever is cool.'

Lou imagined Will running his fingers through his floppy fringe, his cheeks pink.

'I'll phone you then. Bye, Will.'

'Okay. Speak soon, Louisa.'

Poor Will. If he had any idea what a disaster zone she was, he'd run for cover. She'd call him in the New Year to let him off the hook. And to thank him again for all his research.

After a few minutes' wait at the bus stop on the High Street, Lou boarded an almost empty bus. It took a route away from town, across the road bridge over the motorway, along the bypass and out into the open countryside. As it wound down small roads through villages, Lou relaxed back into the seat. She had never taken this bus before. Outings always involved heading in the opposite direction, towards the bright lights of Northampton.

Like a kid pressing her nose to a toyshop window, she watched the villages pass by. Each one was a version of the last, with quaint pubs, neat churches, and rows of cottages with puffs of smoke fluffing from their chimneys. This chocolate-box world was just a bus ride from her own life, yet she had never known it existed.

They reached a sign – *Please drive carefully through beautiful Buryton* – and Lou rang the bell. The bus deposited her at a picture-perfect village, just like all those she had passed through. She checked the address and found the house; a small, whitewashed cottage just off the village green, with a holly wreath on the front door.

Through the open curtains, she could see an old lady sitting in a high–backed armchair before a fire, a standard lamp behind her. On a small table lay a roll of wrapping paper and some children's toys. A board game. A wooden truck. The lady smiled as she folded the paper around the truck, sealing it with tape and pressing on a bow.

Could this be Mrs Hart's Elizabeth? What if it was? What could Lou possibly say to her? *Oh hi, I've travelled from the past to meet you. You know, the past you travelled back to when you were a kid. I think you were an evacuee from London in the Second World War and lived at Hill House for a few years. Fancy chatting about that?*

Lou backed away from the window, but it was too late. The old lady looked up. She leant forward and waved. Oh no! Who did this old woman think was lurking outside her house? A neighbour? A relative? Using the arms of the chair, the lady eased herself up and made her way slowly across the room.

Lou watched. She couldn't run away now. What to say . . . what to say . . .

The door opened and the lady looked up at her. 'Hello, dear,' she said and smiled.

'Mrs Elderman?' Lou said.

'Yes, dear. But you can call me Elizabeth. Come in then. I've been expecting you.'

She should back out now. Leave this old lady in peace. Before Lou could protest that she really wasn't expected and must be confused with someone else, Elizabeth fussed her through the door and into the living room. 'Sit yourself down and get warm by the fire. There's more coal in the scuttle if you need it. I'll pop the kettle on.'

Elizabeth helped Lou out of her parka and disappeared into the hall.

For reasons she couldn't fathom, Lou felt compelled to do what Elizabeth asked of her. She sat in the armchair on the other side of the fire and took in the details of the warm, homely room with its beams and low ceiling. A Christmas tree stood in the corner in a bucket decorated with pink crepe paper. Silver tinsel was draped around framed prints on the wall and photographs of babies, children, and weddings on the mantelshelf.

Elizabeth reappeared, pushing a trolley of jangling tea things. 'My son, Michael, gave me this last Christmas,' she said. 'It's a godsend for when I have visitors. I do like tea to be served properly, don't you?' She eased herself down into her armchair. She was so close to Lou that their knees almost touched. 'Sugar, Denise?'

Oh, no! 'Mrs Elderman, I'm really sorry. I think you might have mistaken me for someone else.'

With no outward sign of concern that there was a stranger in her house, Elizabeth continued to pour the tea. 'You're not Margaret's niece then? I did wonder where your bag was.'

'My bag?'

'Avon ladies usually carry their wares in a special bag, don't they? Come to think of it, I wasn't expecting Denise until next week. And Christmas Eve would be a strange time to call. But if you're not Margaret's niece, who are you?'

What could she say that wouldn't scare this too-trusting lady out of her wits? 'I'm a friend of a friend of yours. A very old friend, I think. I should probably have phoned before coming.'

'Oh, how lovely. Which friend? When you get to my age, you've lost so many that it's nice to get back in touch with any that are still around.'

Elizabeth picked up the cup and saucer. As she handed the tea to Lou, Lou said, 'I know her as Mrs Hart, but you might know her as Leonora. Leonora Mandeville.'

The cup and saucer began to shake, the spoon rattling against the teacup. Lou took it from Elizabeth and placed it back on the trolley. Elizabeth pulled a hankie from the sleeve of her sweater and held it to her face.

'I'm sorry,' Lou said. 'Would you like your tea?' She picked up Elizabeth's cup and saucer but put them back down when Elizabeth slowly shook her head.

Great job, Lou. She had rushed headlong into this meeting. If she had paused for even a second to consider how it would play out, she might have thought twice about barging in on this old lady and scaring her half to death. Lou looked up to find Elizabeth staring at her.

'I shouldn't have said anything,' Lou said. 'I shouldn't have come into your house upsetting—'

'I've waited so long,' Elizabeth said quietly. 'I knew, I just knew, that one day someone would come. And here you are.'

'I can leave if this is too painful for you.'

'Painful? It's not painful.' Elizabeth's face burst into a smile, taking Lou by surprise. She half-laughed, half-cried as she said, 'It's wonderful. It's a miracle. I've waited most of my life to meet somebody else who knows . . . Oh my dear, oh my Good Lord! For the longest time, I thought I might be quite insane. But here you are. Proof that I'm compos mentis after all. Unless we are sharing an hallucination.'

'It's a possibility,' Lou smiled, relieved that she hadn't given Elizabeth a heart attack.

Elizabeth took Lou's hands in hers. 'Where are my manners? I haven't even asked your name.'

'My name's Louisa Arnold.'

'Louisa Arnold,' Elizabeth said, trying the sound of it. 'What a pretty name. You can have no idea how wonderful it is to meet you, Louisa.' She gave Lou's hands a squeeze. 'Please, don't be coy. I can sense your reluctance. You need to understand that I've had a whole lifetime to come to terms with my experiences at Hill House. Nothing you say will shock me. I may be old, but I have a strong heart. I'm desperate to hear about Leo. Tell me, Louisa, how is she? And her family? Are they all well?'

'They were when I last saw them.'

'Which was when?'

'This morning.'

'This morning!' Elizabeth clapped her hands together. 'This calls for something a little more celebratory than tea.' She directed Lou to the dresser and a bottle of sherry. 'Would you mind, I'm as giddy as a kipper. I'm afraid I'd spill it.'

Lou got up, poured two glasses and handed one to Elizabeth.

'So,' Elizabeth said after taking a sip. 'Is Leo still a young woman? She must be married if you know her as Mrs? Does she have children?'

Did she? With a sense of shame, Lou realised how little she knew of Mrs Hart's life. 'She's widowed and has no children that I know of. But she does have a niece and two nephews who she adores and who adore her.'

'Oh, that's wonderful. Leo deserves to be loved. She has a huge heart. She welcomed me into her life so warmly.'

'She has never forgotten your friendship. That's why I'm here.' *Slowly Lou, take it carefully.* 'You see, Mrs Hart has no idea when or where I came from. But to help me understand my situation, she confided in me about you and the life you'd shared as children. She confessed that as a child she was some kind of vessel for Hill House.'

Elizabeth nodded. There was not even a hint of surprise.

'When you left,' Lou continued, 'a letter arrived to say you had married a major and moved to India. Mrs Hart – Leonora – found it hard to believe but had to accept it. She's always desperately wanted to know what became of you. She's been so kind to me that I thought the least I could do was try to find you.'

'Oh, my dear Louisa, I hate to think that Leo was pained by my departure. I never intended to leave Hill House, you know. It took me as much by surprise as my arrival had. Hill House had been my home for so many years and the Mandevilles had been so good to me. It was the place where I grew from a child into a young woman.' She looked hesitant for a moment, then said, 'But I'm sure you don't want to hear the ramblings of an old lady.'

'Oh, I do. Please go on,' Lou said.

Elizabeth took another sip of sherry. 'I was lost, you see, when I arrived. The Mandevilles welcomed me into their home with such warmth and kindness. My entire family – my parents and grandparents – had been killed in an air raid. Our beautiful home, on a square in Kensington, was reduced to a pile of rubble. I only survived because I had been spending the night at a friend's house. My older brother was an RAF pilot and my parents had received news only the week before that his aeroplane had gone down in the Channel and he was missing. It was a terrible time. A terrible time.' Elizabeth shook her head. Lou encouraged her to take a sip of sherry.

'I was twelve years old and all alone in the world. A sad little orphan girl. With no family to look after me, I became the responsibility of the authorities and they put me on a train from Euston to the countryside. The carriages were full of children wailing for their mothers. It was pitiful. After many hours, we arrived at a station and were taken to a church hall where families chose which of us to take in. I was so dreadfully upset and angry. I didn't want to be selected by somebody I didn't know. I'm sure they were all kind and well meaning, but I wanted none of it. So, I slipped away when nobody was looking. I had no idea where I was going, but just outside the church was a set of gates to a house. I ran up the drive, hoping to escape before my absence was noticed. I looked through the windows of the house and found all of the rooms quite empty. What little furniture remained was covered by dustsheets. The house was clearly deserted. I decided then and there that I would set up home in that abandoned place. I was a resilient little spirit and resolved to fend for myself. I explored the grounds to see whether I might catch a trout in the lake for supper. I don't know how I thought I would catch anything with no rod or line! When I arrived back at the house empty-handed, I went in search of an unlocked window to slip through. I hoped I might find a forgotten jar of jam or tin of sardines inside. I was astonished when the front door opened, and a butler appeared. He insisted I come inside. There were fires in the grates, furniture in every room and not a dustsheet in sight. A lovely lady introduced herself as Lady Mandeville. She said they had been expecting me and that I was a distant relative. But I knew that couldn't possibly be true. They were so different to anyone I had ever known, their clothes and hair, everything about them. When I was introduced to Lady Mandeville's daughter, Leonora, she promised that we would be the very best of friends. I was in a dream. But it was one I never wanted to wake up from. You see, I had nothing to go back for. After a few days, I began to think that this was what happened to children who lost their family, they were allowed to choose the life they wanted to go to. Even so, I knew that I shouldn't talk about my previous life, that it was somehow forbidden. Soon, days in Hill House turned to weeks, weeks to months and months to years. I was so very happy there with the Mandevilles and Leo. I could come and go as I pleased from the house and always remained in that wonderful Victorian world. Soon it was my old life that began to feel like a dream. I never forgot it, but I was able to distance myself from the horrible memories. I was educated with Leo, and we shared our lives, our thoughts, our hopes, our dreams. I'm afraid I rather turned Leo's head. We planned that we would go to university together. If men could, why shouldn't we? I had been raised to believe that I was the equal of any man. My mother and father were intellectuals and rather revolutionary in their thinking and my grandmother had been a campaigner for universal suffrage. The beliefs my real family instilled in me never left.'

Elizabeth paused. She looked into the fire and then back to Lou. Lou felt no need to speak, enthralled as she was by Elizabeth's story.

'I always knew Leo was somehow the key to my being at Hill House, but I also knew that I wasn't supposed to say anything to her about my life before. After I had been there for a few years, she began to talk in her sleep. The first time I heard her, I was afraid she was ill. I soon learned to listen to what she had to say. She told me things about Hill House. How I was chosen. After my sixteenth birthday, she began to say other things, alarming things. She told me that I should prepare myself and that I had to go home. As far as I was concerned, I was home. The messages went on for weeks and I tried to convince myself that they didn't mean anything. Finally, I was so disturbed that I decided to ask Leo directly whether she knew she had been talking in her sleep. At the same time, I confided in her about the death of my family. She said that we mustn't talk about it in earshot of the house. She was right, we shouldn't have talked so openly . . .'

'You don't have to continue—'

Elizabeth held up her hand. 'I must. It's just that this is the first time I've talked about any of this.' Elizabeth took a deep breath. 'Where was I? Oh, yes, I remember. One day, soon after I confided in Leo about my previous life, I went to the village to choose a gift for Lady Mandeville's birthday. It was a trip I had made many times before. But that day, when I returned to Hill House, the grounds were full of men. I couldn't believe my eyes. They were soldiers. Canadian soldiers. Playing croquet and sitting in wheelchairs on the lawn, smoking cigarettes. There were cars on the driveway and the men listened to a wireless. I was no longer in the Victorian times. I dropped my parcel and ran inside the house. A woman in a nurse's uniform stopped me and asked whether I was a visitor. I pushed past her and ran up to the room I shared with Leo. Only it wasn't our room any longer, it was the bedroom of two officers, who were somewhat surprised at my bursting in on them and rather shocked when I became hysterical. They called for help and two nurses escorted me to another room where they sat me on the bed. The vicar from St Mary's was in the house and came to speak to me. He had been holding a service for the men too infirm to attend church. He asked my name, and I was just able to give it before I started screaming again and a doctor was called to sedate me. When I woke, many hours had passed. It was dark and I thought I was back in my room until a man sitting beside the bed took my hand and spoke to me. He said he was my brother, Frank. I thought I was dreaming again, that I had lost the ability to distinguish between reality and fantasy. Frank was so kind and gentle. He explained that after his aeroplane crashed into the sea he had been picked up by a German ship and was a prisoner for most of the war. After the Red Cross secured his release, he began to look for me and had just that day arrived at the place I had been sent to as an evacuee and was last known to have been.'

'Which was St Mary's church.'

Elizabeth nodded. 'I was in such a state, torn between joy at finding my brother and the devastation of leaving the Mandevilles, that I had some sort of breakdown and was admitted to a hospital in London. When the doctors pressed me as to where I had been for five years, I said that I couldn't remember. After a few weeks, they stopped asking and let me go, putting my loss of memory down to the shock of the air raid and the return of my brother. There were so many genuinely ill and wounded people, and in every respect, I was healthy, so there was little point in my taking up a hospital bed. I went to live with Frank in his small flat in Pimlico. But Louisa, the world I returned to was foreign to me. It was a world of cars and cinemas and radio and jazz music and aeroplanes. Everyone was rightly happy that the war had ended, but for me it was still raging. I had lost everything I knew – Hill House, the Mandevilles, Leo – but what right had I to be sad when my brother had been returned to me? Frank was all that kept me sane. He was a wonderful brother and we helped each other adjust to the new lives we found ourselves thrust into. I never asked him about his time in captivity and he never asked about my disappearance. It was easier to live in the present than the painful past.'

Tears began to spill from Elizabeth's eyes. Putting her glass aside, she wiped them with her handkerchief.

'You really don't have to continue,' Lou said.

'I'm old, Louisa. If I don't tell of it now, I might never get the chance.' The earlier vigour in Elizabeth's voice had faded to a whisper. She held up her empty glass. 'Perhaps another splash will perk me up.'

Lou collected the sherry from the dresser, poured a large measure into Elizabeth's glass, and left the bottle on the tea trolley.

'So, Leo received a letter saying that I had married a major?' Elizabeth said. 'Well, that wasn't far from the truth. Soon after I moved into Frank's flat, an old RAF pal of his came to visit. Monty. He was a lovely man. Impeccable manners. And he had a rather dashing moustache.' Elizabeth smiled. She took a sip of sherry and brightened a little. 'He was old-fashioned in his ways, and I found that reassuring. Throughout our courtship, he was so kind and so very patient with me. He made me feel safe and loved. When he proposed, I knew that he would make a wonderful husband. Six months after we married, Monty secured a position in the diplomatic service, and we relocated to India where he was posted. We travelled the world and had our two sons, Michael and David. Wherever we went, I worked with the local Red Cross, helping mothers and their babies. I like to think that I was able to make a difference. When Monty retired, we returned to London. I never forgot Hill House, but while Monty was alive, I didn't visit. I felt it would have been a betrayal; as though my old life meant more than the life we had created together. But when he died ten years ago, I moved here. My sons had spread their wings and I wanted to return to a familiar place. This village was once part of the Hill House Estate, and I remembered it from my other life. I revisited Hill House itself just once. It was so upsetting to see the disrepair it had fallen into. It wasn't the house I remembered at all. I decided then that I wouldn't delve into what had happened to the Mandevilles and Hill House. Call me a sentimental old woman, but even now I prefer to remember them as they were. I can't bear to think of anything bad having happened to them. It was enough to know that I had returned to live close to the place I had always considered home.'

Elizabeth wiped her eyes again and Lou decided against filling her in on any details. It would only distress her.

'Listen to me,' Elizabeth fussed. 'I've been going on and haven't asked you a thing about your experience. How long have you been at Hill House, Louisa? What date is it there now?'

'Christmas 1913. I first went in last week and I've been in and out a few times. The time seems to move at the same pace there as it does here.'

'You're free to come and go across the times as you please? Oh, Louisa, you are truly blessed. When I crossed back to my own time the door to the past closed behind me forever.'

'I suppose Hill House has its reasons for what it allows,' Lou said.

'And are you enjoying your time there?'

Lou tried to hide a smile. 'Yes. It is wonderful.'

'I know what you're thinking, Louisa, I recognise that look,' Elizabeth said. 'You're wondering why you have been chosen above all others. Why it is you who has been given this gift. Do you think I haven't asked myself that question every day for the last seventy years?' She placed her glass on the table. 'I've had enough time to develop a theory, if you'd like to hear it.'

'Please.'

'May I ask you a question?'

Lou nodded.

'Have you recently experienced a tragedy so great that you feel you can't go on living? A tragedy that has shaken you and your beliefs to the very core?'

Lou hesitated before nodding again.

Elizabeth clasped her hands. 'I'm almost ashamed to admit it, but the day I ran away from the church hall, I considered filling my pockets with stones and wading out into the centre of the lake. Imagine a child so without hope. Hill House took me in when I needed it to. Do you see Louisa, Hill House saved me. It engineered my arrival and my departure. I can't explain why or how. All I know is it did. I have come to understand that the pain I suffered on my departure was the price I had to pay. I had to sacrifice something for the life that had been returned to me. That sacrifice was the loss of the best friend I ever had. But it was a price worth paying for the wonderful life that I have lived since. I married a man I loved, I travelled, I have children and grandchildren, even great-grandchildren. And I'll spend Christmas Day with all of them tomorrow.' Her eyes fell on the wrapped parcel on the table, then she pointed to the photographs on the mantelshelf; images of children in school uniform, babies, large family gatherings and a black and white photograph of a bride standing beside a man with a huge moustache.

'I'm so glad,' Lou said. 'Really I am.'

'But you think nothing good will come to you. I can see it in your eyes,' Elizabeth said softly.

'I don't know . . .'

Elizabeth took hold of Lou's hands. 'Be patient, Louisa.'

Lou glanced at the clock on the chimneybreast. It was three o'clock.

'I've kept you talking too long,' Elizabeth said. 'Will you return to 1913 now? Tell me, does the tradition of the Christmas Eve Ball live on?'

'It does.'

'Oh, Louisa, what a treat you are in for. Drink it all in, savour every experience Hill House has to offer. When the time comes to leave, let it be with a full heart for the experience you have had. Promise me you will.'

Lou smiled. 'I'll try.'

'Good.' Elizabeth gave Lou's hands a final squeeze before releasing them. 'Now, how are you getting back to town?'

Lou looked at her watch. 'There's a bus in ten minutes.'

'Then you must leave. But before you go, I have something to show you.' Elizabeth eased out of her chair, crossed the room and took a box from a cupboard in the dresser. She removed the lid and with great care, handed it to Lou.

'I kept them all this time,' Elizabeth said, stroking the threadbare stomach of a little teddy bear with one button eye and a nose rubbed bald. It was nestled beside a small scent bottle and a pale brown luggage tag bearing the words 'Elizabeth Goodwill' in pencil so faded it looked like the ghost of a name. 'When I arrived at Frank's flat, I found them in my handbag. I had no idea how they got there. I hadn't seen my teddy bear or tag since the day I arrived at Hill House. The scent was the gift I had chosen for Lady Mandeville that final day.'

'You managed to take things with you?' Lou said. 'I lose everything when I go back and forth.'

Elizabeth's eyes glittered when she said, 'Hill House has its own rules that are beyond anything we can understand. It works its magic and shows us that what we consider to be impossible can happen every day. While we're not watching, marvellous, inexplicable things are at work. We – you and me – are living proof that miracles can happen.' Elizabeth closed the lid and returned the box to the dresser. She paused with her back to Lou, then turned to face her once more. 'I probably shouldn't ask this, I imagine it's breaking every rule, but if the opportunity arises, would you tell Leo that I have lived a good life. Reassure her. Let her know that every day I count my blessings that she was – is – the best friend I have ever had.'

TWENTY-SEVEN

All the way back to town on the bus, on the short walk from the High Street, and past St Mary's, Lou felt like a tiny rowing boat buffeted on a wide and endless ocean. Each piece of information, each fact she had learned that afternoon and over the last few days, became waves crashing over her bows.

Almost without noticing, Lou passed through the gates. Blinding snow whipped about her like ocean foam. Through the confusion of darkness and whiteout, soft smudges of colourful light glowed. Lady Mandeville's Chinese lanterns. By their dim light, Lou wove an unsteady path up the drive. She pulled at the lapels of her coat and put her head down. Halfway up the drive and through the eerie quiet of the snow, a different sound came out of the darkness. Lou imagined it was the wind whistling through the branches of the trees in the woods. Its volume rose.

Louisa. Louisa!

It couldn't be . . . She tried to see through the blizzard. Surely nobody would have ventured out of the house on foot in this storm. It was too early for any guests to have arrived. In any case, no guest would know her name.

Louisa. Louisa!

There it was again! She stopped and strained to hear.

We need you. We trust you!

She spun around. Her mind was playing tricks on her. There was nobody and nothing apart from the dense white of the snow and the smudges of light.

Lou entered the house through the conservatory and, trailing melting snow, she made her way through the billiard room. If she could get back to her room unnoticed, she might just be able to get a grip on her thoughts.

Out in the hall, the maids were so busy hurrying this way and that with trays of crockery and cutlery that they barely had time to dip a curtsey. Lou slipped past a footman bearing a tray of glasses and made her way up the stairs with minimal fuss. She managed to get halfway along the landing when a door she was passing opened, and a maid flew out with a dress over her arm. Before the maid could close the door behind her, a voice called from within.

'Louisa. Come in, do.'

The maid disappeared, leaving Lou before the gaping door of Emma's bedroom.

'I'm sure you're busy getting ready,' Lou said.

'Nonsense.' Emma was seated at the dressing table and spoke to Lou's reflection in the mirror. 'Fielding has gone to stitch the hem of my dress. Come and entertain me for a few minutes. You can spare that for me, can't you?'

Lou checked along the corridor before stepping inside and closing the door behind her. This guest room was similar to hers but the feel of it was very different. Any number of dresses hung from the open wardrobe doors, while accessories for each had been laid out on the bed – gloves, necklaces, headbands and feathers. There wasn't an inch of space on the dressing table between bottles and jars and potions and lotions.

Amidst this chaos sat Emma, surveying her face in the mirror, tweaking the corners of her eyes as though to tease out non-existent wrinkles. Her hair, not yet dressed, hung in a long, dark coil down her back. 'My lord, where the devil have you been?' she laughed. 'You look as though you've been dragged through the proverbial hedge!'

Looking past Emma, Lou saw her own reflection; bedraggled hair, brown overcoat, heavy boots and skirt, all so ugly in this room of sequins, powder puffs and feathers. 'I went for a walk,' she said to her feet.

'In this awful weather? What a funny thing you are. Sit down, won't you?'

Lou lowered herself awkwardly on to the chaise beside the dressing table, her legs too long to sit comfortably on the seat too close to the floor. Emma took a cigarette from a box on the dressing table. She offered Lou the box, but she shook her head.

'What a stroke of luck you passing-by like that,' Emma said, biting the end of the cigarette. With a click, she lit the tip from the flame of a large crystal desk lighter and blew a stream of smoke towards the ceiling. 'I've been hoping to bump into you to see how you've got on with the little challenge I set you.'

'Challenge?' Lou echoed.

'Don't tell me you've forgotten.'

'I'm sorry?'

Emma frowned in irritation. 'The little matter of a man called Tom?'

Lou's boat, already rocking wildly, hit a wave as hard as a wall. Abandoning the oars, she gripped the sides, desperately fighting the surge threatening to tip her overboard.

'Well?'

'Well, what?'

'What on Earth has happened to you, Louisa? Has the walk outside frozen your mind? I thought women like you were always as sharp as a needle.'

Lou's eyes snapped to Emma's face. *Women like you.* What was that supposed to mean? Was Emma trying to belittle her, dressing up her dressing down as friendship? If she was, then it was the kind of friendship a little boy might have with a spider, just before pulling off its legs. Christ, she had even made her sit on a low seat so she could look down on her.

'Louisa?' Emma said, grinding out the cigarette in an ashtray, 'are you all right?'

'I'm fine. Thank you.'

'Well, you don't look it. Are you ill? Aunt Leo said you've been a bit under the weather. I'll ring for some hot beef tea. My nanny used to swear by it when—'

'I said I'm fine.'

'Oh, I see.' Emma turned her back on Lou. 'There's no call to stay on my account. At any rate, Fielding will be back soon with my dress.' She picked up the puff and slammed it against her chest, unleashing a dense shower of powder. Lou saw something unfamiliar in Emma's eyes in the mirror as she tried to avoid looking at her own reflection. It was a sadness, a softness almost. Beneath the devil-may-care attitude, the poise and performance, Emma was just a woman in love with a man. A woman who had been counting on Lou to scatter rose petals across the path to her beau.

A bag of rocks sank in Lou's stomach, cutting her insides on the way down. Her feelings for that man – Emma's man – ran as deep as if their roots had been planted in soil for a lifetime. But this was Emma's reality, not hers. One day soon she would leave. This bashing of heads was a waste of time and energy. Even if this were her reality, Tom would choose the woman at the dressing table, angrily rearranging the coil of her hair.

'You should hit me over the head with that enormous lighter of yours.'

'I beg your pardon?' Emma said.

'It might knock some sense into me.'

Emma turned to face Lou. A wicked grin played on her lips. 'Do you know, I really like you, Louisa. You're so different from the run-of-the-mill women one finds out here in the sticks. And the boring ones in Town. There's something about you. Something I can't quite put my finger on. Not many women have the wherewithal to stand up to me. We might be friends, you and I. So come on then,' Emma leant forward in anticipation, 'tell me all. I've seen you and Tom huddled in corners. Were you speaking about me? Tell me you were.'

'We were . . . we have . . . on more than one occasion.'

'And what did you say?'

'I told him he should marry you.'

'As bluntly as that!'

'Perhaps not quite.'

'Tell me *exactly* what you said.'

'I can't really remember.'

'Try. I must know what hand I am playing with him.'

'I suggested that a marriage between two great families would be good for the Mandevilles.'

'And what did Tom say?'

Lou wouldn't put words in Tom's mouth that he might be held to. But neither did she have to quote him verbatim. 'He said that he would only marry for love.'

'And?'

'And what?'

'My God, Louisa. It's like getting blood from a stone! *And . . . did he say that he loves me?'

'Not in so many words.'

'Oh.' Emma slumped back in her chair.

'But he was receptive to the prospect of love,' Lou said. 'He knows that a good marriage will help his family. He's well aware of the obligations that his position and title brings.'

Emma looked thoughtful. 'I'd say that's progress,' she said. 'If he understands that, then he must realise that there are not many – if any – other women in our circle who would afford him the position that I could. Anything else?'

He asked me whether I thought he should marry you and I didn't answer. 'No, nothing.'

'But he was receptive, which is good. Oh, Louisa. You can't know how happy you've made me. Tonight feels like the night. I'm sure something will happen. And if it does, then it's in no small part thanks to you.'

TWENTY-EIGHT

In her bath, neck deep in warm water, Lou finally had the time to stop and think. She pressed her big toe to the tap. It was time to formulate a plan.

Elliot had provided tangible evidence of George's gambling activities and debts, including the lies he had told the loan sharks in Northampton. There had to be a crime in there somewhere – securing money by false pretences, forging documents about a fictitious company. In many ways, it was better than the accusation that George was involved in Riley's death. That sounded awful, but it was true. If she accused him, it would be her word against his. Whereas Elliot's statement was proof and there was a willing witness to back it up. But now that she had the evidence at her fingertips, what should she do with it? She could present it to Lord Caxton. But what would happen then? Would he throw his son on the mercy of the loan sharks? Or would he close ranks to protect the family name?

Lou took up a sponge, heavy with water, and held it over her head. Squeezing it, she allowed the warm water to run down her face. What if the revelation of George's debts did Charlotte more harm than good? It was entirely possible that in a bid to see his son settled, Lord Caxton might take a pitchfork and force George and Charlotte up the aisle.

And what of Elizabeth Goodwill? She had burst in on that poor woman, frightening her half to death and for what? She couldn't tell Mrs Hart that her old friend missed her; Mrs Hart had been very specific in her instruction that Lou was not to reveal any details about her own time. At least her promise to Elizabeth had been a half promise, unlike her promise to Emma. That had been a full-blown promise to help her marry. Yet she had lied to Emma about Tom's feelings.

Tom. In response to his name, a charge ran through Lou's body.

She balled her hands into fists and brought them crashing down into the water. 'You shouldn't have brought me here,' she said to the marbled walls. 'I can't help anyone. I don't know what to do. I'm going to muck it up.'

The water had cooled. She shivered and pulled her knees to her chest. The pipes in the walls began to gurgle. She watched as the hot tap slowly turned and water gushed out, warming her from the feet up. First the voices outside, and now the tap turning in response to her thoughts. . . Nothing about Hill House could surprise her anymore.

The prospect of being primped for a party was as appealing as being thrown into sackcloth and ashes and paraded through a street lined by a baying mob. Even so, when Sally arrived, Lou sat obediently at the dressing table.

'Are you happy in your work?' Lou asked. It was an attempt to direct her thoughts to something – anything – other than her non-existent 'plan'.

Sally pushed a pin into her hair, securing a coil in place. 'Happy? I can't say I've ever given it much thought. I suppose I am. At any rate, I'd much rather be working than sitting idle at home every day. Not that I'd get much chance of that with Albert under my feet.'

Lou smiled. It was impossible not to smile whenever she thought of those blonde curls and that button nose. 'But if you could have any job – any job in the whole world – what would it be?'

She watched Sally in the mirror. Sally pinched another strand of hair and held it out in a straight line, the tip of her tongue poking from between her lips as she twisted the strand and gave the question serious thought. 'I suppose I'd like to do this all of the time. Doing hair, being around nice clothes, putting powder and rouge on ladies' faces, sewing on the odd loose button or stitching up a hem. Now that would suit me down to the ground.' She laughed. 'But I might as well wish to fly to the moon as to become a lady's maid. It'll be back to cleaning windows and scrubbing the hall floor for me when you go home. A housemaid is what I am, and a housemaid is what I'm likely to stay.'

A light bulb flashed on in Lou's mind. Perhaps she shouldn't. Oh, what the hell. 'Sally, I'd like you to go to town on me tonight.'

'Go to what?' Sally asked, her expression a blank.

'Push the boat out, you know, make a meal of me. Show everybody at the party your genius in transforming a sow's ear into a silk purse. You never know who might be there and be in need of a new lady's maid.'

'Oh, Miss,' Sally chuckled. 'The things you say. In any case, it's a pleasure to get you ready for any evening. You're so obliging. And you're naturally very pretty. You don't need half the make-up that some ladies do.'

'Stop it,' Lou laughed. 'You'll have me blushing. And I mean it. Tonight, I am in your hands entirely. Do with me what you will.'

Sally stood back, assessing Lou's reflection like a florist

sizing up a mound of freshly cut buds. A smile spread across her face. 'Very well, I will.'

Sally had Lou turn away from the mirror so she couldn't see her work in progress. With much teasing and fussing, she finished Lou's hair before setting about her make up. It involved so much powder, rouge and kohl, that Lou began to wonder whether this had been such a good idea after all and whether, when she next looked in the mirror, she might see Coco the Clown staring back.

When the makeup was done, Sally dressed Lou. She paid particular attention to tying the laces of the corset as tight as she could; so tight that Lou had to hold on to the bedframe to allow Sally to dig her knee into her back to get purchase.

After much pulling and preening, Sally decided that Lou was ready. As she secured the clasp of a necklace around Lou's neck, there was a knock at the door.

'Come in,' Lou called.

The door opened and Charlotte rushed in. She came to a dramatic stop. 'Oh, Louisa!' she exclaimed. 'Just look at you.'

Lou performed a twirl. 'Am I presentable?'

'Presentable! You look like a princess. Doesn't Miss Arnold look like a princess, Sally?'

'She certainly does, Miss Charlotte.'

Lou turned to look at her reflection to see what all the fuss was about. A breath caught in her chest. She touched her hair, which was pulled back from her face, a tendril curling at each temple. Her complexion was clean and fresh with a tasteful hint of colour on her eyes and cheeks. And the dress . . . oh, the dress! The bodice sat high up on her waist and a round neckline dropped to her cleavage. A string of pearls sat in the dip where her collarbones met. She twisted from side to side, watching the silk of the darkest, midnight blue flow like water, circling her hips and legs. 'It's a miracle. I look . . .'

'Beautiful!' Charlotte said. 'Sally, I insist that you help *me* dress for Christmas lunch tomorrow too. I had no idea you had such skills. Where have you been hiding them all this time?'

Sally blushed and Lou smiled. Perhaps her meddling didn't always have to end in complete failure.

After helping Lou pull on her long evening gloves, Sally took her leave. The instant she left, Charlotte dragged Lou to the window seat, reminding her of the promise she had made to watch the arrival of the guests together. They sat half facing each other, their bodies twisted to look out of the window.

The snowstorm had subsided, leaving behind a velvet black sky, the stars speckles of white. Headlights of cars snaking up the drive shone on the snow, and the coloured lanterns glowed like fairy lights. William and the second footman, dressed in livery of impeccable blue and gold, stepped from beneath the portico at regular intervals to hold open car doors for men in tails and women draped in furs. Charlotte knew each of the guests by name.

'Isn't it splendid?' she said, pressing her nose to the window, her breath clouding the glass.

Lou studied an old woman decorated with feathers and dripping in so many jewels that they seemed to be weighing her down. 'I've never seen a show quite liked it.'

'Mama would be pleased to hear you say so. Oh look!' Charlotte rubbed the condensation from the window and pointed to a family just arrived. 'It's Melinda Forbes! Her father is a magistrate. We used to play together when we were small. How grown up she looks tonight. I do believe she is wearing her grandmother's tiara!' In an instant, Charlotte's giddy mood evaporated. She slumped back, folding her arms across her chest.

'What's wrong?' Lou asked.

'Nothing,' Charlotte sighed. But in the same breath she added, 'I sometimes think my family will never allow me to grow up.'

Lou looked at Charlotte's face. She was so young and so beautiful, with her whole life to look forward to. Unless George Caxton had his way. *Tread carefully, Lou. Don't scare her.* 'Charlotte, do you really want to go to university? I mean really.'

'More than anything. But it's hopeless isn't it, when my family are so against it? Except for Aunt Leonora, of course.'

'You do know I would do anything to help your cause, don't you?'

Charlotte smiled. It wasn't the usual smile that lit her whole face, but a resigned, sad sort of smile. 'Thank you, Louisa. But I'm afraid that my father will never be convinced. Oh, blast it.' Her hands dropped to her lap. 'Why can't they see I'm no longer the little girl who used to sit up here and watch the guests arrive as I was too young to go down to the party? If I try to join in conversations about politics or suffrage, they look at me as though it's a passing fancy. But why shouldn't I do something useful with my life? I think I'd make a jolly good doctor or solicitor or teacher. My brain works just as well as any man's, doesn't it? Not that you would know that if you spoke to my mother. If she has her way, by this time next year I shall be married off to some starchy military man or a boring prig of a country oaf who will have me tied to his dusty old house, producing a whole herd of babies, like a heifer. If that happens, I shall die, I know I shall.'

An icy blast travelled down Lou's spine. 'Don't you ever stop fighting, Charlotte. Keep shouting. Make them hear you.'

'But I'm just so tired of it all, Louisa. When do you get to the point of saying, *that's it, enough, I give in?*'

Lou took Charlotte by the shoulders. 'Never! Not while there is breath in your body.'

Charlotte's face broke into a broad grin. 'Oh, Louisa, you are so different to anybody I've ever known. When I'm with you I believe that my dreams really could come true.'

'Good. Because they can. They will. You just have to believe in yourself.'

Charlotte flung her arms around Lou's neck. 'I know this will sound perfectly silly since you've been here less than a week. But truly, I love you as though you were my own sister.' She kissed Lou on the cheek.

'If I ever had a sister, I'd want her to be exactly like you,' Lou said. 'Now come on, let's get you to the party.'

As they made their way down the corridor, Charlotte picked up her pace, dragging Lou with her.

Lou freed her hand. 'You go ahead. I'll catch up.'

'If you insist, but don't be long. The bubbles in the champagne will pop and there's nothing more upsetting than flat champagne.'

Charlotte ran towards the landing, the long sash of her pink dress trailing behind her. By contrast, Lou took her time, running her hand along the wooden banisters. She approached the landing and a bubble of voices and music floated up from the hall below. Down there, amongst friends and extended family, was every member of the Mandeville and Caxton clan. Lou gripped the banisters. As she backed away from the top of the stairs, the hidden door on the landing opened. A face appeared, looking furtively around.

'Oh, m'lady,' Mary said. 'I was hoping to find you still up here.' She beckoned and Lou was only too happy to join her behind the door in the cramped space midway up the twisting flight of stone steps. Mary leant over the handrail, looking first up, then down. 'Monsieur Gotti will skin me alive if he realises I'm missing,' she whispered. 'But I had to come and tell you something right away.'

'I don't want you to get into trouble on my account.'

Mary pressed her finger to her lips. 'Noise travels down these stairs, m'lady.' She leant against the wall. Lou joined her, the wall cold against her bare arm. 'You remember I told you about Bertha, the maid from Caxton Hall who's sharing my room?' Mary said quietly.

Lou nodded.

'Well, last night I asked if she knew anything about why Mr Caxton might not like the Mandevilles. She went quiet, all of a sudden like and said she knew nothing and then . . .' Mary peered over the handrail again. 'Then this morning, when I was peeling potatoes, she asked me to come and help her with something in the larder. Only she didn't want help, she was bursting to tell me something she did know after all. It seems Bertha's uncle was the under butler at Caxton Hall when Mr Caxton was still a boy – still Master George – and there was an *incident*. Bertha's uncle said that Miss Emma had a kitten that she adored but which Master George didn't care for. When he thought nobody was watching he'd poke it with a stick and pull its whiskers. This *incident* happened when Captain Mandeville – Master Thomas, as he was then – was staying at Caxton Hall for a few days on his holiday from school. Apparently Master George used to follow Master Thomas everywhere, like a shadow, showing off. Always desperate to impress his older cousin, he was.'

Mary moved in closer and lowered her voice still further. 'When the kitten went missing, Miss Emma cried and cried. Lord Caxton had the servants hunt the house and grounds for it. But they couldn't find hide nor hair of the poor thing. Then, a few days later, Master George took Master Thomas down to the lake. He pulled out a sack weighed down by stones and what do you think was inside?' She paused, her voice taking on a tone of horror. 'It was Miss Emma's kitten! It had scratched Master George and he was so angry that he drowned the poor thing. Bertha's uncle said that Master George showed it off to Master Thomas thinking he'd be impressed. Only he wasn't. Like any right-minded person would, Master Thomas went directly to his uncle and told him what Master George had done. Lord

Caxton was furious. He took his riding crop to Master George and told him that he was ashamed to call him his son. He said if Master George dared breathe a word of how that kitten died to anybody, especially Miss Emma, he would take him out on to the lawn and flog him for the entire household to witness. Soon after that, Lord Caxton sent Master George away to a very strict school in Ireland.'

Mary looked at Lou, her wide eyes full of anticipation. Lou didn't say a word.

'Did I do wrong in coming to tell you this, m'lady? Mr Caxton is my better after all—'

'No, Mary!' Lou snapped. 'That *man* is not your equal, never mind your better. You did absolutely the right thing in coming to tell me.'

'I'm so glad. I wanted it to be my way of showing how much my family appreciates what you've done for us. Father got a good price for all of those lovely things and the medicine has made mother much better.'

'You don't need to thank me,' Lou said. 'I'm happy for your family. Go on, you'd better go back to the kitchen before you're missed.'

Mary curtseyed. 'Thank you, m'lady. And Merry Christmas to you.'

TWENTY-NINE

With Mary's footsteps echoing down the stone stairs, Lou retreated to the carpeted landing. Closing the door behind her, she leant against the wall. A normal little boy might try to impress a playmate by jumping off a wall or climbing a tall tree. A normal little boy wouldn't kill his sister's pet and parade it as a prize.

A phrase raced around Lou's head – *show me the boy and I will show you the man*. Was it really possible that in revealing his cousin's awful act to Lord Caxton, Tom had set in motion the downward spiral of George's relationship with his father? And in doing the honourable thing, had Tom fired the starter's pistol on George's vendetta against the Mandevilles? Surely no right-minded person would drag a childhood slight into adulthood, using it as a reason to kill and destroy. Could George be a sociopath? A psychopath? Whatever twisted reality he inhabited, in his mind Tom had betrayed him and therefore must be made to pay.

In a fog of confusion, Lou descended into the cacophony of the party. The hall was so full of people that there was hardly space to move. Bainbridge stood at the front door, announcing the arrival of guests who Sir Charles and Lady Mandeville greeted. Maids in black dresses and crisply starched aprons waited to take coats and hats to the small cloakroom off the vestibule. Guests circulated, moving from room to room, as maids and footmen in their fine livery, squeezed between them with trays of food and drinks.

'Louisa!'

Charlotte stood on tiptoe in the doorway of the ballroom, beckoning. Lou eased through the throng. If she could, she would form a human shield around that girl to protect her. Charlotte grabbed her hand, pulling her into the ballroom. 'Look!' she exclaimed. 'Isn't it wonderful!'

Lou's mouth fell open. High above the couples packing the dance floor, waiting for the music to begin again, candles blazed in the chandeliers. Light caught in the crystal pendants and sparkled in the mirrors lining the walls. The blue curtains at each of the four tall doors leading out to the garden were decorated with lengths of crystal pendants threaded together, giving the illusion of icicles and, at the far end of the room, the musicians sat before a backdrop painted to resemble a palace of ice. The ballroom was barely recognisable as the cold, empty room Lou had first seen a few days ago.

'Isn't it marvellous?' Charlotte shouted to make her voice heard as the musicians struck up a tune. 'Mama has outdone herself this year! Wait until you see the dining room. Monsieur Gotti has created a swan from ice and there are ice creams in the shape of fruit – pineapples and peaches and . . . oh, what else was it, Melinda?' she asked a long-faced, horsey-looking girl in a peach meringue confection of a dress.

'I believe Colonel Hampton said they are called *guavas*,' the girl answered.

'That's it. Guavas!' Charlotte laughed. 'Louisa, this is Melinda Forbes. Melinda, this is Louisa Arnold, my newest but very dearest friend.'

Lou had hardly said hello when a swarm of young men descended on Charlotte and Melinda, desperate to scrawl their names on the dance cards secured with blue ribbons around their wrists. *Please won't one of you lovely young men sweep Charlotte off her feet. Elope with her tonight. Get her far away from here as quickly as possible.*

Worried that her presence might have the dampening effect of a chaperone, Lou made her way back out into the hall. The heat from the fires and so many bodies was starting to make her cheeks flush. In the mirror over the mantelpiece, she caught a glimpse of her reflection. In the fine dress with jewels and perfect hair and makeup, she hardly recognised herself. Surely with so many people here, nobody would notice if she slipped away. She looked towards the stairs but sensed someone behind her.

'Good evening, Lou.'

She closed her eyes, steeling herself, and then she turned to face the owner of the voice. She was momentarily struck dumb by the sight of him dressed in tails, a perfect white bow tie at his collar, his hair neatly slicked to one side.

'I haven't seen you to speak to for a few days,' Tom said, filling the silence she left. 'Aunt Leo says you have been ill. Are you well now?' A crease appeared between his eyebrows.

'I'm fine. Thank you.' She wanted to apologise for getting drunk and crying over his shirt, but the words refused to come.

'I have something for you,' Tom said. He slipped his hand inside his breast pocket and produced a dance card. With great care, he secured it around her wrist, tying the blue ribbon into a bow. His thumb pressed into her palm. 'I've put my name against the dance you owe me. There's no point in striking it out, I won't forget which it is.'

'Tom! Louisa!'

Lou snatched her hand free.

'Don't you look just charming, Louisa,' Emma said. She

sidled up to Tom and slipped her arm through his, oblivious to the unspoken words hanging in the air.

'And you look beautiful, Emma,' Lou said.

'Oh, this old frock!' She pinched the thin strap of her crimson ball gown dismissively. 'You couldn't be an absolute sweetheart, could you, and dance with this dapper chap as much as you can possibly bear this evening. You'd be doing me a huge favour.' Emma squeezed Tom's arm. She spoke as though their earlier conversation in her room had not taken place. 'I'm going to be busy catching up with old friends tonight and I'm sure Tom would appreciate being spared the clutches of a horde of hungry spinsters.' Emma looked up at Tom. His expression didn't alter.

'I'm not much of a dancer,' Lou said. Of course, Emma wanted her to occupy Tom's time, keeping him away from other women. In Emma's eyes, dowdy, unremarkable Lou was hardly a woman at all. And definitely no threat.

'Nonsense,' Emma laughed. 'I'm sure you're a perfectly pretty dance partner. Although I must say you do look rather pale. It's such a pity you weren't well enough to join us at the shoot yesterday. You missed quite a scene, didn't she, Tom. One of the beaters spotted a suffragette lurking in the woods and he was rather too keen on hunting her down with the dogs. Imagine! You saw her too, didn't you, Tom?'

Lou made the mistake of looking at Tom. He seized her in the grip of his blue eyes. 'I may have caught a glimpse of her,' he said.

Lou felt her cheeks colour. The running around in the woods had been for nothing. He had seen her. Through the spell of Tom's gaze, she became aware of Emma staring at her. Almost imperceptibly Emma's top lip twitched. She released Tom and grabbed Lou's hand. 'Come on. I'll introduce you to some of my friends. Perhaps you're right; you're not well enough to dance after all.'

Emma was forceful in dragging her away and Lou was powerless to resist. She glanced over her shoulder, but Tom had already disappeared; swallowed up in the mêlée.

With Emma still gripping her hand, Lou found herself in the dining room where a feast of extravagant proportions had been arranged on pristine white tablecloths decorated with rows of shimmering silver sequins. Monsieur Gotti's life-sized ice carving of a swan took centre stage, surrounded by the fruit-shaped ice creams so admired by Charlotte and Melinda. Trays of tiny bite-sized canapés ran the length of the table among joints of cold meat that a footman stood ready to carve. Emma released Lou's hand and took up a napkin. She selected an oyster smothered in caviar from a mound of crushed ice in a vast crystal bowl. Raising it to her mouth, she tipped the shell and swallowed the small piece of meat whole before dabbing a glistening spot of liquor from her lips. 'Heavenly,' she said, the tang of the sea on her breath. 'Lady Mandeville is certainly going to be a hard act to follow. But with Father's money, who knows what spectacular parties *I* shall be able to throw at Hill House.'

To a casual listener, Emma's words would have meant nothing more than she hoped one day to be mistress of this house. But to Lou, they dripped with an altogether different meaning.

'What happened back there,' Lou said, 'with Tom. It didn't mean anything. There was nothing going—'

'Of course it didn't mean anything.' Emma's words slammed down on Lou's with the precision of a guillotine. 'But Louisa,' she said, discarding the empty shell on a platter with a resounding ring, 'do not make me regret taking you into my confidence. It's important that you know I despise traitors. You're not a traitor, are you, Louisa?'

'No.'

'And you were listening the other evening when I told you about Sir Charles' debts?'

'Of course.'

'Then you know that only *I* can dig the Mandevilles out of the financial hole they have found themselves in with my father's money. And since you know that, then we understand each other. As you said earlier, Tom wants to marry me.' She grabbed Lou's wrist. 'I'm going to speak to my friends. You must join us. I insist.'

They joined a group of people and Lou instantly forgot the names that Emma rattled off by way of introduction. Two men fought to hand Emma a glass of champagne. When she touched the arm of the man whose glass she refused, saying she would accept his next, he visibly grew a few inches taller. She laughed at another's joke and the blush in his cheeks showed she had made him feel wittier. When she encouraged a plain girl to tell a story, the girl basked in the light of Emma's attention. Emma Caxton was the very epicentre of her universe. She was so at ease, so captivating; a planet with stars circling around her. Tom might not realise it yet, but he would be drawn into her gravity, powerless to resist, like everybody else. Had Emma known that when she asked Lou for help? Had getting Lou onside been Emma's way of saying 'hands off, he's mine'? So what if that had been Emma's intention? Wasn't that what Lou wanted too? Because whatever she felt for Tom, it was nothing compared with how important it was to see him married. She was a speck of grey matter floating in the dark sky, waiting to burn up in the atmosphere. If she were to be remembered at all after she left, it would be with a vague, fleeting memory of a reasonably pleasant woman who had spent a Christmas as their guest. In the history of this house and family, she was nothing.

Looking up, Lou found Emma staring at her. The corner of her nose rose in what could have been interpreted as a snarl. She looked like her brother. Lou turned away. She had made an enemy of the woman she was supposed to be helping. *Bravo, Lou. Bravo.*

'If I may,' one of the men said, taking hold of Lou's dance card.

'I'm sorry, it's full.' She snatched her hand away and made a break for the hall.

Most of the guests had dispersed, joining the dancing in the ballroom or the admiration of Monsieur Gotti's creations in the dining room. Lou clasped her sides. She shouldn't have let Sally tie her corset so tight. She tried to take a deep breath, but it barely filled the bottom of her lungs. Starved of oxygen, her head swam. She stood beside the Christmas tree feeling like a lump of clay on a potter's wheel, spinning around, out of control, pulled and pummelled into this shape and that by so many hands that she no longer knew who or what she was.

'I haven't seen you dance yet. Why is that?' It was the voice of the chief potter.

She drew in a shallow breath before turning to face him. 'Have you been spying on me?'

'You're evading my question.'

'I haven't danced because I don't feel like it.'

'Ah. Then I'm afraid I'm about to make you do something against your will.' Tom crooked his arm and offered it to her.

Lou glanced towards the dining room, half expecting Emma to appear. 'It's not a good idea.'

'A deal's a deal.'

She stared at his arm. She had to do this. It was expected. Not only that, but part of her – a very large part – wanted to touch him again, just once more. She placed her hand in the crease of his elbow. His bicep contracted beneath his black sleeve, and she had to focus on putting one foot in front of the other.

Tom led her on to the dance floor. He took her left hand and placed his free hand on the small of her back. Every step that Sally had taught her in the privacy of her bedroom slipped from her memory. 'I can't do this . . . I don't remember how.'

The pressure of Tom's hand on her spine was constant. 'Let me lead you. I'll take it slowly.'

Tom set off and Lou summoned up the steps, silently counting them to keep her mind on track. *One and two and three and four.* Why did it feel like Tom was pressing against her when in fact he was keeping a respectable distance? *One and two and three and four.* Her body tingled as though an electric charge arced, breaching the gap between them in a shower of sparks. She couldn't see Tom's face but stared at his shoulder until she was sure he must feel it burning through his jacket and into his skin. *One and two and* . . . she stepped on his toes, but he didn't flinch . . . *three and four.* With the beat more or less established, she managed to corral a small section of her brain into making sensible thoughts. She couldn't afford to waste this opportunity. She may never have Tom to herself again.

'Tom, I need to ask you something.'

'Oh?' His words whispered in her hair.

Calm, Lou, focus. She swallowed.

'Will you promise to support Charlotte if she asks your father for permission to enrol at university?'

A pause. *One and two* . . . 'What makes you think my father will listen to me when it comes to decisions on my sister's future?'

'You can try.'

Another pause. Longer this time. 'Is Hill House so awful that a woman needs to escape it to find happiness?'

'No . . . no! Not at all. I just believe that it's what Charlotte needs to do or . . . or . . .'

'She will wither and die like an orchid in my father's hothouse?'

How did he do it? How did he reach inside her mind and pluck out the thoughts she had yet to form into words?

'Very well,' he said. 'I'll plead Charlotte's case to my father. On the condition that you do something for me.'

'Anything,' she sighed, a wave of relief washing over her.

'Tell me why you ran away when you saw me in the woods yesterday.'

She stumbled, stepping on his feet again.

'Do you know how reckless that was? You could have been shot.'

Three and four . . . He looked down at her. The crease had returned to his brow. Was he rummaging around in her thoughts again? If he were, he would see that yesterday, like now, she was running away from her feelings for him. That it was taking every ounce of self-control to hold back. Because in her world, in another time and place, free from the straitjacket of strict manners and the promise to steer him into the arms of another, she would have kissed him. Kissed him and never stopped.

The music ended. Couples applauded. The band struck up the next song. Other guests began to move around them and Tom escorted Lou from the floor. They stood to one side.

'You're trembling,' Tom said.

'I . . .'

A person coughed beside them, bringing the world of the party crashing through their private moment.

'Tom. Miss Arnold,' Edward said. With his hands in his pockets, he rocked back on his heels.

Tom cleared his throat. 'If you're looking for a dance partner, I'm afraid you'll be out of luck with Louisa. She's playing her dance card rather close to her chest this evening.' His jollity, for once, sounded false.

Edward ran his fingers through his fringe. 'It's you I rather wanted to speak to, Tom.'

'Oh?'

Lou felt Tom tense beside her. Did he think Edward was about to reveal all about his affair? Depending on how much Edward had drunk, it was possible he could blurt out anything.

'Father has opened a good malt in the billiard room,' Tom said. 'Perhaps we should take our conversation through there.'

'No, it's all right, really. What I have to say can be said in front of Miss Arnold. You see . . . I felt it right . . . that's to say I had it pointed out to me that . . . look here, Tom, I just wanted to apologise for my shocking behaviour since you've been home. I've had a rum time of it recently, which is no excuse, I know. But . . . well, we're brothers and I'd hate to think there was bad blood between us. Especially as you'll be returning to barracks after the New Year.'

Tom sighed. 'There's no need for apologies, old man. You should come and visit me in Norwich, it certainly seems as though you could do with a break. I'm sure I can arrange a day's leave to show you the sights. And I'd be glad of your company.' He held out his hand. 'No hard feelings.'

Edward took his brother's hand and smiled. 'No, no hard feelings.'

'Are we all having a good time?' Emma had appeared without any of them noticing. 'I thought I'd better come and find you, Tom. We're up next. *The Gay Gordons* followed by *The Royal Scottish Quadrille*. What a hoot! Your mother never misses an opportunity to remind us of her heritage. It wouldn't surprise me if one Christmas she didn't decorate the whole house in her clan tartan!'

Emma's grip tightened around Tom's arm. Lou read her message loud and clear: *This man is mine, and don't you forget it.*

'If you'll excuse me,' Tom said and dutifully led Emma to the floor. Did he have a furrow in his brow, Lou wondered? Or was that wishful thinking? After a moment, Edward excused himself. Shoulders slumped, head sagging, he headed for the door, no doubt intent on finding comfort in his father's whisky bottle. Poor Edward. He exuded sadness, consumed as he clearly was by desire for what he couldn't have.

Alone, Lou stood and watched the dance commence. Tom and Emma took up position in a large circle of couples, Lord and Lady Caxton in front of them, Sir Charles and Lady Mandeville behind. Each man placed an arm around his partner's shoulders and each woman clasped her man's hand. The band struck up a Scottish jig and the circle began to move, taking a few steps forward then a few steps back, before the partners came together once more. After that, the circle started again. As hard as she tried not to, Lou couldn't help staring at Tom's arm around Emma, her hand holding his. When they came together, they were in perfect time; Emma's dress swirling as Tom span her around. Their parents laughed, Lady Mandeville beaming each time she looked at them. Tom appeared to be enjoying himself too, with a partner who matched him step for step; a partner who didn't stamp on his feet. When a portly man wrong-footed his equally portly wife and they stumbled into Tom, he laughed, brushing off their apologies. Instantly he took up position again. He was in Emma's orbit, drawn to the pull of her gravity. They would marry. Lou was certain of that now.

The mass of bodies picked up speed. Round and round they went, the music and laughter growing louder, steps quickening, until everything in the ballroom became a blur of colour and noise. What was she still doing here? Tom was going to marry Emma. He had made his peace with Edward and had promised to plead Charlotte's case to go to university. She was no longer needed here. She had to jump off this merry-go-round. Now. She turned to leave, but found her path blocked.

'I say,' George Caxton said, running his finger across his top lip. 'You scrub up all right.'

His breath stank of whisky. Sir Charles' good malt, no doubt.

Lou tried to step past him, but he used his physical bulk to block her. He snatched her dance card.

'Good God,' he laughed harshly. 'You unfortunate wretch.

A single dance and with *Mandeville*. Well, we'll soon sort that out.' He took a pencil from his pocket and twisted the end to propel the lead. Before he could scrawl his name, Lou whipped her hand away, leaving his pencil to jab the air.

'Well, well, well,' he grinned, returning his pencil to his pocket. 'Looks like I have a feisty filly on my hands. And you know what I do with a disobedient horse, don't you?' He leant in closer. 'I break her.'

Lou was on the potter's wheel again, thrown off centre, spinning around and around. The walls began to sag, threatening to collapse in on themselves. What if she hadn't done enough to push Tom into Emma's arms after all? It was possible that he was stubborn enough to resist. If something happened to him, Charlotte would be left exposed and vulnerable to this man who was beyond kindness and mercy of any sort. A man so intent on exacting revenge that he would resort to murder. Again. She had to act and act now. It made her skin crawl, but she touched George Caxton's hand. 'I don't want to dance,' she said, hoping to mimic Emma's flirtatious purr. 'Why don't we go somewhere a little more . . . private?'

George's eyes slid over her body. It felt as if someone was running a dirty floor cloth across her naked flesh. It was a price worth paying if George fell for her amateur attempt at seduction.

George grabbed her wrist. 'Your room or mine?'

'Neither,' she purred again. This game was dangerous enough without going anywhere alone with him. She parted the curtains at one of the doors that led out to the garden. George followed her into the small bay. The curtains closed, plunging them into semi-darkness.

'I know your sort,' George said, his voice low, 'you like the excitement of getting caught, don't you? All that guff about votes for women, when what you really want is a seeing to by a real man.'

He grabbed her, but she pushed him away. 'Not so fast.'

He smirked and she tried to ignore his tongue flicking to lick the corner of his mouth.

'Going to make me work for it, hey?' he said. 'I wouldn't have put you down as *that* sort of girl. But I warn you, I like the thrill of the chase and I always get my quarry.'

The stench of his breath filled her nostrils so that she could almost taste it. She swallowed. She was going to do this. She was really going to do this. 'I know what else you like,' she said, running her finger down his lapel.

'I bet you do, you bad girl.'

He tried to kiss her, but she pushed him away again. 'You like to be in control, don't you?' she purred. 'You like everybody to know what a powerful man you are.'

'Come here and I'll show you just how powerful I am.'

She leant in as close as she could bear. 'You like to drown defenceless kittens, don't you?' she whispered, lighting the touch paper and standing over the firework rather than retreating to a safe distance. 'What's wrong, George? Cat got your tongue?' She waited, but he didn't respond. Perhaps she'd been too subtle. Amongst his host of crimes, he may have no recollection of Emma's kitten.

Beyond the curtains, the guests clapped as a tune ended. As the next began, George shoved Lou violently, catching her off guard. Had it not been for the door behind her, she would have landed on the floor. His meaty hands pressed her shoulders back against the glass.

'What's your game?' he hissed in her ear. 'Are you in league with *him*?'

'No . . . no . . . it's not him,' she tried to turn her face away.

'Ah, what's this? Is the little girl frightened? If I were you, I would be very frightened. Very frightened indeed.'

Her heart thumped. Something Stephen had taught her when they were small came rushing back. When a boy in her class had spent a whole term bullying her, Stephen's advice had been simple; 'Never let the bastard see that you are scared.'

'You're the one who should be frightened,' she said, fighting to bring her voice back under control. She had no choice but to go straight in with the big gun while she still had the benefit of surprise. 'What about Riley? I know everything about him.'

George's reaction wasn't at all what Lou had anticipated. There was no look of horror or fear at being presented with his crime. Instead, he laughed. 'I can see that Mandeville has been dripping poison.'

'This has got nothing to do with Tom.'

'No? Never reveal your soft underbelly, don't you know that? Riley,' he played with the name like rolling a boiled sweet around his mouth before spitting it out. 'He was a spineless idiot. He should have learned when to hold his tongue. *Thomas Mandeville this, Thomas Mandeville that.*'

'Tom knew Riley?'

'Knew him? They practically lived in each other's pockets at school. I may have been exiled to that hovel in Ireland, but I had my spies. Riley was under Mandeville's spell. He fawned over him. Mandeville made him something of a protégé. I can't imagine anything worse than being at his beck and call. There were rumours that there was more than friendship between them. Oh, wait a minute, it was me and my spies who started those rumours. Shame they never stuck. Why the shocked face?' George stuck out his bottom lip.

'I . . . I . . . '

'Whose tongue has puss got now?' He leant in closer. 'It was a blessing for poor Riley to be put out of his misery. It made me feel wretched just looking at his sorry face.'

'You killed Riley because he was Tom's friend?'

George tutted and shook his head. 'Now, now, Miss Arnold, I took you for a moderately intelligent woman. I never said I killed Riley. He killed himself. The coroner said so. You need to be more careful if you don't want to find yourself up before the judge on a charge of slander. Anyway, it was best all around. Having him reveal my debts to my father would have been far too tedious.'

A surge of adrenaline rallied Lou. She had found *his* soft underbelly. 'What would your father say if he knew what you got up to in the back room of The White Lion now?' She waited a second for the flicker of realisation in George's eyes before adding, 'If you ever harm a single Mandeville, I will see to it that your father finds out about your gambling debts and that you are ruined.'

George laughed again. 'Angry words, Miss Arnold. But you need a little thing called evidence to back up a threat like that.'

'How about a signed statement revealing your debts and details of a fictitious mine in South Africa. I'm sure a few men in Northampton, as well as your father and the police, would like to see—'

Before she could finish, George's hand was around her throat. 'How dare you threaten me!'

She tried to push him away, but she was no match for his strength. She kicked out but it only seemed to spur him on. He pressed his body against hers, pushing her so that the door handle dug into the small of her back.

'If I were to silence you tonight, nobody would be any the wiser,' he said.

'Someone else holds the proof. If anything happens to me or any of the Mandevilles, they are under instructions to deliver the evidence directly to the police and your father.' It was a lie, of course, but she had to say something or George was going to snap her neck and leave her slumped behind the curtain where nobody would find her until the morning.

George's fingers tightened around her throat. She twisted from side to side, but it did no good. She tried to cry out, but the sound wouldn't come. Even hitting him had no effect. He fumbled at her clothes, lifting her skirt, forcing his knee between hers and parting her legs. *Oh no, oh God no . . .*

'Since you love your precious Mandevilles so much, I'll leave your bones here for them to pick over. Once I've had my fill.'

He forced his lips over hers, his hand clawing at her underwear. His tongue rammed into her mouth. She did the only thing she could, she bit down, hard. George stumbled back, clutching his mouth. Lou held her throat, gasping for breath, the iron taste of George's blood on her tongue.

'You twisted little bitch!' George yelled. He stared at his hand. The sight of his blood enraged him, and he charged – but she was ready. Remembering Stephen's advice on what to do if facing up to a bully failed, she raised her knee, and with stunning accuracy, made contact with George's groin. He collapsed and fell back through the curtains, writhing on the floor, spluttering a string of expletives as stunned guests looked down at him.

Lou grasped the door handle and ran out into the cold night air, the curtains billowing behind her.

With no thought to the bitter chill or the flimsiness of her satin slippers, she ran across the lawn, snow swirling around her. She kept to the darkness and away from the lanterns that illuminated the drive. Any number of guests must have spotted her hiding behind the curtains when George fell through. He was, no doubt, at that very moment, portraying her as some kind of deranged harpy, placing himself as the innocent victim so that everyone would believe she had launched an unprovoked attack on him, before running after her. All the planning, all the good she had tried to do, had been undone with one swift knee to the groin of a future peer. She had to get away before he caught up with her.

THIRTY

CHRISTMAS EVE 2013

Lou stumbled on in the blackness, her breath coming in thick, hot gasps. Abruptly the dark gave way to the murky orange glow of streetlamps. The rumble of traffic replaced the crunch of dancing slippers in snow. Freezing rain lashed at Lou's cheeks and eyes. Still running, she swiped her fringe from her face. There was no time to stop, no time to think, no time to acclimatise. If she could cross the boundary of time, why not George? The memory of his thick, hot fingers crushing her windpipe, made her increase her pace, pushing on up the steps and over the footbridge. There would be nobody to hear her cries for help. She sprinted along the empty road, all the while fumbling in her pocket to find her key. She forced the key into the lock, slammed the door behind her and collapsed against it, her heart pounding like a jackhammer breaking through concrete.

A figure emerged from the living room, framed in a rectangle of light. For a blood-churning moment, Lou imagined George had crossed the boundary and somehow found his way to her house. The hall light snapped on. She placed her hands on her knees and sank against the door.

'What are you sneaking around for?'

'I'm not sneaking around,' she panted.

'Why are you out of breath?'

'I was running to get in. It's pouring down out there.'

Stephen shrugged and headed for the kitchen. Lou followed him. She had never been more pleased to see her big, strong brother.

'Drink?' Stephen asked.

Lou nodded. She fell into a chair, dazzled by the brightness of the strip light. Stephen rinsed two glasses and swept some takeaway cartons from the table to make space. He unscrewed the cap of a half-empty bottle of whisky and poured two large slugs. Pushing a glass towards Lou, he picked up his own. 'Down the hatch,' he said and drained his glass before he was in his chair. He poured another slug.

Lou knocked back her whisky. The harsh liquid burned her throat and reinforced the fact that she was here. In the kitchen. At home. As far away from a world of dancing and ice swans and ball gowns as it was possible to be.

Stephen picked up the bottle and Lou held out her glass. She took another slug. This supermarket own brand was sand-paper-rough. Sir Charles' malt, open in the library, would have been silky smooth. 'Where's Dean?' she asked quickly.

'At a mate's,' Stephen said, inspecting the contents of his glass. 'Didn't seem much point forcing him to hang around here. It's not exactly festive.'

'Is he okay?'

'Getting there.'

Stephen ran his hand over his stubble. He was a week past needing a shave and his work t-shirt and trousers – spattered with plaster and unidentifiable plumbing muck – were more than a week past needing a wash. His crumpled face looked like an old man had crept inside and used his skin as a sleeping bag. While she had escaped to live a charmed life of parties and shoots and dresses and other peoples' problems, Stephen had been left to deal with the catastrophe of their real life. Hadn't there been days in the last week when she hadn't woken with the clawing despair of loss? Days when she had managed, for short periods of time at least, to forget their mum completely? 'Stephen, I'm so sorry,' she said, 'for starting that argument last week. For running out. For everyth—'

Stephen threw the contents of the glass down his throat. 'Forget it.'

'But it's my faul—'

'Please, Lou, can you just drop it.' He ran his hand over his hair. 'Going over it again and again won't change anything.' The bottle chinked on the glass as he refilled it. 'Anyway, it was six of one . . .' He left the familiar phrase unfinished as he took a swig of his whisky.

'Half a dozen of the other,' Lou said.

Stephen smiled. Lou wanted to see him smile again. She wanted to make him better and iron out the bags beneath his eyes. 'Least said . . .' she tentatively tried.

'Soonest mended,' Stephen responded. He grinned. 'She always did like her stupid sayings, didn't she? It used to drive me mad. Do you remember when we were kids and she used to make us hug after we had a fight?'

'You loved it.'

'Yeah, right. Almost as much as you.' He held his glass up. 'To Mum,' he said.

Lou chinked her glass to Stephen's. 'To Mum,' she said quietly.

They both downed their drinks. Lou spluttered.

'Lightweight,' Stephen laughed.

For once Lou was grateful that outpourings of emotion and lengthy discussions of feelings weren't their style. An insult delivered with a smile was the closest they would ever get to a gushing show of affection.

Stephen rolled his glass round his hands, staring into it as though the cheap whisky held some deep secret. 'You know it's not your fault, don't you?' he said. 'It was the bastard driving the car, not you.'

Lou swallowed. 'But if I'd come home that night. . . If I'd picked up the dinner instead of going to the pub. . .'

'Yeah, and if *ifs* and *ands* were pots and pans . . .' He tried to smile. 'You were right the other day, you know. We have to find a way to get through this. I've had time to think about it. I shouldn't have been such a git. We have to find a way to move on, you know, stick together. She . . . she wouldn't want us to keep fighting. She wouldn't want us to fall apart.' Abandoning his glass, Stephen turned from Lou. He wiped his eyes on his short sleeve. Lou took his hand, rough and calloused from hard work.

'I'm a soppy bugger, aren't I? Blubbing like a girl.' Stephen sniffed and half laughed. He squeezed Lou's hand so tight that she thought he might break a bone in her fingers.

'Maybe, but you're the only big brother I've got so I guess you'll have to do.'

He laughed properly this time. A laugh full of snot and spit. He turned back to her. 'You know, you're all right really. But don't tell anyone I said that.' As he spoke his eyes fell on her neck. When he spoke again there was a familiar hard edge to his voice. 'What are those red marks on your throat? Has someone hurt you? Is that why you were running? Tell me. I'll kill—'

Someone began to hammer at the front door. It was so loud and such a rapid succession of beats that Lou jumped and Stephen sprang from his seat.

'Stephen, I'm scared—' Lou started. How could she explain George Caxton knocking at their front door?

'Stephen Arnold!' a voice shouted through the letterbox.

'Fuck,' Stephen said, his eyes wide like a cornered cat. He ran to the back door and threw it open. Before Lou could grasp what was happening, the room was full of police officers. One of them knocked Stephen to the floor, twisting his arm behind his back. Stephen let out a cry. 'He's in here!' the officer called.

'What are you doing?' Lou yelled. Nobody bothered to give her an answer. She felt someone take hold of her arms as an officer barged through the back door into the kitchen and out into the hall. He opened the front door, allowing even more officers into the house. Two officers manhandled Stephen to his feet. An officer who appeared to be in charge began firing questions at Stephen. Where was it? Who had he been working with? If he told them, he could make this a whole lot easier on himself.

Stephen said repeatedly that he didn't know what they were talking about; they'd got the wrong man. Lou watched on, struck dumb at their peace so violently shattered.

'Take her into the living room,' the senior officer barked at the female police officer who had hold of Lou's arms.

'Get your hands off her,' Stephen shouted, becoming suddenly animated. 'She's my sister. This has got nothing to do with her. Leave her out of it.'

'So, you admit there's something to leave her out of then?' Looking smug, the senior officer gestured for Lou to be taken away. The female officer half-guided, half-pushed her into the living room. She released Lou's arms and made her sit on the sofa. 'Why don't you do your brother a favour and tell us where he hides it?' she said.

'Hides what?' Lou stared at the officer in absolute bafflement. 'You've made a mistake. My brother's not a criminal.'

The stairs creaked as officers went upstairs.

'You've got no right to be here,' Lou said, getting to her feet. 'This is our home.'

'Sit down and shut up. Unless you want me to arrest you for obstruction'.

Lou did as she was told. She knew this woman's type –

trying to prove that she had bigger balls than a man in a world of men. There was little point in arguing with her.

'Boss!' someone shouted in the hall. The female officer, losing interest in Lou, left to join her colleagues. Lou got up. She'd be damned if she was going to sit there while a swarm of men and women in stab vests invaded her home. But when she looked out into the hall, she wished she'd stayed put.

Stephen's work tools littered the carpet and an officer knelt on the floor, head and shoulders inside the cupboard under the stairs. He was pulling out heavy items wrapped in dustsheets. Another officer was in the process of removing the dustsheets to reveal manhole covers and grates that should have been sealing the drains across town.

The female officer spotted Lou lurking in the doorway. 'Get back in there before I *put* you in there,' she said.

Lou stood her ground. 'I want to see my brother,' she said. Stephen saw her and broke free of the officer who was restraining him in the kitchen.

'I didn't steal any of it, Lou. You have to believe me. I'm just looking after it. I'm not a thief. I didn't know what any of it was. I only did it to pay for Mum's funer—'

Two officers charged at Stephen. They grabbed him and he tried to squirm free. After a struggle, they managed to cuff his hands behind his back. The female officer grabbed Lou's arm.

'Get your fucking hands off my sister!' Stephen yelled. Lou didn't have time to tell the officer restraining Stephen to stop shoving him. Goading him would only heap coals on his temper. With his hands behind his back, Stephen had only one weapon with which to attack. He pulled his head back.

'No, Stephen!' Lou yelled. It was enough of a warning for the officer to dodge out of the way and avoid Stephen's hard forehead bursting the soft cartilage of his nose. Officers swamped Stephen. They bundled him out of the house towards a waiting van.

'You want to thank your sister,' one of them said, catching his breath as he pushed Stephen down the path. 'Do you really want to add assaulting a police officer to handling stolen goods, you bloody idiot?'

The female officer forced Lou to sit on the sofa. She watched in horror as the police searched the living room. Three officers poked around behind the television, pulled books from the shelves, rifled through papers on the coffee table. The female officer told Lou to stand up and she got to her feet. Another officer, wearing latex gloves, pulled the cushions free and rummaged down the sides. What was he hoping to find down there? A manhole cover snuggled amongst the dust and long-forgotten buttons and lost pennies? He pulled the sofa away from the wall and as he looked behind it, he smiled.

'Boss!' he called. The other officers huddled around him and the officer in charge joined them. After much backslapping, he shook his head and said, 'What kind of scrotes steal these? They've got no shame. No respect.'

'They'd have melted them down. And all for a few pounds,' another said. 'Those poor blokes would be turning in their graves.'

There was a ripple of agreement and a round of 'bastards'.

Lou hovered in the corner, unnoticed. The officer tasked with unwrapping the bounty, laid out four brass plaques on the table beside her. Another officer took photographs of them and then they were taken away, but not before Lou had the chance to glance down and scan the list of names. She fell against the wall.

When they finished their search, the police made a cursory attempt to restore the house to its pre–ransacked state. The officer in charge left his card on the table and spoke to Lou but none of his words sunk in. They closed the front door after them and silence was restored – to the house at least.

Lou looked around at the scattered sympathy cards and

discarded latex gloves. Her gut told her that Stephen was telling the truth about not stealing anything; her brother was many things, but he wasn't a thief. He had been arrested because he had carried the burden of paying for Mum's funeral.

Lou gripped her head and sank down the wall. Behind closed eyes, the name engraved into the plaque merged with the sight of the manhole covers in the hall and the glimmer of candlelight in crystal. Music floated around her, arms held her so very close, a hand pressed into the small of her back, traces of woody cologne lingered in the air. She clutched her head tighter. How long had it been since she had danced with him? One hour? Two? Then the crack of gunfire and explosion of shells broke through her thoughts. Men in khaki uniform were thrown into the air like so many rag dolls. She was caught in the eye of a storm, the two lives she had lived for the last week swirling about her. With each passing minute that other life ebbed away. She wanted to seize it, to grasp it to her.

She struggled to her feet, switched off the light and curled up in a ball on the sofa.

THIRTY-ONE

CHRISTMAS DAY 2013

It was dark when Lou woke on the sofa, the bones in her arms and legs fused by the cold. She lay perfectly still, attempting to unravel the events of the previous evening into manageable strands. They resisted, springing back into a tangled mass of confusion. She turned on the lamp and blinked.

Unfurling her body, she sat up, rested her elbows on her knees and let her head hang. It was Christmas Day. She would have laughed at the irony if only her funny bone hadn't been amputated in her sleep.

She picked up the phone and dialled the number on the card the senior officer had left on the table. She asked after Stephen and while the man on the other end of the line went away to check, she went through to the kitchen. Balancing the phone between her ear and shoulder, she filled the kettle and switched it on. An inspection of the tea caddy and fridge revealed only the dust of old tea bags and a dribble of sour milk, a week past its use-by date.

The man returned. 'Your brother's been remanded to go up before the magistrate the day after tomorrow. Don't bother laying him a place at the table. Looks like he'll be eating his turkey sandwiches with us. Sorry.'

He didn't sound sorry. Lou asked if she should get Stephen a solicitor. No need, the duty brief was working on his case. Could she visit him?

'It's not The Savoy, love. We don't lay on afternoon tea for guests.'

Lou chucked the phone down on the table. Steam rose from the kettle and the water rumbled as it came to the boil. Her stomach growled. She scavenged a couple of stale crackers from a tin in the cupboard.

The clock on the oven flashed seven thirty. With any luck Dean had been asleep at his mate's by the time the police ransacked the house and the news wouldn't have reached him yet. None of their neighbours had bothered to knock on the door to see if she was okay, but she knew they would have wasted no time in posting videos of Stephen's arrest online. Lou rescued the phone from where it had landed in a pizza box and wiped it on her jeans. Dean wouldn't thank her for waking him, but it was better than him finding out about Stephen through social media.

She dialled Dean's number and waited.

'Hello, Dean's phone,' a stranger's voice said. It sounded too old to be one of Dean's mates. In a split second, a barrage of awful images vied for position in Lou's head. Dean had been in an accident. An A&E doctor was answering his phone. Dean was hurt. He was . . .

'Hello?' the man said again. There was something familiar about his voice.

'Where's Dean? Is he all right? Is he hurt?'

'No, he's fine. I didn't mean to worry you. He's just popped out into the garden, so I picked up his phone.' There was a pause. 'Louisa? Is that you?'

The years fell away. She began to shake and fought to keep hold of the phone.

'It's . . . I'm your . . . it's your dad here. Are you all right? Sorry.' Her father let out a long sigh. 'Of course, you're not. Shit. I don't know what to say. I'm sorry about Maureen, about your mum. I wanted to get in touch. I thought about sending flowers or coming to the funeral, but I was worried I'd only make it worse . . . Are you still there?'

'Yes.'

'Dean turned up on my doorstep a couple of days ago. He was in such a state. So upset about . . . everything. He's a smashing lad, isn't he?'

'Have you been here? To the house?'

'Yes. I came over yesterday, to collect Dean. I was hoping that you might be home. He's done your mum proud, hasn't he? Dean, I mean . . . Christ, Lou, I don't know what to say. I should have been there to see him grow up. I should have been there for you all. I shouldn't have let it come to this. But you're an adult now; you understand that relationships are . . . complicated. No, you don't need to understand anything. It's my fault.'

Lou could hear children and adults laughing in the background. She recognised Dean's voice. There was a pause and the noise of a door closing. When her father next spoke, the echoing acoustics sounded like he had moved room. 'Sorry. Dean was just outside with the kids and their new bikes. Listen, why don't you come over? Michelle and the kids would love to meet you. I could pick you and Stephen up and you could spend Christmas with us. I could be there in half an hour. No, you've probably got plans. Sorry . . . I'm not saying the right thing, am I? I'm not trying to fix things. I know I can't do that. But I want to help you all. If I can. If it's not too late. Are you still there?'

'Yes.'

'Do you want to talk to Dean?'

What was happening? They were talking as though a conversation between them was an everyday occurrence. 'No. I . . . just tell him I phoned. No, don't do that. Can you hide his phone? I need to tell him something but not over the phone. I don't want him finding out through his messages.'

'Sounds serious. Are you sure you don't want to talk to him?'

'No. Thank you.'

'If you're sure. Look, I'm dropping him home at about seven. Maybe we can have a proper chat then. But Lou, if you need anything, you will call, won't you? Anything at all.'

Really? Was he really acting so normally? 'Okay.'

'Bye then, Lou. Take care of yourself today, love.'

Lou dropped the phone. It landed amongst the shrivelled pepperoni and dried crusts. When she tried to take a swig from a half empty glass of whisky, it knocked violently against her teeth.

Eighteen years without a single word and there he was, a voice on the phone, sounding like he had just nipped out to the shops. The glass fell from her hand. It shattered on the kitchen tiles, splinters flying, whisky splashing up the cupboards and across the floor. Crashing out of the kitchen, she stopped in the dark hall and was confronted by a vivid memory of her ten-year-old self, sitting on the bottom stair in the moonlight.

Long after everyone else had gone to bed she had snuck from her room to begin her nightly vigil. In her pyjamas and slippers, she clutched the paw of her panda, watching the front door, waiting, and promising to be such a good girl if only the door would open. She would help Mummy with the baby and try her very best not to fight with Stephen if only her prayer was answered. On the nights she heard the sobs from Mummy's bedroom, she squeezed her eyes tighter, prayed harder, even promising to give her beloved panda away to another little girl who needed him more, if it would do any good. Most nights she fell asleep on the stairs, waking up cold and alone, to drag panda back to bed and hold him tight, soaking his fur with her tears. Because her daddy hadn't come home.

Her eyes fixed on the bottom stair, Lou finally allowed herself to admit the truth. Her father's departure had ripped out her ten-year-old heart. When she had accepted that she couldn't bring him home, she had built a dam, brick by brick, to protect her tender heart from the pain of knowing that the whispers of adults behind closed doors were true; her daddy had chosen a new family over his old family. He didn't want to be her daddy anymore.

Eighteen years on, she felt that crippling pain of abandonment all over again. Every fibre of her little self had adored her father, yet she had succeeded in convincing herself that if he didn't want her, she didn't need him. He had taught her that to love was to feel pain. That it was safer to harden your heart than let anything or anyone get close enough to hurt you.

And now that voice down the telephone line had brought it all back. It was the voice of bedtime stories, the voice that soothed when she woke from nightmares, the voice of the happy childhood and family life that its owner had stolen from her, stolen from Mum and Stephen and Dean. Even knowing that – even knowing the pain he had made them live through – she wanted to run to him, to have him scoop her into his arms and tell her everything would be all right. But it could never be all right. Any reconciliation now would only happen because Mum had died. She would be trading her mum's life for her dad's comfort.

She grabbed her parka, left the house and lurched up the road with only a haze of drizzle and the moon for company. She should hate him. She should blame him. If he hadn't run out on them, maybe none of this would be happening. Stephen wouldn't have been arrested. Dean wouldn't be a broken boy looking for his father. Mum would still be alive.

Phone me, if you need anything. He had sounded so genuine. So sorry.

She looked up to find that without realising it, her feet had taken her across the footbridge. That bloody thread was reeling her in again. *What do you want with me? I can't help you, can't you see that?* The shattered skeleton of Hill House loomed dark and empty at the end of the drive and her battered heart took another blow.

'I knew it was you.' A woman emerged from behind the abandoned mattress and bags of rubbish, her face obscured by a hood.

Lou's muscles twitched, preparing to make a run for it. 'I haven't got any money, so you can piss off.'

'I don't want your money.' The woman stepped into the pale light of the streetlamp and revealed herself as not a woman at all, but a slight girl. The tension in Lou's muscles melted.

'What do you mean you knew it was me?' Lou said. She was in no mood for playing ridiculous games with a stranger.

The girl stared at the ground. 'You don't recognise me, do you?'

'Should I?'

The girl pulled down her hood. Lou studied her pale complexion, her eyes fixed on the ground, her finger twisting a cotton from her frayed cuff. Finally, Lou took in the hair. It was pulled back into a loose ponytail but there was no disguising the beautiful red waves.

'Alice?' she said. Could this really be the maid who had led the way up the stairs on that first day in Hill House?

'How do you know my name?' Alice asked.

'It's not every day a maid runs away in the middle of the night.'

'They gossiped about me?'

'No. All the staff spoke kindly about you. They miss you.'

Alice dug the toe of her trainer into a crack in the pavement.

'It's crazy, isn't it? I mean, me and you standing here talking about travelling back in time?'

Lou nodded. At least it meant she didn't have to think about her father for a while.

'They're real then? I didn't just imagine it all?'

'No, you weren't imagining it. They're all very real.'

Alice let out a sigh. 'Thank God. Because I thought I was going mad. One minute I'm a maid scrubbing floors and the next I'm squatting in there again thinking it was all just a dream.'

'You're squatting? In Hill House?'

'It's as good a place as any,' Alice said. 'Better probably. It's a bit out of the way so nobody really bothers with it. I did a runner from the hostel the Council dumped me in when I left care last year. It was full of dirty creeps and perverts . . .' She pulled her cuffs over her hands. 'I found out about Hill House when I was in foster care. A kid who was with the same family said if I ever needed anywhere to squat then it was a good place. It's always quiet and once a week a charity hands out food parcels from that church hall up the road. I came here about a month ago. There was no electricity or running water and the house trashed but at least there was nobody to hassle me or scream at my door in the middle of the night. It was just me and my sleeping bag and a camping stove. I only go into town when I have to . . . You were right when you recognised me the day you arrived. I go into Freezerfayre sometimes. But only when I'm really hungry. I only take stuff when I'm desperate.'

'You don't need to explain anything to me.' Lou said. 'We all do what we have to to get by.'

A smile briefly flickered across Alice's lips again. 'I'd been squatting a few weeks when I went looking around the house to see if anyone had left anything useful lying around. That's when everything changed.' Alice started playing with the loose cotton again. 'I went down into the kitchens, and it was all normal. Not like upstairs where it's all ruined. There was glass in the windows, food on the shelves in the pantry, copper pots hanging on the walls. I thought I was dreaming. And then Mrs Moriarty found me. She knew my name and everything and said she'd been expecting me. I played along, waiting to wake up. Only I never did.'

Alice opened her hands, revealing the scabs of healing blisters on her palms. Lou winced. Why had Alice's experience been so different to her own? Why had she been allowed to enjoy the luxuries of a guest when Alice had been forced to work?

'Being a maid was hard work,' Alice said. 'Some nights I was so tired I fell asleep in my clothes. But I didn't care. I was glad to work hard because, for the first time in my life, I felt like I belonged somewhere. The other staff were so nice. They treated me like I was one of them. I had enough to eat every day and a proper bed to sleep in every night.' She paused and chewed her lip. 'I never had a proper family. I was taken off my mum when I was a kid because of her drinking. I never knew who my dad was; I'm not even sure she did. When a social worker told me a few years ago that my mum had died, I didn't feel anything. Growing up in care, you learn quickly not to feel anything. If you do, you hide it.'

'I'm sorry,' Lou said.

Alice shrugged. 'Why? It's not your fault. Anyway, what you've never had you can't miss, right?' She wiped her cuff across her face. 'I came out of Hill House a few times to see if I could. After I saw you last week, I had to know what I was dealing with, so I came out again. When I tried to go back in, everything was gone; the furniture, the ornaments, the people . . . It was just me and my sleeping bag again. I just figured it was another place that had given up on me. Another group of people that didn't want me. You'd think I'd be used to that by now.'

Alice tucked her chin into her collar and wrapped her arms around her body.

Tread carefully; you don't want to scare her off. 'Is it just the staff you miss?' Lou asked.

'What do you mean?' Alice looked at Lou from beneath her eyebrows.

'I know Edward misses you. He told me.'

A proper smile lit Alice's face, her cheeks bloomed with colour. For the first time Lou got a glimpse of the pretty young girl Edward had fallen in love with.

'I didn't mean for it to happen,' Alice said quietly. 'But Edward – Mr Edward – he had this way of making me see him even when I tried not to. There was a day, in the library. I was dusting and he came in to look for a book. He asked me if I liked reading. When I said I did, he made me take a book of poems. He told me to read it and tell him what I thought next time I saw him. Every night, no matter how tired I was, I read a page. I didn't understand it all, but I liked the words. Whenever I saw him after that, he'd talk to me about the poems, about what they meant and . . .' She forced her hands into her single pocket. 'It's so stupid. I mean, how can I feel . . . he hasn't even kissed me . . . how's it possible to fall . . .'

It's easy, Lou wanted to say. 'Have you tried to go back recently?'

'Only every day.'

'Try again now.'

'There's no point.'

'Humour me. Please.'

With a sigh, Alice walked to the gates. It wasn't until her foot was hovering over the boundary that Lou realised the significance of what she was trying to make her do. If Alice disappeared then she was in, which in turn meant that Lou was out. She watched Alice take a step through the gates and stand on the drive and continued to watch as Alice stepped back on to the pavement. With a shrug that said *I told you so*, Alice said, 'Now you try.'

Lou shook her head. 'It won't work. I did something.' Hill House wouldn't want her back. In attacking George Caxton, she had surely severed all ties. *But what if?* A glimmer of hope rose in her as she remembered Bertie's insistence that her doll remain in the house.

'How can you just stand there when there's a chance you can go back?' Alice said. 'I'd be in there like a shot.'

She was talking more sense than Lou had a right to hear. Lou looked towards Hill House. The first glimpse of daylight dawned beyond the abandoned building. She took a deep breath and walked to the gates. *Here goes nothing.*

She crossed the boundary. Night fell. Snow swirled around her. Lady Mandeville's Chinese lanterns glowed in the darkness. Chauffeurs huddled beside the cars lined up on the driveway, the tips of their cigarettes glowing orange. And, at the end of the drive, the lights of Hill House blazed in the dark. It was Christmas Eve again!

Lou took a step back. Out on the pavement she looked through the broken gates. The day once again dawned pink behind the empty hulk of Hill House.

'It worked didn't it,' Alice said. 'You disappeared. Hill House wants you, nobody else.'

'I don't understand.'

'Unfinished business? Whatever it is, there's no chance of anyone else going in.'

What unfinished business and why would Hill House want to take her back to last night? Like a bolt of lightning, it struck her. The envelope in the nightstand. How could she have been so stupid? She couldn't just leave it there. If it was found by the wrong person and they handed it to George, he would crucify Elliot for speaking out against him. She couldn't leave him to face the wrath of George. If she was found to be missing,

George would waste no time in ransacking her room to find the evidence she had threatened him with. She touched her throat. It was still tender. If she went back and George caught her, he would finish the job. She had to make sure that he didn't catch her then.

She checked the clock high up on the steeple of St Mary's. It was almost eight o'clock. 'Meet me here this afternoon. At three o'clock,' she said.

'You're coming back out?' Alice said as though Lou was giving up her claim on a winning lottery ticket.

Of course, she was coming out. She could hardly leave Dean to return to an empty house with police gloves scattered across the floor. She had to be at home to break the news of Stephen's arrest to him and to be by Stephen's side at the magistrate's court. She looked into Alice's confused eyes. It was Christmas morning and this poor girl, who was trying so hard to put on a brave face, had nothing and nobody. In leaving Hill House, Lou would make way for someone who might actually do some good and deserve her place there. 'You want to see Edward again, don't you?'

'I'd die if it meant I could see him just one more time, but—'

'My purse is in my pocket,' Lou said. She shrugged off her parka and forced Alice to take it. 'Put this on. Go and find an open shop and get something to eat.'

THIRTY-TWO

CHRISTMAS EVE 1913

The emotions Lou experienced as she crossed the boundary threatened to overwhelm her; wonder, excitement, fear, hope. As the night surrounded her, she watched the miraculous transition of her shoes into beautiful silk slippers. Turning her face to the sky, she let snowflakes land on her cheeks and melt on her eyelids. Seven hours would surely be enough time to see the papers into safe hands. It was the final act she could perform to try to help the Mandevilles. It might even be enough time to say some goodbyes. The thread gave a sharp tug. The world could spin for another million years, and it would still be too short a time to find the words to say goodbye to one person . . . *Not now, Lou. You have a job to do.*

Icy wind bit into her bare arms and the trailing hem of her dress soaked up moisture from the deep snow as she put her head down and pressed on across the lawn. With the lingering sensation of George's fingers around her neck, she took the path around the side of the house and snuck into the conservatory.

She stood for a moment, damp and shivering, letting warmth seep from the heated floor tiles through the soles of her slippers. Opening the door to the deserted billiard room, she heard music and chatter float in from the ballroom. With one eye on the door to the hall and remembering the wild look in George's eyes, she hitched up her skirt, ran across the room and slipped through the hidden door beside the fireplace.

The winding stone steps headed down to the kitchen and up to the bedrooms on the floors above. If she could just make her way to the first floor unnoticed, then she could slip out on to the landing and sneak to her room. She was only halfway up when the sound of footsteps behind her made her stop.

'Miss! What are you doing here?'

She looked down. Sally was heading towards her.

'Your dress! What's happened to your dress and oh, your hair!'

Lou put her finger to her lips. 'Please, Sally,' she whispered, 'don't give me away. I need to get back to my room without being seen.'

Sally placed her tray of canapés on a step and began to fiddle with Lou's hair. 'Oh Miss, you're soaking. Whatever made you go outside? I'd come and help make you presentable only we're rushed off our feet. I'd be missed and . . . oh, Lord.'

'You don't need to worry. I'm not going back to the party.'

'Not going back to the party?'

'Please Sally, you need to listen to me. I'm leaving tonight, but you can't tell anyone.'

'Leaving?'

'I'm needed at home.' She didn't want to lie to Sally and there was real truth in what she said.

'Of course, Miss. We shall all miss you.'

'I'm truly sorry,' Lou said.

'It's me who should be sorry. I've no right to make you feel bad. I'm nothing to you.'

'Oh, Sally, that's not true. You've no idea how much you mean to me. I would never have survived this last week without your help. You pulled off a miracle and turned me into a lady.'

Sally smiled sadly. 'I succeeded in turning a sow's ear into a silk purse then?'

'You certainly did. And will you do one more thing for me?' Lou slipped her necklace over her head and pressed it into Sally's hands. 'Please give this to Mary. If anyone asks, you should say it's a gift and I want her to have it.'

'Mary?' Sally ran her thumb over the smooth pearls. 'What will a young girl like Mary do with a necklace such as this?'

'She'll put it to much better use than I ever could. And what about you, Sally, I'd like to make a gift to you, to thank you for taking care of me?'

A look of mortification flashed across Sally's face. 'I wouldn't accept anything. I should be offended just to think of it.'

Knowing better than to argue with Sally, Lou backed down. 'Very well,' she said. 'But you can't refuse this.' She put her arms around Sally and pulled her close. After an initial flinch of resistance, Sally gave in to the hug. A lump rose in Lou's throat. 'You take good care of William and that little boy of yours. I'm going to miss you all so much.' She closed her eyes and felt Sally nod. When they parted, Sally quickly wiped her eyes with the edge of her hand.

'You should go,' Lou said, her voice hoarse.

In a final show of dignified deference, Sally curtseyed. 'Very good, Miss,' she said, un-spilled tears in her eyes. She turned, collected her tray and headed away down the stairs.

Lou ran the rest of the way up and emerged at the far end of the landing. She flicked the light switch and made her way along the corridor in darkness; her senses alive, ready to run should any noise sound like an approaching person. Once safely inside her room, she sat at the dressing table, and laid out three sheets of paper. It was clear that she couldn't seek out any of her friends to say goodbye in person; it was a risk too far.

The first letter, to Lady Mandeville, was short: a couple of polite sentences thanking her for her hospitality and apologising for her hasty departure. The second letter took much longer to write. What could she say to Charlotte that wouldn't alarm her? She could hardly make predictions about the future without sounding insane, confirming any such idea that George may have already planted. She settled on a rousing letter, cheering Charlotte on, telling her to make the most of her life, to fulfil her potential, to warn her away from being ruled by men as best she could. She made no promise of returning but neither did she say that she wouldn't. She stopped short of a direct warning to stay away from George.

Let nobody ever tell you how to live your life. Never settle for second best. Fill your brain so full that you feel it will burst and then fill it some more. When you have finished, put everything you have learned to good use. I hope you will remember me fondly as I will remember you. Your friend forever, Louisa.

After sealing both letters in envelopes, Lou looked down at the third sheet of paper. Its blankness stared back at her. She drew more ink from the squat bottle into the pen and placed the nib to the paper. A blot began to form, growing, spreading. The paper soaked up the ink she could not use to form the words she so desperately wanted to say. What she felt for the intended recipient of this letter couldn't be contained on a single sheet of paper. The outpouring of words would spill out over the desk, pour onto the floor and surround her until she drowned in them. It would do neither of them any good for her to lay her soul bare. She had been brought back to tie up a loose end, not unravel another thread.

Dropping the pen, Lou looked at her reflection in the mirror. Her face was scoured clean of make-up and her damp hair hung loose around her shoulders. At no point in the last week had she looked less like Miss Louisa Arnold, a guest of the Mandevilles of Hill House, and more like plain old Lou Arnold from Hill House Council Estate. She pulled a wrap around her shoulders, slipped Elliot's envelope from the drawer, collected up her letters and crept from the room into the corridor.

Downstairs the party was still in full swing. Lou kept close to the wall of the upstairs landing. If anybody spotted her, they would come and see her off. Just short of the secret staff door, she almost tripped over a bundle on the floor. Thinking it was an item of discarded clothing; she was about to step over it when it moved. She stopped. It moved again. Had a dog or cat found its way inside to the warmth? She crouched beside it. It wasn't an animal; it was Bertie, fast asleep and with his face pressed to the banisters. He looked so peaceful that Lou hardly wanted to disturb him. She ran her fingers over his fine blonde curls. 'You be a good boy,' she whispered. 'Cherish your mummy and tell her every day how much you love her. Be sure to give your daddy such big hugs that he'll be able to feel them forever. And if something happens . . . if he ever . . .'

Bertie squirmed. She pulled her hand free. Too late. He rubbed his eyes with little balled fists and blinked at her

'I waited here for you,' he said. 'I'm to put your dolly away tomorrow morning.' He threw his arms around her neck, and she held his small body to hers, rocking him gently, her chin resting on his soft cotton nightshirt. When she prised herself away from him, tears shone in his eyes, just as they had in his mother's.

'I don't want you to go,' Bertie said.

'I don't want to go either. But my family need me. And

someone else needs to come here to take my place. You under-stand that, don't you?'

He nodded.

'Come along now,' she said, putting on her best cheerful voice, 'it's time you were in bed. Father Christmas won't deliver your presents if you're not asleep now, will he?' She held out her hand. Bertie wrapped his warm little fingers around hers and she helped him to his feet. Together they walked to the secret door. She eased it open and ushered him up the first steps to the attic bedrooms. He turned back and waved.

She watched him until he disappeared at the turn in the stairs before she descended the stone steps, heading for the basement. There was no time to dwell, or she might just crumble and she couldn't do that; she had to keep her wits about her. Going down this way was a safer route than navigating the alternative staff stairway into the billiard room, which by now would be full of men enjoying Sir Charles' fine malt. There was no way George would miss out on that. The only other option for leaving the house was to go out through the front door, but that risked facing the fury of George's family and the other guests.

She hovered on the landing at ground level where the steps led down to the kitchen. Monsieur Gotti, Mrs Moriarty and Bainbridge were calling out instructions over the jingle of crock-ery, the chink of glasses and footsteps running across the tiles. Briefly breaking cover, she peered down the stairs. A row of maids stood in a line along the basement corridor, like a row of starlings gathered on a telephone wire. They held trays of food, which Mrs Moriarty scrutinised. After a few adjustments, she nodded. 'Hurry along now, ladies. We don't want to keep the guests waiting.'

The maids headed for the stairs. Lou pressed into a recess, and they hurried past so close that she felt the rush of air around them. She waited for the last maid to disappear before breaking cover again. She ran down the stairs into the empty basement corridor, past Mrs Moriarty's room, the kitchen, the dairy, the stores, and cupboards, and didn't stop until she reached the end where she flung open the door to the outside. She was already halfway up the steps when Bainbridge called out, 'Who's there?'

Snow lay ankle-deep in the yard and Lou slipped inside the stables to the familiar dark warmth, the scent of hay and the sound of horses snuffling. A chair scraped along the floor in the storeroom. Elliot appeared in the doorway.

THIRTY-THREE

They sat opposite each other, two mugs of mulled cider and three envelopes on the table. With an old coat of Elliot's draped round her shoulders, Lou cupped her hands around the hot mug. Between sips of the sweet apple brew, she told Elliot just enough of what had passed between her and George Caxton for his grip to tighten on the handle of his mug. When she finished, he took up the envelope containing his statement and tucked it into the inside pocket of his jacket. There was no need for further explanation; Elliot knew what was needed from him. If the situation ever arose, he would see to it that the envelope and its contents made their way into the right hands.

He glanced at the letters addressed to Lady Mandeville and Charlotte. 'You'll be wanting me to leave them on the post tray in the hall in the morning.'

'Thank you.'

Elliot pushed his chair back and took a coat from the hook behind the door. 'I've to help prepare the cars for people leaving. Will I see you out?'

Lou hesitated. 'Would you mind if I waited here for a while longer?'

'Stay for as long as it pleases you to. Clarence'll keep you company.' At the sound of his name, Elliot's Labrador looked up from the rug in front of the fire and wagged his tail. 'There's cake in the tin if you're hungry and tobacco in the jar on the mantelshelf, if that's more to your taste. I'll say goodnight.' Elliot pulled his cap down.

'Elliot.'

He stopped in the doorway.

'I just wanted to say thank you. For helping me.'

'It's no trouble,' he said. 'My enemy's enemy is my friend.' And with that, the man of few words and honest hospitality, left.

The wind whistled outside, and snow collected on the ledge of the window. Lou got up and stooped to ruffle Clarence's ears. How wonderful it would be to curl up in front of a fire and fall asleep without a care in the world. She wandered through to the stables and stopped at the first stall. Easing in beside Samson, she ran her hand along his sleek coat. He shifted, the straw cracking beneath his hooves. Lou plucked a handful of hay from a bag on the floor, she held her palm out flat and offered it to him. Samson took it with a gentleness that belied his size.

Going from stall to stall, Lou spent a few minutes with each horse. When she arrived at the final stall, she ran her hand over Ambrose's rough mane. It was in the corner of what had remained of this stall that, as a child, she had hidden from Stephen, amongst the debris and charred remnants. If only it were that easy now. If only she could find a quiet corner to hide from the events of this world and her own. She buried her face in Ambrose's sweet-scented warmth. How many times could a heart be plastered and patched up after it had cracked open? Surely a human heart could take only so many poundings before it was damaged beyond repair.

Lou willed the stable door to fly open. Outside, the wind howled, and the snow continued to fall but the door stayed resolutely shut. There would be no more good-natured banter, no more dances, no more lips, cold from the outside, whispering in her ear while she wished they would kiss her. Another crack appeared in the organ shrivelling inside her chest.

She pressed her face to Ambrose's neck, her eyelids growing heavy. Perhaps she could sneak back inside the house and get a few hours' sleep before she had to meet Alice. At least then she wouldn't have to think so hard about what she was about to lose and what she must soon return to.

Ambrose's ears twitched and he shook his head. Lou straightened the blanket over his back and kissed his funny, rough mane before leaving him in peace.

The drive was empty of cars. The party was over. Even so, she couldn't risk entering the house through the front door. The staff had no doubt been instructed to call for help at the first sight of the crazy woman. She followed the path around the side of the house and let herself in through the conservatory. Once inside, Lou stood and listened. How odd it was that a house so full of people could be so quiet. She crept into the billiard room, which was dark except for a fire glowing in the grate. She began to pick her way carefully across the room and was almost at the servants' door when a voice said, 'Good evening, Louisa.'

She stopped, sure that her heart had missed a beat.

'Did I startle you?' Mrs Hart asked. She was sitting in a chair before the fire.

'No . . . sorry,' Lou said. 'I just wasn't expecting to find anyone still awake.'

'And I didn't expect someone to come creeping into the house in the dead of night.'

'I . . . I—'

'You don't have to explain yourself to me.' Mrs Hart took a

decanter from a side table and poured a healthy slug of brandy into two glasses. 'Join me,' she said.

Lou sat in the chair beside her. She rested against the warm leather, waiting for Mrs Hart to mention George. Instead, she picked up her glass and indicated for Lou to do the same.

'Down the hatch,' Mrs Hart said and knocked the drink back in one. She let out a sigh and refilled her glass.

Lou watched the flames sprout from the coals. She clutched her drink and let her eyelids close.

'I understand you are leaving us tomorrow,' Mrs Hart said. Lou's eyes snapped open.

'You mustn't be cross with Sally,' Mrs Hart added, 'she thought a member of the family ought to know. Besides, I had already been alerted by another source. Bertie told me this afternoon that he had been told to put your dolly away. When I asked him by whom, he couldn't say.'

'I'm sorry I didn't tell you in person. It all happened so quickly.'

'At least the forewarning of your departure means we will have the opportunity to say goodbye.'

'Unlike when Elizabeth left.'

'Yes, unlike when Elizabeth left,' Mrs Hart said. The brandy in her glass quivered as she put it to her lips.

It's now or never. 'If I knew something,' she began. 'If I could tell you something about Elizabeth. If I had found something out—'

'Please don't continue, Louisa. I mustn't know anything about the world beyond this world. Beyond my world. No matter how much you might want to tell me. No matter how much I might want to hear of it.' Mrs Hart laughed sadly. 'I have spent most of my adult life railing against any form of oppression or suppression. Yet here I sit, forcing you to keep the truth from me because I must protect this house. Do you not see the hypocrisy?'

'It's not hypocrisy if you're doing it for the right reasons.'

Mrs Hart smiled. 'Ever the diplomat, Louisa. But you mustn't mind me. I'm not quite myself. I'm afraid you've come upon me on my least favourite evening of the year.'

Lou picked at a seam in the arm of the chair. This was fast becoming her least favourite night of the year too. One of them anyway.

'It was a constant source of amusement to my husband – knowing how much I disliked this time of year – that we first met at my mother's Christmas Eve Ball. Years after our first meeting, Frederick told me that he fell in love with me on the spot, because while all the other young women seemed so gay, I hid in a corner like a storm cloud, frightening away any man who might have asked me to dance. Fred always relished a challenge. What a sentimental, foolish man, he was.' Mrs Hart laughed as though at a private joke. 'He was already a captain in the cavalry then and being an eighteen-year-old fledgling revolutionary, I felt honour-bound to dislike him. When he proposed marriage to me that same New Year's Day, I refused outright. It was a ridiculous proposal. I hardly knew the man!' Shadows lengthened across Mrs Hart's face. 'I'm sure you're not interested in the ramblings of an old lady.'

'I am,' Lou said, remembering Elizabeth using the same phrase. She was glad to have something other than herself to think about.

'If you insist,' Mrs Hart smiled. 'Not long into the year after I met Fred, I took a nursing course in secret, then, and much to my mother's horror, I travelled to London to work with a charity helping families in the East End of the city. It was a shock for a young woman like me, who had grown up surrounded by such privilege, to bear witness to the appalling conditions in which some human beings are forced to exist. I honestly cannot count the number of new lives I helped enter this world and how many hands I held as they departed. What little free time I had away from my duties, I spent attending political lectures and rallies. I became a stalwart of any socialist society or movement that would have me. And do you know, throughout all of those years, Fred never gave up on me. Whenever he was home on leave, he sought me out, each time renewing his proposal. I always refused, convincing myself that I didn't want to relinquish control of my life to a man. And then, when I was almost thirty, Frederick tracked me down to the boarding house where I was living in Bethnal Green. He was so earnest in his proposal that I finally accepted. I told everybody that he had worn me down and I felt sorry for the poor, unfortunate man. The truth was that I had seen so much sadness and wretchedness that I no longer wanted to face life without the chance of happiness. I had always found Frederick charming and handsome – although I would never have admitted as much to him. How stupid I had been to deny us both the opportunity of a life together for so long. After we married, Fred never once attempted to discourage me from my work or politics. He even tolerated my turning the parlour of our small house in Putney into a headquarters for my campaigns. He accepted it all as part of the woman I was. The woman he loved.'

The flames of the fire shone in Mrs Hart's eyes, but her voice was quiet when she said, 'Fourteen Christmases ago I left our home and travelled here to pass the festive season with my family as Fred was posted abroad. During my mother's Christmas Eve Ball, a telegram arrived. Fred had been killed leading a cavalry charge in the Transvaal. After that, I returned to Hill House to live permanently. I had lost my appetite for life in London. My nephews and niece became my world. I don't know that I would have survived without my family to fill the void left by the loss of my beloved Fred.' As her story came to an end, the light that usually burned so bright in Mrs Hart seemed to be extinguished.

'I'm so sorry,' Lou said. Her words sounded trite and came

nowhere close to expressing the sadness she felt in the face of such sorrow.

'You are very kind.' Mrs Hart managed a small smile. 'Through the years without Fred, I have taken comfort in the knowledge that he gave his life doing what he was made for. What he loved to do. We can none of us ask more from life than that.'

A swell of love for her friend made Lou want to do or say something. 'May I tell you a story of my own?' she asked.

'I should like that,' Mrs Hart said.

'It's a story about a woman. A hypothetical woman, let's call her Lizzie.'

Lou watched Mrs Hart's face, waiting for a reaction. Mrs Hart stared straight ahead. Taking her silence as permission to continue, Lou said, 'When Lizzie was a young girl, an awful tragedy threw her into the life of another lonely girl. They became such good friends that they grew as close as sisters. Unfortunately, one day Lizzie had to go away. It was as much a surprise to her as those she left behind. Her heart broke for the loss of her friend. But in leaving, she was reunited with the brother she thought lost. Through him, she met a man who became the love of her life. They married and had two sons. They travelled the world and Lizzie worked with women and children in every country they visited. But through all those years, Lizzie never forgot her best friend. Because how can you forget the person who helped mend your broken heart? Lizzie's greatest wish was that her friend should know that she had lived a good and happy life.'

Mrs Hart continued to stare straight ahead. A tear slipped down her cheek. She brushed it away. When another tear fell, it dripped down her cheek and on to her chest. 'Thank you,' she said quietly. Putting aside her glass, she let her hand rest on top of Lou's. 'Now let me tell you the ending to *my* story. Not ten minutes before you came in tonight, Tom was sitting in that chair where you are now. He always takes a drink with me on Christmas Eve. To remember. He was only a boy when Fred died but he was incredibly fond of his uncle. He took the news of his death very hard. I see so much of Fred in the man Tom has become. His kindness, his temperament, his loyalty. But tonight, unlike every other Christmas Eve, Tom needed my comfort. He said that he was sure he wouldn't sleep since he has so much playing on his mind.' She squeezed Lou's hands. 'I would give up all the life I have lived since Fred died for the chance to spend just one more minute with him. I wasted so much time when he could have been mine. Louisa, do not make the mistake that this foolish, stubborn old woman did. Do not leave this house without telling Tom how you feel, without giving him the chance to say what he must. He doesn't know that you are going. I didn't feel that it was my place to tell him.'

Even in the half-light there was nowhere to hide from Mrs Hart's directness. Lou shook her head. 'I can't face another goodbye,' she said. 'It's too painful.'

'If you don't, you will both live to regret it.'

'I shouldn't. It will only confuse—'

'What is meant to be will be, Louisa. You of everyone must know that. But you also know that sometimes fate needs a helping hand.'

Out in the hall, Lou stood before the Christmas tree. Fresh candles had been placed in the branches. Presents wrapped in ribbons were arranged beneath the boughs. Tomorrow morning, the candles would be lit and, as they burned bright, those presents would be handed around. Lou held her wrap tight around her neck. She would see none of it. A crippling pain caught in her chest. It was a physical pain, which she felt in her very core. She would never see him again. Once she left this house, Tom would be gone from her life. Even now she found it hard to picture his face. He was slipping away from her like a figure in a dream. *'Go to him,'* Mrs Hart had said. Never had she wanted to follow an instruction more. But she shouldn't interfere. She should slip away from this family and leave them to whatever the future had in store for them. She closed her eyes. *For once in your life, don't over think a decision. Trust your instincts.*

On the upstairs landing, Lou stopped at a door. A shadow crossed the light beneath. She knocked twice. The shadow came back. A key turned in the lock. The door opened and Tom stood before her, framed by lamplight. He had removed his jacket and tie and his collar was open. He was holding a book.

'Lou?'

She began to shake. *Speak damn it. Speak!* 'Sorry . . . I didn't mean to disturb you. I . . . I just wanted to say goodbye.'

'Goodbye?' Tom took a step towards her. The crease now familiar to Lou appeared between his eyebrows.

'I'm leaving tomorrow, you see. Very early. I wanted to say goodbye before I go. That's all. I'm sorry.'

'Come in.' Tom pushed the door further open.

'I shouldn't, it's not right. If we're seen . . .'

Tom stepped aside. 'Come in.'

THIRTY-FOUR

Lou stood beside the hearth, trying not to look around and disturb Tom's privacy any more than barging into his room in the middle of the night already had. He closed the door, placed his book on the washstand and stood before her with his hands in his pockets.

'What do you mean you're leaving?' Tom stared down at her so that Lou felt he might never look away.

'I've had news from home. I have to go away.'

'Will you return for New Year's Eve? Mother puts on a wonderful Hogmanay meal for a few close friends and family.' The crease in his brow disappeared briefly as he attempted a smile.

Lou shook her head.

'Oh, I see,' Tom said quietly. 'When are you leaving?'

'Early tomorrow morning. I'm being met before sunrise.'

'So suddenly? Will you have time to say goodbye to Mother and Charlotte?'

'I've written to each of them to explain. Would tell them I'm sorry I couldn't say goodbye in person?'

'Of course. They'll be disappointed.'

They, Lou thought. Only they?

An awkward silence fell. Tom rubbed his thumb against his forefinger as though trying to summon words through the action. In the last week, they had found so much to say to each other and now Lou was afraid to open her mouth for fear of what else might come out. 'I should go. It's late.'

'Or early, depending on how you look at it. It is after midnight.' Tom smiled, but it seemed forced. He continued to look at her.

Lou noticed how Tom's shirt gaped, exposing his collarbones. How his Adam's apple moved up and down in his throat when he swallowed. He pulled his hand from his pocket and she saw that his knuckles were bleeding.

'You're hurt.' Lou tried to touch his hand. He pulled it away, hiding it behind his back.

'It's nothing.'

'What happened?'

'It doesn't matter.'

'Tom?'

'If you must know, I let my anger get the better of me. I'm not proud of it but there you are.'

'What did you do?'

'Must you know everything?'

'Not if you don't want to—'

'I hit George. I've a mind to go and do it again.'

'You punched your cousin! Why?'

Tom dug his hands into his pockets and turned from her. When he turned back, there was a look of fury in his eyes. 'What did Caxton do to you? And don't say 'nothing'. I saw you run out into the night after that oaf stumbled through the curtains. I called after you and tried to follow but you'd already disappeared. When the women had finished fussing over Caxton, I sought him out. I demanded that he tell me what he had done to make you run away. He looked at me with that stupid, bloody grin and said . . .' He looked away and then back at her face, intently. 'Did he hurt you?'

'You hit your cousin because of me? Tom, how could you?'

His eyes fixed on her neck. Her wrap had fallen open. She tried to pull it together. It was too late.

'Did he do that?' Tom demanded. 'I swear I'll kill him. I'll wring his bloody neck.' He made for the door. Lou grabbed his arm.

'Tom, don't. What about Emma? How can you hope to marry her if it you go around punching her brother?'

'I have no intention of marrying Emma Caxton.'

'You have to,' she said, releasing his arm.

'I have to do no such thing.'

Why was he being so bloody-minded? 'But she's beautiful and charming and so right for you in every way.'

Tom ran his fingers through his hair, the muscles in his arms tensing. 'For God's sake woman, will you be quiet and listen to me for one second? I'm not going to marry Emma Caxton, because I'm in love with someone else.'

Lou heard herself swallow.

Tom took a step closer to her. 'The woman I love gets two funny little wrinkles in her forehead when she's cross. She hides behind trees in the woods. She smokes cigarettes when she has one too many brandies. She drives me to distraction with her determination to find a solution to every problem, but I know it's because she cares more about other people than she does about herself. And I wouldn't have her any other way.'

'Tom, please don't—'

'While she walks this Earth, there will be no other woman for me.' His voice was soft and low. 'I can't let her leave this house without telling her how much I want her.'

'It's not as simple as wanting.'

'It is, if you want it to be.' He was so close that she could feel the warmth of his body through his shirt. 'Do you want me, Lou?'

Every one of her senses came alive; the sensation of him watching her, waiting for a reaction, the smell of his woody cologne, his closeness causing the hairs on her arms to stand on end. There was nothing, *nothing,* she had ever wanted more than Thomas Mandeville, and there was nothing more overwhelming than the desire burning inside her. She took hold of Tom's hand and kissed each bloodied knuckle. No man had ever loved her enough to fight for her.

Tom cupped her face and she leant into his palm. His lips met hers, his kiss beautiful, tender.

When they parted, Lou was breathless. 'You once told me that you would rather love passionately for an hour than benignly for a lifetime,' she said. 'I want that hour.'

'It's yours.' Tom's second kiss was deeper, and she responded eagerly. They kissed like two starving people, hungry only for each other. His passion was all consuming. She helped him remove her dress, his lips exploring her shoulders and neck.

'The other night you said a man would have to be mad to love you,' he murmured. 'I must be quite insane.' He brushed his lips lightly over the bruises on her neck. 'I will never, *never,* let anybody hurt you again.'

A sensation shot through Lou's body. Every inch of skin was suddenly charged. After all the waiting, now that the moment was here, she didn't want to wait a second longer. She helped him tear off her corset and gasped as, gloriously, Tom's lips found her breasts.

THIRTY-FIVE

CHRISTMAS DAY 1913

For the first time in weeks, Lou slept soundly. When she woke, it was still night. She lay perfectly still, the weight of Tom's arm across her waist, the rise and fall of his chest beside her. She let her breathing fall in time with his, sharing the air that he breathed. Twisting carefully to avoid disturbing him, she looked at his face in the light from the fire, at his closed eyes, his hair on the pillow beside hers. Tom slept peacefully. The sleep of the just; the sleep of the oblivious. For him, they had a future. For him, they had all the time in the world.

The clock on the mantelshelf said four o'clock. Gently, Lou pushed Tom's arm away, she waited for him to settle before slipping from the bed. She stood before his washstand and looked at his private, intimate possessions: hairbrushes, razor, shaving soap, bottle of cologne. She picked up the book he had abandoned when she'd disturbed him.

'Why did you get up?' Tom murmured behind her, his voice full of sleep. His arms slipped around her waist, his chin rested on her shoulder.

'You were reading Plato,' she said.

'Ah, you have caught me out.' He kissed her neck. 'Since I

couldn't look at you directly last night, I settled for the next best thing; reading the words that your eyes had read. It made me feel close to you. You must think me a sentimental fool.'

She turned around and looked up into his eyes. 'No, I think you're the most perfect man I have ever met.'

'Hardly.' He laughed and when he kissed her, she could feel his smile on her lips. 'Come back to bed.'

She wanted to cry out, to yell and scream and tell the world that this was all so unfair. But she knew she couldn't. 'There's something I need to tell you first.'

'Can't it wait?' He kissed her shoulder, and it took all her self-control to resist him.

'Tom, please listen. I want you to know that I don't expect you to wait for me—'

'What?' He laughed, clearly thinking she was joking.

'Where I'm going, I'll have no way of contacting you.'

'Are you going abroad?'

'Yes, with my brothers.' She grabbed his suggestion like a drowning swimmer holding to a life raft.

'And they don't have a postal service where you're going?' He kissed her neck all the way up to her ear.

Focus, Lou. Focus. 'I'll be away for a really long time and long-distance relationships never work. If you meet someone else . . . Tom, I'm giving you my blessing to—'

He silenced her with another kiss on the lips. 'I won't write, if you'd rather I didn't. In any case, I'm a terrible pen pal. But next time I'm on leave, wherever you are in the world, I will find you. I'm afraid you won't get away from me that easily.'

He kissed her again and this time she grasped his sleep-mussed hair, pulling him to her. When they made love, the urgency of their first encounter was gone, replaced by a slow, tender longing. Together they lay, warm and safe beneath the soft sheets with the fire crackling in the grate. Thomas Mandeville connected with something so deep inside her that she hadn't known it existed. And she clung to him as though clinging on to life itself.

When the clock chimed six, Lou reluctantly slipped from Tom's bed and began to dress. She refused his offer of walking her down to the car that she said was waiting for her.

'You're leaving like that?' He frowned at her party dress. 'It's bitter out there. Here, take my coat.'

'I'm being met at the gates. There's no need to worry.'

Tom pulled on his robe and tied it loosely around his waist before collecting her wrap from where it had fallen on the floor. He placed it around her shoulders and holding each end, used it to pull her to him. 'After last night, it's my job to worry about you.'

She was torn down the middle. She looked at the fine hair at the base of each of his fingers and at the white half-moons in each nail. Desperate to make a mental note of every part of him, her eyes flicked to his chest; to his skin, bare where his robe gaped, visible to his navel; to the muscles taught in his stomach, covered by a layer of soft hair.

'Please Tom, if you ever have to go into battle, promise me that you won't be a hero.'

He laughed softly. 'Me? Never.' In that moment, she could see his future as clearly as if it were in the pages of a book. And it broke her heart, utterly. 'Happy Christmas, my darling, Lou.'

He kissed her and she closed her eyes, drowning in the sensation of his arms holding her, his stubble against her cheek, his hands pressing into her hair – imprinting every last drop of Thomas Mandeville's love into her memory.

A chill wind blew into the conservatory as Lou stepped across the threshold. She closed the door to protect the orchids, pausing to look through the window at the outline of their waxy leaves. She gripped the door handle. It would be easy to turn it now, to step inside and run back up the stairs to that gracious, funny, gentle man who had found his way into every part of her. They had said their goodbyes, made promises that she knew neither of them could ever keep. *Tom!* She wanted to shout his name, to have him rush down the stairs, throw open the door, take her in his arms and pull her to him and never let her go. If he did that – if she counted to five and he came for her – it would be a sign that she was free to stay. That she was no longer needed in her old life. That her brothers would cope without her. She peered into the darkness.

One ... two... three ... four ... five ... please ... please ... please ...

No light came on. No sounds of movement from within. She rested her forehead against the cold glass and forced each finger to release its grip on the handle. On the horizon, the first hairsbreadth of pale pink sunlight appeared.

Without looking back, she ran as fast as she could in her dance slippers down the drive. As she reached the gates, she turned for one last look back. There, standing in the window of the room above the front door, was Tom. With the light behind him, he was hardly more than a dark shadow. He raised his hand. Lou kissed her palm and held it up to him, her cracked heart splitting in two.

THIRTY-SIX

CHRISTMAS DAY 2013

Lou crossed the boundary. The sky was dark; the stars and moon out. She had missed every daylight hour of Christmas Day.

'You came back,' Alice said, emerging from the shadows.

'Go on,' Lou said, without looking up.

'Are you okay?'

She felt Alice's eyes search her face.

'Don't waste this chance. Fight for Edward and never let him go.'

'I promise I will, if he'll let me. Are you sure you're okay? You don't look right.'

Lou covered her eyes. 'Just go, before I change my mind.'

'Is there a message? Something I can take back with me? I know what it's like to leave without saying goodbye.'

The thread connecting Lou's soul to the soul inside that house gave a tug so hard she felt it pull at the centre of her chest.

'There is one thing,' she said.

'Anything.'

'Charlotte needs your protection. Do whatever you can to

keep her away from George Caxton. I can't tell you why, it might put your position in Hill House at risk. Just know that there is real danger to Charlotte from George Caxton. There is real danger to any woman from him.'

'I'll do whatever I can, I promise. And Louisa, I'll never forget what you're doing for me. You don't know it, but you're saving my life.'

Alice smiled nervously. She shrugged off Lou's parka and handed it to her. 'I suppose I should see if Hill House wants me then.'

Lou nodded. She watched Alice walk slowly to the gates. Her shoulders rose and fell as she took a deep breath and stepped across the boundary, out of sight. Lou waited. What if she'd got this wrong? It was possible that Alice was still there, just beyond the gates, rooted to the spot after failing to go back, because Hill House didn't want her. Alice wasn't *the one*.

A memory came rushing back to Lou. The text from HR had said that she had until 2nd January to return to work. She still had a week.

Lou ran through the gates. Her shoes skidded on gravel. By the light of the streetlamps out on the pavement, she saw that the drive was empty. Alice had disappeared. Hill House crouched at the end of the drive. The window above the front door was dark. No shadow looked down on her. It was over.

Lou sank to her knees. She had failed. Her promises to help the Mandevilles lay in tatters in that shell of a house. She should never have gone to Tom's room. If she hadn't, there might have been a chance for him and Emma. She had offered herself to him on a plate. Of course, he had accepted. Any man would have accepted what was so easily given. She felt again the sensation of skin against hot skin, the taste of lips, the stroke of fingertips, the realness and wholeness of a man wanting her as much as she wanted him.

Struggling to her feet, she fell through the gates, tripped

over a bag of fly-tipped rubbish, and stumbled up the steps of the footbridge, down the alley and along the road.

She let herself into the empty house, crept up the stairs and crawled fully dressed into her bed. Curling into a ball, she held herself. But she couldn't cry. Nothing felt real. Finally, exhaustion caught her in its grasp, and she slipped into a shallow sleep.

THIRTY-SEVEN

Lou woke, utterly disorientated, her insides stripped raw. With her face pressed into the pillow, she forced one eye open and took in her surroundings. The clothes hanging on the wardrobe door looked like they belonged to somebody else. The titles on the spines of the books on the shelves made no sense. The trinkets on the chest of drawers held no meaning.

Lou swung her legs from beneath the duvet and sat on the edge of the bed. Noises crept through the floorboards from the kitchen below. Pots rattled, plates chinked, the kettle rumbled to the boil. So, she had slept through what had been left of Christmas Day and night, missing Dean's return and the chance to head off the inevitability of someone else telling him about Stephen's arrest.

Leaving her room, Lou made her way downstairs, heading for the kitchen. But when she passed the living room, she doubled back. A Christmas tree stood beside the television. Not the wonky artificial tree they dragged down from the loft every year, but a real tree, in a fancy metal stand. The gold tinsel threaded through the branches, glittered in the bright white light of a string of fairy lights. New fairy lights. The mantelpiece was free of sympathy cards. In their place was a row of Christmas cards arranged around a little wooden Nativity scene. Dean could never have done this on his own. There were no shops open on Christmas Day for him to have bought a tree and he wouldn't have thought to buy a wooden Nativity scene.

Bing Crosby's voice floated from the kitchen. Along with it came the unmistakeable scent of cooking. That definitely wasn't Dean; he could just about heat a tin of beans without setting off the smoke alarm. Mum's cousin, Shirley, must have taken pity on them and come bearing this tree and Nativity decoration along with all the ingredients to cook their Boxing Day lunch. Preparing the words to thank her Auntie Shirley, Lou made her way back through the hall and pushed open the kitchen door.

Nothing in her life up to that point – not even the events of the previous week – could have prepared her for the person standing at the kitchen sink in a Father Christmas apron, peeling Brussels sprouts, humming along to 'White Christmas'.

'Morning, sleepyhead. Merry Christmas!'

Lou collapsed against the fridge, covering her mouth with her hand.

'How's Katie settling in with that lovely new husband of hers? Did you go to the Trafford Centre? I saw it on telly. All those designer shops – it looks wonderful.'

When Lou didn't respond, her mum turned around. 'I didn't hear you come in last night. Was there trouble on the trains?' She smiled over her shoulder as she cut a cross into the base of a sprout.

'Mum?'

'Are you all right, love? You look terribly pale.' Her mum dropped the trimmed sprout into the colander and placed the knife on the edge of the sink. She wiped her hands on her apron and pressed the back of her hand to Lou's forehead. Her skin was cool from holding it beneath the running tap. 'No temperature, you'll live.'

'Mum . . . oh my God, Mum!' Lou cried.

'Here, sit down before you fall down.' Her mum pulled out a chair and helped Lou sit, but no sooner was she in the chair than she was up again, her arms around her mum.

'I've missed you so much. I can't . . . I just can't . . .'

'I've missed you too. But it's only been a week, love.'

'Oh Mum, it's you. It's really you.' Lou cried and laughed at the same time. She kissed her mum's cheeks, touched her warm face and felt her soft hair, freshly washed and straightened.

'Who else were you expecting to find in the kitchen? Dean?' Mum laughed. 'That boy could burn an ice lolly. Speak of the devil.'

'Ding Dong Merrily and all that.' Dean barged into the kitchen wearing a jumper decorated with a giant cartoon reindeer. 'I come bearing gifts for the two ladies in my life.'

He dumped two badly wrapped presents on the table. Shower gel. It was always shower gel; peach for Lou and white musk for Mum. Lou laughed, a laugh verging on hysteria. 'It's Christmas Morning again!' she said.

Dean eyed her like he would Minnie, the old lady who liked to tap dance around the drained fountain in The Arc.

'Get your sister a brandy,' Mum said. 'She's a bit under the weather.'

'Can I have one?' Dean asked.

'Just a small one. And only because it's Christmas.'

'But Muuum,' he whined, 'I'll be eighteen next year.'

'Then next year you can have a large one. Your sister needs it for medicinal reasons.' She placed the back of her hand on Lou's forehead again. 'Are you sure you're not sickening for something?'

Was she? Lou thought. Caught up in the unreality of this moment, the events of the previous week and of last night had momentarily slipped her mind. They came rushing back with the full force of a runaway train. She collapsed into the chair.

'Hurry up with that brandy, Dean,' Mum said. She sat beside Lou and stared at her. 'You can't hide anything from me, sweetheart. Have you had a falling out with Katie? Is that it?' Her voice was so full of concern that Lou wanted to cry. She could never explain what had happened, what was still happening.

At the sound of a key turning in the front door, Mum looked up. 'We're in the kitchen,' she called.

Stephen burst in wearing a Santa hat, his ex-fiancée, Rebecca, by his side. 'Aye Aye fishy pie!' he said, 'Merry Christmas one and all!' He dropped a bag of gifts on the table and kissed the top of Mum's head.

'Morning, Deano. All right, sis. How was Manchester?'

Lou leapt from the chair and threw her arms around his neck.

'Bloody Hell,' Stephen laughed awkwardly. 'What's got into you?'

'Nothing . . . I'm just pleased to see you.'

'Have I missed something?'

Stephen was right to sound confused. In this world, there had never been an argument, since the cause of their fight was sitting there, at the kitchen table. She hadn't stormed out but had been to visit Katie. There had been no funeral to pay for and no arrest. In this world, it looked like Stephen and Rebecca were still engaged. There had been no stolen plaques from the war memorial. The train hurtled towards her again and Lou buried her face in Stephen's jumper. Smothered in her big brother's arms, she heard voices whisper about fevers and flu, walk-in clinics and calling out the doctor. Stephen squeezed her tight. 'You'll be okay, won't you, sis? We'll look after you.' He helped her sit down and she kept hold of his hand. He didn't seem to mind.

'So,' he said, 'what do you want first? The good news or the bad news?'

'Oh, let's have the good news,' Mum said, one eye still on Lou. 'We don't want to hear anything bad on Christmas Day.'

'Well, the good news is . . .' He paused for effect. 'I won twenty pounds on the lottery last night!'

Dean groaned. 'Is that it?'

'Not quite.' Stephen gently freed his hand from Lou's grasp and stood behind Rebecca. He slipped his arms around her waist and patted her stomach. 'The bad news is, it looks like I won't be able to spend it down The Arms. We're saving for a cot.'

'You're not!' Mum shrieked.

Rebecca grinned shyly and tucked her hair behind her ear. 'I'm twelve weeks gone.'

Stephen laughed. 'How's that for a Christmas present? Better than a box of Ferrero Rocher, *Grandma*.'

Mum rushed to Rebecca and Stephen, showering them with kisses. 'Oh, you clever pair!' she gushed, asking about due dates and scans and making a fuss of Rebecca's stomach. 'Have you told your dad yet?'

'We're going to surprise him tomorrow. Hey, and don't you be late, Lou. I'll pick you and Deano up at ten o'clock sharp.'

'What? Why?' Lou asked.

'What's wrong with her?' Dean said. 'We're going to Dad's for Boxing Day. We *always* go to Dad's on Boxing Day.' He looked to Stephen. 'Has she had a bump on the head, or what?'

'Leave your sister alone. She's just tired,' Mum said. She glanced at her watch. 'Come on you lot, we'd best get a move on if we don't want to be late. Dean, get your coat.'

Lou watched the scene unfold around her; her brothers laughing and joking, neither of them in the least surprised at Mum's suggestion they leave the house rather than spend the morning slouched in front of the telly, dipping their hands into a tub of chocolates, waiting for the call from the kitchen that lunch was ready. Mum slipped her apron over her head and hung it behind the door while Dean demonstrated how Rudolph's nose lit up when he pressed a button tucked up inside his jumper. Mum laughed and shooed Stephen and Dean out into the hall. They made a great play of shoving each other, laughing as they both tried to get through at the same time, Mum warning them to watch out for Rebecca.

Lou followed them. Taking the lead from everyone else, she pulled on her coat. As they were about to leave, her mum took a brown envelope from the hallstand. 'I almost forgot,' she said, handing the envelope to Lou, 'this arrived yesterday. Looks official.'

Lou pushed the letter into her coat pocket.

They left the house and Lou slipped her arm through her mum's. They walked along the road, Dean and Stephen dragging up the rear, Mum and Rebecca chatting about nursery furniture. Lou stared at the side of her mum's face. She couldn't let go of her. This might all be a dream. At any moment, her mum might be snatched away from her again.

They stopped at the green to admire the decorations the residents' association had arranged. They were joined by neighbours who Lou knew had moved out months, sometimes years earlier, all greeting each other with, 'Merry Christmas!' Everybody behaved as though this were all perfectly normal. Lou stared in wonder at the usually unkempt gardens cleared of upturned plant pots and discarded children's toys, the broken fences miraculously mended with new wooden posts and panels, and the potholes in the road that had been filled.

She looked at the multicoloured bulbs strung around the bare branches of the trees on the green and the illuminated reindeers arranged at the base of their trunks. She had lived here her whole life but had never heard of a resident's association. And the Council had cut the trees down years before. All around her, everything looked almost familiar. Almost, but not quite. As though the world had shifted on its axis, knocking everything ever so slightly off kilter, making everything just a bit . . . nicer.

The crowd that had converged on the green began to move off. Lou buried her face in her mum's shoulder, walking without knowing where they were going. When she did eventually look up, she gripped her mum's arm tighter.

The momentum of the crowd carried them along, up and over the footbridge. The pavement on the other side was clear of rubbish and abandoned mattresses. The walls were free of graffiti. The gates had been fixed. They were back on their hinges, the filigree freshly painted, the gold lions shining at the top. Lou faltered. But she couldn't stop now. She couldn't turn back. She had to see this through. She had to make sense of this world that had somehow transformed overnight.

Side by side with her mum, Lou crossed the boundary. And there, at the end of the drive, stood Hill House. Its pale Portland stone gleamed and smoke billowed from the tall chimneystacks. Hill House was alive again.

'Lou . . . Lou . . .'

She heard her mum's voice as though from a distance.

'You're shaking, love. I really think you're coming down with something. Maybe I should take you home.'

'I'm all right, really.'

'If you're sure?' Mum smiled. 'I'm glad. It wouldn't feel right for any of us to miss out on Hill House Christmas carols.'

So, this is what they did every Christmas Morning in this world; they didn't watch *The Wizard of Oz* and gorge on Quality Street, they came to Hill House to sing carols.

Lou and her mum followed Stephen, Dean, and Rebecca up the drive and through the door into Hill House. The hall was full of people in coats and scarves, accepting gingerbread from trays offered by other people dressed as maids and footmen. Aside from her neighbours and the people in ill-fitting costumes, everything was just as Lou had left it only hours earlier – the tulip mosaics on the floor, the marble statues, the fire roaring in the hearth, the Mandeville crest on the chimney-breast, a huge Christmas tree beside the fire. For a single heart-beat, Lou considered running up the stairs.

'Would you care for some?' A lady dressed in a long tweed skirt and white blouse held out her tray of gingerbread. Stephen and Dean greedily accepted.

'Doesn't your costume look gorgeous,' Mum said.

'Thanks,' the woman said. 'We're supposed to be the people who lived here one hundred years ago. I drew the long straw. I'm one of the ladies of the house. The sister of the baronet: Mrs Leonora Hart.'

'Lou, Lou, are you all right, love?' Mum's face swam into Lou's field of vision. 'You're shaking like a leaf.'

'I'm fine.' How could she say that Mrs Hart would never wear a crocheted shawl? It would have been silk and jewel-coloured, never dowdy brown wool.

'Oh, there's Jo and the other girls from work.' Mum stood on tiptoe and waved through the open ballroom door. 'Let's pop in and tell them Stephen and Rebecca's news, they'll be thrilled.'

'I'll wait out here,' Lou said. In response to the uncertain look on her mum's face, she added, 'I'm okay. I just need a bit of space. Go on, you go and see your friends.'

'Okay. But if you need me, you will shout. Promise?'

'Cross my heart.'

Lou watched as Mum took Rebecca's hand and led her and the boys into the ballroom. Last night that room had been full of people dancing in their Edwardian finery and now it was packed with people from the town, gathering to sing carols. In the midst of them was her mum. Her mum. She was really there, smiling, pointing at Rebecca's stomach, her cheeks flushed from the warmth and excitement. Tomorrow Lou would spend Boxing Day with her dad. While she had slept, her whole world had changed. She was living a miracle. But it was only a miracle to her. To everyone else, this was all perfectly normal.

From somewhere inside the ballroom a piano struck up the opening chords of 'Away in a Manger'. The staff and final stragglers made their way inside to join the singing, leaving Lou alone before the Christmas tree. She stared into the branches. Amongst the modern, faux-antique plastic decorations, she saw the most beautiful baubles. The delicate glass, once crisply transparent, had grown cloudy, but the prized decorations had survived the last one hundred years. As had the bricks and mortar of this house. But the friends she had left yesterday, made as they were of fragile flesh, would by now all be long gone, having met their awful fates – all because she had failed them.

The reflection of a person standing behind her shone in one of the baubles. 'Happy Christmas, Lou,' a man's voice said.

Lou spun around.

'Surprised to see me?' Will asked.

'What are you doing here?'

'I came to see you.'

'Me? What . . . How . . .?'

'Everyone comes here on Christmas Morning.' Will smiled. 'Take a deep breath, Lou. You're doing a brilliant impression of a goldfish.'

Lou did her best to slow the rate of her breathing.

'Better?' Will asked.

She nodded.

'Good. Come with me.'

Lou followed Will away from the hall and the singing, and into the morning room. Like the hall, it was just as she remembered. The sofas, plump cushions and rugs were a little faded and worn around the edges, but they were all still there. Only now there was a rope barrier stopping anyone going further than a few feet into the room. Within the boundary of what could be explored was a brightly lit glass cabinet full of photographs, each accompanied by a small, typed card interpreting its significance to the story of the family whose history this cabinet contained. The Mandevilles.

'Wait there a second,' Will said. 'I've got a surprise for you.'

A surprise. Was he kidding? Her world had turned into one giant surprise. She scanned the photographs and cards behind the glass, but couldn't make sense of any of it.

Will returned, pushing a wheelchair. The old man hunched over with a blanket across his knees lifted his chin from his chest. His thin lips formed a smile.

'Bertie!' Lou took his hands, feeling the crooked bones beneath his delicate skin.

'You haven't changed at all, Miss Louisa,' Bertie said. As he spoke, his eyes shone. 'It seems like only yesterday that I last saw you.'

'For me it was,' she whispered. 'Last night you were a little boy hiding at the top of the stairs. And now . . . What's happening to me, Bertie? Am I really here? Did I dream everything that happened last week? Am I dreaming now?'

'No, Miss Louisa, you're not dreaming. None of this has been a dream,' he said.

Lou looked from Bertie to Will. He was smiling. 'So, you know my great-granddad Albert,' he said.

'Your great-granddad?'

'And I believe you met my Auntie Julie last week.'

'But you're an archivist . . . at the library . . . I saw you there . . . you helped me.'

'I am. And I did,' Will said, still smiling.

Bertie lifted his chin from his chest again. 'You see, Miss Louisa, William has inherited my gift. And it is a gift. The most wonderful gift that can be bestowed on a person.'

'You're a . . . a . . .' She struggled to find a suitable word. 'You're a *cipher* for Hill House. Is that what you are?'

'Something like that,' Will said.

'You know about . . . about me and what happened.'

'A little,' Will said. 'I know about a young woman called Louisa Arnold who helped the Mandevilles and in helping them, she helped my family.'

'But last week Hill House was a wreck. It was—'

'William, please take me to the cabinet.' Bertie released Lou's hands and Will pushed him to the glass cabinet. With what was clearly a considerable effort, he pointed to the photograph of a family group, a mother and father with four children – two boys, a girl and a babe in arms. They were dressed in what Lou recognised as the fashion of the nineteen twenties.

'Who do you see?' Bertie asked.

Lou peered into the faces. 'I don't know.'

'Look more closely,' Bertie said.

Lou moved in closer but stopped short of pressing her nose to the glass. It took a few moments. 'It looks like . . . well, it looks like Edward. And Alice.'

'Lady Alice,' Bertie corrected. 'She was a godsend to the Mandevilles.'

'Alice?' Lou said. 'We are talking about the same person? Alice the maid.'

'The very same,' Bertie said. 'She had to fight to be accepted but she took strength from Mr Edward's love for her. After they married Lady Alice worked alongside Mr Edward to keep Hill House going. Together they were able to see the place through the lean years. They worked tirelessly to save their home. Land had to be sold, of course, but with them together at the helm, Hill House thrived.'

Lou looked at Alice's beautiful dress, her hair neatly pinned up, her children around her and Edward's hand on her shoulder. She was almost unrecognisable as the sad creature Lou had watched walk through the gates. Lou was still grasping what had happened to Alice when Bertie said, 'You'll be interested in what happened to the rest of the Mandevilles too.'

Lou swallowed and nodded slowly.

'Shortly after the ball you attended that last Christmas before the Great War, Lord Caxton arranged a position for his son with the Colonial Office in India. George Caxton may not have faced justice for his crimes in this country, but he wasn't so lucky when he was implicated in a ring of corruption and a murder in Calcutta. When her father died Lady Emma and her husband took over the running of Caxton Hall. She had a family and was happy. And she was a great supporter of Miss Charlotte.'

'A supporter?'

Will put a hand on Bertie's shoulder. 'You take a rest, Granddad, I'll explain. You see, Lou, Charlotte Mandeville was a trailblazer for the rights of women. She was one of the first women to study at Cambridge. The tradition had always been for the Mandeville heir to become the local MP, but that changed with Charlotte. Edward really wasn't cut out for politics, so it was Charlotte who stood for parliament. But not until the nineteen thirties, after Sir Charles passed away at a ripe old age. Charlotte represented this constituency for over twenty years and made an amazing job of it.'

'Sir Charles lived . . . and Charlotte was an MP.' Lou had to say it aloud to believe it. Sir Charles hadn't killed himself. Charlotte hadn't married George. The bright young girl in a pretty pink dress with a fondness for weather machines and playing cards had made it. She'd only gone and made it!

'She married a young officer who became the local doctor. They did so much good for this town,' Bertie said. 'A veteran from the war, he was. Survived a terrible injury. Carried the scars on his face for the rest of his life. He met Miss Charlotte when she treated him at Mrs Hart's hospital.'

'Mrs Hart turned the house into a hospital.' Lou smiled. 'I can believe that.'

Bertie pointed out a series of photographs of young men, some in pyjamas, others in uniform, some with bandages covering wounds, others on crutches or in wheelchairs. They all had one thing in common – they were photographed in and around Hill House; taking tea in the morning room, enjoying a meal in the dining room, fishing in the trout lake, smoking and drinking over cards in the billiard room or sitting in the wicker chairs in the conservatory amidst Sir Charles' flowers.

'Mrs Hart insisted that Hill House be turned into a hospital for soldiers during The Great War,' Will said. 'But it was on one condition – that it treated all ranks, not just officers. And that no man wore the invalid blue uniforms. Mrs Hart was adamant that each wore his normal uniform, a civilian suit, or the silk pyjamas she had the wealthy ladies of the area donate. She set up one of the guest rooms as an operating theatre for the surgeon who came up from London once a week, and she led the nursing team, mainly made up of the maids. Lady Mandeville took care of the men's pastoral needs, sitting by their beds, helping them write letters home, arranging silver service dinners, cards, and billiards and croquet tournaments, for those able to take part. Every man was welcomed at the door by Mrs Hart, no matter the time of day or night. Some of them arrived in a dreadful state with gangrene and dysentery but nothing fazed Mrs Hart, she oversaw the care of every man, regardless of his rank or his injuries. The archive is full of letters from ex-patients thanking her and the doctors and nurses. There's an extract from my favourite letter sent to Mrs Hart.' Will pointed to a letter in the cabinet and read it out.

When I arrived at Hill House, I wasn't sure I even wanted to live. The pain was unbearable, although I'm sure not as severe as many of my fellow patients. You sat with me that first night and made the world seem a gentler and kinder place. I knew then that if there were people such as you in the world, it was a world I wanted to return to.

'It didn't end there,' Will said. 'Mrs Hart's legacy lived on, and Edward and Alice saw to it that Hill House served as a hospital in the next war too.'

'For Canadian servicemen,' Lou said.

'Of course,' Will smiled. 'You've met Elizabeth. She gave one or two of those Canadian officers a scare back in the day! She's a staunch supporter of Hill House now. She volunteers two days a week as a room steward to show visitors around. She's through in the ballroom at the concert. You'll have to say hello.'

'I don't think so,' Lou said. 'When I visited her last week, I said this house was a wreck. It wouldn't make any sense if I spoke to her now.'

'Don't worry, Louisa,' Bertie said. 'Elizabeth's memory of your conversation will be a little altered, but she will remember you. How could she forget meeting another person who has shared her adventure?'

'But how do you know she won't think I'm mad? And how do you know so much about what it was like before . . . before this changed last night. Mrs Hart said everything happened while she slept.'

Bertie's pale eyes gleamed as he looked first at Will and then at Lou. 'Mrs Hart may have known more than she let on to you. She may have played a greater role in your experience – and that of Elizabeth – than either of you realise.'

'But—'

'We can't tell you more,' Will said. 'Just know that we know.'

'William,' Bertie said, 'please pass the photograph in the frame to Louisa.'

Will handed her a photograph of a little girl in a silver frame. Her blonde hair was scooped into bunches and, with her shoulders shrugged, she looked like the photographer had caught her mid-laugh.

'A pretty little thing, isn't she?' Bertie said.

Lou took in the girl's sweet, upturned nose and her wide blue eyes. 'She's related to Charlotte, isn't she?'

'She's Miss Charlotte's great great-granddaughter. Her name is Louisa. As is her mother's. And her grandmother's.' The skin around Bertie's eyes crinkled as he smiled. 'We never forget those we have loved. Those who have touched our lives and made it better. You do understand what you have done, don't you?'

Lou shook her head.

'You, Louisa, you did all of this.' Bertie's eyes flicked around the room. 'Your love and kindness saved the Mandevilles and, in saving them, you saved all of us who lived and worked here. Even without knowing what you had done for them, the staff spoke of you fondly. My mother in particular. She credited you with arranging for her to become Miss Charlotte's lady's maid. We went with her wherever she travelled, and she saw to it that I had a good education. That is all down to you.'

'It's not possible,' Lou said, 'I'm not that important.'

'What more evidence do you need that you have been crucial to the survival of this house?' Will said. 'You, Louisa Arnold, are as important in the history of this house as Elizabeth Goodwill, Lady Alice Mandeville, and all of your like that went before and have come since. Your actions while you were in Hill House set in place a chain reaction. With Hill House and the

Mandevilles at the heart of this community, this town has always thrived. There has been employment. There's not the crime there is in other towns. People actually want to live here. Don't you see that in altering the future of your town, you also saved your mother?'

Lou shook her head. 'I can't have. It's my fault that my mum died.'

'It wasn't your fault,' Bertie said. 'It's because you are attuned to other's feelings – their fear, their hopes, their destinies – that you blamed yourself.'

'Even if that's true, I've done nothing to deserve her coming back . . . I want her back, of course I do. But I can't believe anything I did deserves such a miracle.'

Bertie smiled. 'And there, my dear Louisa, is the reason that Hill House chose you. You can't even see that you have deserved this reward. That you have earned it through your self-less sacrifice.'

There was a moment of silence before Will placed his hand on his great-grandfather's shoulder. 'Do you want me to explain?'

Bertie shook his head. He opened his mouth but closed it before uttering a word. When he spoke, his voice cracked. 'None of the Hill House men that went to The Great War came home again. Not my own dear father and not . . .'

'Tom?' Lou said. In the bombardment of information, she had allowed herself to believe there was a flicker of hope. Tom may not have married Emma, but that didn't mean he hadn't married at all. It didn't mean he had gone to France. But if Edward had become the baronet, it was because Tom had no longer been alive. . .

Lou's legs gave way. Will stepped forward and caught her.

'He should have married Emma,' Lou said.

'No, Lou,' Will said. 'He shouldn't. That's just what you told yourself.'

'It's my fault. It's all my fault.'

Bertie reached and took her hand again. 'Some people have a destiny so important that it cannot be altered. Mourn for the man you lost, Miss Louisa, but never, *never*, mourn for the man he was. Louisa . . . Louisa . . . Please listen to me. There's a parcel in Captain Mandeville's room for you. Miss Charlotte and my mother placed it in his desk. Everyone in this household has been under strict instructions that the desk should never be unlocked by anyone other than Miss Louisa Arnold. With each passing year nobody expected you to return. Except for me and now William.'

'What is it? I can't take any more surprises.'

'We don't know,' Will said. 'Charlotte and Albert's mother, Sally, refused to tell anyone.'

'My mother would only say that there was something in Captain Mandeville's effects sent back from France that was for you and you alone.'

Gently releasing his hold on her, Will pulled a key from the pocket of his jacket. He pressed it into her hand. 'It's the key to Captain Mandeville's desk,' he said. 'You'll find his room already unlocked for you.'

'I can't,' Lou said, staring at the key crossing her palm.

'Nobody will notice if you go upstairs now.'

'Go on,' Bertie said. 'You know you must. You know he wants you to.'

THIRTY-EIGHT

For the second time in less than twelve hours, Lou hesitated outside Tom's bedroom. But on this occasion the singing downstairs reminded her there was no time for indecision. She pushed the door open and, as she crossed the threshold, an invisible hand reached inside her chest and gripped her heart.

There were books laid out on the table as though the reader had just placed them down, an ashtray, complete with cigarette stubs on the arm of the chair, a pair of riding boots beside the fireplace, and a battered suitcase beside the bed.

Lou clutched the key. The teeth biting into her hand brought back to herself. If she was going to go rooting around in this room, then she had to do it now, before someone came and found her and wanted to know what the hell she was doing sneaking around where she had no right to be.

Summoning what little historian's dispassion she could muster, she crossed the room, but in the few steps it took to reach the desk, all trace of control fizzled away. Her hand shook as she turned the key in the lock and pushed up the roll top lid. The dry wood rattled as it laboured along the metal tracks and a musty smell escaped. It was the scent of old paper, of ink dried to a crust in an open bottle, of pencil shavings that had lain where they had fallen one hundred years earlier. And, amidst the bottles and papers and shavings, sat a parcel. Lou stared at it for a moment. She reached and ran her fingertips over the brittle brown paper, a swell of nerves surging in her stomach. Who was she to open this package that had been hidden for a century; which had become a part of the fabric of this house, a part of its mythology? She fingered the string holding the paper in place. Who had wrapped this parcel so neatly and taking such great care? Had it been Sally, or Charlotte, or both? Charlotte. She had lived. She had not just lived, she had thrived. And along with Sally, she had wanted Lou to have whatever this parcel contained.

A breath escaped Lou's lips and before she could talk herself out if it, she pulled the end of the string. The neat bow unravelled, and a flurry of fibres drifted to the floor. She carefully prised back the paper.

Wrapped inside the neat folds was a slim buff-coloured volume, its once pristine leather cover now worn, faded and water-stained. Lou pressed the surface of the book, her heart aching. Every memory attached to the book seeped into her fingertips. She saw Tom in the library, smiling at her, teasing that he only read Shakespeare's sonnets. She saw herself pretending to read the philosophy before the fire in the morning room when she was so sure that she could help the Mandevilles. But most vivid of all was the memory of Tom standing before her last night, confessing that he had read Plato's words to feel close to her. He had taken this book to France with him. Had he read Plato's words again to feel close to her? A piece of paper stuck from the pages of the book. She pulled it free. Yellowed with age, the story torn from the page of a newspaper was dated 30 August 1914. Beneath the headline 'The Fall of A Hero', and in large bold text, was a quote from Sir Charles.

On that summer's day, in a field in France, the glorious sun that was Thomas set for the final time. While there is a Mandeville alive, he will be remembered. But the world in which we must all now live will be a darker place without him; without our boy.

Each word cut like a razor to Lou's soul. Pain seeped from Sir Charles' words and cried out from this shrine a grief-stricken family had created so their boy would not be forgotten. The Mandeville's pain was her pain. Their boy, her boy.

The words of the obituary formed a border around a black and white photograph of Tom in uniform. It wasn't the splendid uniform of braid and feathers of his mother's painting down in the hall, but a studio portrait in which he wore khakis and puttees and a cap. He looked so normal, so like Lou's Tom.

She closed her eyes tight. 'Please take me back to him. Even if just for a minute.'

This house had spoken to her outside in the storm, it had turned on the hot water tap when she was cold, it had taken her back one hundred years. It could do this one thing, couldn't it? She closed her eyes, picturing Tom sitting in the chair beside the fire. But when she opened her eyes again, she was back in the cold room. Loneliness stretched out like a road with no end. There was no way back. Tears began to stream down her cheeks. A sob made her chest heave. She took the book in her hands. The spine, broken through use, fell open at a well-thumbed page. A passage had been underlined; a few words written in the margin in grey pencil:

Every heart sings a song, incomplete, until another whispers back. Those who wish to sing always find a song.

LA,

You are my reason. You are my song.
TM. 22nd August 1914

Lou's hands began to tremble. She willed herself back to last night; to Tom's smile as he had kissed her; to their hands grasping at her corset in their desperation to get to one another; to his lips tracing the curve of her waist and stomach. She could still smell him on her skin, in her hair. They had slept in that bed, kicking away the sheets because the heat of their bodies was the only warmth they needed. That bed would never know them again, it would be forever empty, forever cold.

You said you'd find me, Tom. You promised. I can't face a world without you in it. I just can't. Why did I let you go? Afraid that her tears would spoil the book, she dug in her pocket. Pulling her hand free, she found that she was clutching not a tissue, but a grubby handkerchief, embroidered in the corner with two initials. *TM.*

She collapsed into the chair beside the fire and muffled her cries with the handkerchief that still smelled of woody cologne. A travel rug draped over the back of the chair slipped down and rested about her shoulders. Behind Lou, the curtains billowed although the window was closed and the air outside was perfectly still.

'There you are,' Mum said, easing through the throng in the hall. 'You missed a gorgeous concert.' She joined Lou to look up at the portrait beneath the stairs. 'I've always liked that painting. He's very handsome, don't you think? With kind eyes.'

Lou pressed the book-shaped bulge in the pocket of her parka as the crowd parted, making way for a wheelchair.

Will brought the chair to a stop. 'Hello again, Louisa. We

wanted to catch you before you leave. This must be your mum. It's lovely to meet you, Mrs Arnold.' Will held out his hand. 'I'm William Morrison and this is my great-grandfather, Bert.'

Not used to shaking hands, Lou's mum blushed as she took Will's hand. 'Are you friends of Lou's?' she asked, sounding a tad confused.

Bertie lifted his chin from his chest. 'Louisa is a tremendous friend to us. And to Hill House.'

'Lou's been helping with . . .' Will paused as though working out how to phrase his words. 'With a long-term regeneration programme of Hill House.'

'Has she now?' Mum slipped her arm through Lou's. 'Well, our Lou has always loved history.'

Bertie's eyes came to rest on Lou. 'Louisa still doesn't fully appreciate what she's done for us. The help she has given.'

'That's my Lou all over,' Mum said, squeezing Lou's arm. 'She's always hiding her light under a bushel. And I'm sorry, gentlemen. You'll have to excuse her today. She's a bit under the weather. She goes quiet when she's poorly. Always has, even when she was a little girl.'

Bertie's blanket fell from his knees. Lou's mum knelt to collect it from the floor. As she tucked it around Bertie's lap, checking that he was okay, Will took a step closer to Lou. 'You'll be all right, I promise,' he said, his quiet words lost to anybody but her. 'You'll always have friends at Hill House. And you've got my number. Phone me. Anytime. I'll always be there for you, Lou.' He ran his fingers through his fringe and made to turn away. Lou stopped him.

'Will, I just want to thank you,' she whispered. 'For everything.'

'It's us that should be thanking *you*. Perhaps in the New Year you'll let me take you for that meal. You know, we could catch up.'

'I'd like that. But it'll be my treat.'

Will smiled. 'I know better now than to argue with you, Louisa Arnold.'

He took her hands in his and gave them a gentle squeeze before taking the handles of the wheelchair. Bertie and Will said their goodbyes, Will turning the wheelchair in the direction of the ballroom.

'They were nice, weren't they?' Mum said. 'And you're a dark horse, I had no idea you were helping here. What is it, some kind of volunteering project?'

Lou nodded and moved in closer to her mum.

'You're still not right, are you? Come on then, let's get you home. I'll make you a nice hot chocolate. If you're good, I might even let you have one of the gingerbread men I made yesterday. How does that sound?'

Lou rested her head on her mum's shoulder. Keeping her hand over the book in her pocket she walked slowly by her mum's side. Together they left Hill House.

THIRTY-NINE

Extract from the private diary of Lieutenant Christopher MacIntyre, 12th Lancers

On 22nd August 1914, my regiment was in rear of the 5th Cavalry Brigade, having spent a day covering the infantry columns advancing north. We had passed a pleasantly warm day in the grounds of a local chateau, the men playing football, the officers chatting about cricket. As was his way, Captain Mandeville had spent a good portion of the morning and afternoon with his nose in a book. He spent so much time reading from a small volume of Latin philosophy that the men had begun to refer to him affectionately as the Librarian. At about 4.00 p.m., I was ordered to take my troop to a small village lying some 10 kilometres from the Franco-Belgian border. Along with another troop from my squadron, we were under the command of Captain Mandeville and had orders to round up what was thought to be a patrol of the enemy spotted in an orchard.

On arrival, I ordered my troop to dismount and we proceeded on foot to locate the enemy in the trees; Captain

Mandeville and B troop remaining in the rear. Almost imme-diately we came under heavy fire and it became apparent that we faced a far greater enemy force than expected. As I reached my position in the firing line, I received a bullet through my left thigh. Clearly recognising the impossibility of this mission and no doubt with a desire to preserve lives, Captain Mandev-ille gave the order to retreat. But it came at the same time the enemy charged.

From my position on the ground, I ordered a handful of my men to hold their position as long as possible to allow the remainder of my troop to get back to their horses, some 100 yards to the rear. Again, Captain Mandeville gave the order to retreat. As I found I could not put any weight on my leg, I emptied my revolver at the charging enemies at close range. The first German to reach me was about to club me on the head with the butt of his rifle. Quite naturally I closed my eyes in anticipation of the blow. When I received none, I opened my eyes to find that my would-be assailant had fallen, having taken a bullet to the temple. It is then I saw that Captain Mandeville had dismounted and was running through the orchard towards me. Having emptied his revolver, he took a rifle from one of my retreating men. With him was another man, a Lance Corporal from B squadron who I recognised as Hughes, the regimental boxing champion. Captain Mandev-ille ordered the remainder of my troop to retreat while he and Hughes kept the enemy at bay. This order, my men finally obeyed. I then felt myself hauled on to Hughes's shoulders. He ran to the rear with me slung about him like a sack while Captain Mandeville provided covering fire.

In the confusion, the rest of the squadron had retreated further back. Only one horse remained; Samson, Captain Mandeville's own hunter, brought out after his cavalry issue horse had developed colic. Captain Mandeville ordered Hughes to place me on Samson and to share the saddle. This,

Hughes refused to do. Captain Mandeville called a command and, without so much as a nudge, that most magnificent of horses carried me away through the trees. I gripped the reins and was able to look back, to see Captain Mandeville and Hughes standing shoulder to shoulder, engaged in a fierce battle with the approaching twenty or so Germans.

It wasn't until later that evening that we received word from the farmer who owned the orchard. He and his family had witnessed the fight from their house and had seen Captain Mandeville and Hughes fall. They were taken to the local doctor and his nurse, who rendered what medical assistance they were able but both men succumbed to their wounds later that same afternoon; Hughes of a haemorrhage caused by gunshots received to his leg and Captain Mandeville from two wounds, one to the stomach, the other to his chest. They were buried in a local cemetery since by that point the village had fallen into enemy hands. We were assured they had received a proper Christian service.

I have more reason than most to be grateful to Captain Mandeville and Lance Corporal Hughes. Had Captain Mandeville not given the order to retreat when he did, many more men would have died that day and were it not for his actions, I should be in a plot in a graveyard in northern France.

Captain Mandeville was the very best of officers; his utmost concern was always for the welfare of his men. On that day, he sacrificed himself so that I and the other men might live. That was a measure of the man.

FORTY

22ND AUGUST 2014

In a rural village in northern France, a young woman leaves a café bar. Blinking in the midday sun, she clutches a map that the landlady has drawn on the back of a paper napkin. She crosses the square where a group of old men play pétanque. Their faces are brown and cracked like the bark of the chestnut tree beneath which some take shade. The balls crack, throwing up a shower of sandy dust.

The men smile as they watch the young woman pass by. She is the stranger who arrived the day before to stay for a single night in the guest room above the bar. The previous evening, they all watched her slowly drink a glass of red wine. Today, in her pretty blue dress and with her hair neatly styled, she reminds them of how women dressed when they were young. For a moment, each man recalls the first woman he fell in love with.

Following the map, the woman navigates the back streets, emerging on to a side road. Opposite a terrace of neat houses with waffled orange roofs, she stops for a moment to steel herself for what she is about to do. She smoothes out her dress and runs her fingers over her hair, before passing through the iron gates.

The air is still, and the sun warms the skin of her bare arms. Not twenty yards away, she sees the two bleached-white stones. Dignified in their simplicity, they stand apart from the grey angels and urns of the civilian monuments. Her pace slows as she approaches but her pulse quickens. She focuses on the name on one of the headstones. A warm breeze brushes the fair hairs on her arms, and she feels him close by. She kneels on the neatly maintained square of grass and runs her fingers over the grooves of his name, of his regiment and of the date he died; one hundred years ago to the day. Her heart fills with love, with sadness and with pride. She understands now what she couldn't a few months ago; they had to sacrifice their love to save their families.

The handful of locals in the cemetery tending graves hear a moped buzz in the distance, they hear grasshoppers chirp in the neighbouring field. But the young woman hears none of them. She takes an envelope from her bag, postmarked December 2013. She opens a letter and reads it aloud. In two weeks' time she will become a trainee teacher in a school in a town in central England. A school that needs good teachers and where she can make a difference. Carefully she slips a book from her bag. The leather is warm to the touch. She opens the pages and begins to softly read aloud. The few people that hear her voice don't understand her foreign tongue and pay her no mind.

When the warmth leaves the day and the sun begins to dip, she takes a grubby white handkerchief from her pocket and unfurls it to reveal a small, wilted flower picked in a garden in another country. Placing the wild rose at the base of the head-stone, she closes her eyes and leans forward to kiss his name. The breeze whispers past her ear. She bites her lip. She doesn't want him to see her cry. When she stands, the pattern of grass criss-crosses her knees. She looks at his name one last time before turning away. This parting is only temporary. She knows that one day they will meet again.

A LETTER FROM THE AUTHOR

Dear reader,

I would like to say a huge thank you for reading *A Time to Change*.

I hope you enjoyed meeting the Mandevilles for the first time and getting to know Lou and Tom. It would be wonderful to have you follow the journey of Hill House and its very special guests in future Mandeville books!

If you want to join other readers in hearing all about my new releases and bonus content, you can sign up here:

www.stormpublishing.co/callie-langridge

If you enjoyed this book and could spare a few moments to leave a review that would be hugely appreciated. Even a short review can make all the difference in encouraging a reader to discover my books for the first time. Thank you so much!

I have a passion for social history and particularly exploring the huge impact that the First World War had on how we live now. I spend a huge amount of my free time visiting old houses, imagining all the lives that have lived within their walls. Bringing this to life with the Mandevilles and their special guests at Hill House is a constant joy.

Thanks again for being part of this amazing journey with me. I love to hear from my readers through my social media channels, so please feel free to find me for a chat. I hope you'll stay in touch as I have so many more stories and ideas to share with you!

All the very best,

Callie Langridge

facebook.com/CallieLangridgeAuthor

twitter.com/CLangridgeWrite

instagram.com/Callie%20Langridge

ACKNOWLEDGMENTS

This book is very special to me. When I began writing it, I had no clue who my First World War ancestors were, and it can be a daunting process to find them. Good fortune intervened and I inherited a box of documents that introduced me to the people in my family who served, who died and who survived. I was also introduced to my ancestors left behind at home. This book is retrospectively dedicated to all of them.

I would like to thank everyone at Storm who has helped me repolish this book – particularly Kathryn, Vicky and Oliver. Thank you to the writers who were with me from the very first page - Susie Lynes, Zoe Antoniades, Sam Hanson and John Rogers. Thank you to my wider writing gang – Emma Robinson, Lisa Timoney, Clarissa Angus, Claire McGlasson, Emilie Olsson, Kate Riordan and Bev Thomas. And thank you to my non writing pals who provide inspiration, fun and encouragement - Kim, Virginia, Emma and Val.

And thank you in particular to my cheerleader in chief, Pete x